THE HORUS HERESY®

Other Novels and Novellas

Many of these titles are also available as abridged and unabridged audiobooks.
Order the full range of Horus Heresy novels and audiobooks from
blacklibrary.com

Audio Dramas

*Download the full range of Horus Heresy
audio dramas from
blacklibrary.com*

Also available

THE HORUS HERESY®

EYE OF TERRA
Edited by Laurie Goulding

BLACK LIBRARY

A BLACK LIBRARY PUBLICATION

Hardback edition first published in 2016.
This edition published in 2017 by
Black Library,
Games Workshop Ltd.,
Willow Road,
Nottingham, NG7 2WS, UK.

10 9 8 7 6 5 4 3 2 1

Produced by Games Workshop in Nottingham.
Cover and internal illustrations by Neil Roberts.

A CIP record for this book is available from the British Library.

ISBN 13: 978 1 78496 373 6

See Black Library on the internet at

blacklibrary.com

Find out more about Games Workshop
and the world of Warhammer 40,000 at

games-workshop.com

Printed and bound by CPI Group (UK) Ltd, Croydon, CR0 4YY

THE HORUS HERESY®

It is a time of legend.

The galaxy is in flames. The Emperor's glorious vision for humanity is in ruins. His favoured son, Horus, has turned from his father's light and embraced Chaos.

His armies, the mighty and redoubtable Space Marines, are locked in a brutal civil war. Once, these ultimate warriors fought side by side as brothers, protecting the galaxy and bringing mankind back into the Emperor's light.
Now they are divided.

Some remain loyal to the Emperor, whilst others have sided with the Warmaster. Pre-eminent amongst them, the leaders of their thousands-strong Legions are the primarchs. Magnificent, superhuman beings, they are the crowning achievement of the Emperor's genetic science. Thrust into battle against one another, victory is uncertain for either side.

Worlds are burning. At Isstvan V, Horus dealt a vicious blow and three loyal Legions were all but destroyed. War was begun, a conflict that will engulf all mankind in fire. Treachery and betrayal have usurped honour and nobility. Assassins lurk in every shadow. Armies are gathering.
All must choose a side or die.

Horus musters his armada, Terra itself the object of his wrath. Seated upon the Golden Throne, the Emperor waits for his wayward son to return. But his true enemy is Chaos, a primordial force that seeks to enslave mankind to its capricious whims.

The screams of the innocent, the pleas of the righteous resound to the cruel laughter of Dark Gods. Suffering and damnation await all should the Emperor fail and the war be lost.

The age of knowledge and enlightenment has ended.
The Age of Darkness has begun.

CONTENTS

THE WOLF OF ASH AND FIRE

Graham McNeill

"A son can bear with equanimity the loss of his father, but the loss of his inheritance may drive him to despair."

– The Black Tacitus of Firenze

"The mind is its own place, and in itself can make a heaven of hell, a hell of heaven."

– The Blind Poet of Kaerlundein

'I WAS THERE,' he would say, right up until the day he died, after which he spoke only infrequently. 'I was there the day Horus saved the Emperor.' It had been a singular moment, the Emperor and Horus shoulder to shoulder in the fiery, ash-choked depths of the scrapworld. Blood-lit in the broil of combat for almost the last time, though only one of them knew that.

Father and son, back to back.

Swords drawn and their foe all around.

As perfect an encapsulation of the Crusade as any later immortalised in paint or ink.

Before remembrance of such times became a thing to be feared.

THE SCRAPWORLD OF Gorro; that was where it had happened, deep in junkyard space of the Telon Reach. The greenskin empire that once claimed dominion over its stars was in flames, assailed on all sides by the inexhaustible armies of the Imperium. The aliens' empire was being overturned, their muddy fortress-worlds burning, but not quickly enough.

Gorro was the key.

Adrift in the distant light of a bloated red sun, where no planet had ever been wrought by inexorable time and gravity, it drifted on an erratic path. Not a wanderer, an intruder.

Its destruction was made the Crusade's highest priority. The command came from the hand of the Emperor himself, and his most favoured and brightest son answered this call to arms.

Horus Lupercal, primarch of the Luna Wolves.

GORRO WASN'T DYING easy.

Any expectation that this would be a swift strike to the heart was dashed the moment the Sixty-Third expedition surged towards the system boundary and saw the scale of the scrapfleet protecting it.

Hundreds of vessels, pulled back from the fighting at the core of the Reach to defend its warlord's planetoid citadel. Vast corpse-ships brought to hellish life with flaring plasma reactors at their heart. Warhulks welded together from rusted wreckage scavenged from celestial graveyards and returned to life by hideous mechanical necromancy.

Anchoring the fleet was a colossal, hollowed-out asteroid fortress, a mountainous rock encrusted with pig-iron and ice. Kilometres-wide engine cowlings were bolted deep into its bedrock and its craggy surface was thick with immense batteries of orbital-howitzers and mine-lobbers. It lumbered towards the Luna Wolves as rabid scrapship packs raced ahead like feral, club-wielding barbarians.

The vox howled with baying static, a million tusked throats giving voice to the primal instinct of the ork.

The engagement volume became a swirling free-fire zone, an impossibly tangled mass of entwined warships, collimated laser fire, parabolic torpedo contrails and explosive debris fields. Void-war engagements normally fought at ranges of tens of thousands of kilometres now began so close that ork marauders with crude rocket-packs were launching boarding actions.

Atomic detonations fouled the space between the fleets with electromagnetic distortion and phantom echoes, making it almost impossible to separate what was real and what was a sensor ghost.

The *Vengeful Spirit* was in the heart of the fiercest fighting, its flanks ablaze with broadsides. A hulk tumbled away, bludgeoned into molten submission by multiple decks of concentrated explosive ordnance. It trailed scads of burning fuels and arcing jets of plasma. Thousands of bodies spilled from its ruptured innards like spores from a fungal mass.

There could be nothing subtle in such a fight. This wasn't a battle of manoeuvre and counter-manoeuvre, it was a brawl. It would be won by the fleet that punched hardest and most often.

And right now, that was the orks.

THE VENGEFUL SPIRIT's superstructure groaned like a living thing as it manoeuvred far faster than anything as massive should ever be asked. Its ancient hull shuddered under thunderous impacts, and the deck vibrated with the recoil of multiple broadside decks firing in unison.

Space between the brawling fleets was thick with debris storms, atomic vortices, duelling attack squadrons and flash-burning vapour clouds, but within Lupercal's flagship, discipline held firm.

Cascading data-slates and shimmering wire-frame holos bathed the vaulted strategium in a rippling, undersea light. Hundreds of mortal voices conveyed the shipmaster's orders, while chattering machine tickers recited damage reports, void strengths and ordnance firing schedules over the binary cant of Mechanicum priests.

A well-drilled bridge crew in battle was a thing of beauty, and were it not for the caged-wolf pacing of Ezekyle Abaddon, Sejanus might have been properly able to appreciate it.

The First Captain slammed a fist on the brass rim of a hololithic table displaying the engagement sphere. The scratchy, flickering threat vectors burped with angry static, but the grim picture of battle surrounding the *Vengeful Spirit* didn't alter.

Greenskin warships still vastly outnumbered those of the Luna Wolves, outgunning them and appearing – in defiance of all reason and sense – to be outmanoeuvring the commander.

It was most vexing, and Ezekyle's choler wasn't helping.

Nearby mortal crew, their faces limned by data-light, turned at the sudden sound, but looked away as the First Captain glared at them.

'Really, Ezekyle?' said Sejanus. '*That's* your solution?'

Ezekyle shrugged, making the plates of his armour grate together and the gleaming black of his topknot shake like a shaman's fetish switch. Ezekyle loomed, it was his *thing*, and he tried to loom over Sejanus as though he actually thought he could intimidate him. Ridiculous, as it was only the topknot that made him taller.

'I suppose you have a better idea of how to turn this

disaster around, Hastur?' said Ezekyle, glancing over his shoulder and careful to keep his voice low.

The pale ivory of Ezekyle's armour gleamed in the light of the strategium. Faded gang markings survived on those plates that hadn't been replaced by the armourers, faded gold and tarnished silver. Sejanus sighed. Almost two hundred years since leaving Cthonia, and Ezekyle still held onto a heritage best left in the past.

He gave Abaddon his best grin. 'I do, as it turns out.'

That got the attention of his other Mournival brothers.

Horus Aximand, so like the commander with his high, aquiline features and sardonic curl of the lip that they called him the truest of the *true sons*. Or, if Aximand was in one of his rare, lighter moods, *Little Horus*.

Tarik Torgaddon, the idiot joker whose dark, saturnine features had avoided the transhuman flattening common among the Emperor's legionaries. Where Aximand would puncture the humour of any given moment, Torgaddon would seize upon it like a hound with a bone.

Brothers all. The confraternity of four. Counsellors, war-brothers, naysayers and confidantes. So close to Horus, they were likened unto his sons.

Tarik gave a mock bow, as though to the Emperor himself, and said, 'Then please enlighten us poor, foolish mortals who are grateful merely to bask in the radiance of your genius.'

'At least Tarik knows his place,' grinned Sejanus, his finely sculpted features robbing the comment of malice.

'So what *is* your better idea?' said Aximand, cutting to the heart of the matter.

'Simple,' said Sejanus, turning to the command station behind them on a raised dais. 'We trust in Horus.'

✠ ✠ ✠

THE COMMANDER SAW them coming and raised a gauntlet in welcome. His perfect face was all finely chiselled lines, piercing ocean-green eyes flecked with amber and freighted with aquiline intelligence.

He towered over them all, the broad sweep of his shoulder guards swathed in the pelt of a giant beast slain on Davin's plains many decades ago. His armour, white-gold even in the battle light of the strategium, was a thing wrought from wonder and beauty, with a single staring eye fashioned across the breastplate. Graven across its vambraces and pauldrons were armourers' marks, the eagle and lightning bolt of Lupercal's father, esoteric symbolism that Sejanus didn't recognise and, almost hidden in the shadows of overlapping plates, hand-scratched gang markings from Cthonia.

Sejanus hadn't noticed them before, but that was the commander for you. Each time you stood in his presence you saw something fresh to delight the eye, some new reason to love him more.

'So how do you think it's going so far?' asked Horus.

'I have to be honest, sir,' replied Tarik. 'I feel the hand of the ship on me.'

Lupercal smiled. 'You don't have faith in me? I'd be hurt if I didn't know you were joking.'

'I am?' said Tarik.

Horus turned his gaze away as the strategium shook with a pounding series of percussive impacts on the hull. Shells from the many guns of the asteroid fortress, judged Sejanus.

'And you, Ezekyle?' said Horus. 'I know I can rely on you to give me a straight answer and not fall back on superstition.'

'I have to agree with Torgaddon,' said Ezekyle, and

Sejanus suppressed a grin, knowing that admission would have cost Ezekyle dearly. Tarik and Ezekyle were so alike in war, but polar opposites when the killing was done. 'We're going to lose this fight.'

'Have you ever known me to lose a fight?' the commander asked of his namesake. Sejanus saw the imperceptible tilt at the corner of Lupercal's lips and knew the commander had engineered the First Captain's answer.

Horus Aximand shook his head. 'Never, and you never will.'

'A flattering answer, but a wrong one. I am as capable of losing a fight as any other,' said Horus, putting up a hand to forestall their inevitable denials. 'But I'm not going to lose this one.'

Lupercal ushered them to his command station, where what looked like a skeletal armature of gold and steel with embedded portions of pale meat stood plugged into the main battle hololith.

'Adept Regulus,' said Horus. 'Illuminate my sons.'

The emissary of the Mechanicum nodded and the hololith bloomed to life. The commander's station gave a clearer rendition of the battle, but, if anything, that only made his current orders more confounding.

The hololith's low light shadowed the commander's eye sockets while sheening the rest of his face in deep red. The impression was of an ancient chieftain squatting at a low-burning hearthfire in his wartent, gathering his generals on the eve of battle.

'Hastur, you always had the best grip on void tactics,' said Horus. 'Take a look and tell me what you see.'

Sejanus leaned over the hololithic plotter, his heart swelling in pride at Lupercal's words. It took an effort of will not to puff his chest out like one of the III Legion peacocks. He took a deep breath and stared at the grainy, slowly-updating schemata of battle.

The greenskins made war without subtlety, no matter in what arena the battle was fought. On land they came at you in a berserk horde, braying, foaming and smeared with faecal warpaint. In space their rad-spewing reaver-hulks stormed into the fray with every gun-deck throwing out shells and atomic warheads with abandon.

'Standard greenskin tactics, though I baulk at dignifying this mess with the term,' said Sejanus, swaying as sequentially enacted orders from the commander's station threw the *Vengeful Spirit* into a savage turn. Echoes of crashing detonations travelled through the flagship's structure. Whether they were impacts or outgoing fire was impossible to tell.

'Their sheer force and numbers is bending our line back on itself,' he continued, as Regulus shifted the focus of the hololith to highlight the fiercest fighting. 'The centre is retreating from that asteroid fortress, we just don't have the guns to hurt it.'

'What else?' said Horus.

Sejanus pointed to the slowly rotating image. 'Our right and upper quadrants are being pushed out too far. The left and lower quadrants are the only ones holding firm.'

'What I wouldn't give for another fleet,' said Tarik, nodding at an empty region of space in an upper quadrant of the volume. 'Then we'd have them on two flanks.'

'No use wishing for what we don't have,' said Little Horus.

Something wasn't right, and it took a moment for the suspicion to crystallise fully in Sejanus' mind.

'Adept, bring up the tally of enemy launch-to-impact

ratios,' he ordered. Instantly, a glowing pane of data light appeared in the air before Sejanus. He ran his eyes down the statistics and saw his suspicion confirmed.

'Their damage capability assessment is far above average,' he said. 'They're on-target with over seventy-five per cent of their launches.'

'That's got to be a mistake,' said Ezekyle.

'The Mechanicum do not make *mistakes*, First Captain,' said Regulus, his voice like steel wool on rust and pronouncing *mistakes* like the vilest of curses. 'The data is accurate within tolerances of local parameters.'

'Greenskins are as likely to hit their own ships as any other,' said Sejanus. 'How are they doing this?'

Horus pointed towards the crackling outline of Gorro and said, 'Because these greenskins are atypical in that I suspect they are ruled, not by warriors, but by some form of tech caste. It's why I petitioned Adept Regulus to join the Sixteenth Legion in this prosecution.'

Sejanus looked back at the display and said, 'If you suspected that, then it makes all this doubly confusing. If I may be candid, my lord, our fleet tactics make no sense.'

'What *would* make them more tactically sound?'

Sejanus considered this. 'Tarik's right. If we had another fleet element *here*, our current strategy would be sound. We'd have them between hammer and anvil.'

'Another fleet?' said Horus. 'And I am supposed to simply conjure one from thin air?'

'Could you?' asked Tarik. 'Because that would be really useful right now.'

Horus grinned and Sejanus saw he was savouring this moment, though he couldn't imagine why. The commander looked up to one of the tiered galleries rising up behind the command deck. As if on cue, a solitary figure stepped to the ironwork rail, bathed in the lambent glow of a spotlight whose arc of illumination was too providential to be accidental.

Slender and spectral in her white gown, the *Vengeful Spirit*'s Mistress of Astropathy, Ing Mae Sing, pulled back her hood. Gaunt-cheeked and with sunken, hollowed-out eye sockets, Mistress Sing was blind to one world, while being open to another secret world Sejanus knew little about.

'Mistress Sing?' called out Horus. 'How long now?'

Her voice was faint. Thin, yet with an authority that carried effortlessly to the main deck.

'Imminent, Primarch Horus,' she said with a faintly scolding tone. 'As well you know.'

Horus laughed and raised his voice for the entire strategium to hear, 'You're quite right, Mistress Sing, and I hope you will all forgive me this little moment of theatre. You see, something magnificent is about to happen.'

Horus turned to Adept Regulus and said, 'Send the manoeuvre order.'

The adept bent to the task, and Sejanus asked, 'Sir?'

'You wanted another fleet,' said Horus. 'I give you one.'

SPACE PARTED AS though cut open by the sharpest edge.

Amber light spilled out, brighter than a thousand suns and simultaneously existing in many realms of perception. The blade that cut the void open slid through the passage it had made.

But this was no blade, this was a void-born colossus of gold and marble, a warship of inhuman proportions. Its prow was eagle-winged and magnificent, its length studded with vast cities of statuary and palaces of war.

It was a starship, but a starship unlike any other.

Built for the most peerless individual the galaxy had ever known.

This was the flagship of the Emperor himself.

The *Imperator Somnium*.

Flocks of battleships attended the Master of Mankind. Each was a titanic engine of void-war, but the immensity of their master's vessel rendered them ordinary.

Still crackling with shield ignition, the Imperial warships surged into battle. Molten spears of lance fire stabbed into the exposed rear and flanks of the greenskin hulks. A thousand torpedoes slashed through space, followed by a thousand more. A glittering flurry of booster contrails painted the void in a web of glittering vapour-wakes.

Ork ships began exploding, gutted by timed warheads or cut in half by precision-aimed lances. Secondary explosions rippled through the hamstrung xenos fleet as raucous plasma reactors achieved critical mass and engines running insanely hot spiralled into explosive death throes.

The ork attack paused, turning to face this new threat.

Which was just what Horus Lupercal had been waiting for.

The XVI Legion fleet – which had been on the verge of being overwhelmed – halted its dispersal, its vessels turning about with astonishing speed and banding together in mutually-supporting wolf packs.

And what was once a fleet in apparent disarray transformed in minutes to a fleet on the attack. Individual greenskin vessels were overwhelmed and bombarded out of existence. Larger groups banded together, but they were no match for two coordinated war fleets led by the galaxy's greatest warriors.

The greenskins drew together around their monstrous

asteroid fortress as the *Vengeful Spirit* and the *Imperator Somnium* bore down upon it. Escorting warships blasted a path through the stricken reaverhulks, clearing the way for Horus and the Emperor to deliver the killing blow.

Coming in at oblique angles, both ships raked the asteroid with unending broadsides. Void flare and electromagnetic bursts from the cataclysmic volume of ordnance wreathed the hulking fortress in flaring detonations. This was planet-killing levels of fire, the power to crack open worlds and hollow them out as thoroughly as ceaseless industry had done to Cthonia.

At some unseen signal, the Imperial vessels pulled away as hellish firestorms engulfed the asteroid. The nightmare machinery at its heart, which empowered the guns and engines, exploded and split the rock apart.

Geysers of green-white plasma energy, thousands of kilometres long, arced around its corpse in crackling whips of sun-hot lightning. Like attracted like, and the lightning sought out the plasma cores of the greenskin vessels and ripped them apart in coruscating storms that burned everything it touched to ash.

Barely a handful escaped the tempest of destructive energies, and those that did were savaged by the prowling wolf pack squadrons.

Within the hour of the Emperor's arrival, the ork fleet had been reduced to a vast cloud of cooling debris.

An incoming vox-hail echoed through the *Vengeful Spirit*'s strategium. The storms of plasma boiling in the greenskins' graveyard made inter-ship vox choppy and unreliable, but this transmission was so clear the speaker could have been standing next to Lupercal.

'*Permission to come aboard, my son?*' said the Emperor.

✠ ✠ ✠

THE MOMENT WAS so sublime, so unexpected and so awe-inspiring that Sejanus knew he would remember it for the rest of his life. It had been a long time since Sejanus had found himself awed by someone other than his primarch.

The Emperor went without a helm, his noble countenance bearing a wreath of golden laurels about his brow. Even from a distance it was the face of a being worthy of eternal fealty, conceivable only as an impression of wonder and light. No god ever demanded respect and honour more. No earthly ruler had ever been so beloved by all.

Sejanus found himself weeping tears of unbridled joy.

Father and son met on the main embarkation deck of the *Vengeful Spirit*, and every legionary aboard had mustered to honour the Master of Mankind.

Ten thousand warriors. So many that every Stormbird and Thunderhawk in the deck had been flown out into the void to make room.

No order had been given. None had been needed.

This was their sire, the ruler who had decreed the galaxy to be humanity's domain and wrought the Legions into being to turn that dream into reality. No force in the universe could have kept them from this reunion. As one, the Luna Wolves threw back their heads and loosed a howling cheer of welcome, a pounding, deafening roar of martial pride.

Nor were the legionaries the only ones who came. Mortals came too – waifs and strays the Luna Wolves had swept up in the course of the Great Crusade. Itinerant poets, would-be chroniclers and promulgators of Imperial Truth. To see the Master of Mankind in the flesh was an opportunity that would never come again, and what mortal would miss the chance to see the man who was reshaping the galaxy?

He came aboard with three hundred members of the Legio Custodes, god-like warriors cast in the mould of the Emperor himself. Armoured in gold plate with crimson horsehair plumes streaming from their peaked helms, they carried shields and long polearms topped with armed photonic blades. Warriors whose sole purpose was to give their lives in order to protect his.

The Mournival followed Horus at the head of the entire First Company, marching in a long column alongside the warriors of the Legio Custodes.

As all warriors do, Sejanus measured them against his own strength, but could form no clear impression of their power.

Perhaps that was the point.

'Jaghatai taught it to me,' said Horus in answer to a question of the Emperor's. 'He called it "the *zao*". I can't pull it off anything like as fast as the Warhawk, but I make a passable fist of it.'

Sejanus saw Horus was being modest. Not enough to keep pride from his voice, but just on the right side of arrogant.

'You and Jaghatai were always close,' said the Emperor as they marched between the proud lines of Luna Wolves. 'Of all of us, even me, I think you know him best.'

'And I hardly know him at all,' admitted Horus.

'It is how he was made,' said the Emperor, and Sejanus thought he detected a note of profound regret.

They marched between the thousands of cheering legionaries, leaving the embarkation deck and moving up through the grandest processionals of the *Vengeful Spirit*. Companies of Luna Wolves peeled off the higher they went, until only Ezekyle's Justaerin elite and the Mournival remained.

They marched down the Avenue of Glory and Lament, the soaring antechamber with embossed columns of dark wood that bore the weight of a shimmering crystalline roof, through which the roiling, plasmic death throes of the greenskin fleet could be relished. Coffered panels running fully half the length of the avenue bore hand-painted lists of names and numbers, and the march to the bridge only stopped when the Emperor paused to kneel by the newest panel.

'The dead?' asked the Emperor, and Sejanus heard the weight of uncounted years in that simple question.

'All those where the *Spirit* was present,' said Horus.

'So many, and so many more yet to come,' said the Emperor. 'We must make it all worthwhile, you and I. We must build a galaxy fit for heroes.'

'We could fill this hall a hundred times over and it would still be a price worth paying to see the Crusade triumphant.'

'I hope it will not come to that,' said the Emperor.

'The stars are our birthright,' said Horus. 'Wasn't that what you said? Make no mistakes and they will be ours.'

'I said that?'

'You did. On Cthonia, when I was but a foundling.'

The Emperor stood and put a mailed gauntlet upon Lupercal's shoulder, the gesture of a proud father.

'Then I must prove worthy of your trust,' said the Emperor.

THEY MET LATER, when the order for war had rung out all across the *Vengeful Spirit*. There was much yet to be done, battle group formations to be decided upon, assault preparations to be run through and a thousand other tasks to be completed before the attack on Gorro could begin.

But first *this*.

'I don't have time for your pointless little ritual, Hastur,' declared Ezekyle. 'I've a company to ready for war.'

'We all do,' said Sejanus. 'But you're doing this.'

Ezekyle sighed, but nodded in acquiescence. 'Fine, then let's get on with it.'

Sejanus had chosen a seldom-visited observation deck in the rear quarters of the ship for their meeting. A vivid screed of plasma storms blazed beyond the crystalflex dome, and forking traceries of lightning danced on the polished terrazzo floor. The walls were bare of ornamentation, though scratched with Cthonian murder-hexes, bad poetry and gruesome images of murdered aliens.

A deep pool of fresh water filled the heart of the chamber, glittering with starlight and made bloody with light from the system's bloated red star.

'It's not even a proper moon,' said Ezekyle, staring at the pallid reflection of Gorro in the mirror flat waters.

'No, but it will have to do,' answered Sejanus.

'The Justaerin are going to be fighting alongside the Emperor,' said Ezekyle, mustering one last objection to a ceremony he'd never liked being party to. 'And I'll not have us shown up by those golden martinets.'

'We've been doing this since Ordoni,' said Tarik, kneeling to set the gleaming silver of his gibbous moon token next to Aximand's half-moon medal at the edge of the pool. 'It's what keeps us honest. Remembering Terentius.'

'I don't *need* keeping honest,' snapped Ezekyle, but he too knelt to place his lodge medal. 'Terentius was a traitor. We're nothing like him.'

'And only by constant vigilance will that remain so,' said Sejanus, and the matter was settled. He set his crescent-moon token next to those of his brothers and said, 'The Legion looks to us. Where we lead, they follow. We're doing this.'

Sejanus drew his sword and his Mournival brothers drew theirs. The XIII Legion favoured the short, stabbing gladius, but Lupercal's sons bore long-handled war blades, capable of being wielded one-handed or as brutal double-handers.

'Who are we?' asked Sejanus.

'We are the Luna Wolves,' said the others.

'Beyond that,' said Sejanus, almost growling the words.

'We are Mournival.'

'Bound together by the light of a moon,' roared Sejanus. 'Sworn to a bond that only death will break.'

'We kill for the living,' shouted Ezekyle.

'We kill for the dead!' they cried in unison.

Their swords lowered, each warrior resting the tip of his blade on the gorget of the man to his left.

Sejanus felt Ezekyle's sword at his neck as he held his own on Aximand, who in turn placed his at Tarik's neck. Lastly, Tarik placed his sword on Ezekyle, grinning at the faintly treasonous action of baring a blade to the First Captain.

'You have your Censures?'

Each warrior held out a folded square of oath paper that would normally be used to record an objective to be achieved in battle. Such oaths would be affixed to a warrior's armour, a visible declaration of martial intent.

Each Mournival brother had written upon their paper, but instead of a deed of honour, they had chosen a punishment for failure. These were Oaths of Censure, something Sejanus had instituted in the wake of the war in the Ordoni star cluster against the traitor Vatale Gerron Terentius.

His brothers had resisted the idea, claiming that to threaten punishment was to impugn their honour, but Sejanus had insisted, saying, 'We hold to the essential, unchanging goodness of the Legions, in their rational appraisal and rejection of evil. We invest our primarchs with divine qualities, with moral and rational faculties that make them both just and wise. We simplify the complexity of the galaxy by believing there is an unbreakable wall between good and evil. The lesson of Terentius is that the line between good and evil is all too permeable. Anyone can cross it in exceptional circumstances, even us. Believing that we *cannot* fall to evil makes us more vulnerable to the very things that might make it so.'

And so they had reluctantly agreed.

Sejanus held out his helmet, its transverse crest pointed to the deck. His censure paper was already in the helmet, and the other three dropped their punishment in with it. Then, each warrior reached inside and selected a paper at random. Aximand and Ezekyle tucked theirs into their belts. Tarik placed his into a leather loop on his scabbard.

Sejanus had read of the tradition from the ancient texts of Unity, where the ochre-painted warriors of Sarapion each crafted censures and cast them into a vast iron cauldron on the eve of battle. Each man would file past and draw a punishment should they fail their king. None knew which punishment they had chosen, thus no warrior could devise a lighter punishment and expect to receive it himself.

By the time the drop pods launched, each of the

Mournival would have an Oath of Censure wax-sealed onto a secret place upon his armour.

In the years since the first censure had been written, not one had ever been read.

And none ever will, thought Sejanus.

THE OATHS OF Moment had been sworn, the straining Stormbirds let fly. The Luna Wolves were en route to Gorro. Drop pods and gunships in the tens of thousands raced to the surface, ready to hollow the scrapworld from the inside out.

Gorro's death was to be won the hard way.

Field technology unknown to the Mechanicum bound the layered depths of Gorro together, and those same technologies made it virtually invulnerable to bombardment.

Macro cannons capable of levelling entire cities barely scratched its rust-crusted surface. Magma bombs and mass drivers with the power to crack continents detonated in its atmosphere. The lethal radiation of destroyer warheads dissipated into the void, half-lives of tens of thousands of years degraded in hours.

Lupercal watched his warriors race to battle from the golden bridge of his father's vessel. He wished he was part of the initial wave, the first to set foot on Gorro's alien surface. A wolf of ash and fire, bestriding the world as an avenging destroyer god.

Destroyer? No, never that.

'You wish you were with them, don't you?' asked the Emperor.

Horus nodded, but didn't turn from the viewing bay.

'I don't understand,' said Horus, feeling the might of his father's presence behind him.

'What don't you understand?'

'Why you wouldn't let me go with my sons,' said Horus.

'You always want to be first, don't you?'

'Is that so bad?'

'Of course not, but I need you elsewhere.'

'Here?' said Horus, unable to mask his disappointment. 'What good will I do from here?'

The Emperor laughed. 'You think we're going to watch this abomination die from here?'

Horus turned to face the Emperor, now seeing his father was girt for battle, towering and majestic in his gold-chased warplate of eagle wings and a bronze mantle of woven mail. A bluesteel sword was unsheathed, rippling with potent psychic energies. Custodians attended him, weapons at the ready.

Upon the largest teleporter array Horus had ever seen.

'I believe you call it a speartip, yes?' said the Emperor.

A BLAZE OF light, a vertiginous sense of dislocation and a world out of joint with itself. No sense of movement, but a powerful sense of time. Phosphor bright light faded from Horus' eyes, replaced by a furnace coal glow of seething workshops and volcanic fissures.

The bridge of the Emperor's flagship was gone.

In its place was a vision conjured straight from his youth.

Cthonia rendered in iron and mud.

Horus had explored the very depths of his adoptive home world, beyond the deepest ore-delvings, where the insane and the crippled waited to die. He'd even ventured beneath the dripping cadaver pits, avoiding the screeching murder-haruspex with their disembowelling knives and organ cloaks.

Cthonia was a warren of nightmarish rookeries filled

with unimaginable horrors at every turn, its claustrophobic tunnels lit with pulsating light from magma fissures. Thick with ash, a toxic miasma clogged the lungs, fouled the eyes and stained the soul.

This was just like that. Bowing ceilings laced with knotworks of rusted reinforcement, caged bulbs that sputtered with fitful light and a fug of sulphurous fumes.

The scrapworld stank of hot iron and flames, of oil and sweat and waste matter left to rot. The chamber was rank with the stench of beasts, as though the herds of livestock were kept here and never mucked out. This was the fetor of the ork, ammoniac and strangely redolent of spoiled vegetable matter.

A thousand or more greenskins roared to see several hundred armoured warriors appear without warning in the midst of the wide chamber. Every ork was encased in rusted plates of hissing iron, strapped and bolted to their swollen bodies. Horus' suspicion of a ruling tech class was all but confirmed at the sight of the wheezing pneumatics, cracking power generators and hissing, lightning-edged weapons.

'At them!' bellowed the Emperor.

Much to Horus' chagrin, the Custodians moved first, bracing their spears and letting fly with an explosive volley of mass-reactives from their guardian spears. The Justaerin opened fire a heartbeat later and the ork line bloomed with fiery detonations.

Then the Emperor was amongst them.

His sword was a bluesteel shimmer, too fast to follow with the naked eye. He moved through the orks without seeming to move at all, simply existing at one point to kill before appearing elsewhere to reap greenskin lives by the score. Each blow struck with the force of an artillery impact, and shattered bodies flew from his sword as though hurled aside by a bomb blast.

Nor was his sword the Emperor's only weapon.

His outstretched gauntlet blazed with white-gold fire, and whatever the flames touched disappeared in explosions of red cinders and ash. He battered orks to bonelessness with bludgeoning blows, he crushed them with invisible coils of force and he repelled their gunfire with thoughts that turned their rounds to smoke.

They came at him in their hundreds, like iron filings to the most powerful magnet, knowing they would never find another foe so deserving of their rage. The Emperor killed them all, unstoppable in his purity of purpose.

A crusade of billions distilled in one numinous being.

Horus had fought alongside the Emperor for well over a century, but the sight of his father in battle still had the power to awe him. This was war perfected. Fulgrim could live a thousand lifetimes and never achieve anything so wondrous.

Horus fired his storm bolter, decapitating a monster with twin rotating hooks for hands. It spun around and gutted another greenskin that stared stupidly at its unspooling entrails for a moment before collapsing. Horus followed his father into the mass of alien flesh and steel. His sword slashed low, taking the leg from a towering ork of absurdly oversized machine-musculature. He crushed its skull beneath his boot as he pushed over its thrashing body.

The Justaerin fought to his left and right, a solid wedge of black-armoured terminators battering their way through an ocean of iron-hard green flesh. Ezekyle led them with characteristic bullishness: shoulders squared against the foe, fist sawing back and forth like a relentless piston as his twin-bolter spat explosive death.

Horus had waged every form of warfare imaginable, but never relished it more than in a bloody broil with the greenskin. Hundreds of greasy bestial bodies surrounded him, howling, yelling, screaming and braying. Fangs snapped on his vambrace. Roaring cleavers shattered on his shoulder guards. He shrugged off every impact, rolled with every blow, killing his attackers with pure economy of force.

Stinking alien viscera coated him, hissing from the blade of his sword and the barrels of his storm bolter. Next to him, Ezekyle slew with furious urgency, pushing himself to the limit to stay by his primarch's side.

The Custodians hewed the orks with precisely aimed blows of their guardian spears. They could wield them in lethally inventive ways, but this was not the place for elaborate fighting styles. Here it was kill or be killed. Strikes that would end any other life form thrice over had to be repeated again and again just to put a single beast down.

The orks fought back with all the primal, animalistic fury that made them so dangerous. Even terminator armour could be breached, legionaries killed.

The orks were doing both.

At least a dozen Custodians were dead. Perhaps the same again in Justaerin. Horus saw Ezekyle go down, a colossal spiked mace, twice the height of a mortal, buried in his shoulder. An ork war-captain, ogryn-huge, wrenched the mace clear and swung the weapon around its immense body to deliver the death blow.

A shimmering sword sliced in to block the descending mace.

Bluesteel, two handed and wreathed in fire.

The Emperor rolled his wrist and the monstrous weight of the spiked head fell from its wire-wound haft. The Master of Mankind spun on his heel and the fire-edged sword licked out in a shimmering figure of eight.

The towering greenskin collapsed in four keenly-sliced segments. Its iron-helmed head still bellowed defiance as the Emperor bent to retrieve it from the deck. He waded into the orks, the roaring war-captain's truncated torso in one fist, sword in the other.

Horus dragged Ezekyle to his feet.

'Can you fight?' demanded Horus.

'Aye,' snapped Ezekyle. 'It's just a scratch.'

'Your shoulder is broken and the bone shield on your left side is fractured. As is your pelvis.'

'They'd need to break every bone in my body keep me from your side,' said Ezekyle. 'As it is for you and the Emperor, beloved by all.'

Horus nodded.

To say more would be to shame Ezekyle. 'No force in the galaxy will keep me from his side.'

As if Ezekyle's words were a dare to the galaxy, Gorro convulsed in the grip of a violent quake that ripped up from far below.

'What was that?' asked Ezekyle.

There could be only one answer.

'The gravitational fields keeping Gorro coherent are spinning out of control,' said Horus. 'The scrapworld is tearing itself apart.'

No sooner had Horus spoken than the deck plates buckled throughout the chamber. Metres-thick sheets of steel ripped like paper as geysers of oily steam belched from the depths. Bulging walls collapsed inwards and debris rained from the splintering ceiling. Cracking fissures spread across the bloody ground, tearing wider with every second as Custodians, Justaerin and orks fell into the scrapworld's fiery depths.

Horus fought for balance, pushing to where he saw the golden light of the Emperor surrounded by greenskin marauders.

'Father!' yelled Horus.

The Emperor turned, one hand outstretched to Horus.

Another quake struck.

And the scrapworld swallowed the Emperor whole.

SEJANUS HAD NO idea where they were. Everything was smoke and ash and blood. Three of his squad were dead already, and they hadn't even laid eyes on the enemy. Red light painted the interior of the smoke-filled drop pod, dripping wet where Argeddan and Kadonnen's bodies had been explosively gutted by spikes of penetrating debris. Feskan's head rolled at his feet, leaving spirals of blood on the floor.

The drop pod's boosters had failed and what should have been a controlled landing with the rest of the Fourth Company instead became a violent descent through hundreds of layers of honeycombed scrap towards Gorro's core.

According to the squalling, static-filled sensorium on his visor, his company was around two hundred kilometres above him. The reek of scorched metal and rotten food poured in through tears in the side of the drop pod.

Sejanus heard the booming, clanking, screeching sound that was the hallmark of greenskin technology. And behind that, the guttural bark-language of orks. The sound had a grating metallic quality to it, but he didn't have time to dwell on that now.

'Up!' he shouted. 'Up now! Get out!'

His restraint harness endlessly ratcheted as the deformed metal tried to unlock. He wrenched it away and pushed himself upright, turning to rip his bolt pistol and sword from the stowage rack above. For good measure, he took a bandolier of grenades as well. The rest of his squad followed suit, freeing and arming themselves with complete calm.

The base of the pod was canted at a forty-five degree angle, the drop-hatch angled towards the ground. Sejanus kicked the emergency release. Once, twice, three times.

It gave, but only a little.

Two more kicks finally freed it, and the panel fell out with a heavy clang. He dropped through the hatch and spun out from underneath its groaning remains. One by one, the survivors of his squad joined him on the scorched ruin of the deck. They followed him out from under the drop pod, bolters ready.

The ground was rumbling, the after-effects of a quake or something more serious? Powerful forces travelled through the ironwork lattice of Gorro. Metal and crushed rock lay in dust-wreathed heaps.

Sejanus looked up to see a rain of debris tumbling from the high ceiling, a wire-tangled hole marking their drop pod's entry to the crackling, lightning-filled vault.

Smashed machinery surrounded the crashed pod. Spars of metal and bodies had been pulverised by their impact and the quake. Arriving this deep had caught the half-dozen ork survivors here by surprise, but the clanking, smoke-belching things closing in on them weren't greenskins.

At least not of the flesh and blood variety.

'Throne, what are they?' said Sejanus.

Heavily armoured in what appeared to be all-enclosing suits of crudely-beaten iron, he'd taken them for ork chieftains, brutish war-leaders able to demand the heaviest armour, the biggest, loudest weapons.

But that wasn't what they were at all.

Their skulls were metal, as were their bodies. No part of them was organic, they were entirely formed of rusted iron, perforated vent chimneys hulking buzz saws and enormous cannons with flanged barrels.

Hundreds of tiny, shrieking, green skinned menial *things* surrounded them. Cackling, mean-looking serviles by the look of them, though even they were augmented with primitive bionics. Some carried smoking ad-hoc pistols, others held what looked like miniature blowtorches or tools more surgical than mechanical. Sejanus dismissed them as irrelevant.

The clanking, hissing metal greenskins stomped towards them and a hail of wild fire blasted from their guns. Sejanus skidded into cover. The gunfire was hopelessly inaccurate, but there was a *lot* of it. Grating speech that sounded like a machine badly in need of oiling ripped from the ironclad orks.

It always surprised Sejanus that the greenskin had mastered language. He supposed it was to be expected, given the incongruent levels of technology they possessed, but that so bestial a race *communicated* offended him on a gut level.

Shells exploded overhead, tearing through the heavy machine sheltering him. Almost immediately after, the snapping, cackling servile creatures swarmed over the top. They were tiny, virtually inconsequential. Until one started blowtorching the side of his helmet.

Sejanus pulverised it with a sharp headbutt. It exploded

like a green blister over his helm. He rolled and wiped the stinking mess of its demise from his visor. They were all over him, cutting, stabbing and shooting with their tiny pistols.

He scraped them off. He stamped on them like insects.

He had dismissed them as irrelevant, and individually they were. But throw a hundred of them into a fight, and even a legionary had to take them seriously.

Because while he was killing them by the score, the ork ironclads were still coming. The swarm kept attacking, fouling the joints of his armour with their ridiculous little tools, screeching with glee as they sawed serrated blades into seams between plates. The rest of his squad fared little better, fouled like prey beasts in a net.

'I don't have time for this,' he snarled, snapping off the string of frags from his belt. He snapped the arming pins and lobbed them into the air.

'Brace for impact!' shouted Sejanus, dropping to a crouch with his arms over his head.

The frags blew out with a rippling thunderclap of sequential detonations. Red-hot shrapnel scythed out in all directions. Fire engulfed Sejanus, and the overpressure threw him forward against the hulking machine. His armour registered a few penetrations where the creatures had managed to weaken the flexible joints at his knees and hip, but nothing serious.

The serviles were gone, shredded to bloody scraps on nearby machinery, like leavings from an explosion in a doll manufactory. Only a few remained alive, but even those were no threat. He rose to his feet, slathered in alien blood, and aimed his pistol at the oncoming ironclads.

'Take them,' ordered Sejanus.

The Glory Squad, that's what they called the warriors Sejanus commanded. Dymos, Malsandar, Gorthoi and the rest. Favoured by Horus and beloved by all, they had more than earned the name. Some thought the name vainglorious, but those who had seen them fight knew better.

Malsandar killed a beast with twin blasts from his plasma carbine, the ironwork effigy going up like a volcano as the searing beam set off a secondary detonation within it. Gorthoi put another down with a slamming right hook from his power fist, going on to tear it limb from limb as though he were back in the kill-pits of Cthonia.

Dymos and Ulsaar kept another at bay with concentrated bursts of bolter fire while Enkanus circled behind it with a melta charge. Faskandar was on his knees, his armour aflame and ceramite plates running like melting wax. Sejanus could hear his pain over the vox.

Sejanus picked his target, an ironclad with enormous bronze tusks welded into a serrated metal jaw. Its eyes were mismatched discs of red and green, its body a barrel-like construction with grinding pneumatics and beaten-metal weapon limbs. He put his bolt-round through the centre of its throat. The mass-reactive detonated and blew its head onto its shoulder in a shower of flame and squirting bio-organic oils.

The thing kept coming, raising a heavy, blunderbuss-like weapon with a flared muzzle. Sejanus didn't give it time to shoot and vaulted from cover. His boots thundered into its chest. The ironclad didn't fall. It was like slamming into a structural column.

A claw with monstrously oversized piston-driven motors snapped at his head. Sejanus ducked and thumbed the activation stud on his chainsword's hilt. The saw-toothed blade roared to life and he hacked through the last remnants of spurting oils and whirring chains holding the ironclad's head in place.

Its horned skull fell to the deck, and Sejanus stamped down on it. Metal splintered, and viscous fluid, like that cocooning the mortal remains of a mortis brother within his dreadnought, spilled out alongside a twitching root-like spinal cord. Sejanus felt his gorge rise as he saw what lay within the iron skull.

A spongy, grey green mass of tissue, like a fungal cyst of knotted roots filled the skull. Two piggish, red eyeballs hung limp on stalks from the broken metal, both staring madly up at him from the ruin of the metallic skull.

His horror almost cost him his life.

The headless ironclad's snapping claw fastened on his chest and lifted him from the deck. Black smoke jetted from the exhausts on its back as its pincer claw drew together. The plates of his armour buckled under the crushing pressure. Sejanus fought to free himself, but its grip was unbreakable.

Mars-forged plate cracked. Warning icons blinked to life on his sensorium. Sejanus cried out as his bones ground together and blood began filling the interior of his armour.

He braced his feet against the ironclad's chest and twisted to bring his pistol to bear. The red eyes within the slowly draining helm were looking up at him, relishing his agony. The bolt-round exploded and the brain matter of the ironclad and its body convulsed with its destruction. The claw spasmed, dropping Sejanus to the deck.

He landed badly, his spine partially crushed. White light smeared his vision as palliatives flooded his body to shut the pain gate at the nape of his neck. He'd pay for that later, but this was the only way to ensure there *was* a later.

Sejanus took a moment to restore his equilibrium.

The other ironclads were dead.

So too was Faskandar, his body reduced to a gelatinous mass by the fire of the unknown greenskin weapon. Dymos knelt beside their fallen brother.

'He's gone,' he said. 'Not enough even for an Apothecary.'

'He will be avenged,' promised Sejanus.

'How?' demanded Gorthoi, belligerent to the point of requiring admonishment.

'In blood. In death,' said Sejanus. 'Our mission is unchanged. We move out and kill anything we find. Does anyone have a problem with that plan?'

None of them did.

Dymos looked up at the ragged hole their drop pod had torn.

'The rest of the company's got to be hundreds of kilometres above us,' he said. 'We're on our own down here.'

'No,' said Sejanus, 'we're not.'

His armour's systems were picking up an Imperial presence.

'Who else is this deep?' asked Malsandar.

Sejanus had never seen this kind of signature, but whoever it was, not even the electromagnetic junk fouling the air and the hostile emissions from the ork machinery at scrapworld's core could obscure his presence.

Only one person would be visible this deep in Gorro.

Sejanus grinned. 'It's the Emperor.'

✠ ✠ ✠

HORUS DROPPED DOWN through the scrapworld's interior, a pearl-white angel trailing wings of fire as he fell. He'd jumped without a second's hesitation, blind to any thought other than following his father.

The quake had ripped the structure of Gorro apart. Its sedimentary levels of agglomerated junk were coming undone. Layers were separating and compacted debris was crumbling as its structural integrity collapsed at an exponential rate.

That meant two things.

Firstly, Horus was able to follow roughly the same route his father had fallen.

And secondly, the spaces opening up below him were getting wider, meaning his descent was getting faster. He smashed down through warrens of dwelling caves, stinking feeding pits and labyrinthine workshops that blazed with emerald fire.

Horus endured impacts that would have killed even a legionary as the scrapworld's death throes tossed him around like a leaf in a hurricane. He looked up, seeing tiny figures in black and gold falling after him.

Justaerin and Legio Custodes.

They'd followed him down, heroic and selfless.

But, ultimately, doomed.

They weren't primarchs. They could not endure what he could.

He saw Justaerin incinerated by a gout of plasmic fire billowing from a ruptured conduit. Custodians who dropped in arcing dives were smashed by falling debris or deforming structural elements. Their limp, lifeless bodies followed him down into the depths.

Eruptions flared up from the depths in kilometres-long forks of lightning. Ork war-machines exploded and swirling contrails of wildly corkscrewing ammunition ricocheted from every surface. Some of it struck him, scorching his armour and blistering his flesh.

Horus dropped through cavernous spaces filled with towering engines that no adept of Mars would ever dare build, let alone get to function. The world spun around him as Gorro's structure twisted and screamed with its imminent destruction. Cliff-like walls slammed together, giant girders wrought from the keels of wrecked starships bent like wire, and gouts of molten metal poured from collapsing foundries.

Horus slammed into a wall that might once have been a deck plate. Angled enough to slow his descent, but only just. The ground below was a nightmarish mass of cascading debris and fire. Horus punched his fist through the metal, ripping a jagged furrow in his wake to slow his descent.

Even with his speed reduced, Horus still slammed into the ground too hard. He bent his knees and rolled through the flames, feeling the heat of them scorch his armour and reach through to his flesh.

The deck plate shuddered and tore free of its moorings.

It tipped him over a yawning abyss limned in blue-white radiance from below. For a second, Horus was held aloft in an incandescently bright void of competing gravitational forces, wrenched in a thousand directions at once. Then one force, stronger than all the others combined, took hold of him and drew him down.

Horus fell and only at the last instant managed to right himself. He slammed down, bending his knee and punching a crater into the ground with the force of his impact.

For an instant he couldn't believe his senses.

The space in which he'd landed was a vast, spherical chamber where endlessly reconfiguring gravimetric forces were at play. There was no up or down, no cardinal direction in which gravity would act. Lightning leapt from enormous brass orbs spaced at random intervals around its inner surfaces, and a dizzyingly complex series of impossibly inverted walkways and gantries surrounded a colossal vortex of energy. At least a thousand metres wide, it seethed like a caged beast of plasma fire. Lashing silver fire forked from its expanding mass, tearing at Gorro's structure and breaking it apart.

As blinding and mesmerising as the runaway plasma reaction was at the scrapworld's heart, it was to a beleaguered golden light that Horus' eye was drawn.

The Emperor was fighting his way through a howling mob of the largest greenskins Horus had ever seen. Most were the equal of a primarch in stature. One even dwarfed the Emperor himself.

His father fought to reach a fragmenting ring of iron surrounding the blinding plasma core, but the greenskins had him surrounded.

This was a fight not even the Emperor could win alone.

But he was not alone.

SEJANUS AND HIS Glory Squad fought through the disintegrating ruins of the scrapworld in the old way. No subtlety, no finesse. Like a raid on a rival warlord's territory back in the day, when all that mattered was brute force and shocking violence. Where you stabbed and bludgeoned and shot until you either killed everyone in front of you or were dragged down in blood.

His armour was pearl-white no more, but slathered in viscera. He'd been forced to discard his pistol when a mechanised slug creature had latched onto it and tried to detonate the ammunition. His sword broke on the armoured skull of another ironclad, spilling its disembodied, fungal brain to the deck.

None of that mattered.

His fists were weapons.

His mass was a weapon.

Enkanus and Ulsaar were gone, murdered with motorised cleavers and energised hooks.

All that mattered was that they reach the Emperor.

Sejanus had settled into a rhythm of battle, that cold void within a warrior where his world shrinks to a sphere of engagement. Where the truly great are separated from the merely skilled by virtue of their ability to be aware of everything around them.

Dymos fought on his left, Gorthoi his right.

They pushed ever onwards, wading knee deep in greenskin blood and flesh. The stench of the abattoir and offal pit was overpowering, but Sejanus blocked it out. The raging tide of orks was a mass of green flesh clad in beaten armour. They saw more of the ironclads, and many other technological abominations that made them seem almost comprehensible.

In the course of the Great Crusade, Sejanus had seen many examples of the crudely effective greenskin technology, but what lay beneath the surface of the scrapworld were orders of magnitude more advanced and abhorrent.

The Emperor's signal never once wavered in his visor, though every other return fizzed and screamed with distortion.

Ahead, Sejanus saw a ragged archway through which spilled blazing white light. The Emperor lay beyond it.

'We're here,' he gasped, even his phenomenal

transhuman physique pushed to the limits of endurance by this fight.

He stormed through the archway and into a vast, spherical chamber with the brightest sun at its heart.

'Lupercal...' breathed Sejanus.

HORUS' SWORD WAS broken, his twin bolters empty of shells. The sword had snapped halfway along its length, the edge dulled from hewing countless greenskin bodies. He'd fought his way onto a stepped bridge, killing scores of monstrously swollen orks to reach a crumbling ledge just below the Emperor.

Blood drenched him, his own and that of the orks.

His helmet was long gone, torn away in a grappling, gouging duel with an iron-tusked giant with motorised crusher claws for arms and a fire-belching maw. He'd broken the beast over his knee and hurled its corpse from the bridge. Rogue gravity vortices hurled it up and away.

More of the greenskins followed him onto the bridge, grunting and laughing as they stalked him. Their grim amusement was a mystery to Horus. They were going to die, whether he killed them or they were burned to ash by the colossal plasma reactor's inevitable destruction.

Who would laugh in the face of their death?

The Emperor fought an armoured giant twice his height and breadth. Its skull was a vast, iron-helmed boulder with elephantine tusks and chisel-like teeth that gleamed dully. Its eyes were coal-red slits of such vicious intelligence that it stole Horus' breath.

Horus had never seen its equal. No bestiary would include its description for fear of being ridiculed, no magos of the Mechanicum would accept such a specimen could exist.

Six clanking, mechanised limbs bolted through its flesh bore grinding, crackling, sawing, snapping, flame-belching weapons of murder. The Emperor's armour was burning, the golden wreath now ashes around his neck.

Chugging rotor cannons battered the Emperor's armour even as claws of lightning tore portions of it away. It was taking every screed of the Emperor's warrior skill and psychic might to keep the mech-warlord's weaponry from killing him.

'Father!' shouted Horus.

The greenskin turned and saw Horus. It saw the desperation in his face and laughed. A fist like a Reductor siege hammer smashed the Emperor's sword aside and a fist of green flesh lifted him into the air. It crushed the life from him with its inhuman power.

'No!' yelled Horus, battering his way through the last of the greenskins to reach his father's side. The mech-warlord turned his spinal weapons on Horus, and a blistering series of lightning strikes hammered the walkway.

Horus dodged them all, a wolf on the hunt amid the ash and fire of the world's ending. He had no weapon, and where that wasn't normally a handicap to a warrior of the Legions, against this foe it was a definite disadvantage.

No weapon of his would hurt this beast anyway.

But one of its own…

Horus gripped one of the warlord's mechanised arms, one bearing the spinning brass spheres and crackling tines of its lightning weapon. The arm's strength was prodigious, but centimetre by centimetre Horus forced it around.

Lightning blasted from the weapon, burning Horus' hands black. Bone gleamed through the ruin of his flesh, but what was that pain when set against the loss of a father?

With one last herculean effort, Horus wrenched the arm up as a sawing blast of white-edged lightning erupted from the weapon. A searing burst of fire impacted on the mech-warlord's forearm and the limb exploded from the elbow down in a welter of blackened bone and boiling blood. The beast grunted in surprise, dropping the Emperor and staring in dumb fascination at the ruin of its arm.

Seizing the chance he had been given, the Emperor bent low and surged upwards with his bluesteel sword extended. The tip ripped into the mech-warlord's belly and burst from its back in a shower of sparks.

'Now you die,' said the Emperor, and ripped his blade up.

It was an awful, agonising, mortal wound. Electrical fire vented from hideous metal organs within the wreckage of the greenskin's body. It was a murderous wound that not even a beast of such unimaginable proportions could take and live.

Yet that was not the worst of it.

Horus felt the build up of colossal psychic energies and shielded his eyes as a furious light built within the Emperor. Power like nothing he had ever seen his father wield, or even suspected he possessed. All consuming, all powerful, it was the power to extinguish life in every sphere of its existence. Physical flesh turned to ash before it and what ancient faiths had once called a soul was burned out of existence, never to cohere again.

Nothing would ever remain of he who suffered such a fate.

Their body and soul would pass from the finite energy

of the universe, to fade into memory and have all that they were wiped from the canvas of existence.

This was as complete a death as it was possible to suffer.

That power blazed along the Emperor's sword, filling the greenskin with killing light. It erupted in a bellowing golden explosion, and lightning blazed from the coruscating afterimage of its death, arcing from ork to ork as it sought out all those who were kin to the master of Gorro. Unimaginable energies poured from the Emperor, reaching throughout the entirety of the chamber and burning every last shred of alien flesh to a mist of drifting golden ash.

Horus watched as the power of life and death coursed through the Emperor, saw him swell in stature until he was like unto a god. Wreathed in pellucid amber flames, towering and majestic.

His father never claimed to be a god, and refuted such notions with a vengeance. He had even castigated a son for believing what Horus now saw before him with his very own eyes...

Horus dropped to his knees, overcome with the wonder of what he was witnessing.

'*Lupercal*!'

He turned at the sound of his name.

And there he was, his wolf on the hunt.

Sprinting along the bridge was Hastur, howling his name over and over while pumping a fist in the air. He had fought beyond the limits of endurance and sanity to stand at the side of his primarch and his Emperor.

The wondrous light behind him was eclipsed by blue-white plasma, and Horus turned to see the Emperor silhouetted in the cold fire of Gorro's seething core.

His back was to Horus, sword sheathed at his hip and arms raised high. The same golden fire that had so comprehensively destroyed the greenskin warlord dripped from his spread fingertips like immaterial fire.

Horus had no knowledge of the insane mechanics behind the greenskin power core, but any fool could see that it was spiralling to destruction. The powerful tremors shaking Gorro apart was evidence enough of that, but to see the bound starfire straining against its bonds was to know it for certain. Had the death of the Mech-Warlord been the final straw in breaking whatever bonds of belief held its monstrous power in check?

How long would it be before it exploded? Horus had no idea, but suspected it would be long before any of them could escape the depths of the scrapworld.

'This can't be how it ends,' whispered Horus.

'No, my son,' said his father, gathering the golden light within him once again. 'It is not.'

The Emperor clenched his fists and the air around the seething plasma ball *folded*. It turned sickeningly inwards, as though reality was merely a backdrop against which the dramas of the galaxy were played out.

And where it folded, the spaces behind were horribly revealed, great abysses of crawling chaos and unlimited potential. Howling voids where the combined lives of this galaxy were but motes reflected in the cosmic dust storm. An empyrean realm of the never-born, where nightmares were birthed in the foetid womb of mortal lust. Things of void-cold form writhed in the darkness, like a million snakes of ebon glass coiled in endless, slithering knots.

Horus stared deep into the abyss, repulsed and fascinated by the secret workings of the universe. Even as he watched, the Emperor drew the fabric of the world together, sealing them around the greenskin plasma core. The effort was costing him dear, the golden light at his heart waning with every passing second.

And then it was done.

A thunderous bang of air rushed to fill the void left by the plasma fire, and the backwash blew back into the chamber in a gale of sulphurous wind.

The Emperor fell to one knee, his head bowed.

Horus was at his side a heartbeat later.

'What did you do?' said Horus, helping his father to his feet. The Emperor looked up, colour already returning to his wondrous features.

'Sent the plasma core into the aether,' said the Emperor, 'but it will not last long. We must withdraw before the warp fold implodes and takes everything with it. The entire mass of this scrapworld will be soon crushed as surely as if it had fallen into the grip of a black hole.'

'Then let's get off this damn thing,' said Horus.

THEY WATCHED THE final death agonies of Gorro from the bridge of the *Vengeful Spirit*. With the Mournival before them, the Emperor and Horus stood at the ouslite disc from which he had planned the void war against the scraphulk fleet.

'The greenskins will never recover from this,' said Horus. 'Their power is broken. It will be thousands of years before the beast arises again.'

The Emperor shook his head, drawing a shimmering orrery of light from the disc. Gently glowing points of light rotated around the edge of the disc, scores of systems, hundreds of worlds.

'Would that you were right, my son,' said the Emperor.

'But the greenskin is a cancer upon this galaxy. For every one of their ramshackle empires we burn to the ground, another arises, even greater and ever more deeply entrenched. Such is the nature of the ork – and this is why their race is so hard to destroy. They must be eradicated wholesale or they will return all the stronger, time and time again, until they come at us in numbers too great to defeat.'

'Then we are to be cursed by the greenskin for all time?'

'Not if we act swiftly and without mercy.'

'I am your sword,' said Horus. 'Show me where to strike.'

The Emperor smiled, and Horus felt his heart swell in pride.

'The Telon Reach was but a satrapy of the largest empire we have ever encountered, one that must fall before the Crusade can continue,' said the Emperor. 'It will be magnificent, the war we will wage to destroy this empire. You will earn much honour in its prosecution, and men will speak of it until the stars themselves go out.'

'And this is it?' asked Horus, leaning over the glowing hololith. First one, then dozens, and finally hundreds of worlds were outlined in green.

'Yes,' said the Emperor. 'This is Ullanor.'

AURELIAN

Aaron Dembski-Bowden

~ DRAMATIS PERSONAE ~

The Primarchs

LORGAR AURELIAN	Primarch of the Word Bearers
FULGRIM	Primarch of the Emperor's Children
ANGRON	Primarch of the World Eaters
HORUS LUPERCAL	Primarch of the Sons of Horus
PERTURABO	Primarch of the Iron Warriors
ALPHARIUS OMEGON	Primarch of the Alpha Legion
MAGNUS THE RED	Primarch of the Thousand Sons
KONRAD CURZE	Primarch of the Night Lords
MORTARION	Primarch of the Death Guard

The Word Bearers Legion

ARGEL TAL	Lord of the Gal Vorbak
KOR PHAERON	Captain, First Company

The Emperor's Children Legion

DAMARAS AXALIAN	Captain, Twenty-ninth Company

Inhabitants of the Great Eye

INGETHEL THE ASCENDED	Viator of the Primordial Truth
AN'GGRATH THE UNBOUND	Guardian of the Throne of Skulls
KAIROS FATEWEAVER	Oracle of Tzeentch

'Three things cannot long be hidden: the sun, the moon, and the truth.'

– Ancient Terran proverb

'I wish, with every fibre of my soul, that I had killed him when I had the chance. That momentary flicker of disbelief and sorrow, that second's hesitation for the abhorrence of fratricide, cost us more than anyone can measure. Horus leads the Legions into heresy, but Lorgar is the cancer in the Warmaster's core.'

– The Primarch Corax

'All I ever wanted was the truth. Remember those words as you read the ones that follow. I never set out to topple my father's kingdom of lies from a sense of misplaced pride. I never wanted to bleed the species to its marrow, reaving half the galaxy clean of human life in this bitter crusade. I never desired any of this, though I know the reasons for which it must be done.

But all I ever wanted was the truth.'

– Opening lines of the *Book of Lorgar*,
First Canticle of Chaos

PROLOGUE

HERALD OF THE ONE GOD

Colchis
Many years ago

THE ARCHPRIEST WATCHED from the cathedral window as his city burned below.

'We should do something.'

His voice was a bass rumble, yet edged by a softness that smoothed his words into something almost delicate. His was a voice made to reason, to question, to reassure – not to scream and froth and rage.

The archpriest turned from the window. 'Father? When will the fires stop burning?'

Kor Phaeron walked across the chamber, his wizened scowl deep-set on his face, like a scar cut into old leather. He busied himself with the scrolls on the central table, his thin lips moving as he read each one in turn.

'Father? We cannot remain here while the city burns. We must help the people.'

'You have not spoken since we claimed the Cathedral

of Illumination.' The ageing man glanced over for the merest moment. 'And your first words after winning this war are to ask when the fires will be drowned? You have just conquered a world, boy. You have greater matters to concern yourself with.'

The archpriest was a young man, beautiful in a way that transcended notions of physical attraction. His tan skin gleamed with tiny tattoos of gold-inked scripture. His eyes were dark without being cold, and he could spend days without smiling, yet never seem sinister.

He turned back to the window. In his mind's eye, he'd always pictured the crusade's end in this very place, the avenues of the City of Grey Flowers flooded by cheering crowds, their joyous prayers reaching into the skies, shaking the slender towers of their former rulers.

The reality didn't quite approach it. The streets were crowded, that much was true, but crowded with rioters, looters and clashing bands of robed warriors, as the last lingering remnants of the Covenant's defenders fought to the last against the tide of invaders.

'So much of the city is still aflame,' the archpriest said. 'We must do something.'

Kor Phaeron murmured to himself as he read the tattered parchments.

'Father.' The archpriest turned again, watching the older priest discard another scroll.

'Hmm? What is it, boy?'

'Half of the city is ablaze. We must do something.'

Kor Phaeron smiled, the expression ugly but not unkind. 'You must prepare for your coronation, Lorgar. The Covenant has fallen, and the Old Ways will be cast down as blasphemy against the One God. You are no longer merely Archpriest of the Godsworn, you are the Archpriest of all Colchis. I have given you a world.'

The golden figure turned back to the window, eyes narrowed. Something crept into his voice then, something rigid and cold, a foreshadowing of all that would be in the centuries to come.

'I do not wish to rule,' he said.

'That will change, my son. It will change when you see that no one else around you is as fit to rule as you are. In a moment of realisation, it will change out of your own selfless need. That is how it always works for men of power. The road to every throne is paved with good intentions.'

Lorgar shook his head. 'I wish for nothing more than our people to see the truth.'

'The truth *is* power.' The other priest went back to the scrolls. 'The ignorant and the weak must be dragged into the light, no matter the cost. It doesn't matter how many bleed and cry out on the way.'

Lorgar watched his new city burn, seeing his followers slaughter the last of the Old Ways' blasphemers in the streets below.

'I know I have asked so many times before,' he said softly, 'but does it not give you pause, even as the crusade ends? You once believed as they do.'

'I still believe as they do.' Kor Phaeron gave an assured smile. 'But I believe as you do, as well. I keep to my old faith that there are many gods, Lorgar. Your One God is simply the most powerful.'

'He will come to us soon.' The archpriest looked to the darkening sky. Colchis was a thirsty world, and rainclouds rarely made a call in the heavens. 'Perhaps a year from now, but no longer. I have seen it in my dreams. On the day he arrives, his vessel will descend through a storm.'

Kor Phaeron came closer, resting his hand on the taller man's forearm. 'When your One God comes, we will see if I was right to believe you.'

Lorgar was still staring up at the blue sky, watching it become choked by the rising smoke from the burning city. He smiled at his mentor's words.

'Have faith, father.'

Kor Phaeron smiled then. 'I have always had faith, my son. Have you ever dreamed this god's name? The masses will ask for it, soon enough. I cannot help but wonder what you will tell them.'

'I do not believe he has a name.' Lorgar closed his eyes. 'We will know him only as the Emperor.'

PART ONE
THE SEVENTEENTH SON

ONE

FRATERNITY

The *Vengeful Spirit*
Four days after Isstvan V

EIGHT OF HIS brothers were present, though only half of them truly stood in the room. The absent four were nothing more than projections: three of them manifested around the table in the forms of flickering grey hololithic simulacra, formed of stuttering light and white noise. The fourth of them appeared as a brighter image comprised of silver radiance, its features and limbs dripping spiral lashes of corposant witchfire. This last projection, Magnus, inclined its head in greeting.

+*Hail, Lorgar,*+ his brother bred the words within his mind.

Lorgar nodded in return. 'How far away are you, Magnus?'

The Crimson King's psychic projection showed no emotion. A tall man, his head crested by a sculpted crown, Magnus the Red refused to make contact using his one remaining eye.

+Very far. I lick my wounds on a distant world. It has no name but that which I brought to it.+

Lorgar nodded, not blind to the nuances of hesitation in his brother's silent tones. Now was not the time for such talk.

The others acknowledged him one by one. Curze – a cadaverous, pulsing hololithic avatar of himself, gave the barest suggestion of a nod. Mortarion, an emaciated wraith even in the flesh, was hardly improved by this electronic etherealness. His image faded in and out of focus, occasionally dividing in the bizarre mitosis of distance distortion. He lowered the blade of his Manreaper scythe in greeting, which was in itself a warmer hail than Lorgar had been expecting.

Alpharius was the last of those present through long-range sending. He stood helmed, while all others were bareheaded, and his hololithic image was stable while each of the others suffered corruption from the vast ranges between their fleets. Alpharius, almost a head shorter than his brothers, stood scaled in crocodilian resplendence, his reptile-skin armour plating glinting in the false light of his manifestation. His salute was the sign of the aquila, the Emperor's own symbol, made with both hands across his breastplate.

Lorgar snorted. How quaint.

'You're late,' one of his brothers interrupted. 'We've been waiting.' The voice was a graceless avalanche of syllables.

Angron. Lorgar turned to him, dispensing with any attempt at a conciliatory smile.

His warrior brother stood hunched in the threatening lean that characterised his body language, the back of his skull malformed from the brutal neural implants

hammered into the bone and wired into the soft tissue
of his brainstem. Angron's bloodshot eyes narrowed as
another pulse of pain ransacked through his nervous
system – a legacy of the aggression enhancers surgically
imposed upon him by his former masters. While the
other primarchs had risen to rule the worlds they'd been
cast down upon, only Angron had languished in captivity,
a slave to techno-primitives on some forsaken backwater
world that had never deserved a name. Angron's past still
ran through his blood, nerve pain sparking in his muscles with every misfired synapse.

'I was delayed,' Lorgar admitted. He didn't like to look
at his brother for too long at a time. It was one of the
things that made Angron twitch; like an animal, the
lord of the World Eaters couldn't abide being stared at,
and could never hold eye contact for more than a few
moments. Lorgar had no desire to provoke him.

Kor Phaeron had once made mention that the World
Eater's face was a sneering mask made of clenched knuckles, but Lorgar found no humour in it. To his eyes, his
brother was a cracked statue: features that should have
been composed and handsome were wrenched into a jagged, snarling expression, flawed by muscle twinges that
bordered on spasms. It was easy to see why others believed
Angron always looked on the edge of fury. In truth, he
looked like a man struggling to concentrate through epi-
leptic agony. Lorgar hated the bleak, crude bastard, but
it was hard not to admire his unbreakable endurance.

Angron grunted something wordless and dismissive,
looking back at the others.

'It has been nine days, and we know our tasks,' he
growled. 'We are already spread across the void. Why
did you gather us?'

Horus, Warmaster of the cleaved Imperium, didn't answer immediately. He gestured for Lorgar to take his place around the table, at Horus' own right hand. Unlike his Legion's sea-green ceramite, Horus stood clad in layered, dense armour of charcoal black, adorned with the glaring cadmium Eye of Terra on his breastplate. This last sigil, the symbol of his authority as master of the Imperium's armies, had its black core refashioned into a slitted serpent's pupil. Lorgar wondered, as he met Horus' pale, elegant smirk, just what secrets Erebus had been whispering into the Warmaster's ears in recent months.

Lorgar took his place between Horus and Perturabo. The former presided at the head of the table, all pretence of equality done away with in the aftermath of Isstvan. The latter stood in his burnished, riveted war plate, leaning on the haft of an immense hammer with an admirable air of casual disregard.

'Lorgar,' Perturabo murmured in greeting. Two-dozen power cables of various thicknesses plugged directly into the Iron Warrior's bare head, even at the jawline and temples, linking him to the internal processes of his gunmetal-grey armour. Chains draped over the tiered plating rattled as he gave a cursory nod.

Lorgar returned it, but said nothing. His dark eyes drifted across the others, seeking his last brother.

'So.' Horus' indulgent smile was all teeth. 'We have gathered again, at last.'

All eyes fell upon him, except for Lorgar's. The seventeenth son's distraction went unmarked as Horus continued.

'This gathering is the first of its kind. Here, now, we unite in one another's presence for the first time.'

'We gathered on Isstvan,' Angron grunted.

'Not all of us.' Alpharius' colourless hololithic image still hadn't turned its helmeted face. The projection's voice held little in the way of corruption-crackle, and just as little emotion.

The nine Legions had scattered after Isstvan. With a galaxy to conquer and great armies to raise on the long road to Terra, the Legions loyal to Warmaster Horus broke apart into the void, boosting away from a world left dead in their wake.

Angron narrowed his eyes, as if fighting to remember. He nodded agreement a moment later. 'True. Lorgar refused to come. He was *praying*.'

Horus, his handsome features lit from the low glow of his gorget, offered a smile. 'He was meditating on his place in our great plan. There is a difference, brother.'

Angron nodded again without really committing to agreement. He seemed to care for nothing but shrugging the conversation from his shoulders and moving on to other matters.

Horus spoke up again. 'We all know the costs of the coming campaign, and our destinies within it. Our fleets are underway. But after the, shall we say, unpleasantness of Isstvan, this is the first time we have gathered as a full fraternity.' Horus gestured with an open palm to his golden-skinned brother. Intentionally or not, the movement was threatening when made with the massive clawed Mechanicum talon sheathing his right hand. 'I hope your meditations were worthwhile, Lorgar.'

Lorgar was still staring at his final brother. He'd not taken his eyes off the last figure since he'd looked away from Perturabo.

'Lorgar?' Horus almost growled now. 'I am growing

ever more weary of your inability to adhere to established planning.'

Curze's chuckle was a vulture's caw. Even Angron smiled, his scarred lips peeling back from several replacement iron teeth.

Lorgar slowly, slowly reached for the ornate crozius mace on his back. As he drew the weapon in the company of his closest kin, his eyes remained locked on one of them, and all physically present felt the deepening chill of psychic frost riming along their armour.

The Word Bearer's voice left his lips in an awed, vicious whisper.

'You. *You are not Fulgrim.*'

TWO

BLOOD AT THE COUNCIL TABLE

TIME CHANGES ALL things.

The son that had never found a place in his father's empire was not the same soul that drew his weapon now. Lorgar was already moving before even the keenest of his warrior brothers knew what was happening.

Fulgrim had a scarce moment to draw a breath, to instinctively reach for his own weapon in a futile attempt to ward the coming blow.

Lorgar's crozius mace struck with a bell's toll, echoing around the war room. Fulgrim crashed into the back wall – a porcelain doll in shattered ceramite – and crumpled to the ground.

The golden primarch turned his fierce eyes upon his other brothers. 'That is not Fulgrim.'

The others were already advancing, drawing their own weapons. Lorgar's crimson armour, painted in honour of his Legion's treachery against the Throne, reflected the stuttering hololithic avatars of the four brothers present only in spirit.

'Stay back,' he warned those that still advanced upon him, 'and heed my words. That wretch, that *thing*, is not our brother.'

'Peace, Lorgar.' Horus approached, his own armour joints purring with low snarls. In times past, the merest threat of a confrontation had been enough to quell Lorgar from any rash action. He'd scarcely ever spoken a harsh word to any of his brothers, nor had he ever relished the many times they'd rebuked him for his perceived flaws. Unnecessary conflict was anathema to him.

As they faced him now, even Horus was wide-eyed in the changes wrought since Isstvan. The Word Bearers primarch clutched his maul in both red gauntlets, defying his brothers with narrowed eyes. In the voice of a poet turned to hate, he warned 'Stay back,' a second time.

'Lorgar.' Horus lowered his voice, softening it to match his brother's. 'Peace, Lorgar. Peace.'

'You already knew.' Lorgar almost laughed. 'I see it in your eyes, brother. What have you done?'

Horus gave a brittle smile. This had to end now. 'Magnus,' he said.

The psychic projection of Magnus the Red shook its crested head. 'I am on the other side of the galaxy, Horus. Do not ask me to contain our brother. Keep order on your own flagship.'

Fulgrim moaned as he began to rise from the decking. Blood made lightning trails down his face from the edges of his lips. Lorgar rested an armoured boot on the prone primarch's chestplate.

'Stay down,' he said, without looking at Fulgrim.

Fulgrim's pale, androgynous features twisted in false amusement. 'You think you–'

'If you speak,' Lorgar kept his boot on the fallen pri-march, 'I will destroy you.'

'Lorgar,' Horus growled now. 'You are speaking madness.'

'Only because I have seen madness.' He met his broth-ers' eyes in turn, looking from one to the other. The kindest among them looked upon him with pity. Most were merely disgusted. 'I alone know what the truth looks like.' He pushed down with his boot, pressing on Ful-grim's shattered ribcage, driving ceramite armour shards into the broken body. Fulgrim choked on blood. Lorgar paid it no mind.

Horus turned to the others with a melodramatic sigh. Indulgence was plainly writ across his handsome features, as if sharing some old jest between the rest of his family.

'I will deal with this. Leave us for now. We will recon-vene shortly.'

The hololithics flickered off immediately, but for Alpharius, who stood watching Lorgar for several moments longer. Magnus the Red was the last to fade, his projected self nodding to Horus at last, and dispersing like mist in the wind. For several moments, his sourceless voice hung in the empty air. *To manifest here requires a significant effort of will, Horus. Bear that in mind next time.*

'The Cyclops is right,' one of the others objected. 'We delay over nothing. Let the fanatic claim what he wishes. We will restrain him and be done with it. We have a war to plan.'

Horus sighed. 'Just go, Angron. I will summon you back from the *Conqueror* when we are ready.'

In the clash of irritation and amusement that coloured most of their discussions, Perturabo and Angron trudged from the war room; one speaking, the other listening.

With the chamber sealed again, Lorgar aimed the immense maul at Horus' bare head.

'So you send them away to protect a secret that should never be kept. Do you think they will suspect nothing? If you believe I will allow you to concoct a tale of my insanity to aid in your deception, you are misleading yourself.'

Horus wouldn't be baited. 'That was incautious, Lorgar. Explain your actions.'

'I can see the truth, Horus.' Lorgar risked a glance down at whatever was wearing his brother's skin and armour. 'His soul is hollowed through. Something nestles within this body, like eggs layed inside a host.' Lorgar raised his eyes again. 'Magnus would have sensed it also, had he not been drained from sending his image such a great distance. This is not Fulgrim.'

Horus released a breath. 'No,' he admitted. 'It is not.'

'I know what this is.' Lorgar rested the mace's spiked head against Fulgrim's temple. 'What I cannot understand is how this happened. How have you allowed it to come to pass?'

'Is it so different from your own Gal Vorbak?' the Warmaster countered.

Lorgar's gold-inked features, ruthlessly similar to their father's, broke into patient sympathy. 'You do not know of what you speak, Horus. One of the Neverborn, puppeteering the soulless body of our own brother? There is no balance of human and divine elements here. No graceful alignment of two souls in harmony. This is desecration, blasphemy, not ascension.'

Horus smiled. Lorgar could always be relied upon to seethe with such theatrics. 'Consider this another unpleasant truth. I did not orchestrate Fulgrim's demise. I am merely containing the aftermath.'

Lorgar exhaled slowly. 'So he is dead, then. Another sentience rides within his body. This husk is all that remains of Fulgrim?'

Horus' reply was preceded by a grunt of annoyance. 'Why does it matter to you? You and he were never close.'

'It matters because this is a perversion against the natural order, fool.' Lorgar spoke through perfect, clenched teeth. 'Where is the harmony in this joining? A living soul annihilated for its mortal shell to house a greedy, unborn wretch? I have walked in the warp, Horus. I have stood where gods and mortals meet. This is weakness and corruption – a perversion of what the gods wish for us. They want allies and followers, not soulless husks ridden by daemons.'

Horus said nothing. He didn't even respond to Lorgar's insult, though his lip curled.

Lorgar cast his eyes down to the fallen primarch. Fulgrim, whatever was within him, stared back with blood flecking the pale skin around his eyes.

Get off me, the voice ghosted through Lorgar's mind. It wasn't Fulgrim's voice. It wasn't even a close approximation.

+Be silent!+ he psychically pulsed back, with enough force to make Fulgrim tremble.

Lorgar... The creature's voice was weaker, raspier, a tremulous breath of wind. *You know my kind. We are kin, you and I.*

The primarch of the Word Bearers moved away, his sneer painted plain. The desperation in the creature's silent voice made his skin itch.

'How did this happen?' he asked Horus.

The Warmaster watched Fulgrim rise. Lorgar did not – he spat onto the decking and tossed his crozius onto the table. Its ornate spiked head sent cracks lightning-bolting across the table's surface.

On his feet, Fulgrim was a slender, willowy figure – svelte even in his contoured war plate. Lorgar saw none of the grace when he turned: he saw only the sickening unlight behind his brother's eyes, and the intelligence of another being at the body's core.

Fulgrim smiled someone else's smile.

'Lorgar,' he began, using Fulgrim's curiously tender voice.

+I will learn your true name and banish you back into the warp. Perhaps in its tides, you will relearn restraint.+

He held back as he forced the speech into the other's mind, but it was still harsh enough to make Fulgrim snort blood onto his lips.

Lorgar... I–

+You have desecrated the flesh in which you ride. Nothing more. This is not the holy union of humanity and Chaos. You violate the purity of the gods' Primordial Truth.+

Fulgrim sagged back against the wall. Blood was running from his eyes.

'Lorgar.' Horus rested his unclawed hand on his brother's shoulder. 'You are killing him.'

'It is not "him". It is an *it*. And if I wished to kill it, then it would already be destroyed.' Lorgar narrowed his eyes at Horus' restraining grip on his shoulder.

+Remove your hand, Horus,+ he sent.

Horus obeyed, though he tried not to. The Warmaster's fingers shivered as they withdrew, and his grey eyes flickered with unhidden tension.

'You have changed,' he said, 'since crossing blades with Corax.'

Lorgar gathered his crozius and rested the immense maul on his shoulder guard. 'Everything changed that night. I am returning to my ship, brother. I must think upon this... this foulness.'

THREE

MAGNUS AND LORGAR

HE DID NOT wait long, nor had he expected to. Indeed, his brother awaited him in his chamber.

'We must speak, you and I.'

The phantasm's form rippled, bright with witchfire, beaming myriad reflections across the angled walls of Lorgar's inner sanctum. The chamber was cold, always too cold, and the air was forever moist as it ran through the filtration system. The primarch missed the dry climes of Colchis.

He rested *Illuminarium*, the immense crozius maul, against the wall.

'Magnus,' he said to the wraith. The figure formed of silver fire gave a graceful bow.

'It has been a long while since we spoke anything of substance.'

Once, not so long ago, he would have smiled to see his wisest, most powerful brother. Now, the smile read false, and didn't reach Lorgar's eyes.

'You exaggerate. We have spoken many times in recent years.'

Magnus' remaining eye followed his brother's steps as Lorgar moved over to his writing table.

'Our last talk of any real worth was in your City of Grey Flowers, almost half a century before. Have anything beyond the shallowest pleasantries passed between us since then?'

Lorgar met Magnus' eye. The silvery form flickered as Lorgar's voice resonated around it.

+Times change, Magnus.+

The Cyclops visibly shuddered, though he kept smiling. *'I felt that, even here. You have grown strong.'*

+I saw the truth on the very Pilgrimage you demanded I never make. And after Isstvan, a veil lifted from my eyes. There is no longer any need to hold back. If we restrain ourselves, we will lose this war, and humanity will lose its only chance at enlightenment.+

The distant primarch's image wavered again. For a moment, Magnus looked pained.

'You scream your strength into the warp without care. A vessel must sail with the aetheric tides, Lorgar, lest it break against them.'

Lorgar laughed, a gentle, patient sound. 'A lecture, from you? I have seen your past and future, Magnus. You stand with us only because our father exiled you. You stand as the crowned king of a Legion of the damned.'

'My Legion? Of what do you speak?'

Lorgar felt his brother's questing probes, the softest psychic touch within his skull. It took the barest effort to hurl the insidious psi-touches aside.

+If you ever seek to pry into my thoughts again, I will make sure you regret it.+

Magnus' smile became forced. *'You truly have changed.'*

'Yes,' Lorgar nodded, writing upon a scroll. 'Everything has changed.'

'What did you mean about my Legion?'

Lorgar was already distracted as he worked. 'Watch for the greatest snarl in fate's skeins, brother.' He dipped the quill into an inkpot and resumed his scribing. 'You are not free of the flesh-change your Legion once feared. Beware those among your sons that fail to embrace it as the gift it is.'

Magnus fell silent for some time. The only sound in the room was the scritch-scratch of Lorgar's quill-tip, and the omnipresent bass murmur of the generators on the enginarium decks.

'Fulgrim is–'

'So it seems.' Lorgar stopped writing long enough to look up. 'How long have you known?'

Magnus moved to the wall, reaching out as if his ethereal fingers could touch the paintings of Colchis hanging there.

'I knew it as soon as I reached into Horus' war room.' He withdrew his fingers, curling them back with slow care. *'Like you, I am no stranger to the entities within the warp. One of them animates his body now. '*

+Entities? Name them as they are, brother. Daemons.+

Magnus' image wavered again, almost discorporated in the winds of Lorgar's silent voice.

'Control your strength, Lorgar.'

Lorgar went back to his writing. 'You should have told me the truth years ago.'

'Perhaps.' The melancholy bleeding from Magnus was almost strong enough to caress the skin. *'Perhaps I should have. I sought only to protect you. You were so certain, so arrogant in your beliefs. '*

Lorgar spoke as he kept writing. 'I stand at the right hand of the new Emperor, commanding the second-largest Legion in the Imperium. You are a broken soul, leading a shattered Legion. Perhaps I was never the one that needed protection, nor did my arrogance lead to my downfall. You cannot claim the same, Magnus. We both knew the truth, but only one of us faced it.'

'And such a truth.'

Bitter amusement lapped at Lorgar's senses.

'The galaxy is a foul place. We are only making it fouler. Have you considered that it might be better to die in ignorance than to live with the truth?'

Lorgar repelled his brother's creeping emotions with a burst of irritation. The spectre shimmered again, almost dissolving into the air.

+Have *you* considered it, Magnus? If so, why do you yet live? Why did you not surrender to the howling death that came for you, when Russ broke your spine over his knee?+

Magnus' ghost-image laughed, but it was a forced sound, barely reaching Lorgar's mind. *'Is this what we have come to? Is this the bitterness you have hidden from all of us for half a century? What did you see at the end of your pilgrimage, my brother? What did you see when you stared into the abyss?'*

+You know what I saw. I saw the warp, and what swims within its tides.+ He hesitated a moment, feeling his fingers curl, forming fists in his rising rage. +You are a coward, to know of the Primordial Truth yet fail to embrace it. Chaos Incarnate is only grotesque because we see it with mortal eyes. When we ascend, we will be the chosen children of the gods. When–+

'Enough!'

Three of the paintings burst into flame; the crystal sculpture of the Covenant's tower palace shattered into worthless glass chips. Lorgar winced at his brother's psychic release. He had to sniff blood back into his nose.

'I am finished with this petty banter. You believe you know the truths behind our reality? Then show me. Tell me what you saw at the end of your accursed pilgrimage.'

Lorgar rose to his feet, extinguishing the small fires with a gentle gesture. Frost glinted on his fingernails as the flames hissed into nothingness, starved of air. For a moment he felt a twinge of regret, that he and his closest brother should be reduced to this.

But time changed all things. He was no longer the lost one, the weak one, the one brother plagued by doubt.

Lorgar nodded, his eyes thinned to dangerous slits.

'Very well, Magnus.'

PART TWO
THE PILGRIM

FOUR

A DEAD WORLD

Shanriatha
Forty-three years before Isstvan V

HE TOOK HIS first steps onto the world's surface, hearing the soft percussion of his steady breathing within the enclosed suit of armour. Targeting cross hairs moved over the emptiness in a sedate drift, while the delicate electronics of his retinal display listed his own bio-data in ignorable streams.

Slowly, he moved into the wind. Dust crunched underfoot, soil so absolutely dead and dry that it defied the possibility of life. His musings were accompanied by the rattle of grit in the breeze, clattering against his thrumming armour plating.

For just a moment, he turned and looked back at his gunship. The racing winds were already painting it with a fine layer of the powdery red dust that existed in abundance on this world.

This world. He supposed it had once possessed a name,

though it had never been spoken by human lips. Its bleak, rusty desolation reminded him of Mars, though Terra's sister world was a bastion of industry with few wild lands remaining. It also laid claim to calmer skies.

He didn't look up; he didn't need to, for there was nothing new to see. From horizon to horizon, a blanket of tortured clouds bubbled and churned, thunderheads crashing together to make tides of white, violet, and a thousand reds.

The warp. He'd seen it before, but never like this. Never around a world. Never in place of true weather. Never crashing through thousands of solar systems in a migraine tide, like a nebula rotting in the void.

'*Lorgar*,' said a genderless, breathless voice behind him, from a place where no one had been a moment before.

He didn't spin to face it, nor did he bring his weapon to bear. Instead, the primarch turned slowly, his eyes laden with patience and a bright, too-human curiosity.

'Ingethel,' he greeted the aberration. 'I have sailed into the mouth of madness. Now tell me why.'

INGETHEL SLITHERED CLOSER. Its claim to a humanoid form ended at its waist, which became the thick, ridged tail of a deep-sea worm or serpent. Mucous membranes along its underside were already coated with dust. Even its torso was human in only the loosest sense: four skeletal arms reached from its shoulders, in divine mockery of some ancient Hindusian deity, and its skin was a grey, mottled spread of dry leather.

'*Lorgar*,' it said again. Malformed teeth clacked together as the creature's jaw chattered. What had once been the face of a human female was now a bestial ruin – all fangs and dusty fur, with a leonine mouth that couldn't close around its deformed dental battlements. One eye stared, swollen and ripe with blood, bulging from its socket. The other was a sunken, useless nugget half-buried in the beast's skull.

'*Why did you choose this world?*' the creature asked.

The primarch saw its throat quiver with the effort of speech, but no human words left the trembling jaws.

'Does that matter?' Lorgar wondered. His own voice emerged from the snarling vox-grille in the mouth of his helm. 'I do not see why it would.'

'*From orbit, you must have known several things – you cannot breathe the air of this world, nor is there any sign of life upon its surface. Yet you chose to land and journey across it.*'

'I saw the ruins. A city drowned in the dust plains.'

'*Very well,*' it said, as if expecting such an answer. The creature hunched its shoulders against the wind, turning its head to shield its swollen eye. From its spine and shoulder blades rose several black pinions of burned bone – an angel's wings, with no muscles or feathers.

'What are you?' Lorgar asked.

The beast's tongue bled as it licked its armoury of teeth. '*You know what I am.*'

'Do I?' The primarch towered above any mortal man, but Ingethel was taller still, rising high on its coiled tail. 'I know you are a creature incarnated without a soul. I see nothing of the same life I see in humanity. No aura. No glimmer in the core of your being. But I do not know what you are – only what you are not.'

The wind picked up, tearing at the parchment scrolls fastened to Lorgar's war plate. He let the storm claim them, not watching as they were ripped away, flapping in the air. A retinal warning flashed by the edge of his right

eye, it was proclaiming another fall in the temperature.
Was night falling? Nothing had changed in the sky above;
no sun could be seen, let alone one that seemed to be
setting. Lorgar cancelled the warning with a blink at the
pulsating rune, just as his armour began to hum louder.
The back-mounted generator growled as it churned out
more power, entering a void-thaw cycle.

'It is over two hundred degrees below the point water
would freeze,' he said to the monster. 'Almost as cold as
naked space.'

*'Another reason I wonder why you chose to walk upon
this world.'*

Lorgar bared his teeth behind the granite-grey faceplate.
'I am armoured to survive such extremes. What are you,
to stand here and ignore an atmosphere cold enough to
turn blood to ice in the time it takes the human heart
to beat a single pulse?'

*'This is where the realm of flesh and spirit meet. Phys-
ical laws mean nothing here. There is no limit on what
might be. That is Chaos. Endless possibility.'*

Lorgar took a deep breath of the clean, recyc-scrubbed
air of his war plate. It tasted of ritual cleansing oils, coppery in his sinuses. 'So I could breathe here? I would
not freeze?'

*'You are unique among the Anathema's sons. All of your
brothers are whole, Lorgar. You alone are lost. They have
mastered their gifts since birth. Your own mastery will
come with understanding. When it does, you will have the
strength to reshape entire worlds on a whim.'*

Lorgar shook his head. 'I am bred from the best of
humanity, but I am still human. You may stand unarmoured in this storm. It would destroy me in a moment.
We are too different.'

The creature faced the primarch, its swollen eye cataracted by a film of red grit. *'Only one difference exists between the warp and the flesh. In the realm of flesh, sentient life is born ensouled. In the realm of raw thought, all life is soulless. But both are alive. The Born and the Neverborn, on both sides of reality. Destined for symbiosis. Destined for union.'*

The primarch crouched, letting dust fall through his gauntleted fingers. 'Neverborn. I have studied the history of my species, Ingethel. That is no more than a poetic word for "daemon".'

The creature turned its back to the wind again, but said nothing.

'What is this world called?' Lorgar looked up, but did not rise. The dust hissed away in the racing wind, leaving his fingers in a gritty stream.

'The eldar called it "Ycressa" before the Fall. After the birth of Slaa Neth, She Who Thirsts, it was named "Shanriatha".'

The primarch gave a soft laugh.

'You know the meaning of this word?'

'I learned the eldar tongue when my Legion first met them. Yes, I know the meaning of the word. It means "never forgotten".'

The daemon flicked a slit tongue over its maw, heedless of the bloody scratches it inflicted upon itself. *'You have met the soulbroken?'*

'The soulbroken?'

'The eldar.'

Lorgar rose to his feet, brushing the last of the dust away. 'The Imperium has encountered them many times. Some expeditionary fleets have clashed with them, to drive them from Imperial space. Others have passed in peace. My brother Magnus was always one of the more lenient when encountering them.' He hesitated for a moment, turning to the creature. 'Your kind know of my brother Magnus, do they not?'

'The gods themselves know Magnus, Lorgar. His name is threaded through destiny's web as often as your own.'

The Word Bearer looked back to the horizon. 'That gives me little comfort.'

'It will, in time. Speak of the soulbroken.'

He continued, slower now. 'My Legion encountered them not long after we sailed from Colchis the very first time. A fleet of eldar, their vessels built of bone, drifting through the void powered by immense solar sails. I met with their farseers, to determine their place in mankind's galaxy. During those weeks, I mastered their tongue.'

Lorgar took another breath, thinking back to that time. 'It was easy to despise them. Their inhumanity made them cold – their skin stank of bitter oil and alien sweat, and their vaunted wisdom came at the cost of sneering condescension. What right did a dying breed have to judge us inferior? I asked them this, and they had no answer.'

He laughed again, the same gentle sound. 'They named us *mon-keigh*, their term for so-called "lesser races". And yet, while they were easy to hate, there was much to admire in them, as well. Their existence is a tragic one.'

'And what of your Legion?'

'We destroyed them,' the primarch admitted. 'At great cost, in both warships and loyal lives. They care for nothing but survival – the ferocious need to continue their existence saturates their whole culture. None of them ever die easily, nor do they fall cleanly.'

He paused for a moment. 'Why do you name them "soulbroken"?'

If such a thing as Ingethel could be said to smile, it did so now. *'You know what this place is. Not this world, but this whole region of space, where gods and mortals meet. A goddess was born here. Slaa Neth. She Who Thirsts.'*

Lorgar looked to the sky, watching the cosmic after-birth raging above. He knew without being told that this storm would rage forever. And it would spread, over the coming centuries, engulfing ever more solar systems. It would spread far and wide, opening to peer into the galaxy's core like a god's staring eye.

'I am listening,' he said quietly.

'In her genesis, brought about by the eldar's worship, she claimed the spirits of the entire race. They are the soulbroken. When any mortal dies, its spirit drifts into the warp. It is the way of things. But when the eldar die, they are pulled right into the maw of the goddess they betrayed. She thirsts for them, for they are her children. She drinks them as they die.'

Together, the daemon and the Emperor's son began to move west. Lorgar moved against the wind, his helmed head lowered as he listened to the creature's psychic speech. Ingethel closed its eyes as best as its deformed face allowed, its slithering passage leaving a sidewinder trail in the dust.

The marks they left didn't last long, for the storm soon obliterated all evidence of their passing.

'Something you said, it matches the Old Ways of Colchis.' He quoted verbatim from the texts of the very religion he'd once overthrown in the name of Emperor-worship. 'It is said that "upon death, the unshackled soul drifts into the infinite, to be judged by thirsting gods"'.

Ingethel made a choking, coughing gargle. It took Lorgar a moment to realise the creature was laughing.

'*It is the core of a million human faiths throughout your species' lifespan. The Primordial Truth is in humanity's blood. You all reach for it. You all know that something awaits after death. The faithful, the loyal, will be judged kindly and reside in their gods' domains. The faithless, the unbelievers, will drift through the aether, serving as prey for the Neverborn. The warp is the end of all spirits. It is the destination of every soul.*'

'That is hardly the heaven promised in most human faiths.' Lorgar felt his lip curling.

'*No. But it is the same hell your species has always feared.*'

The primarch couldn't argue with that.

'*You wish to see the ruins of this world.*' Ingethel weaved as it slithered alongside him.

'This was once a grand city.' Lorgar could make out the first fallen towers on the horizon, shrouded in generations of carmine dust. Whatever tectonic devastation had claimed this world long ago had dragged the city into a crater, spilling its spires to the ground. What protruded from the earth now resembled the ribcage of some long-dead beast.

'*These ruins were never a true city. When the soulbroken fled the goddess' birth, the survivors boarded vast domed platforms of living bone, carrying the remnants of their species into the stars on a final exodus.*'

'Craftworlds. I have seen one.' Lorgar kept trudging forward, into the wind. 'It was magnificent, in its own alien, chilling way.'

Ingethel's chittery laugh wasn't quite stolen by the wind. '*Many of the fledgling craftworlds failed to escape Slaa Neth's birth scream. They dissolved in the void, or fell to die on the faces of these abandoned worlds.*'

Lorgar slowed in his pace, casting a glance at the dae-mon. 'We walk to the grave of a craftworld?'

Ingethel rasped another laugh from its malformed jaws. *'You are here to witness wonders, are you not?'*

AND SO THEY came to a dead city, fallen from the void to bury itself in the world's lifeless dust.

Red-stained bone architecture reached as far as the eye could see, jutting from the fundament with all the grace of a mouth filled by shattered teeth. Lorgar and his guide stood at the crater's lip, staring down into the grave of the alien void city.

The primarch was silent for some time, listening to the howl of the wind and the accompanying grit-rattle against his armour. When he spoke, he didn't break his gaze from the ancient annihilation below.

'How many died here?'

Ingethel raised itself higher, peering down with its foul eyes. Four arms spread in a grand gesture, as if laying claim to everything the daemon beheld.

'This was Craftworld Zu'lasa. Two hundred thousand souls burst in the moment Slaa Neth was born. Unguided, with madness rampant in its own living core, the craft-world fell.'

Lorgar felt a small smile take hold. 'Two hundred thou-sand. How many in the entire eldar empire?'

'A whole species. Trillions. A decillion. A tredecillion. A goddess was born in the brains of every living eldar, and tore itself into the realm of cold space and warm flesh.'

The daemon hunched itself, leaning with all four arms on the crater's edge. *'I sense your emotions, Lorgar. Pleas-ure. Awe. Fear.'*

'I have no love for the galaxy's xenos breeds,' the

primarch confessed. 'The eldar failed to grasp the truth of reality, and I feel no sorrow for them. Merely pity that any being can die in ignorance.' He took a breath, still staring down at the buried craftworld. 'How many of these failed to escape the goddess' birth?'

'A great many. Even now, some drift in the warp's tides – the silent homes of memories and alien ghosts.'

Lorgar ignored the wind tearing at his cloak as he took his first step on the crater's slope.

'I sense something, Ingethel. Something down there.'

'I know.'

'Do you know what it is?'

The daemon wiped its abused eyes with careful claws. *'A revenant, perhaps. An echo of eldar life, breathing its last, if it still breathes at all.'*

Lorgar drew his crozius maul, his thumb close to the activation rune. The weapon caught the tumultuous light above, reflecting the storm on its burnished spines.

'I'm going closer.'

FIVE

ECHOES

GHOSTS WALKED THE streets, wraiths of wind and dust, forming tantalising shapes in the tempest. They lived at the edge of his vision, slaughtered by the storm each time Lorgar sought to see them more clearly. There, a fleeing figure, obliterated back into the breeze the moment Lorgar turned to see it. And there: three reaching, shrieking maidens, though there was nothing more than whirling dust when the primarch turned again.

He clutched the crozius tighter. Ahead, always ahead, there thrummed that aching sense of something barely alive – weakened, trapped, almost certainly dying. The bleak resonance reaching into his mind spoke of something like a caged, diseased animal: something that had been dying for a long, long time.

Lorgar moved with care, stepping around dust-coated rubble, treading through the skeleton of a city. The gritty wind carried distant voices in its grip – inhuman voices, screaming in an alien tongue. Perhaps the gale played tricks of its own, for even with a grasp of the eldar language, he couldn't make out the words being cried into the storm. Trying to comprehend individual voices merely made the others louder, eclipsing any hope of focus.

As he moved deeper through the emaciated city, Lorgar ceased turning at every half-formed image, unfocusing his eyes and letting the teasing wind shape whatever it chose. In the thrashing gusts, faint spires stood at the corners of his eyes, alien towers reaching up with impossible grace into hostile skies.

The primarch looked back, seeking Ingethel and seeing nothing.

+*Ingethel*,+ he reached out with his stuttering psychic sense, unsure if the call even pierced the wind. +*Daemon. Where are you?*+

The storm howled louder in answer.

TIME SEEMED TO lose its grip. Lorgar's thirst grew raw, though he never slowed in weariness, all the while walking for over seventy hours beneath an unending dusk. The only certain evidence of time's passing was his retinal chrono, which degenerated into unreliable fluctuation at the tip of the seventy-first hour. The digital display began to pulse with random runes, as if finally surrendering to the unnatural laws of this warp-drowned realm.

Lorgar recalled Argel Tal's face: gaunt, almost vampiric in its skeletal ferocity, when the warrior had claimed his vessel had sailed the warp's tides for half a year. To Lorgar and the rest of the fleet, the *Orfeo's Lament* had been gone no longer than a few heartbeats.

Idly, he wondered how long would pass in the material universe while he lingered here, walking along the shores of hell.

What little of the craftworld's architecture remained above ground was a victim of erosion, worn down and scarred by the blistering winds. Lorgar stalked down yet another avenue of dust, his boots grinding down on the ancient rock. Perhaps this had once been an agricultural dome, fertile and forested with xenos flora. Perhaps it had been nothing more than a communal chamber, though. Lorgar sought to restrain his imagination, refusing to let it be stirred further by the dancing shapes in the dust storm.

Another hundred metres, scuffing through worthless soil, and the curious, queasy ache of struggling life began to throb below his boots. To his left, to his right, nothing but the fallen towers of a dead civilisation.

The primarch crouched to grip a fistful of the red soil. As before, he let it fall through his fingers, watching as it was snatched away by the wind. The presence, such as it was, waxed and waned in arrhythmia. Lorgar took a breath, aiming a thin pulse of psychic energy to trickle downward. He felt nothing in response. Not even a tremor of awareness. It could've been a metre below the ground, or all the way down to the world's core. Either way, it was a weak, irregular thing; seemingly untouchable and only barely reminiscent of life.

Sentience resided in hiding, but it didn't feel alive.

Curious.

He pushed deeper, scenting, seeking, but the same buried core of resistant nothingness met his questing touch.

In grudging defeat, Lorgar withdrew his hesitant psychic probing, curling his perception back into his skull's senses.

That did it. Even as he was cursing his erratic talents, he felt something stir beneath, burrowing upward. The presence beneath the sand chewed its way up, an icy bloodhound sentience straining to sniff after his retreating psy-caress.

Lorgar recoiled on instinct, shuddering at the sense of desperation wrenching closer from below. With gritted teeth, he forced a blast of repellent thought back at the grasping presence – the psychic equivalent of smashing a drowning man's fingers as he grasped for a lifeline. The presence ebbed for a moment, regrouped, and clawed upwards again.

Its crest broke the surface: raw feeling crashing against the primarch's mind in a splash of cold ferocity, absolutely devoid of any other emotion. Lorgar staggered back from the fountain of rising awareness, deflecting its jagged intensity as best he could. When the hand burst from the sand, the primarch already stood with his crozius in his fists.

He watched, shielding his mind from a spit-spray of formless psychic hate, as the statue of a dying god dragged itself from a grave of scarlet soil.

It couldn't stand. In its struggles to rise, the creature crawled closer, hands digging into the earth to find loose purchase. But it couldn't seem to stand. The primarch watched it crawl, unable to see any distinct spinal injury along its cracked armour plating. The long mane of hair falling to either side of its snarling death-mask face looked to be composed of smoke. It streamed out, captured by the wind, a slave to the storm's breath.

Lorgar backed away with slow care, boots crunching the dust, his own features bare of anything beyond curiosity. Whatever the crippled thing was, its wrath poured from it in an aura of physical pressure. Lorgar took another retreating step, still watching closely.

For all the god-statue's majesty, it was plainly ruined
by supernatural decay. A husk crawled where once a great
entity would be striding over the land. Lorgar saw its banished glory when he narrowed his eyes, peering at the
flickering after-images through his lashes. A being of tectonic armour plating: with eyes of white flame; a heart
that beat magma over bones of unburnable black stone;
a towering manifestation of incarnate rage and holy fire.
Lorgar saw all of this through the swirling sand, and even
smiled as the wind formed a false heat haze around the
creature – another weak echo of what should have been
truly majestic.

Had it been able to stand, it would have risen taller
than a Legiones Astartes dreadnought. Even prone and
destroyed, it was an immense thing, leaving a wretched
trail in the dust.

He almost pitied it, in this devastated incarnation. Its
black skin was faded to a greyish charcoal, split in old
cracks that bled smoke into the storm. Lava-blood had
dried to a sluggish flow of ember sludge; scabby crusts
spoke of its own blood cooling, drying as it left its body.
Where eyes of witchfire had once blazed, hollow eye
sockets twisted in sightless, feral expressions.

'I am Lorgar,' he told the crawling god. 'The seventeenth
son of the Emperor of Man.'

The god bared black teeth and grey gums, seeking to
shout. Nothing but ash left its snarling lips, spilling onto
the sand beneath its chin, while the psychic aftershock
of the denied scream battered uselessly against Lorgar's
guarded mind.

It crawled closer. Two of its fingers broke against the
ground. Congealing magma oozed from the stumps,
blackening as it dried.

'I know you can hear me.' The primarch kept his voice calm. His crozius hammer flared with energy, lightning sparking in a mad dance over its spiked head. 'But you cannot answer, can you?'

He took another step backwards. In response, the god's statue gave another soundless roar.

'I see you cannot.' The primarch's smile faltered. 'Nothing is left of you but this dull ache of unquenchable hatred. That is almost tragic.'

Lorgar.

+*Ingethel?*+ He reached for the daemon's voice. +*Ingethel? I have found… something. An echo. A wraith. I believe I will put it out of its misery.*+

It is an avatar of Kaela Mensha Khaine.

Lorgar nearly shrugged. +*The name means nothing to me.*+

The war god of the soulbroken. You have disturbed the city's heart, bringing living warmth to the coldest of places.

He returned the psychic equivalent of a snort. +*Whatever it once was, it is dying now. It has been dying for a long time, entombed beneath this poisonous soil.*+

As you say. A pause. A sense of amusement. *Lorgar. Behind you.*

The primarch turned from the crawling god, to face the slender figures walking from the gritty wind. He could see nothing in the way of detail; they were silhouettes in the storm, drifting closer, curved blades in their hands.

A dozen, two dozen, all ghosting closer. Not a single one of them betrayed the warm resonance of living sentience.

'Mon-keigh,' whispered the wind. 'Sha'eil, Sha'eil, Sha'eil.'

He knew the word. Sha'eil. Hell. A place of absolute evil.

Lorgar blasted each of the silhouettes apart with focused projections of psychic force. It took no more than a moment's focus. Heat haze shimmered in the wake of their discorporation – the primarch laughed as he realised he was wasting his strength on mirages.

A groaning, grinding moan rang out from behind. Lorgar turned again, in time to see the god's statue finally rising to its knees. From the red sand, it drew forth an ancient and cracked blade. Through clenched teeth that wheezed with ash, it coughed its first words.

'*Suin Daellae,*' growled the withered god. The blade in its hands, used more as a crutch than a weapon, streamed with unhealthy black smoke, but didn't burst into flame.

Lorgar watched the trembling creature with a cautious eye. +*Suin Daellae,*+ he sent to his distant guide. +*I am not familiar with the words.*+

The Doom that Wails. It is the name of the blade in its hands.

Lorgar watched the avatar topple again, crashing onto its hands and knees. +*I almost feel pity for the thing.*+

He was aware of the daemon taking form behind him, shaping itself from the wind, but felt no compunction to turn and face it.

You should not pity it, Lorgar. There is a lesson in this.

The primarch was sure there was, but he cared little for such unsubtle teachings. The avatar's skin cracked and peeled away by each of the statue's joints.

'I am ending this,' he said aloud.

As you wish. Ingethel's words drifted back.

Lorgar stepped forward, his mace heavy in his hands.

Remember this moment, Lorgar. Remember it for what it is, and what it stands for.

He drew closer to the collapsing statue and raised his crozius high, every inch the image of an executioner.

The avatar's cracking hand gripped his armour greave. Another of its fingers broke off.

'I will end the misery of your ignorance,' said Lorgar, and let the hammer fall.

A SINGLE STRIKE. A blow to the back of the head.

The crash of iron against stone. The hiss of dust captured by the wind. The rattle of grit against sealed ceramite.

'There is a lesson here.'

On the red soil, an outline of black ash marked the shape of a god's grave.

'Lorgar. Do you see it?'

Lorgar turned back to the daemon. Ingethel was slavering, its jaws dripping with clear saliva that somehow failed to crystallise in the intense cold.

'Do you see?' it asked, unblinking. *'A divine being can be as ignorant, as lost, as blind as any mere mortal. They can be as stubborn in their defiance, and just as grave a threat to the truth. Look at the revenant you destroyed – an echo of a faith that failed long ago. Now it is gone, this world can heal, untainted by false and heathen belief. Do you see?'*

The irritation left his vox-grille as a raucous grunt. 'You asked that question of my son, Argel Tal, and I do not wish for the same blunt instruction. Yes, Ingethel. I see.'

'Even a god may die, Lorgar.'

He laughed again. 'Subtlety is poison to you, isn't it?'

'Even a god may die. You will remember those words, before the end.'

The daemon's silent tone gave him pause. 'You speak of the end as if you know its outcome.'

'*I have walked the paths of possibility. I have seen what might be, and what is almost certain to be. But one cannot see what will be, until it has become what was.*'

Lorgar no longer felt like laughing. 'What is most likely, then? How will this end?'

The daemon licked its maw clean of dark ash and red dust. '*It ends as it began, Emperor's son. It ends in war.*'

TWO WORDS WERE all it took.

'Show me.'

PART THREE
IN WAR

SIX

THE ULTIMATE GATE

'I KNOW THIS place,' he whispered into the silence. 'This is the Eternity Gate.'

Lorgar stared down the endless hall – wide enough to admit a thousand men marching abreast, long enough to house every banner of honour from each of the Emperor's regiments. A hundred thousand banners, just in range of his genhanced eyesight. A million reaching beyond it. Two million. Three.

More and more and more, as far as the eye could see, proudly heralding world after world clutched in the Imperium's grip. Each world had raised countless regiments, their war flags hanging here to form an infinite tapestry. The hall itself, stretching for hours upon hours, was part cathedral, part museum, part sanctum of honour.

In the furthest reaches, shadowed by the darkness abounding, stood two wolf-masked Warhound Titans, their city-killing guns trained upon the marble steps leading towards the great gate they guarded.

The portal itself defied description. Words such as 'door' and 'gateway' implied comprehensible scope, something mortal minds could fathom without difficulty. This was no such thing. To construct such a barricade must have taken a full quarter of the remaining adamantium deposits on Mars, even before the ornate gold was added in layers upon the outer core of dense ceramite plating.

A barrier so grand, so impossible in scale and majesty, could only be protecting the secrets of one soul, above all others. Lorgar had been here but rarely, for the Eternity Gate was the portal to his father's innermost sanctum, where the Emperor kept his personal genetic laboratory sealed away from his sons and servants.

For a time, Lorgar stood beneath the company banners of an army regiment hailing from a world called Valhalla. The imagery upon the flags was one of a white world and cloaked men raising pennants in the Emperor's service. Lorgar had never set foot upon their world and wondered how far it lay from Terra in the night sky. Perhaps its people were as cold and unwelcoming as the frost upon which they trod.

'Why did you show me this?' he asked, turning from the hanging banners.

Ingethel slid from the shadows, the fur around its swollen eye dark and wet with secreted fluids.

'Are you weeping?' Lorgar asked the thing.

'*No. I am bleeding.*'

'Why?'

The daemon's uneven jaws clicked together. '*It does not matter. Tell me, what do you see in this place?*'

Lorgar took a breath, tasting the hot and sweat-ripened air of his armour's internal ventilation. 'Can I breathe here?'

'Yes. We are no longer on Shanriatha.'

Lorgar disengaged the seals at his collar and lifted the helm clear. Cold air caressed his face, while his next breath pulled a welcome chill into his burning lungs.

He turned his calm, scholarly eyes upon the daemon. 'How did we leave the dead world?'

'We are there, and we are here. You will understand one night, Lorgar. For now, explanations are a waste of time and breath. Some truths cannot be contained by the mortal mind.'

The primarch smiled to hide the curl of his lip. 'For a guide, you are doing precious little guiding.'

'I am an emissary. A viator.' Ingethel slithered along the lush red carpet, leaving a slug's smear. *'You are here, for all that it matters. You can breathe here, and die here, if we are not careful. The warp is everything and nothing, and you are adrift in its tides.'*

'Very well.' That would do, he supposed, for now.

'Do you hear that, Lorgar?'

Lorgar took another refreshing breath, letting the chill fill his chest. 'Battle, in the distance?' He shook his head. 'This vision is a lie. The Imperial Palace has never been besieged.'

'No? You look upon this endless chamber with mortal eyes. Use an immortal's sight.'

Easier said than done. His sixth sense, never reliable, was a curled core within his mind, suddenly resistant to being unlocked in this place. With concentration, he managed to pry his psychic gift open, as if pulling apart the fingers of a stiffened fist.

Lorgar managed to say 'I…' before he was drowned in the battle raging around him.

✠ ✠ ✠

GHOSTS WAGED WAR in every direction, their spectral bodies falling victim to the bite of each other's bolters and blades.

The illusion was complete enough to force his body into a physical response – a quickening of the heart, a shallowness of breath, the crucial urge to draw steel and leap into the fray. He considered himself a seeker, a scholar before a soldier, but the battle's intensity demanded instinctive reaction. Through clenched teeth, Lorgar watched warriors in the clashing shades of Legiones Astartes armour fighting and dying at his feet.

Amongst their chaotic ranks were beings of twisted inhumanity, their wrenched faces and bleeding bodies serving as ironclad evidence of their Neverborn origins. Claws snapped and cleaved; fleshy tendrils of barbed skin lashed and coiled in strangling embrace; eyeless faces howled above the grating clatter of bolters. Thousands upon thousands of warriors, mortal and immortal alike, grinding and slaying, shrieking and roaring. Many bore wings of flame and smoke, while others soared to the high ceiling on chiropteran pinions, casting bats' shadows on the fighting below. These last daemons hurled the struggling bodies of captured Imperial Fists down, bombarding the warriors below with their own brothers.

Lorgar released a breath he hadn't realised he'd been holding. In a voiceless exhalation, he said the words, 'Witness before me, the very heart of heresy.'

Ingethel hunched next to him. A reflection of the tumult showed plain in its swollen eye. *'Your own words, Emperor's child?'*

'No. A quote, from an old Covenant text.'

Lorgar stared as a towering figure, taller even than a primarch, waded through a broken phalanx of Imperial

Fists. The creature was clad in cracked fragments of ceramite armour, warped into a colossal image of legionary
purity. The brutal familiarity of a Mark II snarl-mouthed
helm had become a jawed monstrosity, crested by great,
curved horns of iron and ivory. Its hands, once human
fists in armoured gauntlets, were swollen into gnarled
claws ending in scything black barbs, akin to a bird of
prey's talons. Even from this distance, the aberration
reeked of something poisonous – a perversely pleasant,
cloying malignancy, promising death the moment its
sweetness ever touched a tongue. The lethal, deceptive
scent poured off the leviathan in waves.

'That creature.' Lorgar watched with wide eyes. 'It
wears the armour of the Legions, but I cannot mark its
allegiance.'

Ingethel gestured with its two left arms. *'Do you see
the warriors clad in cardinal red?'*

Lorgar couldn't fail to see them. An entire Legion
unknown to him, their bolters crashing as they advanced
in mixed ranks with the bellowing Neverborn. Imperial
Fists fell back before them, their numbers diminishing
with each passing moment.

'They are the Bearers of the Word.'

'They…'

'Yes, Lorgar. They are.'

And they were. His Legion, his own loyal sons,
armoured in a shade of spilled blood and oxidised iron.
Prayer scrolls marked their armour, their piety declared
with defiance even as the parchments were ripped and
scorched in the heat of battle. Many helms bore horns
in mimicry of officer crests, and every shoulder guard
showed a daemon's twisted visage, wrought in blackened bronze.

Watching them brought their chants to life. Who were these warriors, to adorn themselves in skulls and daemons' faces, chanting ritual verse as they advanced? What had become of his Legion?

Ingethel pried the thoughts from Lorgar's mind. *'The future holds many changes, primarch.'*

He didn't answer. Lorgar moved among the warring Legionaries, utterly ignored by all of them. The warriors moved to fire around him, but paid no more heed to his existence. With a hesitant shove, he pushed one of the red-clad Word Bearers' shoulder guards. The warrior cursed at a missed shot, moving aside and adjusting his aim. The bolter started up its thunderous refrain a moment later.

Surrounded by advancing legionaries, the primarch looked back to his guide. Ingethel slinked closer, its sinuous, muscled worm's body parting the crowded warriors with the same ease.

'This moment is fifty years distant from when we stand on Shanriatha.'

'Why do they wear red?'

Ingethel reached to one of the Word Bearers, its nails streaking over the daemonic visage on the warrior's pauldron. The legionary hesitated; for a moment Lorgar wondered if the daemon had made their presence known. Instead of noticing them, the warrior reloaded, immediately adding his fire back to the assault.

'The Legion's old armour was cast aside to herald the changes taking hold of humanity. They are no longer the Bearers of the Emperor's Word, Lorgar. They are the Bearers of yours.'

'This cannot be true.' The primarch flinched as a bolt shell detonated nearby, killing the Word Bearer closest to him. 'You have still not told me what that creature is – the one that wears the armour of my Legion five decades from now.'

He watched it move, its bunched musculature in concert with the exposed power cables and layered crimson ceramite armour. As it pulled one of the Imperial Fists apart with its immense claws, the black smoke misting from its wings was an acidic shadow, slowly eating into the golden armour of every Imperial Fists warrior nearby.

'Throne of the God-Emperor,' Lorgar whispered. In the great beast's grip, the bisected Imperial Fist fought on, firing his bolter down into the daemon's face. The armoured creature hurled the warrior's legs aside, turning its corrupted helm from the shells cracking against its faceplate. Lorgar watched in silence as the winged daemon slammed the halved Imperial Fist onto its taurine crown, impaling the legionary on its right horn. That, at last, stilled the warrior's defiance. His bolter fell from his hands, clattering down the shadow-wrapped wings. The daemon fought on, untroubled by the weight of the armoured torso punctured onto its ivory crest.

'What is that thing?' the primarch asked again. 'Its soul is… I do not have the words for it.' Lorgar stared through the grinding crash of unfolding carnage, peering to see beneath the monstrosity's flesh. Where a flaring emanation would pulse in a living being, and a hollow chasm would swallow light within one of the Neverborn, this creature possessed both. An ember burned hot in the blackness beneath its skin.

'It is not human.' Lorgar's voice was strained by the effort it took to pierce the black mist shroud rising from the creature's wings. 'But it was.' He turned his eyes to Ingethel. 'Wasn't it.' The words weren't a question.

This time, Ingethel's tone betrayed some of the daemon's own hesitation. The moment inspired some
reluctance, perhaps a reverence, in the daemon itself.

'That is your son, Lorgar. That is Argel Tal.'

A peal of thunder roared from the Eternity Gate itself,
as another winged figure landed amidst the melee.
Its wings were torn and stained, ragged with rips and
the white feathers streaked by blood. Its armour was a
shattered ruin of split steel and burnished gold, while
its face was masked by a golden helm. The blade in its
hands rippled with psychic flame, bright enough to sear
the sight from a watcher's eyes.

'No,' Lorgar managed to whisper.

'And that is your brother,' the daemon pressed. *'Sanguinius, Lord of Angels. This is how Argel Tal will die.'*

LORGAR FROZE AFTER the first step forward. He began a
breath in the hall before the Eternity Gate, and released
it under a sky tortured by groaning volcanoes.

The air had a ripeness to it – that spoiled, blackening reek of an open tomb. Despite the horizon aflame
and choking on ash from the erupting mountains, little
warmth reached his exposed skin. No wind stirred to
freshen the air. The ground quivered in a prolonged
shudder, giving a low, moaning rumble of tortured tec-
tonics far below the grey earth. The planet itself objected
to what was taking place on its surface.

Lorgar's vision couldn't penetrate the blanket of ash
swallowing the sky. To cover the heavens like that, the
volcanoes had to have been erupting for months, at the
very least.

He turned to the daemon, sensing its approach from
behind.

'Where are we? Why did you bring us here?'

'A nameless world. We are here because you saw all you needed to see.'

The primarch laughed without intending to. Just as he mustered enough control to speak again, a second burst of laughter broke from his lips.

'I fail to see the amusement, Lorgar.'

'You show me my armies laying siege to my father's palace, allied with daemons, waging war against my brothers, and you ask why I wished to see more than a handful of seconds?' Lorgar shook his head, the laughter dying down. 'I am finished with being led by the nose into your prepared lessons, creature.'

Ingethel drooled. *'Watch your tone when addressing one of the gods' chosen.'*

'I am here by my own choice. I will leave here by the same virtue.'

'Yes.' The daemon stood straighter, eliciting several wet cracks from its vertebrae. *'Keep telling yourself that, Lorgar.'*

The primarch gripped his crozius, aching to draw the weapon and wield it out of spite, swinging it in anger, reasserting control over life through the use of violence. In this, he was as any of his brothers, and he knew it. The desire was always there. What better way to bend reality to one's desire? Bleed those who would defy your choices and there is no longer any opposition. The destroyer's way was always an easy one. It fell to the builders, the visionaries, to do the difficult work.

Lorgar did something none of his brothers would have done in his place. He released the weapon, leaving it undrawn, and took a calming breath.

'I am here to learn the truth of the gods, Ingethel.

And you are here to show it to me. Please do not force my temper.'

The daemon said nothing.

Lorgar stared into its bloated eye, still weeping ichor. 'Do you understand me?'

'Yes.'

'Now tell me why you summoned me here. I heard the call of this place, the shrieking of my name through the solar storms. I came to maturity on a world where our ancient holy texts spoke of this dead alien empire as a heaven for humanity. I want answers, Ingethel. I want them now. Why have I been shaped from birth to be brought to this place? What does fate want of me?'

The daemon drooled again. Its gums were bleeding now and two if its arms were curled close to its glistening chest.

'What is wrong with you?'

'I am nearing the end of this incarnation. My essence sits uneasily in this cage of bone and flesh.'

'I have no wish to see you die.'

'I will not die, as you perceive the concept. We are the Neverborn. We are also the Neverending.'

Lorgar swallowed a pulse of irritation, not letting it rise to the fore. 'True immortality?'

'In the only possible way.' The daemon looked to the horizon, just as Lorgar had done only minutes before. Its gaze milked over, going turgid with thought. *'You ask a question, despite already knowing its answer. You are here, now, because you have been summoned. You are here, now, because your life was engineered to ensure this moment took place. You are here, now, because the gods wished it. In the tangled skeins of time's web, I have seen innumerable possible futures where you never came to us, Lorgar.*

'In one, you died in youth, the golden child-martyr of Colchis, slain by assassins seeking to restore the Old Ways. When the Imperium came to reclaim you, they found a world dead by its own hand, lost to the crusades of bitter fanatics.

'In another, you were poisoned only three nights after retaking the capital in your holy war for the hearts of Colchis' people. You were murdered by the wine in your cup, with the poison placed there by the hand of one you called Father, for he feared you could no longer be manipulated.

'In another, you were not the master of your own temper, much like many of your brothers: in a confrontation with Sanguinius, you sank a knife into his back, and were in turn butchered by Horus for your sin.

'In yet another, you defied the Anathema – the creature you name the Emperor, falsely considering it to be human – and you were executed by your brothers Curze and Russ. Your heart was cut from your corpse, and a great sorcery of alchemical and genetic power was wrought upon all who shared your bloodline. Your Legion was poisoned, reduced to madness, and finally annihilated by the fleets of the Ultramar Kingdom.

'In another, you–'

'Enough.' Lorgar felt pale, and suspected only his gold-inked skin hid that very truth. 'Enough, please.'

'As you wish.'

The mountains continued to rumble with distant bellows as the world breathed fire into its own sky.

Lorgar opened his eyes at last. 'Why me? Why was I brought here? Why not Horus or Guilliman? They are the generals I will never be. Why not Sanguinius or Dorn?' He laughed then, a sneering, private snort. 'Why not Magnus?'

Ingethel grinned, insofar as its mangled mouth would allow. *'The gods have touched many of your brothers in ways both obvious and occluded. One of them bears wings upon his back. Is that part of your Emperor's genetic intent? Did he not wish to destroy all religious reference? Why, then, would he breed a son that stands as an angel incarnate?'*

Lorgar brushed the point aside. 'Enough cryptic idiocy. Why not Magnus? He is the most powerful of us all, without a shadow of doubt.'

'Magnus. Magnus the Red. The Crimson King.' Ingethel laughed inside Lorgar's mind, and gestured out onto the plains. *'He is already with us, whether he admits it or not. He came to us without needing to be summoned, and without ever considering the notion of faith. He came for power, because that is why all things of flesh come to us. And in five short decades, when the galaxy begins to burn, he will come here himself.*

'Behold this very world, Lorgar, in fifty years.'

SEVEN

CITY OF LIGHT

FOR A MOMENT, to even face the light was painful. Silver in its artificiality, as cold and far removed from the warm gold of a natural star as could be imagined. Shadowing his face from the austere glare, Lorgar looked across the plains where Ingethel had gestured.

Shapes resolved themselves into an uneven skyline. Lorgar knew it instantly, for he had studied there for almost a decade, living among its people and coming to adore them as he loved the people of Colchis.

'Tizca.' He said the word only after swallowing his horror. Cracked spires of human ingenuity; great pyramids of white stone, pale metal and shattered glass; city walls fallen to nothing more than lumped rubble – this was the great and enlightened city of the Thousand Sons, reduced to the edge of devastation.

'What madness do I see before me? What lies cruelly given shape?'

'Tizca will burn in the crucible of the coming war. It must be so.'

'I will never allow this to come to pass.'

'You will allow it, Lorgar. You must.'

'You are not my master. I would never hold faith in a god that controlled its worshippers. Faith is about freedom, not slavery.'

'You will allow this to come to pass.'

'If this is the future, Ingethel, I will tell Magnus in the past. When I return to the Imperium, it will be the first thing to leave my lips.'

'No. This is the final incident in Magnus' illumination. Betrayed by the Emperor, betrayed by his own brothers, he will bring his city to the warp in order to escape final destruction. Here, he forges a bastion for the war to come.'

'What war?' Lorgar spat the words. 'You keep speaking of betrayals, of crusades and battles, as if I can already see into the same futures you describe. Tell me, damn you, what war?' Lorgar started to move towards the ruined city, but Ingethel gripped his armoured shoulder.

'The war you will begin, but will never lead. The war to bring all these truths to the Imperium. You came to find the gods, Lorgar. You have found them, as they always intended for you. Their eyes are turned towards humanity now. We said this to Argel Tal, as we say it to you now – humanity must embrace the truths of divine reality, or suffer the same fate as the eldar.'

Lorgar looked back to the city.

'You already knew it would come to war. A holy crusade, to bring the truth to Terra. Too many worlds will resist. The Emperor's grip on their lives is too complete, too merciless. The Anathema starves them of any chance to grow

*on their own, so they will languish – and then they will
die – while shackled by his narrow vision.'*

The primarch smiled, the expression a mirror of his
genetic father's own faint amusement. 'And in place of
order, you offer Chaos? I have seen what walks on the
faces of those eldar worlds lost in this great, drowned
empire. The seas of blood and the cities of howling
Neverborn…'

'You look upon an empire that failed to heed the gods.'

'Even so, there are horrors no human will willingly
embrace.'

*'No? These things are horrors only to those who look
upon them with mortal eyes. Without belief in the true
gods, humanity will fall to its own faithlessness. Alien
kingdoms will break the Imperium apart, for humanity
lacks the strength to survive in a galaxy that loathes your
species. Your expansion will fade and diminish, and the
gods will smite all who turned from the offer of true faith.
Your kind can embrace the Chaos you speak of, or it can
taste the same fate as the eldar.'*

'Chaos.' Lorgar tasted the word, weighing it on his
tongue. 'That is not the correct word, is it? The immaterial realm may be one of pure Chaos, but it is changed
when bonded with the material universe. Diluted. Even
in this Great Eye, where the gods stare into the galaxy,
physical laws are broken but it is not a place of pure
Chaos. It is no random ocean of seething psychic energy.
It is not the warp itself, but a meshing of here and there,
the firmament and the aether.'

The primarch breathed in the ashy air, feeling it tickle
the back of his throat. 'Perfect order would never change.
But pure Chaos would never rise in the first place. You
desire a union.'

He turned to Ingethel. Blood ran from both the daemon's eyes now, darkening its fur in bleak lightning
streaks.

'You need us,' Lorgar said. 'The gods need us. They cannot claim the material realm without us. Their power is
strangled when they have no prayers or deeds offered
in worship.'

*'Yes, but the need is not a selfish one. It is a natural
desire. The gods are masters of Chaos as a natural force.
The warp is every human emotion – every emotion from
any sentient race – made manifest into a psychic tempest.
It is not the enemy of life, but the result of it.'*

Lorgar breathed deeply, tasting more of the ash on the
wind. He said nothing, for there was little to say. Argel
Tal had brought these words back with him, and now
they were Lorgar's to hear first hand.

*'Chaos seeks symbiosis with life – the Ensouled and
the Neverborn in natural harmony. Union. Faith. Power,
Lorgar. Immortality and endless possibility. Sensations
beyond mortal comprehension. The ability to feel maddening delight at any agony. The gift of ecstasy even when
you are destroyed, making even death a great joke, knowing you will incarnate in another form over and over until
the suns themselves go black.*

*'And when the stars die, Chaos still lives on in the
cold – still perfect, still exultant, still pure. This is everything humanity has ever dreamed of – to be unchallenged
in the galaxy, to be omnipotent above all other life, and
to be eternal.'*

Lorgar would no longer look at the fallen city. 'You
have chosen poorly. I am pleased and proud to have
discovered the truth. I am honoured to be chosen by
beings powerful enough to be considered divine by the

truest meaning of the word. But I will struggle to bring this light to humanity. I cannot win a war against the god sat upon the Terran Throne.'

'Life is struggle. You will strive, and you will succeed.'

'Even if I believed all of this…' Lorgar's blood ran cold. 'I have one hundred thousand warriors. We will be dead the moment we make planetfall upon the Throneworld.'

'You will attract more, as you liberate world after world. It is written in the stars – after you sail from here, your Legion no longer spends years crafting perfect worlds venerating the Anathema as the God-Emperor. You will crush resistance beneath your boots, and draw fresh, faithful humans into your service. Some will be slaves in the bowels of your warships. Others will be your flock, to shepherd them toward enlightenment. Many more will be taken into your genetic harvester asylums, and bred into legionaries.'

The primarch resisted the urge to curse. 'I am growing increasingly uneasy with you discussing my future in such definite terms. None of these events have happened yet and may never occur. You have still not answered the one question that matters. Why must it be me?'

'It has to be you.'

His teeth clenched together, hard enough to squeak. *'Why?* Why not one of the others? Horus? Sanguinius? The Lion? Dorn?'

'Each of the other Legions would die for their primarchs, and lay down their lives for the Imperium. But the Imperium is the cancer killing the species. Even when some of your brothers turn against the Emperor, they will fight to command the Imperium. Only the Word Bearers will die for the truth, and for humanity itself.

'Faith and steel must now be joined. If humanity becomes an empire instead of a species, it will fall to alien claws

and the wrath of the gods. It is the way of things. What has happened before will happen again.'

Lorgar pulled a sealed scroll from his belt, unrolling it with exaggerated care. Red dust clung to the parchment from the surface of Shanriatha, as did a few speckles of blood from carnage beneath the Eternity Gate. They dotted the cream page, bold against the pale paper, almost like tiny wax seals.

His son's blood. The lifeblood of one of his Legion, fifty years from now. A warrior destined to die on the home world of humanity, countless systems away from where he'd been born. Had that warrior even been born, yet?

Lorgar screwed up the parchment, destroying the Colchisian cuneiform scripture, and let it fall to the cold ground.

'Is Magnus here now? Are we here, fifty years from the night I entered the Great Eye?'

'Yes. Where we stand now is mere days after something humanity will come to recall as the Razing of Prospero. Magnus fell victim to his own arrogance, and now resides in the tallest tower of his broken city here, lamenting the destruction of his Legion and the death of his hopes. He intended only the best, but his curiosity saw him damned in the eyes of the Emperor. He looked too deep, too long, into ideals the Emperor did not hold.'

Lorgar nodded, expecting nothing less. It was hardly unprecedented, after all. His own Legion – a hundred thousand Word Bearers kneeling in the dust of Monarchia...

He shook his head, looking back to the city, and the tower at the heart of it.

'Why does he come here, to the empyrean?'

'To hide where the Emperor's dogs cannot catch him. He is here to lick his wounds. For his sins, Magnus was sentenced to censure. He chose exile over execution.'

Lorgar started walking.

'I am going to speak with him.'

'You will not be allowed to stand before the Crimson King.'

He didn't need to turn to know the daemon was smiling. 'We will see,' he called over his shoulder.

There was no answer. Ingethel was gone.

HE WAS THREATENED by an abortion wearing the cardinal red ceramite of the Thousand Sons Legion.

'Denlcrrgh yidzun,' it demanded. A bronze bolter was wrapped in the quivering flesh-coloured tentacles it used as arms. Behind this lone sentry, the fallen city wall of Tizca rose in mounds of rubble.

Lorgar breathed a slow exhalation. Even from a dozen metres away, the Thousand Son reeked of spoiled meat and the rich, coppery tang of aetheric secrets. What remained of its face looked as if it had melted down the front of its skull.

'I am Lorgar, Lord of the Seventeenth Legion.' He gestured to the bolter in the thing's limbs. 'Lower your weapon, nephew. I am here to speak with my brother.'

Another attempt at speech left the Thousand Son's ravaged features as a meaningless blur of syllables. It seemed to recognise its own inadequacy in this regard, for a gentle, cultured voice drifted into Lorgar's mind a moment later.

+I am Hazjihn of the Fifteenth Legion. You cannot be what you appear.+

Lorgar buried his discomfort beneath his father's smile.

'I could say the same words to you, Hazjihn.' The ground gave a particularly violent shudder. Glass shattered in the lowest levels of the closest pyramid as more rocks tumbled from the ruined city wall.

+*The Crimson King tells us we are the only human life on this world.*+ Hazjihn's dripping face snuffed back a mouthful of air in ungainly respiration. +*You cannot be Lord Aurelian of the Word Bearers.*+

Lorgar spread his hands in a display of unarmed beneficence. 'You know me, Hazjihn. Do you recall the evening I lectured on the Khed-Qahir Parables, in the west garden district of the City of Grey Flowers?'

The bolter lowered a fraction. +*I recall it well. How many of my Legion's warriors were present that night?*+

Lorgar nodded in respect to the Thousand Son. 'Thirty-seven, among a mortal crowd of over twenty thousand.'

The warrior's sloping eyes blinked slowly. +*And what is the fiftieth principle of Qahir?*+

'There is no fiftieth principle of Qahir, for he died of a consumptive sickness soon after penning the nineteenth. The fiftieth principle of Khed is to maintain cleanliness of flesh and iron as surely as one would maintain purity of soul, for the external inexorably bleeds into the internal.'

The warrior lowered his bolter. +*You may yet be a deceiver, but I will take you to my lord. He will judge you with his own eye.*+

Lorgar inclined his head again, this time in thanks. He followed the limping figure of Hazjihn, ascending the mounds of rubble to enter the city proper. The warrior's halting stride set his armour's servo joints snarling.

Lorgar watched the warrior's limping movements. Whatever benefits the mutations offered, they were hidden by the Legion's armour. Above all, a randomness lay in Hazjin's corruption. Lorgar couldn't help contrast it to the shaped, yet lethal warping of Argel Tal in his previous vision. His own son's alterations had all the hallmarks of malicious intent, as if a greater intellect had kneaded the Word Bearer's flesh, rewriting his life at the genetic level, crafting him into a living engine of war.

Hazjihn's mutation showed no such design. If anything, he seemed diseased.

'Nephew.' Lorgar kept his voice soft. 'What has happened to you? How many of my brother's sons are as changed as you are?'

Hazjihn didn't look back. +*This place, this world, it has altered so many of us. The Powers bless us, my lord.*+

Blessed. So the daemon Ingethel had spoken the truth: physical considerations faded when one embraced union with the gods. With psychic mastery and the ascension of consciousness to immortal levels, evidently the struggles of the flesh were increasingly irrelevant. Perhaps it made a sick kind of sense: when one was omnipotent, functions of the flesh hardly mattered. Power to such a degree overshadowed lesser concerns.

Yet even for one who prided himself on his enlightened perspective, it was a bitter pill for Lorgar to swallow. The truth may be divine, but that hardly rendered it any more appealing to the human race. Some truths were too ugly to be easily embraced.

A rancid, unwanted smile claimed his mouth for a moment. It would be a crusade, then. Another crusade to bring the truth to the masses at the point of a sword.

Humanity would never, could never, be relied upon to reach its own enlightenment. He found it the sorriest, saddest aspect to the species.

'How long have you been here, Hazjihn?'

+*Some of us insist it has been months. Others claim mere days have passed. We cannot record the time accurately, for it flows in all directions. Chronometers dance to tunes of their own devising.*+ The warrior made a strangled gargle, approaching a laugh. +*However, the primarch tells us mere days have passed in the material realm.*+

Lorgar. Ingethel's voice, not Hazjihn's. *Turn back. This future is not yours to see.*

The primarch held his tongue as they walked into Tizca, the City of Light.

As he looked upon Magnus, Lorgar reconciled logic with emotion, forging both into understanding. This was not the Magnus he knew – this was Magnus five decades older.

In fifty years, he had aged a hundred. The Crimson King had abandoned the pretension of armour, clad now in nothing more than divine light that left aching after-images in the minds of all who looked upon him. Yet beneath the psychic grandeur, a broken brother stared at Lorgar's arrival. His remaining eye showed little of its former pearlescent gleam and his features, never those of a handsome man, were now cracked by time's lines and the ravines of tortured thought.

'Lorgar,' the figure of Magnus said, breaking the library's stillness and silence. The witchlight roiling from him in waves illuminated the scrolls and books lining the walls.

The Word Bearer entered slowly, his purring armour joints adding to the breach of silence. Standing too near Magnus bred a painful tingling behind the eyes, as if white noise had evolved into a physical sensation. Lorgar turned his gentle gaze aside, taking in his brother's collection of writings. Immediately, his glance fell upon one of his own books – *An Epilogue to Torment* – written the very same year he had won the crusade against the Covenant's Old Ways on Colchis.

Lorgar traced a gloved fingertip down the book's leather spine. 'You do not seem surprised to see me, brother.'

'I am not.' Magnus allowed himself a smile. It only deepened the lines marring his face. 'This world holds endless surprises. What game is this, I wonder? What incarnated hallucination am I addressing this time? You are a poor simulacrum of Lorgar, spirit. Your eyes do not burn with the fire of a faith only he and his sons understand. Nor do you bear the same scars.'

Magnus remained standing by his writing desk, but made no move to go back to his reading. Lorgar turned to him, narrowing his eyes at the glare.

'I am no apparition, Magnus. I am Lorgar, your brother, in the final nights of my pilgrimage. Time, as you see, is mutable, here.' He hesitated. 'The years have not been kind to you.'

The other primarch laughed, though the sound held no humour. 'Recent years have been kind to no one. Begone, creature, and leave me to my calculations.'

'Brother. It *is* me.'

Magnus narrowed his remaining eye. 'I grow weary of this. How did you ascend my tower?'

'I walked, in the company of your warriors. Magnus, I–'

'Enough! Leave me to my calculations.'

Lorgar stepped forward, hands raised in brotherly conciliation. 'Magnus...'

+**Enough.**+

The explosion of whiteness stole all sense, save for the feeling of falling.

PART FOUR
CHOSEN OF THE PANTHEON

EIGHT

QUESTIONS

HE OPENED HIS eyes to see a familiar horizon, boiling in rebellion against the laws of nature. Dusk claimed this world, which was surely Shanriatha. Yet he could breathe now. And the temperature, while cold, was far from lethal.

Slowly, Lorgar picked himself up from the sand. The parchment scrolls were gone from his armour, burned away in the face of Magnus' sorcerous dismissal. A tightness in his lungs didn't bode well. He felt the muscles in his throat and chest clenching in uncertain spasm.

Not enough oxygen in the air. That was all. He reached for the helm mag-locked to his belt, and resealed his armour. The first breath of his internal air supply was surprisingly soothing. He breathed in the incense of his armour's sacred oils.

Only then did he see Ingethel. The daemon lay curled upon itself on the ground, a foetal nightmare slick with the slime of gestation. Red sand clotted its moist skin.

He kicked it gently, with the edge of his boot. Ingethel rolled, baring its bestial features to the evening sky. Neither of its eyes could close, but both had made the attempt. They *snicked* open, and its jaw cracked as it heaved itself from the sand. The moment the daemon righted itself, blood gouted from its maw in a hissing flood. Things writhed in the pool of stinking liquid, squirming into the sand as soon as they came into contact with the air. Lorgar had no desire to examine them any closer.

'Daemon,' he said.

'Not long now. Soon. This flesh will rot away. I will need to incarnate again.' Its bones clicked and cracked as it rose to its slouched height. *'It cost me much, to pull you from Magnus' tower.'*

'My brother would not speak with me.'

'Your brother is a tool of the Changer of the Ways. Are you still so blind, Lorgar? Magnus is a creature unaware of his own ignorance. He is manipulated at every turn, yet believes himself the manipulator. The gods work in many ways. Some of humanity's leaders must be lured by offers of ambition and dominance, while others must be manipulated until they are ready to witness the truth.'

The primarch spoke through clenched teeth. 'And I?'

'You are the chosen of the pantheon. You alone come to Chaos from idealism, for the betterment of the species. In this, as in all things, you are selfless.'

Lorgar turned and began walking. The direction was irrelevant, for the desert was a featureless sprawl as far as the eye could see.

Selfless. Magnus had once accused him of the same thing, making it sound more like a critical flaw. Now the daemon used it with a honeyed tongue, as his greatest virtue.

It didn't matter. Immune to vanity, he would not be lured by silken words. The truth was enough, despite the horror of it all.

'Do I survive this crusade?' he asked aloud.

Ingethel dragged itself alongside his bootprints, slower now, its breath sawing in and out of heaving lungs.

'The Imperial Great Crusade is already over for you. All that remains is to play the role fate offers.'

'No. Not my father's crusade. The true crusade, yet to come.'

'Ah. You fear for your life, if you turn against the Terran Emperor?'

Lorgar kept walking, a relentless trudge over the sand dunes. 'The vision of Magnus said I had suffered in his era. At some point in the coming five decades, I must struggle to survive. It stands to reason that I may die. If you have stared down the paths of possible futures, you must know what is likely to occur.'

'Once the betrayal breaks across the galaxy, there are countless moments in which you may meet your end. Some likelier than others.'

Lorgar crested another dune, pausing to stare down at yet more endless desert. 'Tell me how I die.' He looked at the daemon, fixing it with his gentle glare. 'You know. I hear it in your voice. So tell me.'

'No being may know its future written out before it, in absolute terms. Some decisions will see you almost certainly dead. On a world named Shrike, if you interfere in an argument between Magnus the Red and the brother you name Russ, there is a concordance of possibility that you will be slain in their duel.'

'And?'

'If you ever draw a weapon against your brother Corax,

in a battle you can never win, you are almost certain to die.'

Lorgar laughed at the maddening unlikelihood of it all. 'You cannot offer me choices I will not have to make for many years.'

The daemon sprayed spit as it growled. *'Then do not ask questions of the future, fool.'*

Lorgar had no answer to that, though he found the daemon's tone amusing. 'Where are we?' he said at length. 'Shanriatha again?'

'Yes. Shanriatha. The past or the present, perhaps a possible future. I cannot say.'

'But the air isn't as cold as the void, here.'

'The warp changes all things, in time.' Ingethel paused, seeming to sag. *'Lorgar. You must be aware of the task ahead of you. I cannot remain incarnate for much longer, so hear my words now. In the course of the Emperor's Great Crusade, you will come to many worlds. Those populated by alien breeds are useless to you. For the next few decades, let your brother primarchs purge those. You have a more solemn duty.*

'Find the worlds rich in human life. Find those with harvestable populations for your armies, with as little deviation from purestrain humanity as possible. Your Legion is one hundred thousand strong now. Over the next five decades, you must add a thousand warriors each year. For every legionary to fall, you will replenish your Word Bearers with two more.'

He shook his head, still staring out at the sea of dunes. 'Why have you brought me back here? What lesson is there in this?'

'None. I dragged you from Magnus' chamber with crude force, not guile. It was not my intention to show you this

world again. Something else pulled you here. Something very strong.'

Lorgar felt his skin crawl at the creature's tone. 'Explain yourself.'

Even with its bloody, inhuman face, Ingethel's worthless eyes were wide in something not far from fear.

'You did not believe even the chosen of the pantheon will be allowed to leave the realm of the gods without first passing their tests, did you? It was chosen that the gods would elect one vizier to send, to stand judgement upon you.'

The primarch drew his crozius with slow, careful intent. 'If this is all proceeding as planned, why then do you tremble in fear?'

'Because gods are fickle beings, Lorgar, and this was not the plan at all. One of the gods has overstepped the boundary, and violated the accord. It must wish to test you itself.'

He swallowed. 'I do not understand. Which god?'

He heard no answer. Ingethel's psychic shriek went through him like a blade. For the first time since the maiden on Cadia had become his daemonic guide, he heard the girl within the creature.

She was screaming with it.

NINE

THE UNBOUND

THE SOUND BEGAN as the promise of thunder. Lorgar raised his head just as the tortured sky went black.

A gargoyle shape cast darkness across the clouded heavens, blasting wind downward from its beating wings. He saw it descending in a graceless spiral but, despite his eye lenses tinting to reduce the greasy glare of warp space, he could make out little detail in the figure's form.

It struck the ground a hundred metres distant, sending up a vast spray of powdery sand. The ground shuddered beneath Lorgar's feet; stabilisers in his armour's knee joints clicked and thrummed harder to compensate for the quake.

Its wings rose first – huge, bestial black wings, the membranes between the muscles and bones as tough as old leather, cobwebbed by thick, pulsing veins. Scarred fur coated much of its body, while the rest of its bunched musculature was encased in great brass armour plating. Its horned head defied easy description – to Lorgar it resembled nothing but the malicious features of Old Terran's greatest devil-spirit, the Seytan, as seen in some of the oldest scrolls. It did more than tower over any mortal man – it stood above them as a colossus. Its fists, each the size of a legionary, gripped two weapons: the first, a lashing whip that thrashed of its own accord, sidewinding across the sands; and the second, an immense axe of beaten brass, its surfaces encrusted with dense metal runic scripture.

It stalked from the crater it had made, each fall of its armoured hooves sending tremors through the world's surface.

The targeting reticules and streams of biological data across Lorgar's retinal displays offered no insight at all. One moment they listed details in a runic language the primarch had never learned. The next they told him nothing was there.

When he spoke, his voice was a breathless exhalation, crackling through the lowest frequency of his helm's vox-grille.

'What, in my father's name, is *that*…?'

Ingethel had slithered away while Lorgar stood rapt, yet it still heard his voice. Hunched upon itself, doubled over and leaking fluids from every orifice on its head, the daemon's psychic sending was a weak stroke.

'The Guardian of the Throne of Skulls. The Deathbringer. Lord of Bloodthirsters. First of Kharnath's Children. The Avatar of War Given Form. In the mortal realm, it will come to be known as An'ggrath the Unbound.

'It is the revered champion of the Blood God, Lorgar. And it has come to kill you.'

He opened his mouth to reply, but all sound was stolen in a tempest of breath as the creature roared. The scream was loud enough to disrupt the electronics in the prima-rch's helm, causing his aural intakes and retinal displays to crackle with static. Lorgar tore the helm free, choos-ing to breathe the thin air over fighting deaf and blind.

His lungs reacted immediately, clenching like twin cores within his chest. The granite-grey helm fell to the sand by his boots. Fear didn't clutch at him, the way it would a mortal. He feared nothing but failure. Defiant irritation set his skin crawling, that the deities would test him this way. After all he had endured. After being the one soul to seek the truth.

Now this.

Lorgar raised his maul, activating the generator in the haft. A rippling energy field bloomed around the weap-on's spiked orb head, hissing and spitting in the wind. Sparks streamed away from its spines, like halogen rain.

The daemon thundered closer, step by step.

'This was never part of the Great Plan. You are not a duellist to match the Lion. You are not a brawler to match Russ, nor a fighter to match Angron, nor a war-rior to equal the Khan. You are not a soldier like Dorn, nor a killer like Curze.'

'Be silent, Ingethel.'

'Kharnath has violated the accord. Kharnath has vio-lated the accord. Kharnath has v–'

'I said be silent, creature.'

The winged daemon roared again, its fanged maw wide, and the veins in its taut throat as thick as a man's thigh. Even braced against the gale, Lorgar was forced back several metres in a skidding slide over the gravel. The primarch breathed a stream of Colchisian invective and, as the stinking wind died down, he replied with a shouted challenge of his own.

Before sanity could wrest control of his limbs, he was charging, boots pounding onto the red sand, his crozius raised in both hands.

THE FIRST BLOW struck with the force of a gunship falling from the sky, and with an impact at the same volume. The cleaving blade crashed against the golden maul, both weapons banging together and locking fast. Sparks sprayed from the elbow joints of Lorgar's armour as the muscle-mimicking servos overloaded and shorted out. But he did it. He blocked the first blow. In spiteful retaliation for the beast's presence, his crozius kissed the axe's edge with leaping bolts of electrical force. With a cry that wouldn't have shamed a feral world carnosaur, the primarch hurled the bloodthirster's axe backward in a heaving shove, and brought his warhammer to fall on a downstroke, smashing into the creature's knee.

At the moment of connection, faster than mortal reactions could process, the weapon's power field protested at the kinetic treatment and burst outward in a blast of force. Something in the daemon's leg cracked with the wet rip of a tree trunk falling.

First blood. Lorgar was already scrambling back, stumbling over the quaking sand, when the lash found his throat. The spiked coils bit as they wrapped tight, turning the trial of breathing into an absolute impossibility.

In the panicked rush of distorted senses, he saw the creature driven to one knee, its back-jointed bull-legs bent in submission. The primarch's first blow had near crippled it. Had he been able to take in any air, he'd have roared in exaltation. Instead, he crashed to his knees, clawing at the serpentine weapon encircling his shoulders and throat. One arm was pinned to his body by the lash's wrapping caress. The other clutched and pulled, dragging the whip off in a mess of snarling armour joints. For a flickering, red-stained moment, he remembered a painting in his father's palace: a restored oil work of an oceanic sailor – in the era when Terra had possessed such large bodies of water – entangled by a krahkan sea monster.

Lorgar heard the bloodthirster's wings rattling, felt the force of more wind as they beat again. Another acidic spurt of panic knifed through his thoughts: the daemon sought to take off, and drag him into the sky with it.

He rolled into the whip, trapping himself further, for the chance to tear his crozius from the fist wedged against his body. The lash around his throat squeezed in leathery embrace, freed of all resistance now. As he was dragged across the sand towards the daemon, Lorgar hurled his maul one-handed, with a strangled cry and the last of his strength.

It struck the bloodthirster's face with the juicy crack of shattering bone, silencing the victory roar that had been brewing in the beast's lungs. Fangs clattered down onto the primarch's armour in a discoloured enamel hail. One sliced his cheek open with the daggerish fall of a stalactite. Had he been able to breathe, he'd have laughed, but pulling himself free of the slackened whip was taxing enough.

Lorgar's first three steps carried him to his crozius. Numb fingers slapped onto the hammer's haft and he hauled it back into his grip. He turned in time to catch a face full of sprayed blood and spit, shaken from the daemon's broken maw. It stung his skin, even as he wiped it away. The rest ate into his armour with hissing, smoking slowness.

'Let this be finished.' He bared his teeth, unaware how his expression reflected the daemon's. For a wonder, it replied through its broken jaws and architecture of cracked teeth. Its voice was pulled right down from the thunderheads colliding above.

'All the strength in the flesh. And the bitter caress. And the taste of blood on my tongue.'

He knew those words. He knew them well.

Perhaps the beast had intended them as a distraction. Perhaps it was channelling mockery straight from the mouth of a god. Either way, Lorgar met the next attack with a laugh. The bloodthirster's axe crashed against his swinging maul. One of the weapons shattered with the same ease as the daemon's teeth. Metal debris burned in the air, flickering with ghost-white fire, before clattering across the sand.

Lorgar advanced, his maul still raised. 'You quote my home world's holy scrolls to me? Is even this moment supposed to be a lesson? Even *this?*'

The daemon's wings snapped out at full reach, darkening all view of the horizon. The display sent the foetid, spicy reek of spoiled meat emanating afresh from its pinions. It wasn't finished. It wasn't even close. It needed no axe when it bore such claws. It never needed to walk, when it possessed those wings.

But it was bleeding now, and Lorgar's disquiet had long since burned away in the wind. He didn't fear the thing. Every broken fang heralded triumph, as did every droplet of molten brass blood running from its black gums and each grinding crackle from its shattered knee.

'I will not die here,' the primarch promised the daemon.

The bloodthirster's answer was to roar again. This time, it threw the primarch from his feet, sending him tumbling across the rocky ground. Dull snaps sounded from beneath his armour; jagged spurts of pain pinched inside his chest. Even the fibre-cable cushioning wasn't enough to prevent broken bones. He crashed to rest against a jutting rock, and in dragging himself back to his feet, he caught sight of Ingethel – its warmish form coiled as it crouched in the sand.

Cracked ribs stole the strength of his voice, rendering it a wheeze. 'Help me, you spineless bitch.'

Ingethel slithered away, chittering with frightened laughter, leaving a thick sidewinder trail in the red dust.

'You die next,' Lorgar breathed at its retreating back. That, too, was a promise.

But Ingethel could wait. Thumbing the trigger brought his crozius back to electric life, just in time to fall under the shadow again.

Sonic booms rent the air with each thrash of the whip. Its lashing impact carved ravines in the sand – canyons Lorgar rolled to avoid, while desperately evading each strike. Each breath brought fresh pain to his broken bones. Each inhalation was strife in the thin atmosphere.

Another rift in the rocky sand yawned to the side as he weaved away from the touch of the lash. It split the ground with a thunder-clap, throwing him off balance again, beyond the means of armour stabilisers to adjust for. The daemon's immense hand, deprived of its axe, reached to clutch at the prone primarch, and Lorgar reacted purely by instinct. He raised his hand to meet the downward grasp, little caring how his eyes burned and streamed with psychic fire. The great red fist crashed against a psychic barrier, knuckles crackling like loose gravel.

Lorgar struck. The crozius sang its tempestuous song,

thudding against the curled claws and pulverising the black iron bones beneath its flesh. Blood sprayed from the split skin, splashing molten brass across the primarch's gauntlets and chestplate.

The whip lashed back, snake-keen and vicious. It spiralled around his arm and crozius, biting with barbs. Lorgar staggered, his armour joints whining at the sudden, harsh movements as the wounded daemon pulled him closer. Its breath hit him in another rancid blast, though the creature didn't roar. It was done with such displays; as Lorgar leaned back, boots scraping across the sands, he could see the beast's intentions all too easily. Its jaws were already falling open, offering up broken fangs as a weapon where an axe and whip had failed.

In the past, he'd imagined his death more often than he cared to admit – wondering if it would come in the distant cold of a deep-void battle, or the burning warmth of a blade to the back. Despite their vaunted immortality, despite the invulnerability bred into their bones, a primarch was still a being of flesh and blood. One of Angron's snorted witticisms came back to him in those moments Lorgar mused over mortality: if something bled, it could be killed.

Everything bleeds, Lorgar. His brother's words, cutting right to the quick even years after they were first uttered. Tanks bled fuel and coolant. Aliens bled blood and ooze. Angron had never stood upon a battlefield and failed to apply his own brand of tortured logic to the conflict.

Lorgar hauled back against the drag, succeeding in doing nothing beyond pulling the coiled lash tighter. The daemon's clumsy, shattered hand reached for his torso, and the primarch's kick crunched into its thumb, mangling it further.

With a roar, it lifted him from the ground. In the time it took to spit a curse, the beast snapped its jaws on his free arm, cracked incisors scraping across the ceramite. Melted brass droplets dripped from the creature's bleeding gums.

He was not used to pain – at least not physical agony. The pressure constricting his arm was incomparable to anything else he'd experienced. Ceramite split in metallic rips, threatening the sealed integrity of his armour plating. Something in his elbow clicked, then crunched, then snapped entirely. The fist at the end of his arm fell loose, the fingers relaxing, no longer obeying his mind's impulses.

With a fury even his brother Angron would have admired, the primarch wrenched his crozius free with a final scream. The hammer head crashed against the bloodthirster's temple in a cacophony of breaking bone, shattering its cheek, eye socket, and the hinge of its jaw. The grip relaxed immediately, dropping the primarch to the sand.

He landed hard, heaping more abuse on his ruined arm, but kept a grip on his power maul. With a roll through the beast's stampeding hooves, Lorgar struck the creature's other leg, smacking a blow right against the thing's kneecap. This time, the crack of splitting bone was enough to cause him to wince even through his own pain.

The bloodthirster howled as it fell, crippled, to the sand. Worthless legs stretched out behind it. Before the wings could even beat twice, Lorgar vaulted its back, boots clinging tight to the leathery flesh, and pummelled a single strike to its ridged spine. Another tectonic crackle heralded the daemon's backbone giving way for good.

One wing ceased its ignoble flapping, slapping against the sand and twitching with spasms.

The primarch hammered its club-hands aside as they reached back, deforming the fingers beyond use. Only then did he move around to face it once more, meeting its fevered, bleeding eyes. The blood running from its maw was already cooling in the sand, fusing its jaw to the ground.

A nasty smile coloured his lips. 'What did you learn from this?' he asked the creature.

It snuffed at him, almost dumbly bestial but for the enraged sentience drowning in its eyes. Even crippled and broken, it sought to drag itself forward, as if the primarch's very life was some intolerable insult.

'Rage without focus is no weapon at all.' Lorgar raised his crozius. 'Take this lesson back to the Blood God.'

For the second time, his hammer fell, butchering the incarnated essence of a god.

TEN

ORACLE

THIRTEEN SECONDS LATER, Lorgar collapsed alone.

He didn't feel the crozius fall from his nerveless fingers. He didn't feel anything but the breath sawing in and out of his abused body. On instinct, he dragged his broken bones closer, curling upon the sand in foetal echo of the time he spent gestating in his genetic life-pod.

He could taste blood. His own blood. How different it was from the chemical-thick piss running through a legionary's veins, or the molten, sick richness of the dead daemon.

The air is too thin. In his heavy-eyed delirium, his own thoughts came in Ingethel's voice. *And my lungs are pierced by spears of rib.*

For a time he lay there, struggling to stay alive, breathing blood-wet air into weak lungs.

The daemon died with the same maddening dissolution of so many aetheric insanities in this haunted realm.

As for Ingethel, the primarch had no idea. He would check soon. Not yet. Soon. He... he had to...

'No more tests, Anathema's son,' said a voice.

'One last test, Anathema's son,' said another, similar to the first, but somehow flawed. It was as if a botched cloning had lightly scarred the voice's timbre.

The primarch hauled himself over, blinking bloody eyes up at another winged figure. This one was grotesquely avian, with stinking, withered wings and two vulture heads. While it would have towered above a mortal man, it was a hunched and decrepit thing by the standards of its daemon kin, closer in size to Ingethel.

'I am the one sent to judge you,' both heads said at once.

'I am tired of being judged.' The primarch lay on the sand and laughed, though he couldn't think what was funny.

'I bring the chance for a final truth,' said one of the creature's heads, in a corvidian caw.

'I bring the final lie you will hear,' its second head croaked, just as sincere as the first. No shade of amusement shone in any of the four pebble-black eyes.

'I am done with this,' the primarch grunted. Even rising to his feet was a trial. He could feel his bones sliding awkwardly together, jagged pieces of a puzzle that no longer fit cleanly. 'That,' he breathed, 'is most unpleasant.'

'Lorgar,' said the creature's right head.

'Aurelian,' said the left.

He didn't answer them. Limping, he moved to retrieve his crozius from the sand. Its active power field had scorched the ground to black glass. When he lifted it, it had never felt so heavy.

'Ingethel,' Lorgar sighed. 'I am done with this. I have learned all I need to learn. I am returning to my ship.'

There was no answer. Ingethel was nowhere to be seen. The bland desertscape offered no hope of determining direction.

He turned back to the two-headed creature.

'Leave me be, lest I destroy you as I destroyed the Unbound.'

Both wizened heads bobbed in acknowledgement. 'If you could banish the Unbound,' the first said, 'you could easily banish me, as well.'

'Or perhaps I am more than I appear to be,' the second hissed. 'Perhaps you are weaker now and you would fall before my sorcery.'

Lorgar shook his head, seeking to tame his swimming senses. The air was so painfully thin, it made all thought difficult.

'I bring you a choice, Lorgar,' both heads spoke at once, sharing the same serious, watery-eyed expression.

He limped over to his overturned helm, lifting it from the ground and shaking sand from its interior. Both eye lenses were cracked.

'Speak, then.'

The daemon fluttered its wings. Vestigial, skinny things – Lorgar doubted the creature could even fly. Small wonder that it squatted on the sand, leaning upon its bone staff as a crutch.

'I am Kairos,' both heads said at once. 'The mortal realm will come to know me by another name. Fateweaver.'

Lorgar's desire to show respect for the gods' agents had faded somewhat in the last hour. The words came through gritted teeth.

'Get on with it.'

'The future is not entirely unwritten,' both heads spoke again. Their wrinkled features were strained by effort, as if speaking with unity was a great challenge. 'Confluences exist as sureties. There will come a time when war breaks out across the Imperium of Man, and you will once again face the brother you despise.'

Lorgar's kindly eyes, already weary, now grew cold. 'I do not despise my br–'

'You cannot lie to me,' one head said.

'And if you try, I will always see through to the truth,' said the other.

The primarch forced himself to nod, before placing his helm back on. It took a moment for the cracked eye lenses to flicker into clarity, but a grainy picture materialised soon enough. Curiously, Lorgar couldn't see the daemon through his left eye lens, merely the horizon beyond. In his right eye, the creature sat in hunched repose.

'Get on with it,' he growled this time. Three of his teeth were loose and bleeding.

'It will happen at Calth,' the right head said.

'Or it will happen, yet not at Calth,' said the left, though its placid tone wasn't one of argument.

Lorgar still tasted blood in the back of his mouth. His eyes wouldn't stop watering, and he suspected the pain in the bridge of his nose was a mashing break that would need resetting.

'What will happen?'

'You will face Guilliman,' both heads squawked in eerie unison. 'And you will slay him.'

Lorgar hesitated. To consider it, truly, was almost beyond him. Even if there was no way to avert the coming crusade, did it truly have to come to such measures as fratricide?

His own selfishness was a surprise. With a shake of his head, he considered the other side of the coin. Was fratricide worse than genocide? The loss of life would be immense on both sides of the divided Imperium, among the faithful and the ignorant.

He had to focus.

'Go on.'

'I am Kairos, the Oracle of Tzeentch,' said both heads. 'I am bound to always speak one truth and one lie.' The creature rattled its withered wings. Several blue-black feathers, the colour of ugly bruises, drifted from its pinions. 'But this is a moment of great divinity. A nexus of possibility. A fulcrum. The Great Gods have bound me to speak only the truth, in this moment of moments. I am sworn now to stand before the chosen of the pantheon, and offer a choice. Now, and never again, I may speak with one mind. No lies. No words of deceit from one mouth, and words of truth from another. This, now, is too important. The gods are in alignment for the first time in an eternity.'

'And the Unbound?'

Both heads regarded Lorgar with impassive, unblinking eyes. 'Kharnath violated the accord. But the Blood God is still bound by it. Still oathed to it. The pantheon of heaven is kin to the primarch pantheon of your species. They wage war amongst themselves, just as you will wage war against your brothers. Existence is strife.'

'To strive,' the second head added, 'is to live.'

The thought chilled Lorgar's blood. A convocation of warring gods. 'I understand.'

'No,' the first head said. 'You do not.'

'But you will,' the second nodded, 'in the decades to come.'

'I bring you a choice,' added the first head. 'Face Guilliman and slay him.'

'Or let him live,' finished the second. 'And taste the shame of defeat.'

Lorgar wanted to laugh, but the creeping sense of unease held the mirth back. 'How is that a choice?'

'Because of Calth,' both heads replied. One was silently weeping now, the other grinning with beakish malice. Could a bird grin? Somehow, this one did. Lorgar couldn't help but stare.

'You must choose whether you walk a path of personal glory, or one of divine destiny,' said the first head.

The second spoke through its crystalline tears. 'You must choose whether you will stand among your brothers as an equal, with vengeance as your goal, or work in the name of the gods, tasting shame for a greater victory.'

'I am not a vain man.' Lorgar felt his broken ribs aching as they slowly re-knitted beneath his armour and flesh. 'I seek enlightenment for the species, not self-glorification.'

'You will end this war with many scars.' The first head lowered in bizarre respect.

'Or you will end it dead,' added the second, 'in one of a thousand ways.'

'Get–' Lorgar forced the words through a barricade of teeth, '–to the point, creature.'

'Calth,' the first head intoned. 'You will be given one chance – and only one chance – to shed Guilliman's blood. It is written in the stars, by the hands of the gods. If you face him at Calth, you will slay him.'

'But you will lose the war,' said the second. 'You will earn your brothers' respect and awe. You will savour your vengeance. But your holy war will falter. The Emperor's defences will be enriched by too many defenders, drawn there by fates that would otherwise have been denied. You may never even reach Terra.'

Lorgar turned from the daemon, shaking his head in wonder at their offer. Like ruined wings, the remains of his cloak flapped in the breeze.

'Is this prophecy? If I fight Guilliman, I am destined to win, yet I will lose all I sought to achieve?'

The daemon's first head hawked and spat bloody saliva in a thick string. As it coughed, the second head spoke. 'It is prophecy. You will not always be the lost one, Lorgar – the weakest of your brothers. You will find your strength in this faith. You will find fire and passion, and become the soul you were born to be. That is why Guilliman will die at your feet, if you choose to make it so. Fight him at Calth, and you will finish the battle with his blood on your face. You crave that temporal triumph, and it could be yours.'

The first head twitched with sudden movement, regarding him with its beady bird's eyes. 'But the cost is high. To bring about this future, you will be at Calth, instead of standing in the place your species most needs you to be in that ordained hour. If you face your brother Guilliman, and choose human honour over the destiny of your species, you will kill him. Yet in doing so, you will fail in your hopes of setting humanity free from ignorance.'

'I say again, that is no choice at all.'

Both heads laughed. 'Is that so? You are human, whether you choose to confess to it or not. You are a slave to mortal emotions. The primarchs are far from a perfection of the human recipe, despite their individual might.'

'There will come a time,' the first head said, smiling with beak-creaking amusement, 'when your pride and passion will demand that you destroy the Warrior-King of Ultramar.'

The second nodded in accord. 'But weigh the balance, Emperor's son. A moment of personal glory, proving to your brothers that you are ascendant among them... Or paving the way for the future of your species. All prophets make sacrifices, do they not? This will become one of yours.'

'If,' the first finished, 'you live long enough to make it.'

Lorgar said nothing for some time. He listened to the wind toying with his tattered cloak, and the withered feathers on the daemon's wings.

'Show me,' he said in a soft voice.

THE SHIP BURNED.

On the deck around him lay a hundred dead mortals and slain Ultramarines. The walls of the strategium shuddered, venting air pressure and feeding the flames sweeping across the entire bridge deck. Thrones stood in flames. The fire was already cremating those that had fallen in the last few minutes.

Lorgar saw himself at the heart of the flames, his crozius in his gauntlets. The image wore red armour, in mirror of the Word Bearers he had seen at the Eternity Gate, and cast its maul aside with an angry flourish. Whatever battle it had been fighting had taken its toll; the image of himself stood in cracked armour, with its face blackened by burn scarring.

'For Monarchia,' the image of Lorgar raged through bleeding gums and split lips. 'For watching me kneel in the dust of my many failures.'

At first, Lorgar couldn't make out who his image was addressing. Then, with grim and wounded majesty, Guilliman staggered from the flames. Silently defiant even as his armour blackened into a burning ruin, the Lord of Macragge drew a gladius. His helm was gone, baring a face that remained stoic despite a crushed skull. One arm was gone, ending at the elbow. Blood ran in viscous rivulets from the joints of his armour. His white cloak was aflame.

Lorgar's image threw his hand forward. Psychic energy, so intensely golden it aborted direct sight, haloed and crowned his head with three aetheric horns. A wave of unseen force pounded into the Ultramarine liege, hurling him back through the fire and against the wall beyond.

Guilliman crashed to the deck, a twitching, ragged marionette with severed strings. And then, with his remaining hand, he reached for the fallen gladius again.

Lorgar crushed the hand beneath a crimson boot.

'This, my brother, is for every life lost in the name of a lie.' Lorgar hauled the Lord of Macragge up by the throat, smashing him back against the wall even as he strangled him. 'Your fleet burns. Your astral kingdom dies next.'

Guilliman managed to smile.

LORGAR FACED THE twin-headed daemon again.

'I must see more.'

'You have seen all you need to see,' both heads chorused.

'I do not understand. At the last, he seemed amused.' The primarch winced at the pain of his heart thudding against broken ribs. 'How can that be?'

But he knew. At least, he could guess. He had seen that look in Guilliman's cold warlord's eyes before. Not anger. Not wrath. Disappointment, bordering on disbelief. *What have you done wrong this time?* The accusation came in Guilliman's arch, solemn voice, as if proclaimed by their father himself. *What have you ruined now? What lives have been lost because of your foolishness?*

Lorgar's lip curled. 'He knew something. Even as he died, he knew something.'

'He hates you,' said the daemon's first head. 'He was amused to learn he was right about you. That you were, as he always suspected, a traitor in waiting.'

The second head shook in dismissal. 'No. He has never loathed you, Lorgar. You have always imagined his hatred. He does not respect you, for you are too different to find common ground, but your imagination has always been the source of the feud between you.'

The primarch cursed. 'Which one of you is telling the truth?'

'I am,' they both said at once.

Lorgar swore again. 'Enough. Tell me then, if I am not at Calth, where should I be? What path must I walk to enlighten my species?'

'I am not your seer, Emperor's son,' the first head rasped. 'I have given you the choice. You will make it in time.'

'If,' the second added, matching its tone completely, 'you live that long.'

The creature spread its wings.

'Wait, please.'

It didn't wait. 'All will be decided in Ultima Segmentum, Lorgar. Vengeance, or vision. Glory, or truth.'

The primarch raised his hand to plead for more time, but the daemon was gone in the time it had taken to blink.

HE FOUND HIS prey coiled upon itself, curled in some grotesque foetal parody of reptilian gestation.

But all rage had bled from him. He couldn't help but see the young maiden shaman that had whored her life away to become this thing. Not for glory or gain, but for faith. He doubted she existed as more than an echo in the creature's mind, but the idea itself was enough to bleed the anger from his body.

'Ingethel,' he said. 'Do you live?'

Its fingers twitched, several of them, on all four of its hands. The sky was darkening now. With the night came the cold. Lorgar replaced his cracked helm, breathing deep of his internal air supply.

'Ingethel,' he said again.

The daemon's bones creaked as it slowly rose. *'I live. Not for much longer. But for now, I live.'* It turned its monstrous face to his. Cataracts milked its abominable eyes. *'All is done. You have witnessed all that had to be seen.'*

'How much was true?' demanded Lorgar.

'All of it,' replied the daemon. *'Or none. Or perhaps something in between.'*

Lorgar nodded. 'What if there was more I wished to see? You have shown me what the gods demanded I bear witness to. Now show me what *I* wish to see.'

The daemon curled its twiggish arms close against its broad, speckled chest. *'This is permitted. What would you have me show you, Emperor's son?'*

He paused for a moment, seeking the right words. 'I've seen what I must do to ensure victory. I've seen the fate of the galaxy if the Emperor's lies are not challenged. Now, I wish to walk other worlds in this Great Eye. If this is the gateway to the heaven and hell of human myth, show me more of it. Show me the possibilities in these mutable worlds. Show me what the warp can offer humanity, if we concede to this merging of flesh and spirit.'

'I can do all of this, Lorgar. As you wish.'

The primarch hesitated. 'And before I return to the Imperium, there is one thing I must see above any other.'

'Name it.'

Lorgar smiled behind the emotionless faceplate. 'Show me what happens if we lose.'

PART FIVE
CRUSADE'S END

ELEVEN

COUNCIL

The *Fidelitas Lex*
Four days after Isstvan V

MAGNUS WAS SILENT for a long time. Lorgar continued his writing, pausing only to tap the quill into one of the nearby inkpots. The traditionalist in him adored Colchisian rusticism; he couldn't shake the lingering notion that Holy Scripture should not be written upon a data-slate, unless no other implements presented themselves. In truth, he enjoyed the expression of recording his thoughts and prayers through flowing cursive lettering. There was more beauty in such creation, and it gave his apostles something to copy in its entirety.

'Brother,' Magnus said at last. 'I remember banishing that vision of you from my tower. It was mere days ago for me. Strange to think of the games time plays with us, is it not?'

Lorgar finally laid the quill to rest. When he turned to Magnus, it was with amusement in his eyes, and something more. It took his brother several moments to really see it, to truly understand what was different.

Few things in the galaxy could unnerve Magnus the Red, but the sight of absolute conviction burning in the embers of Lorgar's eyes was suddenly revealed to be one of them. He'd seen that look before, in the eyes of madmen, prophets and fanatics of alien races and other human worlds. Above all, he had seen it in the eyes of his father, the Emperor, where it warred with a patient affection. But he had never seen it in the eyes of a brother – never in the eyes of a being who commanded enough power to reshape the galaxy against the codes of the Imperium.

'The Great Crusade is over,' Lorgar smiled. 'The true holy war begins now.'

'*Will you face Guilliman?*'

Lorgar's smile didn't fade, though it took on a kinder warmth, rather than the full and unhealthy heat of fervour. 'My Legion leaves for the Calth system as soon as Horus' council concludes.'

Magnus' image wavered, affected by his own unease. '*That does not answer my question.*'

'The Ultramarines must be crippled at Calth. Their backs need to be broken, lest they race ahead to Terra and bolster our father's defences.'

Magnus struggled to equate the purred assurances of military tactics with his most scholarly brother's soft voice. It all seemed somehow incongruous, yet Lorgar had never looked so bizarrely *complete*. Gone were the furtive, soulful glances and the hesitations before speaking.

The duel with Corax had done more than grant him scars upon his face and throat.

'*That does not answer my question, either,*' Magnus pointed out.

'My fleet will divide. We will storm Ultima Segmentum, for there is more to attack than Guilliman's little empire.'

'*Where? Why?*'

Lorgar's chuckle sent distortions rippling through Magnus' image. 'You may know our plans when you join us fully.'

A chime sounded, followed by a stern, careful voice over the vox.

'*The Warmaster requests your presence, lord.*'

Lorgar rose to his feet, not bothering to take his weapon this time. 'Thank you, Erebus. Inform the *Vengeful Spirit* that I am coming aboard immediately.'

THIS TIME, THE council chamber was almost empty. Lorgar dismissed his warrior escorts, letting Kor Phaeron lead them away. He walked to the central table alone, not concealing his bemusement at the lack of presences in the room.

'Brothers,' he greeted Horus and Angron.

The Warmaster's expression was a sour indication of how he'd cast the atmosphere of indulgent fraternity aside. Angron's distracted scowl showed he'd never paid heed to such a notion, anyway.

'Lorgar,' Horus fairly seethed the name through an insincere smile. Gone was the charismatic demigod so adored by his followers. In his place stood the truth offered by privacy: a brother among kin, and on the edge of black temper.

'I came as requested,' said the Word Bearer. 'I see you have no desire to discuss Fulgrim.'

'You have spoken your piece on our beloved brother. For now, you will have to trust me that all is in hand.'

Lorgar snorted. 'I have seen horrors and truths you are only now beginning to imagine, Horus. It is you who should be trusting me.'

The Warmaster's features were taut and blue-veined. He scarcely looked himself these nights.

'I *have* trusted you, Lorgar. Look at what we brought about in this system. Now it is time for you to repay my trust with some of your own.'

'Very well. But where is "Fulgrim"?'

'He walks the surface of Isstvan Five once more, attending to the withdrawal of his Legion's final forces. Now, enough of such talk. We have a great deal to plan.'

Lorgar shook his head. 'No. Enough planning. We have spent months, *years*, speaking of plans. There is no more to discuss. I am taking my Legion into the galactic east. If all goes well, I will rejoin you on the crusade to Terra. If the battles go badly, then I will still rejoin you, though with significantly fewer warriors.' He ended his assurances with a smile.

Angron stared into the middle distance, distracted by the stabbing thoughts of his neural implants. The occasional tic pulled his facial muscles tight, but he seemed to pay no attention to the conversation.

Horus released a slow breath. 'We have argued over this many times, and I was a fool to let your enthusiasm run as wild as your imagination for this long. You do not have enough warriors to achieve what you plan.'

'And I have told you, brother, my apostles are prepared to sail into Ultramar. We have made pacts with divine forces you still struggle to comprehend. *Daemons*, Horus – true daemons, born of the warp, will answer our summons. Our cargo holds heave with the bodies of faithful mortals, taken from the worlds we have conquered. The Seventeenth Legion has not been idle these last years.'

'You need legionaries.' Horus leaned on the stellar cartography table, his fists eclipsing the galaxy's outermost stars. 'If you divide the Word Bearers fleet according to your desire, you will need more legionaries.'

Lorgar threw his hands up in surrender. 'Fine. Give them to me. Give me a few of your companies, and I will take them with me into the east.'

'I will give you more than that.' Horus gestured to the other brother in the chamber. 'I will give you another Legion.'

Angron turned his scarred features upon Lorgar. His smile was the ugliest thing the prophet had ever seen.

TWELVE

COUNTERMEASURES

THE WORLD STILL smelled of betrayal. The smoky reek of it, thick and piquant, hung heavy in the air.

But then, that was no surprise. The civil war to divide the Imperium had begun there only four nights before. Many of the Legions loyal to Horus were still engaged in the arduous process of withdrawing their forces back into orbit. The pyre marking the final resting place of the tens of thousands of slain warriors was more than an ashen burial ground – it was a beacon of cinders, proclaiming the overthrowing of humanity's stagnant oppressor. The blackened earth and scorched, empty suits of armour from over two hundred thousand legionaries lay at the heart of a tank graveyard. Those war machines suitable for plunder were already claimed by the victorious Legions. The wrecks too far gone to repair sat where they'd died, consigned to rust and corrode when the rebels moved on.

Captain Axalian of 29th Company watched his warriors'

progress from atop the burned-out hull of a Raven Guard
Land Raider. The palatine aquila still stood out upon his
breastplate, as was his right as one of the Emperor's Children Legion. Many of his brothers were already defiling
the Imperial symbol as they altered their armour with
little but their own blades and ingenuity, but he kept his
wargear as pristine as possible. The emblem could be
removed by the tech-adepts once his planet-side duties
were complete. Until then, he would tolerate no damage to the ceramite he'd miraculously managed to keep
unbroken through the insane battle earlier that week.

He had no need to raise his voice. His men, and the servitors working alongside them, operated fluidly and efficiently
with only a little spoken direction. His role was one of
organiser, not an overseer, and he took pride in the smooth
operation taking place in his allotted section of the field.
Axalian watched another of the black-hulled battle tanks
being connected to the lifter claws of an Emperor's Children
transporter gunship. The servitors backed away, and a warrior nearby raised his hand. The captain nodded in reply.

'This is Axalian,' he spoke into the vox. 'Sector Thirty,
requesting clearance.'

'Request acknowledged, Captain Axalian. Please hold.'

Another gunship, this one in the sea-green of the Sons
of Horus, rattled overhead, pregnant with stolen Rhino
troop carriers. About a minute after it, an Iron Warriors
lander shook the ground as it lifted off on guttural engines.

'Captain Axalian,' came the reply from the Techmarine
overseer at Reclamation Command, to the east. *'You are
clear, with five minutes to make your assigned launch window.
If you fail to meet this requirement, you will surrender the
launch window to the next vessel in line. Do you understand?'*

Of course he understood. He'd been doing this for

four days. He'd heard that same refrain, from the same Sons of Horus Techmarine, at least two hundred times.

'I understand.'

'*Your launch window has commenced.*'

He switched vox-channels. 'Thunderhawk transporter *Redeemer*, you are clear for orbital return.'

'*Order received, captain. Launching now.*'

The flyer's thrusters started cycling up. Axalian watched it rise, shuddering with the weight of its plunder.

That was the moment a shadow passed overhead. The Reclamation Command bunker blurted an emergency code in screeching binaric cant across the communications channels.

'Abort!' Axalian called into the vox. '*Redeemer*, this is Axalian, abort launch immediately. Land and cut engines at once.'

The Thunderhawk thudded down heavily on its landing gear. '*Sir?*' voxed the pilot.

'Stay *down*,' said Axalian. 'We have inbound.'

Three of them, and inbound without clearance. He watched the grey gunships roar overhead, spiralling down in landing trajectories, uncaring of the discord they sowed in their approaches.

'Word Bearers.'

With an annoyed grunt, he jumped down from the Land Raider hull. Two of his warriors stood watch over a gang of servitors nearby; he gestured for them to leave their charges and follow him.

'*Self-righteous bastards,*' one of them voxed, '*coming in like that.*'

Axalian was irritated enough not to reprimand the legionary for the breach of protocol. 'Let us see what this is about,' he said.

The gunships were kin to all Legion troop drop-ships: thick-hulled, swoop-winged and avian in a strangely hulking way. With a mechanical unison that could only have been intentional, the three ramps lowered as one. Axalian stood before the closest Thunderhawk, flanked by his guards.

'I am Captain Axalian of the Third Legion. Explain your–'

'Captain,' both of his warriors hissed at once.

Leading the squad of Word Bearers was a towering figure in ceramite painted the red of fine wine. He stalked down the gang-ramp, ignoring how it shook beneath his boots. The primarch's unmasked face was pale, given life and colour by the tattooed stripes of runic scripture inked in gold upon the white flesh. Axalian could claim the honour of standing in the Emperor's presence a number of times, and this being resembled the Master of Mankind more than any other, but for the changes he had wrought to himself in order to appear different.

'My Lord Aurelian,' Axalian saluted.

'Tell me.' Lorgar bared his perfect teeth in something that wasn't quite a smile. 'Where is my brother Fulgrim?'

'THE SCARS SUIT you.'

They faced each other in a mausoleum of tank husks, while their warriors looked on. Thirty Word Bearers held their bolters in loose fists – half of them in their Legion's traditional granite-grey ceramite, the other half clad in betrayers' red. Change had come to the XVII Legion after the Dropsite Massacre. Great change indeed.

Lorgar stood at the head of his phalanx. Fulgrim, clad in burnished purple and gold, needed no such formation. His Emperor's Children surrounded the intruders;

some stood in neat squad rankings in the presence of two primarchs, others remaining by the hulls of battle tanks, awaiting orders to close into formation. All of them sensed the unpleasant tension in the air, few fingers strayed far from bolter grips. Legionaries firing upon brother legionaries may have seemed madness only weeks before, but the age of innocence and inviolate trust was over. They had buried it forever on this very battlefield.

Fulgrim's effortless charm manifested in a warm smile, a brotherly glint in his eyes. He made no effort to reach for a weapon, as if such behaviour were beyond conception.

'I am not making a jest,' Fulgrim said, 'the scars suit you.' He stroked his fingertips along his own pale cheeks, tracing a mirror image of where the scars were carved down Lorgar's face and neck. 'They blend well with your tattooed scripture, almost like understated tiger's stripes. They ruin any hopes of refining your features to perfection, certainly, but they are not entirely unattractive.'

Lorgar's own smile seemed genuine enough to all who looked upon the scene from the sidelines, at least as sincere as Fulgrim's.

'We must speak, you and I, my beloved brother.'

Fulgrim gave an elaborate shrug, his face a guileless picture. 'Whatever could you mean? Are we not speaking now, Lorgar?'

Several of the Emperor's Children chuckled through vox-speakers. Lorgar's smile didn't fade. He said two words into his own open vox-channel. A name.

'Argel Tal.'

CAPTAIN ROUSHAL OF the Emperor's Children destroyer *Saturnine Martyr* covered his eyes as his command deck exploded in light and noise. The peal of thunder shattered several consoles, cracking glass instruments and driving a thick crack through the occulus screen.

He was already yelling into the vox for an emergency containment and repair team, while cursing at his on-board cult of tech-adepts for whatever laxity that had allowed such a grievous malfunction.

Several of the returning shouts insisted it was a teleport flare. Either way, alarms were ringing.

When Roushal dragged himself off the floor, waving a hand through the dissipating mist, the first thing he encountered was the muzzle of a bolt pistol. Fat-calibred and painfully wide, it broke his teeth on the way into his mouth, and rested hideously cold and bitter on his tongue. He tried to swallow. Three of his teeth went down with the saliva. They tasted smoky and bitter.

'Unguh?' he managed to gasp.

The mist cleared enough to reveal the massive arm clutching the pistol, and the Word Bearer in traitors' red to whom the arm belonged.

'My name is Argel Tal,' said the warrior. 'Remain silent, on your knees, and you will be allowed to survive the next hour.'

FULGRIM HESITATED.

'Yes, Captain Axalian?'

The captain needed a second attempt to speak. The primarch was clearly unconnected to the main vox-net, and he was the ranking officer in his lord's presence. It fell to him to apprise the Legion commander of the orbital... situation.

'Lord, we are receiving a mass-aligned signal from forty-nine of our vessels. One signal, coming from the

Saturnine Martyr, is the source pulse. The others are confirmations, aligned to the source message.'

Fulgrim ground his teeth together. The smile died in his handsome eyes. 'And what is the message, Axalian?'

Before the captain could reply, Lorgar clicked his gorget's voxsponder to a louder volume. The voice that came through was crackled by distance distortion, but the words were clear enough.

'This is Argel Tal of the Gal Vorbak. Objectives achieved, my lord. No casualties. Awaiting order to teleport back to our ships.'

Lorgar silenced his vox. 'Now, brother.' He smiled at Fulgrim, and there was no mistaking the absolute sincerity in the expression. 'Let us talk alone.'

Fulgrim swallowed, too composed to ever reveal his discomfort, but unable to force life and colour to his strained features.

'You have changed, Lorgar.'

'So everyone keeps telling me.'

THIRTEEN

LA FENICE

THEY HAD SPOKEN for hours, walking together by the edge of the battlefield, weaving between the barricades and firebases established by the Iron Warriors Legion. They kept their voices low, watching one another with careful eyes, while any legionary or servitor nearby scattered before their slow path. It seemed clear, in no uncertain terms, that the brothers had no wish to be interrupted.

By the time Lorgar left the surface, night had fallen upon the killing fields of Isstvan V. The work continued, with Axalian and his cohorts returned to work hours before, lifting the salvage and leaving the scrap. The captain was close enough to witness the brothers finish their discussions, noting that the XVII Primarch's saccharine amusement had abated, as had the anger simmering within his gaze.

As for Fulgrim, he seemed similarly dispassionate, adopting neither the familiar smile he usually wore in Lorgar's presence, nor the subtle signs of fraternal condescension that had so thoroughly marked their decades of brotherhood.

When the teleport flare faded, Axalian voxed for his waiting Thunderhawk to hold position, and switched communication channels.

'This is Axalian to the *Heart of Majesty*. Priority request.'

The expected delay lasted almost a full minute, before a voice fuzzed back on fragile vox. '*Captain Axalian, priority request acknowledged. How may we illuminate you, sir?*'

'What is the status on the forty-nine vessels with Word Bearers "visitors"?'

Again, the delay. '*Fleet reports indicate the Seventeenth Legion is recalling its embarked guests via teleportation.*'

Ah, III Legion pride at work. No warship captain would confess to being taken by surprise like that, let alone boarded by those they'd trusted. *Embarked guests.* Axalian almost grinned. How delightful.

He was just about to reply when his battle-brother's voice rasped back from the *Heart of Majesty* in the heavens above. '*Captain Axalian, we are receiving conflicting reports on the primarch. Where is Lord Fulgrim? The fleet is calling out for immediate visual affirmation of his location.*'

The captain looked to where the flare of teleportation fog was little more than a disseminating glimmer.

'I had visual confirmation on the primarch until a few moments ago. Inform the fleet, he teleported with Lorgar.'

With morbid curiosity, he listened to the slipstream of voices in conflict across the orbital vox-net. It took almost five minutes for sense to break through and when it did, it wasn't what he'd been expecting.

'*This is the flagship to all vessels. The primarch is aboard.*

Repeat – this is the Pride of the Emperor *to Third Legion fleet. Lord Fulgrim is aboard.'*

THE CHAMBER LAY in darkness. It assaulted the other senses to make up for its lack of the most important one: the smell of decay was a raw musk hanging thick in the cold air, and never before had Lorgar considered that absolute silence could have an oppressive presence all its own.

'Lights,' the primarch said aloud. His voice echoed dramatically, but nothing answered.

'The acoustics in here have always been wonderful,' Fulgrim said, and his brother could hear the grin in those words.

The Word Bearer lifted his fist. A moment's thought wreathed it in heatless, harmless psychic fire, but it was a parasitic luminescence, seeming to eat the darkness rather than banish it. Still, it was enough.

Lorgar regarded the devastated theatre. Whatever last performance had taken place here had been one of supreme decadence. Bodies, already gone to rags and bones, slumbered in cadaverous repose across the chairs and aisles. Discarded weapons and broken furniture lay strewn across the scene. Nothing was unmarked by the black stains of old blood.

'I see your Legion's pursuit of perfection does not extend to cleanliness,' Lorgar said softly.

Fulgrim grinned again. He could see it now, his brother's teeth oranged by the amber witchlight.

'This is holy ground, Lorgar. You of all souls should respect that.'

Lorgar turned and moved on, walking over the bodies toward the stage. 'You are the puppet-slave of a single

god. I am the archpriest of all of them. Do not tell me
what I should respect.'

The stage was riven by damage and darkened by shed
blood. Both primarchs ascended the steps to the platform itself, their ceramite boots forcing the reinforced
wooden boards to creak and whine.

'There it is.' Fulgrim gestured behind the thin, silk curtain. Lorgar had already seen it. He brushed the gauzy
veil aside with the gentle push of a man moving an
unbroken spider's web.

The Phoenician. The painting stole his breath for a
long moment, and he was complicit in his awe, glad
to let it do so. Few works of art had moved him as this
one did.

Fulgrim, triumphant in this rendering, wore his most
ostentatious suit of armour, as much Imperial gold as
Third Legion purple. He stood before the immense Phoenix Gate leading into the Heliopolis chamber on board
his flagship, a vision of gold against even richer gold. At
his shoulders, reaching out in angelic symmetry, the great
fiery pinions of a phoenix cast burning light against his
armour, lighting the gold to flame-touched platinum and
enriching the purple to a deep Tyrian hue.

All of this, from the look of haunting purity in the
pale eyes to the last and least strand of white hair, was
formed from a mortal's craft. To stare with a primarch's
eyes, even from this respectful distance, showed the faint
topography of brush strokes across the canvas. Only the
most divine muse could inspire mortal hands to create
such a masterpiece.

'My brother,' Lorgar whispered. 'What a man you were.
A paragon among wolves and wastrels.'

'He always enjoyed flattery,' Fulgrim smiled. 'Do you

so quickly forget how he sneered at you, Lorgar? Does his disregard slip from your memory so fast?'

'No.' The Word Bearer shook his head, as if reinforcing the denial. 'But he had every right to think less of me, for I was never whole. Not until now.'

The thing wearing Fulgrim's skin peeled back its lips in a smile the true primarch would never have made.

'You asked to see your brother, chosen one. Here he is.'

'This is a painting. Do not mock me, daemon. Not after we at last reached an accord.'

'You asked to see the brother you had lost.' The smile didn't leave Fulgrim's face. 'I have upheld my end of our agreement.'

Lorgar was already reaching for the crozius on his back.

'Peace, chosen one.' Fulgrim held up his hands. 'The painting. Look longer, look deeper. Tell me what you see.'

Lorgar turned again and stared at the exquisite masterwork. This time, he let his eyes slip across the image, seeking no details, merely drifting until they rested where they may.

He met the image's soulfully rendered eyes, and at last, Lorgar breathed through the faintest of smiles.

'Hail, brother,' he finally said.

'Do you see?' the daemon at his side asked. For a moment, for those three words, it wasn't Fulgrim's voice at all.

'I see more than you realise.' The Word Bearer turned to face his brother's captor. 'If you think to relish all of eternity while playing puppeteer to my brother's bones, you will find yourself fatally disappointed one night.'

'You speak the lies of a desperate and foolish soul.'

Lorgar laughed with a rare and sincere grin, perhaps the only expression that ever broke his resemblance to his father.

'Your secret is safe with me, daemon. Enjoy your stewardship while it lasts.'

He gave Fulgrim's shoulder a comradely slap and walked through the aisle still decorated with corpses, chuckling as he left the graveyard theatre.

When he closed the door, he took his witchlight with him, leaving Fulgrim and the painting together in the darkness.

OUTSIDE THE DOORS, Argel Tal waited with his honour guard. Most of the Legion had repainted their armour in the same crimson as the Gal Vorbak – another sign of the changing times. Each of these warriors wore betrayers' red.

'Sire,' Argel Tal greeted him. The horns on his helm lowered as the legionary nodded. Lorgar felt the palpable heat of the man's twin souls – one living, one parasitically leeching from the first in imitation of life, replacing its theft with a symbiotic flood of power.

Harmonious. Pure. Divine. This was the unity of Chaos, when flesh and spirit met.

'My son, tonight we convene the Council of Sanctity, and I will speak once more of Calth. Then, in the hours that follow, I will summon you and your most trusted subcommanders. After the Council of Sanctity has dispersed, I will speak to you not only of Calth, but of what follows it.'

The warrior hesitated before speaking. 'I do not understand, lord.'

'I know. But you will. There is a great difference between glory and sacrifice, Argel Tal. Sometimes, fate takes care of itself. In those times, you may follow your heart and do whatever you will. You may chase the glory you seek. And other times, destiny needs the courage and blood of mankind to force it through to a better future. Even at the cost of passion and vengeance. Even at the cost of a glory most highly deserved. We all make sacrifices, my son.'

Argel Tal bristled, though he sought to hide his offence from his primarch's eyes. 'I would like to believe I know enough of sacrifice already, my lord.'

Lorgar conceded with a nod. 'That is why I turn to you with the truth this evening, and not Kor Phaeron or Erebus. You, like me, have looked into the gods' eyes. And you, like me, have other wars to fight even as the Calth system burns.'

MASSACRE

Aaron Dembski-Bowden

'WE HAVE BEEN summoned,' said Malcharion. 'Not the Army detachments with us. Not the auxilia. Not the Mechanicum. We alone.'

The fleetmaster had opened the council with those words, knowing there would be many warriors who wished to reply to them.

'The highest authority demands this of us,' he continued.

'The Emperor?' called one of his warriors, out of turn. As intended, the question was met with muted grunts of amusement from the ranks.

'The highest authority that we recognise,' Captain Malcharion amended, unsmiling. He was monumentally stern, and not a man to show his amusement even on those rare occasions he actually felt it.

Malcharion's war councils were informal gatherings, though not without certain protocols. Much to the irritation of his subordinate officers, the Tenth Captain of the VIII Legion saw fit to change those protocols without a moment's notice, appropriating traditions of etiquette from other cultures, and even other Legions, seemingly on random impulse.

He claimed it encouraged his kindred to consider new perspectives in the planning and prosecution of warfare. Many of his brethren simply believed he did it out of perverse eclecticism.

His current preference was a distorted mimicry of the Luna Wolves' custom of warriors placing tokens and mementos in the centre to indicate that they wished to speak before their brethren. Aboard the *Vengeful Spirit*, it was common for Luna Wolf officers to place their weapons or helms upon the central table and wait to be granted permission to speak. Here, in the war councils of the VIII Legion aboard the *Covenant of Blood*, Malcharion had decreed that his officers could only use tokens taken from the bodies of fallen foes.

Almost fifty officers were present – shipmasters, centurions, champions, all accompanied by their oathbound honour guards and personal attendants, bringing the total close to two hundred warriors standing beneath the banners of four battle companies.

Every Night Lord present was entitled to speak no matter his rank, which meant that skulls – used as tokens – were in plentiful supply. The oversized, elongated skulls of dead aliens were piled upon the table, each one scratched or painted with the curved runic lettering of the mellifluous Nostraman language. Here and there among the tokens of skinless bone lay exotic weapons and armour fragments of fallen human cultures, from kingdoms either brought to compliance by the VIII Legion, or rendered extinct by it.

Talos looked over the mournful mess taking up most of the central table in disorganised heaps. Whatever order prevailed when the Luna Wolves practised this tradition was absent in the Night Lords' incarnation. Without a Space Marine's eidetic memory, recalling which warrior had placed which relic would have been impossible.

The young Apothecary carried his helm beneath one arm, breathing in the warm, stale air that barely circulated through the cavernous chamber. A sweet reek nagged at his senses, something not far from spoiled food and a strangely musky spice. He found it cloying rather than unpleasant; one didn't join the Night Lords Legion to fight their wars and train aboard their crypt-ships only to balk at the stench of decaying flesh.

Talos spared a brief glance for the hundreds of corpses hanging from the ceiling on industrial chains. Most were human or eldar, their armour cracked by bolts and rent by blades, many of them now little more than sinewy skeletons in broken carapace plate. Several were strung up by their wrists and necks; others by their ankles with their dead hands hanging down towards the gathered officers in beseeching silence. Many of the bodies were wrapped so utterly in binding chains that they hung as though cocooned by the hungry whims of some impossible metallic arachnid.

The Apothecary returned his dark gaze to the briefing. A hololith of the Night Lords armada dominated the air above the relic-strewn table, showing the fifteen vessels of varying classes that escorted the *Covenant of Blood*. Talos watched the warship, his home since leaving Nostramo so many years before, rendered in blue light and flickering as it sailed in formation. The lesser cruisers and escort frigates turned in a slow perimeter dance around their flagship, while the other three Night Lord warships kept close to the *Covenant* at the armada's heart.

Talos had watched his home world die from the *Covenant*'s command deck.

He'd stood there with his closest brothers over two decades ago as the VIII Legion poured fire upon their own birth-world and pulled it apart with the anger of ten thousand guns.

It had been the last great gathering of the Night Lords. A bittersweet fact, at best.

Of all the eighteen Legions, few avoided their own brothers' company with the tactful frequency of the VIII. It was said by many Imperial commanders that they didn't work well with others, but the truth was a little more amusingly bleak.

The Night Lords scarcely worked well with each other.

Apothecary Talos blinked once, inhumanly languid, and turned iris-less eyes upon the figures around the table. Officers from all four companies comprising the 2,901st Expeditionary Fleet had been summoned to the emergency council. The gathering was limited to the warriors of the Legion. Their Imperial Army counterparts and the auxilia officers that had served faithfully – if uncomfortably – at their sides for the last several campaigns remained aboard their own vessels.

Beyond the ever-present thrum of so many suits of active power armour, the gathered warriors were silent and voiceless. No murmurs or whispers passed their lips. They waited, unnaturally quiet, not through discipline but through cold expectation.

Something was wrong. All of them felt it.

Chained skulls rattled against Malcharion's war plate as the fleet lord keyed a command into the central table's hololithic projectors. The fleet display sparked out of existence and another image crackled into audio-visual resolution above the pile of grisly tokens.

First Captain Jago Sevatarion, Praetor Nox of the VIII Legion, stood rendered in jagged light. His crested helm hung at his belt, while his spear, the weapon almost as renowned among the Legions as the warrior himself, rested across one shoulder. Two of his Atramentar warriors flanked him as motionless avatars, their lightning claws silent and still in deactivation. The pale faces of the warriors around Talos looked on, their white skin turned a consumptive blue by the ethereal light.

'Brothers of the Eighth Legion,' said the recording of Sevatar, his voice hissing with vox corruption. 'Wherever you are in this hypocritical empire, whatever campaigns you are prosecuting in its name, our father demands that you join the Nightfall at once.'

Talos noted the vital signs of his squad elevating slightly on his narthecium gauntlet as the First Captain spoke once more.

'The time has come. Make all speed to the Isstvan System.'

THERE WAS NO order to the fleet's dispersal. The warship Foresworn pulled away first, its engines running hot as it veered out of formation and began to breach the barrier from the material galaxy to the realm beyond the veil.

Alarms and klaxons wailed aboard the decks of those warships still sailing in cohesion, but by the time the perimeter vessels were rolling away from the fleeing Foresworn, it was already too late. The vile machinery at her core sent warp lightning coruscating over the vessel's metal skin, and the Foresworn ripped into the great hole she'd torn open in reality.

The two closest escort destroyers, each crewed by several thousand humans, were dragged along helplessly in her wake. Great cyclones of ectoplasmic smoke, veined by lightning and seething with shrieking faces, clawed at the labouring, juddering vessels. These tendrils from the outreaching storm pulled them – unprepared and unprotected – into the warp behind the *Foresworn*.

Talos watched from the *Covenant of Blood*'s bridge. He leaned on the guardrail that surrounded the elevated central platform, where Malcharion's command throne oversaw the workings of the whole deck. No expression marked his face as he witnessed the helpless ships tumbling into the warp's tides, dragged to damnation as their engines failed to pull them free. He thought, briefly, of the thousands of men and women aboard the vessels, filling the corridors with screams as the boiling acid of unreality flooded through the unshielded decks.

A swift death, perhaps, but one that condensed an infinity of agonies into a soul's last tortured seconds.

The *Covenant of Blood* began its own manoeuvres. The deck shuddered beneath his boots. Servitors locked into their stations on mono-programmed instinct, while the crew braced for entry into the Sea of Souls.

Calls for confirmation and explanation rang out from the rest of the fleet, sounding over the speakers set into the command deck's ornate gothic ceiling. They fell silent at a curt gesture from Malcharion's hand, as he sat with statuesque patience in his command throne.

Talos sensed one of his kindred drawing near from the thrum of live armour. He knew who it was without needing to look at the vicinity trackers on his narthecium. Telling squadmates apart by familiarity and instinct became second nature: they walked in different rhythms,

their sweat had different tangs, they breathed with subtly different cadences. A Space Marine's senses bathed
his brain in information at all times.

'Brother,' said Vandred Anrathi, drawing alongside him.

'Sergeant,' Talos replied. He didn't take his black eyes
from the twisting, tumbling warships, now half-swallowed
by incorporeal fire.

Sergeant Anrathi was a warrior of sleek, sculpted features, with the filed teeth of the night-worshipping
tribes that had lived beyond the limits of Nostramo's
crime-choked cities. Despite his barbaric origins, his
composure and self-control were envied by many; few
warriors handled a Xiphon Interceptor with such serenity,
or could oversee an orbital battle with the same tena-
cious precision.

He led Captain Malcharion's command team and
advised the commander on matters of void warfare.
'Quite a sight, is it not?' he asked.

Talos didn't reply. There had been a time when the
extinction taking place would have threaded strains of
bleak fascination through his core. Even in the process
of inflicting excruciation upon the Legion's prisoners,
there was a sense of righteousness in his actions. Agony
and fear were meted out for a cause, for a purpose. Not
by random chance.

But watching his home world burn and break apart had
cooled his capacity to feel sympathy. In truth, he neither
admired nor mourned the destruction now taking place
before him. He felt little, in fact, beyond a vague sense
of curiosity at whether the warp would one day vomit
the stricken vessels back into real space, and what ruin-
ation they might have suffered in its tempestuous grip.

The deck gave a violent shudder at the cry of distant

thunder. *Broadsides*, thought Talos. The *Covenant of Blood* was firing upon its own fleet.

That, at last, made him draw breath to question what was taking place.

'Why?' he asked, turning to meet his sergeant's eyes.

Anrathi grinned more than most of his brothers. He did so now, bearing his elegantly filed teeth. He didn't need to ask what the Apothecary was questioning.

'Because I ordered it, and Captain Malcharion sanctioned it.'

'Why?' Talos repeated. Irritated curiosity narrowed his eyes. He wanted answers, not another of Anrathi's dances around semantics.

'If we kill them now,' the sergeant replied, 'we don't need to kill them later.'

The medicae wasn't fooled. Talos snorted, looking back at the wide, vast oculus screens, now showing the burning hulls of their escort vessels, dying in the black void between worlds, crumbling apart as they futilely sought to limp away. The *Covenant* had been born in the skies above sacred Mars and blessed with a host of weapons capable of levelling cities. The shieldless, trusting warships of its allies had no hope at all.

'This is spite,' Talos said at last. An ache was beginning to form at his temples, cobwebbing its unwelcome way through the meat of his mind. 'We could cripple those we cannot convert. We could simply run, knowing they would never be able to keep pace, even if they learned of our destination. Instead we gun them down out of spite.'

Anrathi's token shrug could have meant either confirmation or defiance. 'Do you pity them, Talos?'

Do I? For a moment, for the barest breath, he did

wonder. The boy he had been long before he stood in midnight clad with his brethren... that child might have stared in awed horror at what he saw. Before empathy, like sympathy, had eroded from the edges of his soul.

He found himself smiling at the idea.

'You know I do not,' said Talos.

'Then why do I sense disapproval in your tone?'

'My disgust is philosophical in nature. If we destroy out of spite, not from purpose or necessity, we lend credence to what the other Legions claim we are. Slaughter enough souls without true cause, and we would be the very monsters our cousins believe us to be. A self-fulfilling prophecy.'

Anrathi rested a gauntleted hand on the younger warrior's shoulder guard. The skulls bound to Talos' pauldron rattled against the ceramite as if whispering to one another in some muted, bony verse.

'I can never tell if you are as naive as you present yourself to be, as deluded as you seem, or if you are simply laughing at all of us behind your eyes, Talos.'

The Apothecary looked back to the oculus screen, watching reality being ravaged by the arcane engines at the *Covenant*'s heart. A wound in space opened up before them, haemorrhaging wrathful antimatter in streaks of fiery lightning, ready to swallow the ship whole.

'Perhaps the truth is somewhere between all three,' he said at last. The pressure at his temples flared, a true migraine ache that leaked through his skull like searing fluid, feeling like an ugly premonition.

'Are you well?' Anrathi asked, his tone one of cautious surprise.

He knows, Talos thought. *He senses it*. Something in the Apothecary's face had betrayed his sudden pain.

'I have never killed another Legionary,' said Talos. 'That is all. I cannot help but wonder what it will feel like.'

'Yet I have seen you kill many, brother. Witnessed the deeds with my own eyes.'

The Apothecary inclined his head, conceding the point. 'Yes and no. Excruciation and execution are not quite the same as murder.'

THE GUNSHIP BLACKENED was a crow of dirty blue and filthy bronze. Bodies of aliens and apostates were fused to the hull with half-melted adamantium chains, the corpses burned away to husks of charred bone upon atmospheric entry. Replacing them between missions was as sacred an act as the warriors of First Claw ever performed together. If no foes presented themselves, the Night Lords of Malcharion's squad weren't above crucifying members of their own human crew to serve in place.

Talos and his brothers stood in the dark as the gunship rocked around them. Each of them had abandoned the rearward restraint harnesses, choosing to stand in the forward bay for rapid deployment, holding onto the overhead handrails. Only the more cautious among them mag-locked their boots to the shaking deck.

'Five minutes,' said Captain Malcharion. 'Helmets on.'

Talos lifted his helm into place, staining his senses in the red of his tactical display. Target cursors flickered and ammunition counts flashed. Nostraman runes scrolled down his eye lenses as he received his squad's life signs and datafeeds. His armour's systems greeted his immersion with squirts of adrenal chem-fire into the implants across his torso and down his spine.

'First Claw, soul count,' ordered Malcharion. The captain's stern tones were raspy with vox breakage.

'Talos, aye,' the Apothecary replied at once.

'Vandred, aye,' said Sergeant Anrathi a moment later.

'Ruven, aye.'

'Xarl, aye.'

'Cyrion, aye.'

'Sar Zell, aye.'

'Acknowledged,' Malcharion voxed over the straining network. 'Second Claw, soul count.'

And on it went as the other claws aboard other landing craft reported in. Talos watched each name-rune in the Tenth Company's ranks briefly chime across his retinal display as their vital signs uplinked to his narthecium gauntlet.

'Ninety-two souls,' Talos voxed at the count's completion. He turned to the captain at the squad's lead. Malcharion was performing the final checks upon his double-barrelled bolter. 'Tenth Company stands ready,' Talos told him.

'Viris colratha dath sethicara tesh dasovallian,' Malcharion murmured in serpentine Nostraman. *'Solruthis veh za jasz.'*

Sons of our Father, stand in midnight clad. We bring the night.

There were no cheers, no solemn oaths, no roars of adrenaline-soaked readiness so common in other Legions. The Night Lords waited in the wake of their traditional words, staring into the darkness through primed target locks – some smiling, some dead-eyed, some silently baring their teeth in cannibal emotions that no mortal could know – all behind skull-marked faceplates.

The gunship heaved, almost dropping from the sky. Talos felt a split-second's nausea before the gene-forged changes in his inner ears compensated. It triggered the pressure in his skull which had, until then, been dissipating.

'Atmosphere breached,' said Malcharion. 'Three minutes.'

No going back, Talos thought. Though in truth they'd broken past the point of no return months ago. Perhaps even years, when they had burned Nostramo under the Night Haunter's orders, to quell the poison seeping into the Legion from its own recruitment harvests.

Xarl was at the Apothecary's side, holding the opposite handrail. His double-handed chainsword was bound across his back, and Talos saw the high crest atop his kinsman's helmet, tall and proud.

'Why are you wearing that?' Talos voxed to his brother across the squad's intra-link. 'It will not be a parade ground down there.'

Xarl turned his bat-winged helm towards Talos, red eye lenses gleaming in the transport bay's gloom. 'Legion pride,' came the reply in his husky, deep voice. 'It feels right, given what we're about to do.'

Cyrion, standing behind Xarl, had affixed his bolter's chain-bayonet, and was testing it by live-cycling it with droning whines.

'That crest is almost as high as Sevatar's,' he pointed out. 'The enemy will mistake you for a hero.'

Xarl grunted. In dismissal or disgust, it added up to the same result. He turned back to face the front.

In the hull-shaking, iron-rattling unquiet that followed, Cyrion looked over his shoulder, where Ruven was distractedly watching lightning ripple across the naked blade of his force sword. It cast watery light across the gunship's interior, ugly and fluid – it would have been just bright enough to hurt the warriors' sensitive Nostraman eyes, had any of them stood unhelmed.

'Will you be keeping to the precepts of the Nikaean Edict down there, brother?'

Ruven, Tenth Company's attached Librarian, gave a charmless sneer. He sheathed the sword, plunging them into true darkness again, and said nothing.

Deprived of his favoured targets for baiting, Cyrion looked across the bay to Talos. Lightning bolts ran down the warrior's faceplate, painted as elemental tear-trails. They glowed scarlet with the light from his eye lenses.

'So,' Cyrion said. 'How are you?'

TRUE TO THE Night Lords' nature, the fight was anything but fair. They'd left the main battle in the Urgall Depression to the forward elements of Warmaster Horus' forces. Malcharion had other plans, which First Captain Sevatar was only too pleased to grant his blessing.

Malcharion had led Tenth Company at the head of its battalion along the southeast ridge, holding back in favour of bringing their Thunderhawks down among the columns of fleeing, wounded Iron Hands struggling on the way to their own evacuating gunships.

Fresh from orbit, unscathed from the day's exhausting fighting that continued to leech the strength of the massacred Legions, the Night Lords had torn into their foes with relentless, joyous abandon.

Half a long and bloody day later, the unending demands of butchery were taking their toll even on the sons of Curze. Their gunships still roamed overhead on strafing runs, gutting the loyalists with relentless volleys of heavy bolter fire and driving them forwards onto the waiting blades of the VIII Legion. But those blades moved slower in arms that were growing weary. Though wounded and scattered, the Iron Hands resisted their slaughter with the tenacity that their Nostraman cousins were learning to lament.

Talos wrenched his chainsword clear of another fallen warrior, ignoring the blood spray that flecked his eye lenses from the blade's revving teeth. His hand was cramp-locked to the grip, his forefinger curled against the trigger and unable to bend away. His muscles were aflame with lactic burns just from the gruelling repetition of raising and swinging his blade, again and again and again.

The Iron Hand on the gore-soaked ground clawed up at the Night Lord, too brutally stubborn even to realise that he was dead. Another swing of the chainblade took off the warrior's reaching bionic arm at the wrist in a spray of sparks, and on the backswing Talos rammed the whining, protesting weapon down into the Iron Hand's throat. The chainsword threw several more of its remaining teeth on the way through the fibre-bundle musculature of the warrior's gorget collar. When the Apothecary pulled the blade clear for the final time, he looked with momentary irritation at the paltry few still attached, rotating loosely on the moving saw-blade.

He tried to hurl the weapon aside. It took two attempts to get his hand to unlock, such was the force of his cramp after six hours of face-to-face fighting.

Just as the sword left his straining grip, something crashed into the side of his helmet with a hammerblow of force, snapping his head back and de-tuning his eye lenses to a mess of red static for the duration of two heartbeats. Talos was hauling himself back up from the mud when another blow pounded him beneath the right arm, knifing through his ribs with a spread of sharp, thick, throbbing pressure. He tasted fyceline gunsmoke on his tongue and blood far back in his throat.

Retinal alarms flashed and flickered, demanding his

attention, cataloguing his exact wounds, even charting the angles of the incoming enemy fire. Up ahead, a trackless, wrecked Rhino transport grew a flickering outline on his retinal imaging: the source angle of the bolt shells that had knocked him from his feet. For a rare moment his own lifesigns took precedence over those of his brothers. Stings lanced through his bloodstream as his armour dispensed pain nullifiers and battle stimulants.

He blind-fired back through the press of warring bodies, holding his bolter one-handed, heartened by the heavy kick of the gun in his fist. There was no cover to take out here in the naked melee. The closest shell of a tank wreck was thirty metres away.

Two of his brothers were nearby, almost close enough to touch. To his left, Xarl was reaving left and right with his immense chainsword, all sense of skill abandoned as unnecessary, carving through exposed joints in black, war-scarred Mark II plate. Cyrion was down in the mud, kneeling atop a convulsing Iron Hand, sawing his bayonet through the dying warrior's neck.

Over the vox, Xarl – who usually waged war in cold silence – was emitting a primal grunting, doubtless feeling his own muscles burning after so many hours of battle. Cyrion was alternating between cursing in reptilian Nostraman syllables and occasionally breaking into laughter. He had a way of laughing without any cruelty, sounding somehow good-natured and generous even as he was tearing out a rival's trachea.

Talos moved ahead, needing to fight his way forward. The ground beneath his boots was a tormented scree of broken ceramite and blood-choked mud; when he wasn't clambering over the fallen corpses he was sloshing in the gore ejected from their bodies. He paused only to

loot the slain for ammunition, firing mercy bolts down
at the dying.

+Cease.+

The word flared in his mind, more visual than audible,
written in flame upon the backs of his eyes. The Apothecary staggered, risking a glance to his side, seeking signs
of the Librarian, Ruven. It took several seconds for his
vision to clear from the mist of migraine fire.

+Cease executing the fallen. Mercy has no place here.+

Talos gave a bestial grunt at the pressure in his head,
a compression at his temples hard enough to make the
bones of his skull squeal under the strain. The sourceless pain of the last few weeks sang harsher and harder
in the wake of Ruven's telepathy.

The Librarian stood with Malcharion – *As he always
does,* Talos thought with a sneer, *guarded by the company's
best blade* – adding his sorcerous lightning to the Tenth
Captain's relentless advance.

'I see all pretence of the Edict has been cast aside,'
Cyrion murmured across the squad's internal link.

The Apothecary ignored Cyrion's baited observation.
'It is not mercy,' he voxed to the figure fighting in Malcharion's shadow. 'It is prudence. Should we advance
too far, and the wounded reform in enough numbers...'

Ahead, Ruven didn't spare Talos a backward glance.
The skin-cloaked Librarian swung his heavy blade, rippling with psychic energy, breeding thunderclaps each
time the sword fell upon scarred black ceramite.

+You have your orders, Apothecary.+

Talos was drawing breath to reply when another
bolt caught him behind the knee, shattering the
machine-muscles of his greave. Two more took him low
in the breastplate a half-second apart, breaking the silver

aquila on his chest and sending him to the ground. He crashed into the blood-churned muck, only for one of the downed Iron Hands to ram a broken gladius blade into his wounded side, triggering a fresh panic of irritating retinal alarms.

'Traitor,' the wounded Medusan breathed, the word a wet crackle through his shattered vox-grille. Talos stared into the warrior's scorched, empty eye socket through the Iron Hand's cleaved faceplate. There was a moment of grotesque fraternal camaraderie, joined as they were by wounds and hatred and the blade gouging through the Night Lord's fused ribs.

Talos levelled his bolter, pressing it to the warrior's flame-ruined face.

'*Jasca,*' he replied in a hiss of Nostraman. *Yes.*

He never pulled the trigger. The Iron Hand's head rolled clear, raked away by a downswing of Xarl's immense, howling chainsword.

'Get up, damn you,' came his brother's distracted command.

With a snarl against the adrenal sting of pain nullifiers, Talos offered up his hand. Taking Xarl's place, Cyrion gripped the Apothecary's wrist and hauled him to his feet.

The pulsing in Talos' head was a ragged, merciless crush now. He could barely see past the blurring runes spilling down his data feeds. The surreptitious neural scans he'd performed aboard the *Covenant* weeks ago had revealed no brain injury, yet the pain came ever more fiercely, day after day.

'Thank you,' he said to his brother.

'How apt,' said Cyrion.

'What?'

Talos was still struggling to clear his retinal alarms. First Claw had sustained no fatalities, but the other squads were beginning to register an infrequent stream of fallen kin. There was gene-harvesting to be done.

Cyrion banged a gauntleted fist against Talos' smoking breastplate, where the silver-forged aquila was reduced to cracked, blackened devastation.

'That,' he said. 'How apt.'

Scrape. Scrape. Scrape.

The warrior crouched in the comforting dark, needing no light by which to carve. Scratching into ceramite wasn't an easy task, but the edge of a Legiones Astartes combat blade did the trick sure enough.

Scrape. Scrape. Scrape.

Each rake of the blade's edge lanced the throbbing boil of pain in his mind. Each long scrape was a relief, though not a release. He could fight the pain, diminish it, but not banish it.

Scrape. Scrape. Scrape.

The sound of carving was a whetstone rasp that echoed from the bare walls. The sound of crude art being born in absolute black. Human eyes couldn't pierce the gloom, but the warrior hadn't been human in many years. He could see, just as he could see on the sunless world, born and raised in a city where light was a sin only the wealthy could afford to indulge.

Scrape. Scrape. Scrape.

It was a scratching percussion to the omnipresent growl of the warship's distant engines. Other sounds intruded upon the warrior's work, but these were easily – *unconsciously* – ignored. Far from his sanctum were the muted moans of men and women toiling on the black decks, and the rattling thuds of bulkheads opening and closing elsewhere on the *Covenant of Blood*. Here in the room with him were the rhythms of a slow-beating human heart and the wet sighing of mortal respiration. He heard these things without truly knowing them. They were sensory nothingness, input without context, not piercing the veil of his ruthless focus.

'Master?' came a voice.

Scrape. Scrape. Scrape.

'Master?'

The warrior didn't look up from his work, even as he lost the instinctive rhythm of his etching.

'Master? I don't understand.'

The warrior breathed in slowly, only then realising he'd been starved of breath, murmuring to himself in a low drone that blended with the ship's rumbling engines. That, at last, was enough to make him raise his head from his carving.

A human stood there in the dark, clad in a filthy Legion uniform, with a Nostraman coin threaded upon on a leather thong around his neck. The warrior looked at the grime-marked man for some time, feeling his parched throat constrict in an attempt to speak the slave's name.

'Primus,' he said at last. The sound of his own voice horrified him. He sounded as though he'd died weeks ago, and a desiccated revenant was speaking in his place.

Stark relief passed over the slave's bearded features. 'I brought water.'

The warrior blinked to clear his vision, reaching for the tin canteen in Primus' hands. He saw the dirt beneath his slave's fingernails. He smelled the stale brackishness of the life-giving fluid in the metal container.

He drank. The pain in his head, already exorcised by his carving, faded further with each swallow.

'How long?' he asked. 'How long have I been here?'

'Twelve days, master.'

Twelve days. When had the massacre ended? *How* had the massacre ended?

He remembered little past Cyrion's lightning-etched faceplate, as his brother hauled him to his feet...

Talos turned to the nearest wall, where a crooked scrawl of Nostraman runes ran along in ugly lines across the dark iron. The lettering crossed itself, seemingly without order. It trailed across the chamber, even onto the deck floor in places, carved by the now dulled gladius blade in the warrior's hand.

'Twelve days,' he said aloud. He was genetically reforged beyond the capacity to feel fear, yet a cold, cold unease trickled through his blood at the sight of all these words he couldn't recall writing.

'There are things in my head,' he said at last. 'Memories that never happened.'

Primus had no answer. Talos expected none. He was already distracted -- the runes marked his own armour as well. Much of it made no sense, though his brothers' names were mixed in amidst the nonsense. Sergeant Anrathi's name was brutally scratched over with the rune symbolising 'exalted'.

One phrase rang through his senses as his black eyes passed across it. A sentence he would never forget.

Written there, in a jagged and childlike incarnation of Nostraman script, were nine words.

It is a curse, the runes read, *to be a god's son.*

BROTHERHOOD
OF THE MOON

Chris Wraight

[Transcript begins.]

*I am Torghun Khan, of the Brotherhood of
the Moon, and the ordu of Jemulan Noyan-
Khan. This is my sworn testimony.*

> Tell me where it started.

From Khella?

> No, from before. You told me you were
on secondment before then.

Very well.

> Hide nothing.

Do you think I would try?

> Some do. I would not recommend it.

IT WAS DURING the fractured time. We had had more freedom then. This changed at Ullanor, they tell me, and
by the time we were all called to Chondax there were
attempts to rein us in. But back then it wasn't like that.

I had taken my brotherhood on a mission to the

plains-worlds of Urj, to re-pacify places we had conquered twenty years before. The Legion had moved on
too soon; the roots were not set deep. It was not a heavy
task – we were out on our own, five hundred mounts,
and a single attack frigate to house them – but it should
never have been necessary.

It took three months. It was a punitive raid, and they
had no stomach for a long fight. We restored the Imperial banner over the system capital, and called in the
Army to resume control. Hakeem was with me, though I
did not know him well. We had served together by then
perhaps… two years? No more than that. He had been
keener than I on the assignment, and I came to appreciate his zeal. We were both Terrans, as were many of my
warriors. It was harmonious.

With that done, we waited for orders. I had expected to
rendezvous with the ordu again – we had already heard
that the muster was underway for something big, but we
did not know what it was. Instead, we were re-tasked,
told to remain away from the main deployments.

This was the road that would take us to Khella, but
not yet.

First came the Tarsch Belt, a string of worlds on the
edge of the Crusade's southern front. The defenders
were humanoid, but barely. I do not know, even now,
if they were some offshoot of our species, xenos or
something else. We killed them, and that was all anyone asked of us.

It was a long journey. We had trouble in the warp on
the way, running it close with the ship. That was why
we had been chosen – resupply in the Belt was proving
difficult, and we were closest. The main force was the
other Legion: the Luna Wolves, as they were then. They

had been fighting for nearly seven months, and had been told to bring it to a swift conclusion.

So we became part of that. I delegated liaison to Hakeem initially, while I was busy digesting the scant tactical data I got from my commanders.

I had no strong feelings about it, at the time. I was curious, no more.

> On your file, it states that you were
initially assigned to the Sixteenth
Legion's recruitment program.
Yes.
> You say you had no strong feelings?
You would be fighting with them.
*I was a White Scar. I had been a White
Scar for a long time. I was a child when
the transfer was made.*
> There is a supposition—
I know of it. It is false.
> We will take this up later. Continue.

THEIR COMMANDER WAS Verulam Moy, of the 19th. He was the senior officer, and had clearly been ordered to accept our help. He didn't like it. He had a much larger contingent – mostly infantry, some mechanised support. Our presence was a slight to him, and we were aware of this, so I determined to do what I could to smooth the way between us.

We arrived prior to an assault on a city-cluster on the ninth world of the Belt, one on the edge of a large open landmass. They had been preparing for our assault for a long time, and were well dug in. They had heavy dome shielding, and Moy judged it best to assault by land. He had used this tactic before – infiltrating under the edge of the void shield dome, knocking out the generators to destroy their coverage, then launching orbital barrages to complete the task.

The Tarschi knew what was coming, and had fortified their land approaches. They did not ask for quarter, though they could not match our joint firepower and I suspect they knew that.

We coordinated assault plans on the bridge of Moy's ship. He wanted to lead the main assault – the 'speartip', he called it. His warriors were practised in this and worked well together. He didn't wish to have the battlefield cluttered with rival vanguards so he gave us the flanks, our forces split in half, each on either edge. That suited us. We could use our speed unhindered, hitting them hard before drawing away and letting the advancing Luna Wolves lead the main assault.

'You will stick to the plan?' Moy asked me, clearly sceptical of our ability to complement his own forces.

I told him that we would. Everything in his body language was adversarial, but there was little he could do – we both had our orders.

It was Hakeem who improved things.

'This is a great honour for us,' he told Moy. 'Your primarch is venerated among our people second only to our own Great Khan. They share the same spirit, I think.'

Moy looked amused at that. Even then, the Luna Wolves were set apart. Comparisons with Horus, with his record and reputation, risked looking ludicrous.

'So you are... what? The Company of the Moon?' Moy asked.

'Brotherhood,' I replied. For some reason, the word seemed foolish to me.

'We had been given your tactical designation. Sixty-Fourth Company.'

'If it makes it easier for you, use that,' I said.

Moy shrugged. 'We are both lunar warriors. We can use our old names.'

I think that might have been an attempt at lightening the mood. I smiled, but Hakeem bowed deeply, and upon rising his eyes met Moy's. It seemed to me then that there was some prior understanding between them that I had missed.

If that made our task easier, though, then I could live with that. I did not think it could be serious.

WE WERE DROPPED into position one hour before the scheduled combined assault. I took the right flank, Hakeem the left. We were a long way from the Luna Wolves' positions, and planned to skirt wide of their intended advance to draw as much fire from the centre as possible.

We were wary of the enemy gunnery – it was precise – but we were also confident in our speed, our bike-mastery. I wished to show Moy what we could do. I wanted the city to be in flames and confusion.

Moy gave the order, and we accelerated, falling into a wide approach pattern. From two kilometres out we started picking up incoming fire. It intensified, and we dragged back in, weaving between the energy beams. I was enjoying it. We took some losses, but they were clearly struggling to target us. We reached the walls ahead of schedule, boosting the jetbikes high to clear the outer parapets.

The defenders fell back, hit on all sides by our incoming lances, giving us room to deploy heavy charges. They were wall-breachers, enough to gouge holes into the perimeter and allow ingress to the advancing infantry. We blew them just as the enemy began to regroup and bring up their heavier weapon pods. Whole sections of barricade crumbled, opening up the city beyond.

I voxed Hakeem, preparing to fall back as we had planned. Our task was complete, and we were now to stage a mock retreat, pulling defenders out from what remained of their defensive perimeter in time to meet the oncoming Luna Wolves.

'*Now we stay, khan,*' Hakeem said.

'What do you mean?' I asked. I could hear over the comm that his position was already being shelled. Soon, mine would be too.

'*These are Horus' sons. They will not respect a fall-back. We hold, though, and our pact will be sealed.*'

I don't know why he chose that moment to spring the new plan on me. Perhaps he judged that under fire I would be more likely to make the snap decision he needed. In any case, as soon as he spoke I saw the attraction of it. I was tired of the endless withdrawals, the strafing and the shams. We were like ghosts, never planting our feet long enough to make a stand. Other Legions were proud of their steadfastness under fire – why could we not be the same?

My warriors were looking to me for orders. Already the volume of fire was picking up, and soon it would become ruinous. I checked the augurs, noting Hakeem's position, the Luna Wolves' ingress routes, the timings and the dispositions...

Then I made up my mind.

'Dismount and hold,' I ordered, pulling my bolter from its holster. 'We will blood them here.'

✠ ✠ ✠

WE TOOK MORE losses. I am not proud of those. We were armed and equipped for fast raiding, not for holding beachheads against heavily armoured enemies, and we lacked the ranged support we needed.

But I am proud of this: we were not dislodged.

By the time Moy's troops caught up, we were dug in deep, preventing the Tarschi squads from linking up amidst the ruined walls. The Luna Wolves marched past us, hitting the flanks of encircling enemy units and shattering them. Then we pushed on, united, burning into the city beyond. Some of us remounted, using the bikes to combine with Moy's infantry. I stayed on my feet, and soon my battle-brothers were ranged in both white and copper-green.

It was a potent mixture. I watched the way they fought. I admired it and sought to emulate it. It is my belief that they did the same. We had become a merged force, and the blood of the enemy was bright upon our twin blades.

I was fighting in the very centre of the city when Moy reached me, his armour spattered and his chainblade glistening.

'That was not what we planned,' he shouted, though there was no anger in it, just surprise.

'Would you have pulled back?' I asked.

He laughed. 'I would not have known how.'

AFTER THAT WE reduced the whole place to ashes. They tell me that the wreckage burned for weeks.

We did not return to the ships that night. Our warriors remained out on the surface, celebrating the victory. There was a rapport there – we were Legions of rawness, and killing together had shown how similar our natures were.

Hakeem returned just after sunset, his armour bearing heavy damage. He was grinning.

'This was a good night, khan,' he said.

'Where have you been?' I asked.

'Learning new things,' he said. 'Will you follow? Moy is waiting.'

And I did follow. I had no reason not to. My battle-spirits were still coursing. I was as euphoric as the rest of my brotherhood. Few victories have ever tasted better to me than that night, for we had cast down expectations as well as the walls.

Moy was waiting outside the entrance to a canvas tent. Guards of his Legion were posted all around it, and torches burned within. I could see the shadows of those moving inside, and hear the sounds of raised voices.

'This was good hunting,' said Moy. There was a vivid light in his eyes, which I took to be the joy of the clean kill. 'It will not be the last we share.'

I was pleased to hear it. 'So what is this, captain?' I asked.

'A gathering of warriors. It is something we do in the Legion. Will you join us?'

Did I feel any reason not to? I do not remember clearly. I do not think so. It seemed... courteous. Hakeem was evidently already familiar with what was going on and went ahead of me, ducking under the tent flaps.

I could hear the chants from my brothers, victory-songs in both Terran Gothic and Chogorian Khorchin. I hesitated on the threshold, looking back at Moy.

'A custom of your home world?' I asked.

'Not of Cthonia. And it has become more than a mere custom now.'

His earlier belligerence was gone. I felt that my attempts

at diplomacy had been successful, and that this was the start of something new for the Legion – something that would see us become less... *isolated*. I felt as if I had achieved this, alongside the military victory, and it made me proud.

So I went inside.

> Here is the supposition: you had always wished to be a part of the other Legion.
I told you, no. Others joined. In the beginning, it felt natural.
> And afterwards?
Until the end, I believed it to be in the cause of justice.
> And Hakeem?
We shared the same views, though he was always further down the path than I.
> Where is he now?
I have already told you. I do not know. Either he died at Prospero, or he is gone.
> But you have a belief.
[pause]
I do not believe he was killed. He will not have recanted. He will attempt to restore things, somehow, to turn them back to the vision he was shown.
> You were weak in this. You were his khan.
I have many errors to regret. Hakeem is not the greatest of them.
> We will come to those. But what of you?

I have told you everything.
> Not yet.
*What more do you wish to know? If
I would enter the tent, given my
time again? If I would return to my
brotherhood? If I would right the wrong?*
> The Khagan will rule.
*I would enter it again. Of course I
would.*
> Be wary. You may yet damn yourself.
*I will not grovel! I am Torghun Khan,
of the Brotherhood of the Moon, and the
ordu of Jemulan Noyan-Khan. In all these
things, I took the path of honour. I
believed in the Great Crusade. I believed
in the Warmaster when all others believed
in him. These things will not be erased.
Now pronounce sentence, or give me a
blade to wield. I can still serve. I can
still fight.*
[pause]
Then what will it be?
[pause]
What will it be? Tell me!
[pause]
I will know my fate.
[Transcript ends.]

INHERITOR

Gav Thorpe

THE ABYSSAL SITULATE would come. Orisons of pain would call him. Lamentable prayers would build the bridge. The ecstasy of faith would open the gate. As he had been instructed, so Torquill Eliphas would obey. As had been laid down in the *Architectus Paternus*, so the Word Bearer would act.

'Soon,' he told his companions. 'Soon the consecration will be upon us and our labours fulfilled. Glories undreamed-of and rewards everlasting shall be ours.'

Clad in armour of dark red and gold – the drab plate of the old Legion obscured beneath layers of enamel just as the old rites had been replaced by new sacraments – Eliphas epitomised the grandeur and celebration of the reborn XVII Legion. The new lacquerwork blotted out his old hierarchical symbols, but in gold and rubies was picked out the icon of the Ark of Testimony Chapter.

He was Chapter Master no longer. Soon, he would be so much more.

He bore a large mace, as much a sceptre of office as a weapon. From the pierced head drifted clouds of crimson incense whose sweet scent left a bitter aftertaste. Its specific compound had been developed to induce a slightly stimulated state, even in the adapted physiology of a Space Marine. Near-constant exposure left Eliphas twitchy, his pupils dilated to the extent that his eyes appeared black. He was never still, his gaze always moving from one point to another, fingers flexing on the haft of the mace and fidgeting with the snakeskin-bound grip of the pistol holstered at his hip.

Eliphas' roaming stare moved across the edifice he had raised, ignoring his two fellow Word Bearers as he spoke.

'Now is the greatest moment of our lives. Now our service shall be renewed and our efforts redoubled that we might herald the Epoch of Changes. An empire laid waste, its ruins a dedication to the Abyssal Situlate. Five hundred worlds drowned in blood, scoured by fire, in revenge for fair Monarchia.'

'It is not enough, Inheritor,' growled Achton. Like his commander, Khyrior Achton wore the new livery of the Legion. On a long stave he bore an icon wrought from eight gilded skulls, set upon an octagon of silvered thigh bones. When he spoke, the vexillary's deep voice was edged with bitterness. 'A thousand worlds would not repair such hurt. The wound is in our souls where no salve can reach.'

The third warrior of the XVII wore the original grey of the Legion, the surface of his armour marked by scripture dedicated to the Emperor – now struck through in many tracts, the meanings of others amended by subtly ironic additions that turned entreaties into insults, benedictions into curses. Though outwardly the least changed of the trio, Gorvael Yoth was the most learned in the works of Lorgar and Kor Phaeron.

While it had been Eliphas' energy and vision that had brought the Templum Daemonarchia into existence, it had been shaped by the knowledge and calculations of Yoth.

Eliphas said nothing as he admired the construction wrought by their slaves, rendered breathless by its magnitude and magnificence. If one looked closely there might have been a wet glimmer in his eye, though he would have claimed it was simply the reflection of Kronus' sun.

The cathedral of impurity towered two hundred metres into the sky, built from the ruins of the flattened city of Typhaedes on the Deimos Peninsula. Though masonry and mortar formed its foundation – looted from court precincts and tithe yards, senatorial palaces and communal solisternia – the true beauty of the edifice was in the human materials bound within its construction. Their sacrifice to honour the Abyssal Situlate would remain forever, an immortal end for benighted mortals. Eliphas looked upon their physical remains and, for a moment, he almost envied them their eternal peace.

Some had been preserved intact, particularly the youngest, their skin like alabaster, their innocent faces raised to the sky with expressions of beatific torment. When he closed his eyes and pictured them, Eliphas could hear the screams of despairing adulation trapped within the transparent lacquer that coated each of the one thousand cherubic figures arrayed in a tightening spiral around the immense pilaster.

The chorus of their death-shrieks vibrated on the very edge of hearing, unheard by the mundane but projecting a clear signal that rippled out across the empyrean.

It would carry Eliphas' message to the Abyssal Situlate and the favour of the great master would fall like manna upon him.

The other nine thousand souls bound within the awe-inspiring monument of the templum had been rendered down to their essence, to the bones upon which weak flesh had been hung. Of these, three thousand were intact skeletons, arrayed artfully as a parade of the dead dancing and feasting as they marched into the heavens. The artistry belonged to Eliphas, but the precisely calculated angles of each body belonged to Gorvael Yoth. Between them they combined the science and aesthetic of the immaterial, that mystical yet attainable balance point between the everyday and the divine, the real and unreal, the mortal universe and the warp. The Golden Gate, it was called colloquially by the lower ranks – a crude euphemism but one that served its purpose. The Templum Daemonarchia would be like a gate once activated, and through it would arrive the Abyssal Situlate to lay down praises upon those that had built such a wonder.

Of the remaining cadavers, all but eight were no more than skulls used to pave the road before the macabre procession and to act as the sacred constellations in the sky above them on this arcane tableau.

The last handful adorned the Primordial Sun of Achton's standard, which would be set upon the monument at the required moment, a lightning rod for all the powers of the Daemonarchia.

Thus would the bridge be built and the path laid.

The entire tower throbbed with latent energy, silently singing with the souls of the blessed deceased. Eliphas could only imagine what it would feel like when the templum was empowered.

With each passing moment he admired anew the wonderfully grotesque lines and confluences of the strangely angled edifice. In places it seemed to bare teeth made of ribs, in others it was as flat and smooth as the gulf between stars, the dark marble seeming to swallow his gaze. Elliptical spirals and geometric concatenations drew the eye in strange directions, making even Eliphas' head spin, despite his artificially augmented sense of balance. The rapidly narrowing point of the tower, the forced perspective against the overcast sky, drew one up into the heavens with vertiginous swiftness.

And it was still not complete. A scaffold of wooden towers and decks linked by rope ladders jutted impossibly from the narrow but soaring building. Pulleys and tackles hung like spider's webs, used to move the immense blocks of basalt and granite, sandstone and marble from the base of the tower to their final positions.

Shaped by a team of seventy-three masons – many of whom had been only too willing to work to Yoth's plans to build the tower rather than become part of it – each block had been stained pale red, anointed with blood from the sacrificed. They were fixed in place with mortar mixed from the same and liberally thickened with bone powder. Thousands laboured at the winches to manoeuvre the great slabs and bricks into place. They worked without harness or rope – more than a hundred had fallen to their deaths in the last two days, and a similar number had been crushed against the growing walls by swaying blocks, or bludgeoned by snapping scaffold.

All in all, a hundred thousand souls of Kronus had given up their tedious mortal existence for the greater glory of the Abyssal Situlate.

The last of the foursome viewing this majestic

enterprise was Vostigar Catacult Eres. He was a little shorter than Eliphas, by just two or three centimetres, but was broader in shoulder and chest. His armour was layered with the polished sheen of gritty white ceramite, contrasting with his blue steel pauldrons and gauntlets. Upon his shoulder was wrought in brass a pair of jaws closing about a planet – the symbol of the XII Legion. If one did not know his allegiance from such colours and icons, it would have been made obvious by his half-shaved skull, the left side of which was studded with exposed metallic implants. Mood-inhibitors and adrenal boosters, Eres and his brother World Eaters referred to them as 'the Butcher's Nails' and seemed oddly proud of the fact that their brains had been tampered with. For Eliphas, such mechanical interference was a contravention of the bond between the corpus and the soul, but he was wise enough not to cause any insult to the temperamental captain.

Eres stood with arms crossed and looked at the templum. Two curved chainswords hung at his hips, and the right vambrace of his war-plate was mounted with a boltgun mechanism fed by a belt of ammunition linked to his modified backpack. The plates at his elbows and knees, as well as his boots, sported serrated blades specially angled to allow him to use his arms and legs as weapons in close fighting.

'This is what you wanted all the bodies for?' the World Eater asked. He turned his incredulous gaze on Eliphas. 'It's ugly. Why would you build such an abomination? What does it do?'

'*Do?*' Yoth sneered and turned on the World Eater before Eliphas could reply. 'It channels. It absorbs. It magnifies. It contorts. It takes the energies of the other-realm and spirals them through a complex system of decantations and alphanumerical mysti-rhythms, until it creates a condensed immaterial formwork derived from quarto-potentials bonded to a semi-scaling decline rift. It is a construction of epic nature – those physical properties you deem ugly are mirrored by a conversely beautiful but invisible balance and poise of preternatural accuracy and function. One might just as well set eyes upon the opening blossom of a dawnrose and complain that the edges were a little ragged.'

Yoth turned breathlessly back to his creation and was clearly about to continue, but Eliphas intervened.

'It is equally a beacon, a bridge and a gateway, kinsman,' he said. He understood his companion's frustration, but it served nobody's purpose to antagonise their ally. Trying to explain to the purely military mind of Eres the aetheric interplays brought about by the unique construction of the templum was akin to describing the glory of a rainbow to a blind fish. He waved a hand in agitation as he struggled to find the words that would convey the multidimensional elegance of it. 'It is… It is both the messenger and the message. The herald and the clarion. The slaver and the slave.'

'I see,' said Eres, tapping the fingers of one hand on his arm as he looked again at the huge tower. 'I thought it was supposed to be some kind of teleporter.'

Eliphas cringed inwardly at the simplistic nature of Eres' worldview, but managed a smile. 'Aye. In a very distant way, it is.'

'Why do we need one?' asked Eres. He opened his arms and gestured towards their surroundings. Typhaedes was a desolate ruin for five kilometres in every direction. 'You have two hundred warriors. I have five times that number.

The people of Kronus are broken. What need do we have of a giant, mystical teleporter?'

'Kronus is a step, a means to a greater end. When the Abyssal Situlate comes before us, we shall be ushered into the new dawn. Forget the petty ambitions of simple conquest, Eres. Not just the fiefdoms of Guilliman, but all of the Emperor's domains shall be ours for the taking. Our goal is not the defeat of a single people – it is the avenging of the Emperor's betrayal of our Legion. No more will we be taken as fools, the lives of our brethren expended for the grandeur of an uncaring god. Not again shall we suffer the ignominy of serving lesser mortals.'

'And your tower will do that, will it?' Eres shrugged. 'How do you turn it on?'

'In all bargains there is a price. It is paid in blood, sweat and toil.'

'I see plenty of sweat and toil,' said Eres. He grinned savagely. 'When do you need more blood?'

'SO, THEIR PLAN has worked?' asked Khordal Arukka.

Eres' second-in-command did not look convinced as the two of them studied the orbital sensor sweeps at the control station in the back of the Achilles-pattern Land Raider transport. A prized headquarters vehicle, gifted to him by none other than Amandus Tyr of the Imperial Fists fourteen years and an age ago when they had fought together at Varleth Gorge. Arukka had slain Captain Nordas Vyre out of hand when he had tried to insist that Eres left the transport behind when departing with Eliphas.

It had been a good signal of loyalty on his part.

'Perhaps,' Eres conceded. He looped back the data readings as he continued. 'I admit, I was confused at first when Eliphas had insisted that we allow a few of the

Ultramarines garrison to escape Kronus on that commandeered warp-trawler. It seemed folly to spare them in itself, and doubly so because they would doubtless take word of what occurred back to their commanders. I argued that the Ultramarines would surely respond and that we lacked the resources for a swift conclusion to the planetary occupation.'

Arukka nodded. 'I thought it oddly diplomatic of you at the time. You should have just taken the idiot's head.'

'The will of Angron was most specific, my brother. We were to extend our full co-operation to the sons of Lorgar. That we were saddled with this foam-mouthed disciple of madness doesn't alter anything.'

'He was exceptionally patronising, captain. He talked to us as though we were simpletons.'

'He was and he did, and but for the demands of the primarch I would have ended him there and then. But you must remember, my brother, that words and deeds are not the same.' Eres tapped a finger to his implant. 'Rage begets rage – that is the pit that awaits us. I have warned you before that we should not waste the gifts of the Butcher's Nails on inconsequential matters. In most concerns, we must kill cold and kill clean. Show no remorse but also feel no pleasure. Overuse of the implants reduces their effect with time, I believe.'

'You are most peculiar for a World Eater, captain. There are few that share your view on the Nails.'

'Which explains why I have been attached to these mumbling Word Bearer morons rather than fighting alongside our Lord Angron.'

Eres paused, and checked the chrono-mark on the orbital readings. Four hours old.

Why had Eliphas not released them sooner?

'Many have thought me a fool, my brother. Their corpses have been forgotten. Eliphas courts disaster when his tongue runs away from him, but he knows that he needs me. It matters not whether I believe his great temple will bring their deliverer or not. He believes it, and that makes him beholden to us.'

'Look at these time codes,' said Arukka. 'The Ultramarines response force must already be in range of the defence stations, but we receive no word that they have opened fire. It seems foolish to allow them to land without contest.'

'That is because we are merely ignorant warriors, my brother,' said Eres. He wound the readings forward and pointed to a screen. 'The drop assault is imminent. Their blood on our ground, that is what the Word Bearers desire. To slay them in orbit, to scatter their atoms to the void, serves no purpose to our incense-huffing companion.'

Eres turned and opened the assault ramp of the Achilles, flooding the interior with daylight. He strode out with Arukka at his heels, and looked up. There was a telltale glimmer in the upper skies – the first glint of descending drop pods would have been missed by any less experienced warrior.

About him were arrayed his one thousand warriors, stationed in and around the templum. Linked by artificial causeways to the tower and each other, eight bunker-like outbuildings guarded the approach to the main gatehouse, forming 'an abyssal star' as Yoth had termed it.

To Eres it was simply a convenient line of defence. World Eaters squads were positioned in the fortifications and amongst the ruins further out from the grotesque edifice.

He looked at it now. The construction had been completed five days ago, the third after receiving confirmation from Eliphas that the Ultramarines had returned, and that the incoming task force numbered only two warships of any size. Had the Ultramarines taken the threat at Kronus seriously, the Word Bearers and World Eaters might well have faced several thousand warriors rather than a mere demi-company.

'They come,' he warned his legionaries across the vox, drawing his chainsabres. 'Remember the request of the Word Bearer. Slay only in the precinct of the templum. Allow some to enter.'

He lowered his voice and addressed Arukka. 'A battle-barge and a strike cruiser. No more than five hundred warriors at most. It seems that Eliphas' gambit has paid off. Concealing our presence has caused the enemy to underestimate the strength required to retake Kronus. Guilliman's sons are about to receive a hot welcome.'

'It feels counter to all of my instinct and training to willingly leave enemy to the rear,' said Arukka.

'We must trust the Word Bearers.'

'Why?'

The inquiry took Eres by surprise, not because it was a bad question, but because it had not occurred to him before. It took him some time to think of an appropriate answer.

'Because if we cannot, this entire endeavour has been a monument to Eliphas' vanity and nothing else. If that is the case, I shall present his head to Angron myself.'

Arukka nodded, accepting his captain's wisdom without comment. He pulled on his helm, its faceplate daubed with a red handprint across the snout and left eye. It had once been a bloody mark left by the first

Raven Guard that Arukka had gutted at Isstvan, but the
blood had dried and flaked away over time, and so he
had decided to commemorate the moment in more per-
manent fashion.

He was not alone. There were other affectations,
some far more disturbing, creeping in across the formal
blue-and-white of the Legion.

Eres did not mind these slips in uniform discipline.
There was little enough incentive for his warriors to band
together as it was. They had heard nothing from their
primarch in over forty days, nor from Legion command.
The presence of Captain Vostigar Catacult Eres was all
that reminded them that they were World Eaters at all,
and he was not about to risk a mutiny by remarking on
the daubed slogans and additions made by his warriors.

The burning lights of the incoming drop pods and
landing craft grew brighter.

'I wonder what it feels like,' said Arukka.

'What's that?'

'Making a drop assault without the Nails. I've always
been too lost by the time I even stepped aboard to worry
about the danger of plunging from orbit onto an enemy
position. These sons of Macragge know exactly what they
are doing. *All* the way down.'

Eres did not reply. His implants were starting to
respond to the change in his physiology and brain activity as the prospect of battle approached. His adrenal
surge was already boosted by his Space Marine augmentations. On top of that, the Butcher's Nails were fizzing
in the meat of his mind.

He shuddered and bared his teeth, suppressing a growl.
It was too soon.

The key to using the Nails properly was not to become

a mindless slayer, as much as many in his Legion allowed themselves. There was a technique, a pattern to follow, that allowed the implant to peak in its effect at just the right moment. The trick was to hold back on the rise to the top of the wave, and then allow oneself to succumb fully, riding it back down into oblivion.

He knew that the desire to kill had to be burning through the nerves of his warriors, but they held back their fire. Not a single volkite beam or bolter shell leapt out to meet the descending enemy craft.

UNOPPOSED, THE ULTRAMARINES crashed down onto the surface of Kronus, thirty drop pods packed with vengeful warriors, ten more unleashing clouds of missiles and blasts of plasma into the surrounding ruins. Gunships rained down fire as they circled, battering shells against the toppled walls and the reinforced ferrocrete of the bunkers.

'The time is at hand, my proud Eaters of Worlds!' declared Eres, opening fire with his bolter vambrace while the Achilles spat forth death from its thunder-fire cannon and multi-meltas. 'Let the enemy know our retort!'

The World Eaters surged from dozens of cover positions, bolters and pistols barking, covered by heavy weapons fire from Word Bearers stationed at murder holes in the lower levels of the templum.

Suddenly surrounded by a mass of foes, the Ultramarines tried to pull back into a defensive formation, the guns of the Thunderhawks overhead silenced by the short distance between both sides. Eres ran in, his chainsabres whirring as bolts from a charging Ultramarines sergeant sparked from his war-plate.

The sergeant had a short-bladed gladius in one hand, his pistol in the other. Diamond-edged chainblade teeth cut through his sword hand, scattering armoured fingers. Eres' other weapon split the pistol's barrel, detonating the bolt in the chamber. Reeling from this, the sergeant took a step back. Eres ripped both blades free and drove them into the Ultramarine's chest, the spinning teeth chewing through the golden blazon and blue ceramite until they churned into bone and organs.

Eres felt a jolt as his Butcher's Nails responded to the carnage unfolding around him. He snarled, taking in a short breath as he looked around.

Brother versus brother. It mattered not.

To fight his fellow legionaries was the ultimate test. If he was stronger than the best of them, then there was no other in the galaxy that could threaten him, save for the primarchs themselves.

He wove his blades in deadly arcs – sometimes together, sometimes apart – punctuating the moments of inactivity between foes with salvoes from his vambrace.

With each death the gorging of his warrior spirit grew and the Nails' effect became more potent. His vision was turning red as combat stimms coursed through his body, threatening to burst his genhanced veins.

There was something else, alongside the well-known euphoria of battle. There was a sense of release with each foe he killed. Every Ultramarine that fell was accompanied by a surge of power. It lingered along his blades with the blood, a miasma on the edge of sensation.

The same was also true of every World Eater that died around him. Eres could almost feel something ephemeral, as though their very *essence* fled their cleaved bodies, trying to soar away but caught in the thrall of the Templum Daemonarchia. It occurred to him, as he struck the head from another foe, that perhaps Eliphas was trying to play him for a fool, luring him into sacrificing his warriors for some greater goal…

The implant reached its perfect pitch, raw sensation and intellectual understanding meeting at an infinitely small point of balance.

Everything was clear and pin-sharp. Each flying drop of blood, each tooth on his sword blades, every scratch upon his armour. He saw the detonation of bolts and the trails of propellant behind them, felt the thunder of the Achilles' guns through his boots, smelled the blood and tasted the sweat on the air.

For an exquisite instant he teetered on the precipice, trying with every mote of will to hold on to his sanity, lifted up above all other creatures in his moment of ecstatic accomplishment.

And then he slipped over the summit and was dragged down into the mindless rage, all thought of grand plans and potential betrayal forgotten.

FROM A SKEWED window a few metres above the base of the tower, Eliphas heard Eres' howl split the air. The World Eater was a blur of death, his armour sprayed with gore as he hacked his way into the heart of the Ultramarines' ranks.

But as much as the XII Legion fell upon the sons of Guilliman with reckless abandon, Eres had been true to his plan. He had positioned his warriors in such a way that there was a path to the Templum Daemonarchia, and along this weakened axis the Ultramarines naturally moved, seeking both refuge from the berserk assault and also to silence the heavy guns of the Word Bearers in the higher reaches.

'It's working!' crowed Yoth. 'Can you feel it?'

'I can,' replied Eliphas. Like a rising flood, the immaterial energy was gathering in the foundations of the tower. It was drawn to the blood-soaked stones, built in ritual, arranged along the occult lines of confluence between realms. He slapped a hand to Yoth's shoulder plate. 'I can feel it, my learned friend. Your calculations are perfect!'

The first of the Ultramarines reached the gate below, staggering into the cold interior as they turned and fired their bolters at the pursuing World Eaters. Eliphas gestured to Achton, who was waiting by a crude stairway to the left, the great icon across his shoulder.

'It is nearly time. With me, proud *sacrificier*.'

The Word Bearers commander raced down the steps and into the beleaguered Ultramarines. His mace left crimson trails of smoke as he smote left and right, cracking open armour and crushing helms.

For all that he had laboured to build the templum for the glory of the Abyssal Situlate, it felt good to smite his enemies in person.

The escaping soulstuff of the dead washed around him, the death cries and passing moans of the departed lingering in his hearing. As more legionaries died, the warp-fluid became a tangible thing, a half-present cloud of fog that was spiralling up to the pinnacle of the templum, guided by the swirl of dedicated corpses adorning the exterior, concentrating and solidifying as though light passing through successive lenses, becoming sharper and more distinct as it spun higher.

'Now, Achton!' he cried. '*Immoria magisterius sanguinia!*'

Eliphas' icon bearer drove the sharpened heel of the

stave through the chest of a dying Ultramarine, pinning the flailing legionary to the ground.

The skulls flared with black fire, hurling Achton half a dozen metres across the floor of the templum as if he had been struck by lightning. His smoking war-plate clattered to a stop against the far wall, cracked open as though something huge had burst out from within. Of the warrior that had worn the armour, nothing was visible.

Set into the corpse of the Ultramarine, the standard started to shine with a dirty golden light that caused even Eliphas to flinch, averting his eyes from its blazing light. When he had recovered, he saw that the head of the icon was slowly starting to spin. The circle described by the orbiting skulls darkened, becoming a black disc that bowed outwards.

Or perhaps *inwards*? The shining surface tricked the eye, making it seem both convex and concave at the same time.

A face formed in the fluid-like blackness.

A proud brow, and unflinching eyes. Lips pursed in agitation.

The Abyssal Situlate.

The Incarnate Entity of the All-Changing Ways. The Guide of the Blind.

Lorgar, Aurelian.

The Urizen. Primarch of the XVII Legion.

Eliphas and the other Word Bearers threw themselves to their knees, all except the Inheritor averting their eyes.

'Lord, a thousand humble thanks for your appearance,' Eliphas called, holding out his hands in supplication. 'You bless us with this visitation. But I beg more. Why do you not walk the bridge we have built? Why would you not pass through the golden arch we have erected in your honour?'

The primarch's lips moved, and as they did the skulls opened their jaws, mouthing in time to the words that issued from the icon, the voice bassy and distorted.

'Eliphas. What cause brings you to disturb me in this awkward fashion?'

'Kronus, revered lord. We beg your indulgence and your presence so that you might witness the holy slaughter. Bless us with your strong arm and sure command, I beseech you!'

'Kronus? What of Kronus?'

'The Five Hundred Worlds burn in your name, Father of Truth. Kronus shall be lit like a pyre in your honour.'

'The Five Hundred Worlds are of no concern to me any longer, Eliphas. I have achieved that which I sought when we came east.'

Eliphas became aware that all had fallen quiet around him. He heard the tread of boots and glanced to his left to see Eres marching into the hall of the templum. The glazed look in his eyes was fading, his gaze slowly focusing on the Word Bearers. Eliphas ignored him.

'But my lord… Monarchia?' Eliphas spluttered. 'What of our retribution against the sons of Guilliman? Are the Ultramarines to be spared the anguish that their callous betrayal deserves?'

'The Ultramarines are no longer of any consequence – my brother Angron and his Legion will hew their pitiful remains. All forces and expeditions of the Word Bearers are to reassemble on the Road of Stars, to follow the primus naviclature to the recall point on Tarsaron.'

'Tarsaron?' Eliphas' voice was almost a whimper. 'What of our works here? What of the great pyre?'

'Obey.'

The image of the primarch grimaced briefly and then

was gone, the icon falling to dust across the body of the Ultramarine.

Yoth rose to his feet and rounded on the commander. 'That is our reward, Inheritor? That is the prize for all our labours?'

'The Abyssal Situlate has spoken,' Eliphas replied, though his voice sounded as hollow as his heart felt. 'The Shadow Crusade is no more. Vanished, like the Great Crusade before it. Lorgar commands. We follow.'

'We fought for Kronus...'

'You fought little,' said Eres, coming up behind Eliphas, his chainswords leaving bloody droplets on the crudely tiled floor. 'Kronus belongs to me. You heard the words of your gene-sire.'

Eliphas thought to argue, but he could see the last remnants of the implant still pushing murderous thoughts into the captain's brain. Outnumbered, facing direct orders from his primarch, Eliphas had little option but to acquiescence to Eres' demand. He said nothing, and started towards the archway that led from the tower.

As he went, he heard Eres speaking to Yoth.

'Why do you call him "Inheritor"?'

'It is how he came by the rank of Chapter Master,' Yoth replied with a bitter laugh. 'During the Purge, he slew the previous leader of the Ark of Testimony, and took his place. Lorgar did not elevate him, saying only that he had "inherited" his command. He never earned his place, and we will never let him forget it.'

ELIPHAS GROUND HIS teeth. He had hoped that Kronus would seal his place in history and allow him to bargain for Lorgar's favour. He had failed.

But it was not the end of his ambitions. Even if he had

to throttle Kor Phaeron and slay a thousand worlds himself, he would get the respect he deserved...

He walked out into the body-strewn surrounds of the templum. Kronus was a stepping stone, as he had said, but now he knew that he could depend upon the primarch for nothing.

The principles had been proven. Now he would enact his plans on a far grander scale. There would be a reckoning. When the time came, Eliphas swore to himself, Lorgar *would* finally take notice, and the name of the Inheritor would be known across the galaxy.

Whether as a curse or blessing, he did not care.

VORAX

Matthew Farrer

Ratiomancer Spaal's legs are heavy-boned machines, bulged at the hip and bent backward at the knee, cored in a nickel-steel alloy. Their mechanisms whine softly as they walk, with splayed, cloven feet clanking on the deck.

His arms are longer than his organic arms were, moving smooth and silent on universal joints and faced with silver. When they were first grafted to him, the palms and backs of the hands were etched with patterns describing the sacred formulae of Old Mars. When he threw down his oaths on the steps of Kelbor-Hal's shrine and renamed himself from calculus to ratiomancer, he took an engraving tool, drilled it into his torso to anoint it with his own blood, and then filed all those old designs away. He can still remember the teeth-gritting vibration coming through the metal into his flesh-body.

It was not long afterwards that the smoothed silver plating began to tarnish and rise in organic-looking blisters that Spaal could neither understand nor explain.

Now his hands look like blighted human limbs instead of the perfect mechanisms that they are. The growths seem to be forming new patterns of their own.

This excites Spaal, although he is not sure why.

It excites him even more to see those hands wrapped around the neck of Enginseer Arrys, their festering patina staining the man's red collar and hood. He gives him a little shake as he drags him backwards down the crawl-way, as though testing that he is still alive. He *knows* Arrys is still alive, of course – he is monitoring the enginseer's vital signs with a battery of inhuman senses. The shake is just to see if he can get a reaction.

He does. Arrys' jaw works and a brief attempt at speech is choked off somewhere down in Spaal's grip.

'No, no, no, *nooooo*,' Spaal croons, rocking the engin-seer as if soothing a baby rather than gripping an enemy by the throat. His flesh-voice is reedy and wavering from lack of use. <Like *this*,> he cants, and sends a hoarse bark of scrapcode into the enginseer's ears.

Even as he continues to pull the half-dead man along, he watches the code hit the aural processors as sound waves, turn into micro-impulses in his mechanised senses and flit into his augmented nervous system to join the infectious code already there. Arrys' systems writhe with metastasising scrapcode structures, building and rebuild-ing themselves, eating away at him from within. Some of the growths have begun to fight amongst themselves over access to the handful of as-yet unspoiled systems. Spaal giggles to see that. He can't wait to see it happen again, writ large across the Imperial manifolds that he can dimly sense around him.

Somewhere in the distance there is a *whoosh* and *clang* as some component of the great Ring of Iron realigns itself, the vibration briefly palpable even through Spaal's heavy metal legs.

Or maybe a ship has docked, or a piece of the vast orbital debris field has caromed off the Ring's armoured hide.

No matter. The Ring is an artefact of the old Mechanicum. Spaal doesn't expect it to last long into Kelbor-Hal's new order – not once this war is all settled and Mars is free to begin remaking itself in earnest.

Spaal's work is part of the very earliest stages of that great work. Small, but not trivial. As peripheral and yet important as… filing the sacred designs off a silver augmetic. What a comparison! Spaal almost code-chuckles at his own audacity as he drags Arrys' limp body along.

Along and ahead, deeper into the humid and electric smoke-filled darkness.

THERE'S ONE DRIVER-LOCK still working, even though there's *so much* potential to misuse them.

Spaal finds that hilarious. The locks are not a military asset, and they surely are of no use to the blockade the Terrans are trying to impose around Mars. They are waste disposal sites, nothing more, designed to shoot reject-mass out into space with enough force to make sure it doesn't simply orbit back in and clutter the void around the Ring.

Well, the orbit is well now and truly cluttered anyway. The view from every port that Spaal has passed is choked with wreckage from the first fighting, and from the early attempts to run the blockade.

And yet *someone* is so obsessed with proper trash disposal that they have kept one of the locks. As if it were just for him.

Spaal code-chuckles again. A working driver-lock is a wonderful thing for a man in his position to have. No end of uses. It has dispatched the corpses of Imperial functionaries he has murdered off into the debris field where they will be safely lost. It has launched out any number of saviour-suits from the Ring's emergency stations, packed not with desperate, evacuating station crew but with special payloads that Spaal has cooked up in his little lair on one of the Ring's depopulated decks. Maybe they won't all be found, but surely a couple of them will. Found and brought in by an Imperial ship crew who think that maybe they've found some missing comrades, men and women who will be taken in by the fake life sign indicators and who will get a wonderful toxic surprise when they break the suit seals. Spaal has become very inventive with the creation of chemical and biological payloads. It has become one of his favourite pastimes.

And then there is Enginseer Arrys. What a wonderful treat! His systems are almost completely in thrall to the scrapcode now, and the predatory un-logic structures incubating in this fertile vessel are hungering to burst out and find new machines to overwhelm. Spaal can hear and feel them rioting in the transmissions coming out of Arrys' augmetics. As he waits for the driver-lock to open its hatch, he gives the twitching man a quick and affectionate pat on the head. Having one of his former Mechanicum brothers to work upon is a treat that grows ever rarer as the Terrans' grip on the Ring of Iron becomes more solid. Spaal is almost sorry that it is time to part company with him.

<You're such a lovely opportunity – oh, you are!> he tells Arrys. There's a clang from the lock shaft and the little

window mists with condensation for a moment. <You're well made, you are. You'll last for who-knows-how-long out in the cold! You're going to be in such pain.> He chuckles again. <Everyone will hear you, too, even if they don't realise it. Oh, all around the Ring you'll go, all among the ships and shuttles, and you'll leave your mark on every little system that hears you. You'll say thank you, won't you, to our dear Mechanicum brothers, for making you with such useful systems and then sending you to me?>

Spaal bounces on his sprung metal legs, shaking the enginseer's body with glee. It will take a few more moments for his lock-picking codes to open the hatch in such a way that won't alert the Imperial controllers, and then he will have to say goodbye to his new friend. Better make the most of these last few moments together.

The hatch opens. Spaal has his back to it and his senses focused on Arrys. It is only some unnameable instinct that makes him turn and look into the face of the thing that crouches in the driver-lock, watching him.

Everything seems to go silent for a moment.

And then Spaal is screaming with his flesh-voice as the shining mantis-like face lunges forward into his own, springing backwards in a blind reflex leap as cutter-mandibles shear the air where his skull was only a split second ago.

He lands, no time to think. Part of the distance his leap bought him has been eaten away – the thing is already half out of the hatch and into the passageway. Spaal takes another step, but his shoulder clips a stanchion and he whirls in the air, falling facedown on the deck; He is listening to his claws scrape and scrabble as he tries to stand himself up again.

There is a deeper, heavier tread underneath that noise. The thing is coming for him.

With a single, brisk chug of actuators, Spaal's arms extend and shove him back to his feet. He whirls to face it, bringing his arms up, shrieking. Behind it, a second one is folding itself through the hatch, trampling the ruin that the first one has made of Arrys' body.

The moment of distraction almost kills him as the thing pulls its arm cannon up close, aims and opens fire even as it strides inexorably forwards.

Spaal screams again, in both flesh-voice and code this time; the sound blows the emergency dismount on the access panels all down the corridor. Suddenly the passage is a mess of steam, vapourised coolant and clanging metal squares swinging out from the walls and dropping from the ceiling. There are just enough of them between Spaal and the metal monster to deflect the first of its rounds and fill the passage with cracking, whining ricochets.

By the time it has readjusted its aim, the passage is empty.

WITH SPAAL'S LEGS folded under him and his arms hyperextended, he scurries down the maintenance crawlspace on all fours like a hyena, yammering one word over and over.

'Vorax! Vorax! Vorax!'

He can't hear his own voice over the constant scream of metal. The lead battle-automaton is keeping pace with him in the passage beyond – tearing away panels, shearing through the bulkhead with its blades and pumping cannon-rounds through any obstacle it cannot rip aside with more than a moment's work. Spaal's 310-degree vision is getting glimpses of the second beast folding itself into the crawlspace and clawing its way along after him, somehow reshaping itself from a striding mantis to a terrifying armoured worm. The grippers pulling it along are wet with Arrys' blood.

That brings a thought to Spaal's mind but, in the instant it takes him to try and process it, the lead Vorax drags the slashed bulkhead open and exposes him, lunging in with no word and no pause.

Spaal pushes off the crawlspace wall in blind terror, and rolls forward under its lunge. Then he is crawling, crawling and skittering, finally scrambling through the hatch at the other end of the passage, howling the lock code in terror-corrupted binaric. But the blades lash out, blocking the hatch from closing, and the Vorax is already head and shoulders through.

It is right on his heels. Feedback fogs Spaal's senses as a hooked blade takes one of his metal feet away below the shin and the power burst ripples through his systems.

He is choking with rage. Rage at himself – stupid, *stupid* – the one working driver-lock, of course it was a trap. They were waiting nearby like predators in the water-hole! He was supposed to be the predator here. They would regret thinking that they could just come and take him. He feels the heat and strain in his shoulder joints as his arms drag him onwards. It is only a matter of–

He is rolled over onto his face again as the floor plating *booms* upwards, the second Vorax bursting from the crawlspace where it had kept pace with him. Spaal felt the impact as he rolls away again, the point of its bladed gun-limb gashing his side, the first machine marching almost on top of him, its insectoid face staring down at him. Spaal leaves a trail of bright blood as he watches the gun muzzles come up.

It is only a matter of time.

Both machines step through the hatch and onto Arrys' body, walking straight through his noospheric link – even as the link dies with Spaal. The children of his scrapcode infestation will be erupting in the Vorax like cancers and abscesses, cysts disgorging parasites and poison into their systems. It cannot be more than seconds away, now.

The code will have them. The Vorax will bow to him or they will burn. Even just to slow them for a few seconds…

As the two machines stand over him, Spaal runs a wrenching reconfiguration pulse through his external transmitters, and then pours all the power he can muster into the code blast. It is a killing blow, a curse from the gods, a Chaos-syntaxed death shout that should shock any system it strikes into immobility. It is what will buy him the time he needs.

The ceiling lights blow. The power regulators in the walls squeal. Spaal even feels a quick shift in his equilibrium as the gravity plates falter for a moment. He has time for a pleased little noise – *<Hehh!>* – before he reaches into the heads of the automata to see what damage he has wreaked.

He finds no damage.

No system indexes. No complex consciousness emulation. His senses, attuned to the near-mystical flows of subtle code, can barely perceive the functions that have driven the machine-beasts so relentlessly after him. There is nothing in the Cybernetica cortex for the scrapcode to drive mad, no web of logic to break down.

There is only the seamless instinct to kill, protected by the purity of its own malice.

Spaal's last thought is: *Wait, I–*

Then the lead Vorax stamps its foot, and the second skewers his now headless corpse on its bladed limb. And without a second's pause the two of them swing about and march away, tracking Spaal's blood in ever more faint footprints through the passageways of the Ring of Iron.

IRONFIRE

Rob Sanders

Idriss Krendl wanted to destroy something beautiful.

The Iron Warriors warsmith was ugliness incarnate. He had once been a specimen of genetic perfection, blessed with the grim visage of a conqueror – the face of his father. That had been before Lesser Damantyne, before the Schadenhold.

Before Barabas Dantioch.

Krendl had taunted his brother for being a cripple, an imperfect reflection of their primarch. It seemed that the galaxy was not without cruel irony when Dantioch had sent Krendl back to their father as a broken warrior. By the time Krendl's reinforcements had arrived, Dantioch was long gone. He had left Krendl buried alive, barely breathing, beneath a mountain of rubble. The Schadenhold had fallen and had decimated armies – Space Marines, even the god-machine, *Omnia Victrum*.

But not Idriss Krendl. Shattered and smashed but still alive, the warsmith had been recovered from the remains of the fortress. He had been saved by his gene-engineered gifts, his body entering a state of torpor. But when chemical therapies and auto-suggestion brought him back to the agonies of the present, Krendl found himself to be a monster. A cripple and an affront to the Iron Warriors about him – a son imperfect, whose every breath shamed their father. But the warsmith survived this indignity – for Idriss Krendl would not be destroyed.

'So, that is it?' Victrus Krugeran said as he reached the crest of the dune. The siege-captain wore the tattered livery of the Dodekatheon: the Brethren of Stone, those who knew what it was to create and destroy. As one of Perturabo's favoured, Krugeran had been placed in possession of two of the Legion's most powerful siege guns, *Eradicant* and *Obliteratus*. This honour had been tarnished somewhat by the fact that Krugeran had been placed in Idriss Krendl's charge.

'That is your target, siege-captain,' Krendl told him.

The two Iron Warriors stood unmoving, wind-blown sand grains collecting in the crooks and ridges of their dun battleplate. While Krugeran's suit was silver trimmed with chevrons and greening gold, Krendl wore armour of sullied chrome.

It was more than just armour. Like some ancient torture device, the suit was shot through with metal rods and skeletal screws that held his broken bones in place. The plate was covered in rivets and bolts, large and small, that gave it a studded or spiked appearance. The brute bionics of his limbs sighed and vented steam, while his head was encased in a cubed wire cage threaded through his shattered skull. The full half of his face had not been saved, and the patchwork of stapled flesh gave way to a grisly crater.

Over his plate Krendl wore the ragged mail cloak of a warsmith – a rank he now held in name only. The 14th Grand Company had been wiped out on Lesser Damantyne and his flagship stolen by the traitor Barabas Dantioch. He had commanded one thousand Iron Warriors intended for the primarch's glorious march on the Throneworld. Now he had but a handful of battle-brothers attached to Krugeran's battery section and its associated divisions.

'It's huge,' the captain admitted, looking at the colossal structure that dominated the northern horizon. 'I've never seen anything like it.'

'Then you've never been to Terra,' Krendl said. 'The architecture, the flourishes and ornamental towers. Size. Defensive capabilities. Walls. The layout of the structures within. These are all comparable.'

'Comparable to what?'

'To the Imperial Palace, to the decadent pile of rubble Dorn and his mongrels work to fortify. To the tomb into which the Emperor has already crawled.'

'That's impossible.'

'I ran the calculations myself,' Krendl said, handing Krugeran a scuffed data-slate. 'I've compared thousands of known fortifications on just as many different worlds. This is as close a match as Perturabo or the Warmaster could hope for.'

'These figures are correct?' Krugeran asked, scanning the stream of data.

'They're correct,' Krendl hissed. 'We are to become part of Imperial history, siege-captain. It starts with us. The first preparations for an attack on the Palace. The first real-world siege simulations. Here we shall discover how to crack the defences of such a fortification.'

'What is this place?' Krugeran asked.

'It's all in the files,' Krendl said, lost in imagined visions of decimation and destruction.

The planet's name was Euphoros. It had been designated One-Forty-One Nineteen and received back into the Imperium of Man after a swift and bloodless compliance action years before. Classified as a garden world by attending adepts of the Administratum, it was appreciated as a place of incredible, almost hypnotic beauty, even by the battle-hungry warriors of the Legiones Astartes who had quietly conquered it. Polychromatic deserts dominated the pleasant poles. The equatorial regions, meanwhile, were a scattered landscape of deltas, floodplains and crystal-clear waterways. There a belt of lush vegetation grew, visible from orbit. The perfume of the mangroves carried on winds that sculpted the southern dunes. Oasis-townships, orbital ports and hinterfields of desert fruits and optimised grain crops punctuated the stunning desolation of the north. The architecture of towering citadels and regional alcazars was an exquisite union of defensive function and elegant artistry, finding an apex of expression in the great polar palaces.

The paradise was inhabited by a technologically advanced civilisation who had called themselves the Euphantine before compliance. Over thousands of years in isolation, they discovered such hedonistic wonders upon their home world, expanded their technological reach, fought off the pirates and marauders of local systems and mined the mineral-rich moon of Phibea, leaving but a hollowed husk in the Euphorosian sky. From the bedrock of Phibea, the Euphantine created a sprawling, fortified palace at the northern pole that housed much of the planet's population. Called the Great

Selenic, it was a grand fortification of kilometre-high concentric walls, domes, hanging gardens and towers that rivalled even the Imperial Palace of Ancient Terra.

'Admitted,' Victrus Krugeran said. 'It is a wonder.'

'And we're going to destroy that wonder,' Krendl said.

'However… warsmith,' Krugeran said, hesitating to use the title. 'You seem to be forgetting something.'

Krendl let the slur wash over him. He knew what Iron Warriors like Krugeran thought of him – of his failure at Lesser Damantyne and the cripple he had become.

'Enlighten me, siege-captain. If you can.'

'The Imperial Palace – when we get there, primarch willing – is defended by the Imperial Army, the Legio Custodes and Dorn's dogs of the Seventh Legion. How are you going to simulate that, *warsmith*?'

'I will improvise,' Krendl shrugged. 'I will give our father and the Warmaster what they truly desire – data, tactical simulations tested in shot and shell, stratagems whose success has already been written in blood.'

'The subjugated population that resides behind these walls, even in their millions, are no match for the sons of Perturabo.'

'And we would hope to command many more siege guns alongside the paltry two with which your battalion has been entrusted,' Krendl said. He did not allow Krugeran any retort. 'You are right, of course. For a true simulation, even one calibrated to the meagre forces at our disposal, we shall need legionaries. We need to see how our own kind might respond to an attack on such a fortress, so that we can factor their presence into our future battle plans.'

'And how are you going to do that?' Krugeran demanded.

'One-Forty-One Nineteen was brought to compliance by the Third Legion.'

'The Emperor's Children?'

'Aye,' Krendl said. 'Fulgrim's deviants took to the worthless beauty of this world and the myriad pleasures of its people. And now, they have an entire civilisation to use and abuse within the mighty palace walls. Lord Commander Lelanthius should have regrouped at his primarch's command, but he dallied and sent half of his force on to Fulgrim at Hydra Cordatus, remaining here with one hundred of his brothers.'

'A hundred legionaries garrison that place?' Krugeran asked.

'In truth I have no idea what depraved things Lelanthius and his warriors do behind those walls. But I know what they are going to do when we attack.'

'We cannot attack the sons of Fulgrim!' Krugeran protested. 'The primarchs are allies. They fight side by side for Horus.'

'As this war rolls on, siege-captain,' Krendl said, 'you are going to have to develop a stomach for such necessities. Our only allegiance is to victory and those standing next to us upon its achievement. All else is ash on the wind, collateral damage in the service of greater death still to come. Remember, I have spilled the blood of our own brothers. Necessity demanded such a sacrifice. Perturabo and the Warmaster too, though they did not know it at the time. You think I care more for warriors of the Third Legion than I do our own primarch's flesh and blood?'

'When Fulgrim hears of this, he will believe the order came from Perturabo. Horus will punish them both. Your sufferings have driven the sense from you, Krendl. What you propose is madness.'

Krendl took the data-slate back. 'Before we entered orbit, I sent a message to Lord Commander Lelanthius. I told him that we had sighted an Imperial Fists flotilla two systems away. There was, of course, no flotilla. He despatched his only strike cruiser – the *Rapture* – to investigate the threat. When Fulgrim finally discovers that his wayward sons have been wiped off the face of this planet, the *Rapture*'s own logs will tell him all he needs to know – that the ship searched for an enemy contingent that had meanwhile launched an attack on Euphoros. Only Perturabo shall learn of the truth, and only when the invaluable data our simulations have provided are in his hand. When our father offers the Warmaster the tactical keys to the Imperial Palace, do you think that Horus will care about the loss of a few Third Legion deviants?'

Victrus Krugeran gave the warsmith a hard glare. 'I don't know that such a plan convinces me of your sanity.'

'You are not here to be convinced,' Krendl told him. 'You are here to rain destruction down upon that fortress. Bring forth your gunners.'

Krugeran's hateful gaze lingered on the monstrous warsmith before he motioned for a pair of Iron Warriors to join them, and Krendl turned his back on the palace that shimmered through the heat of the immaculate desert.

Before him was *Eradicant*, the mountainous centrepiece of the Iron Warrior encampment. Stolen from the Mechanicum on Diamat by the I Legion, the gargantuan mobile artillery piece had subsequently been entrusted to Perturabo before the Dropsite Massacre. *Eradicant* was as long as a Titan was tall, the tracks of its individual drive units sitting in the Euphorosian sands. In the bright light of day, the enormous barrel of a macrocannon gaped darkness and death at them from where its

great system of pulleys and derricks allowed it to rest.
The massive machine bristled with automated emplacements – quad-lasers, flak batteries and mega-bolters silent
and ready to roar to the siege gun's defence. Fat, tracked
ordnance compartments two storeys high stretched for
hundreds of metres, trailing the main gun carriage like
the segmentations of a death world decamillipede.

Trudging through the polychromatic sands, a pair of
Techmarines presented themselves to Krendl and their
siege-captain.

'Brothers Arkasi Achorax,' Krugeran said, 'and Mordan
Vhosk. Overseers and senior gunners of *Eradicant* and
Obliteratus respectively. They are Dodekatheon. The best
artillerists I have.'

'They had better be, siege-captain,' the warsmith muttered. 'They need to be, for what I have planned. Brothers
Achorax and Vhosk, I have heard much about your
mighty siege guns. Captured Mechanicum monstrosi-
ties, given as a gift from one primarch to another, the
pride-foolish Lion El'Jonson thinking to buy the loyalties of our father. El'Jonson shall pay – like those who
stand with him – for his lack of foresight. He will know
its price, brothers, when your guns bring down the walls
of his master's great palace. Then the Dark Angels will
come to know *true* darkness.'

'They truly are wonders,' Krugeran told the warsmith. 'They are bigger than anything fielded by my
brother-captains in the Dodekatheon, or present in the
experimental arsenal of the Stor-Bezashk.'

'Tell me of their wonders,' Krendl said.

'Fully armoured and protected by void shield generators, warsmith,' Achorax said, 'their weaponry can level
a small fortress with ease from miles away.'

'And what if it is my wish to strategically demolish sections of a much larger fortification – say, the Selenic behind me?' Krendl put to them.

'Each weapon boasts an MIU interface chamber,' Vhosk told him.

'For which we have embraced certain adaptations,' Arkasi Achorax added.

'A neural link between weapon and gunner results in unparalleled accuracy, data-streaming, response-calibration and rate of fire,' Vhosk said. 'Not unlike that expected of a Titan's gunnery moderati.'

'To be one with the weapon,' Krendl said. 'An intriguing notion. That truly is excellent, brothers. Your siege guns are everything your captain promised. It is just as well, for Captain Krugeran and myself will be putting our lives in your hands.'

Krugeran frowned. 'My lord? This is the first I have heard of this. It is traditional for brethren officers to oversee the prosecution of the siege barrage from a command vehicle.'

He pointed down at the four Spartan assault tanks that flanked *Eradicant* as an armoured escort. His own, named *Escutcheon*, mounted a lodge banner of the Dodekatheon that turned and twisted in the desert wind.

'And that is where we shall be overseeing the barrage,' Krendl told him. 'Only the command vehicle will be at the heart of our direct assault on the palace.'

Again, Krugeran's face changed at the warsmith's apparent insanity. He went to snarl some rebuke but caught himself. He would not question Krendl in front of Brothers Achorax and Vhosk.

'Just to clarify,' the siege-captain hissed through his teeth. 'You wish to lead a direct assault on *that* fortress?'

'Yes.'

'With my Iron Warriors?'

'With every Iron Warrior under your command,' Idriss Krendl said. 'Though I admit you do not have many, being that of a battery section. It is no grand company, but the primarch has seen fit to grant me a little, with which I shall achieve much.'

'What of the guns themselves?' Krugeran asked, hoping to find a weakness in the unassailable optimism of the warsmith's insane plan.

'As you said yourself, the guns are well protected and can defend themselves if need be. Achorax and Vhosk will command each mobile artillery piece, aided by the servitors and bondsmen assigned to the ordnance sections.'

'Once more – you want to attack the palace, while the siege guns are firing upon it?'

'It really is something,' Krendl said, lifting the bionics of his replacement arm, 'to be at the heart of the battle, rather than monitoring distant destruction from a horizon away. To feel the fires of destruction raging, while the fortress to which you lay siege crumbles about you. It is a feeling I would not deny you, captain. Following my last siege I had a great deal of time to think. While the body heals, it is important to keep the mind active. I worked on new siege tactics and approaches – strategies we can use to defeat the most determined of defences. As I relived the fall of the Schadenhold, billions of tonnes of rock and metal raining down, it came to me. As my bones and my mind broke, the very tenets of my training broke with it. Legion convention suggests that you bombard an enemy position – you break their defences and then you lead assault forces inside. But what if both could be achieved at the same time?'

'You are talking about shelling your own forces,' Krugeran said, shaking his head in disbelief. '*My* forces.'

'If I can survive the unsurvivable,' Krendl continued, 'then perhaps my brothers can too. Perhaps besiegers can attack a fortification *during* a full-scale bombardment rather than following it. Perhaps a redoubtable force, using the eye of the storm as their protection, could strike at the strategic heart of an enemy exposed, an enemy in confusion, while all else about them turns to ash and screams. Who better than the Iron Warriors to put such a strategy to the test?'

'We would be obliterated...' Krugeran murmured, but he could see that his words were lost on the warsmith.

'Not with these new siege guns,' Krendl said. 'Not with the precision advantages mind-linked artillery can bring. Brothers Achorax and Vhosk here – by your own admission, your two best gunners – can monitor our position from the signatures of our suits, and time the impact of their artillery to clear a path before us of walls, structures, emplacements and enemy forces. It will be a feat of transhuman timing and calculation.'

'I implore you, warsmith...'

Krendl did not listen, but turned to the two Iron Warriors before him. They both wore cruel smiles of expectation and bellicose glee. 'Brother Achorax?'

'Let us make history,' the Iron Warrior returned.

'Vhosk?'

'Do you have a name for this stratagem, warsmith?' Vhosk asked.

'I do, brother,' Krendl said. 'I call it Ironfire.'

SEVEN SPARTAN ASSAULT tanks, all in the tarnished silver of the Iron Warriors, tore across the desert flats. Out in

front, trailing the whipping Dodekatheon banner, was
Escutcheon, carrying Siege-Captain Krugeran, Idriss Krendl
and ten Iron Warriors in augmented plate, each carrying a boltgun and boarding shield. The squad stood in
silence, riding out the bumps and rolls of a high-speed
insertion. The drive system roared its automotive fury
and the tracks tore through sand as *Escutcheon* led the
train of tanks in.

Krugeran was wearing his helmet but Krendl could tell
that the battery officer's face was contorted with frustration beneath it. Krugeran was no cowardly soul – the
warsmith understood that. He simply hadn't expected
to die under the fire of his own guns.

Krendl left him with his silent warriors and hauled
himself up front. The assault tank's driver, Brother
Gholic, was strapped into his elevated seat, working the
vehicle's nest of throttles, levers and pedals. With the
optics of his studded helm almost up to the armourglass of the narrow viewport, Gholic gunned the Spartan
across the desert sands.

'As you were, brother,' Krendl said as Gholic went to
acknowledge him. The warsmith leaned in and peered
through the auxiliary port. *Escutcheon* was riding through
the thick sands almost like a ship in the ocean, plough-
ing through the polychromatic desert, the tank's tracks
throwing up a haze of colour and beauty. Before them,
the mighty walls of the Great Selenic reached for the deep
Euphorosian skies. Krendl felt the sights of emplacement
guns upon him, the reach of augurs and the eyes of a
thousand sentries.

All of them were watching, but none of them knew
what to make of the unannounced approach.

'Why aren't they firing?' Gholic asked, his voice a

grille-modulated hiss against the rhythmic rattle and bounce of the tank.

'This world was conquered by the Emperor's Children,' Krendl said, 'if you call what Fulgrim's deviants did here "conquering". They arrived as heralds of a new age but stayed on to become tyrants. The people of this planet know little of the wider conflict. They will not fire on a legionary. Not yet.'

'What if a member of the Third Legion is up on those walls?' Gholic pressed.

'Lelanthius and his warriors will be otherwise occupied, I suspect,' the warsmith said. 'And even if they are up there, what of it? They know our vessel is in the area. We could be carrying messages from Perturabo or Fulgrim at Hydra Cordatus, or even from the Warmaster himself. We are brothers, united by our treachery. Don't worry – first blood will go to us.'

Krendl opened a channel to the other tanks in the column. 'Armour, call in.'

'Truculent, *ready.*'

'Iron Tyrant, *ready.*'

'Ferrico, *standing by.*'

'Incaladion Irae, *right behind you*, Escutcheon.'

'Unbreakable Litany, *awaiting your orders.*'

'Ictus *is ready, warsmith.*'

'*Eradicant, Obliteratus* – report in,' Krendl voxed.

'*Siege gun* Eradicant, *ready to commence firing,*' Arkasi Achorax reported.

'Obliteratus *tracking your progress and awaiting first target,*' came Mordan Vhosk's voice a moment later.

Krendl turned and nodded his caged features at Siege-Captain Krugeran.

'Ready your weapons,' Krugeran said, prompting a

synchronous clunk of boltgun priming mechanisms from the siege squad beyond. Smacking their boarding shields down twice on the compartment floor, the Iron Warriors indicated their readiness. About him, Krendl heard *Escutcheon*'s belligerent machine-spirit powering up the assault tank's flank-mounted lascannon quads and cycling belt-ammunition from trough-feeds into the forward heavy bolter. The gunners were ready too.

'*Eradicant, Obliteratus,*' the warsmith voxed, looking down at the data-slate in his gauntlet. 'You are cleared to fire. Initiate Ironfire, I repeat – Ironfire protocols initiated. Acknowledge.'

'*Ironfire a go.*'

'*Ironfire, go,* Escutcheon.'

Krendl looked from a chronometer on his slate, back to the dirty port window. His broken mind swam with seconds, metres and angles. His mangled lips wrapped themselves silently around a countdown.

'*Eradicant* – this is a call for fire. Grid IF 3-61 72-09.'

'*Grid IF 3-61 72-09, confirmed.*'

'Confirm. Target – curtain wall. Ordnance adjust,' Idriss Krendl voxed back.

The warsmith waited. From kilometres away he heard the thunder of the monstrous siege gun. He waited. And waited. With the armoured column ripping through the multicoloured sands. Krendl could hear the faint whine of inevitable destruction overhead as he counted down under his breath.

'...three... two... one.'

One moment there was a formidable expanse of wall. Moon rock. Architectural flourishes. The smooth line of crenellations. Emplacements of exotic weaponry.

The next there was obliteration: flame, storm, darkness, thunder.

Krendl watched as the curtain wall became a swirling maelstrom of fire and debris, as the Iron Warriors ordnance smeared the structure into shades of destruction. Blasted sand swirled outwards in a blinding storm of grit, and glass streaked with the darkness of soot and ash. Flames tore through this polychromatic assault on the senses, washing off *Escutcheon*'s armoured hull with a hail of masonry fragments that pranged off the thick plate.

'Maintain speed and direction,' Krendl ordered as he felt Gholic ease off the drive. With the thunder of detonation all about the assault tank, and rubble cascading down from the towering wall section, Krendl understood the legionary's concern. 'This is Ironfire!' he roared through the insanity of destruction. 'Embrace it. Become one with the storm. Ride its eye through the obliteration of your enemies!'

Escutcheon plunged through the swirling devastation, its tracks thrashing against the small mountain of rubble that had crashed down in the lee of the demolished wall section. Thrashing the treads against the rocky incline, Gholic kept the Spartan assault tank bouncing and shredding its indomitable path into the Selenic palace.

'Column, stay with us,' Krendl warned the other drivers over the vox. 'Maintain position on our augur signature.'

As *Escutcheon* thundered down the rubble slope on the other side, the smoke and dust began to clear. The warsmith could see the labyrinthine settlements and hab-shacks that dominated the municipal plazas beyond – a small city of brightly coloured tents, stilt-shacks and sand-glass architecture.

'Hit it,' he commanded.

Gholic took the assault tank straight into the buildings, the people and the confusion. Men, women and children of the slums screamed and ran for their lives. Native livestock trumpeted calls of alarm and broke free from their rickety enclosures. *Escutcheon*'s armoured form ploughed through hovels of coloured glass, stilts, steps of second-storey shacks and trailed the coloured materials of market stall awnings. Sand imps were smashed from their cages and flapped through the destruction. The mist-eyed, swarthy citizens of the Great Selenic went down under the tank's thrashing tracks and bounced with bone-breaking regularity off the Spartan's armoured hull. Exotic beasts of burden were smashed across the tank's riveted assault prow. Mechanised wagons of wares and spidery walking limbs were smashed aside and aged repulsor-bikes exploded, dousing *Escutcheon* in fresh flame.

'*Obliteratus*,' Krendl said into the vox. 'Grid IF 4-61 68-07.'

'Grid IF 4-61 68-07, *aye*,' Vhosk returned from the interface chamber of his mighty siege gun.

'Confirm. Concentric wall section. You are cleared to fire… now.'

The Selenic palace had hundreds of kilometres of walls. With the few Iron Warriors at his disposal, the warsmith could not hope to take the fortifications in a traditional siege. But he didn't need to if he used his Ironfire protocols. A small force, shielded from a colossal defending force by surgical ordnance strikes could punch their way through the polar city-palace. Like the Imperial Palace on Terra, the people of Euphoros and their overlords hid behind walls, behind which lay more walls still.

Like the outer curtain, the concentric inner wall vanished in a cacophony of flame and tumbling masonry. Bodies and shattered structures rained down through the billowing, choking dust as *Escutcheon* led the way once more up the mound of rubble that marked the gap.

What the Spartan failed to crush in its track-thrashing path, the seven assault tanks behind pulverised into the ground. Euphorosian homes. Livestock. The bones of palace citizens. As death rained down from *Eradicant* onto the third wall, Krendl kept the stream of strike coordinates coming; his confidence in his strategy and siege guns increased as more Techmarines manned them.

For Siege-Captain Krugeran and his Iron Warriors, the experience was one of noise and motion. The assault tank shuddered as it bulldozed through buildings and bucked as it mounted piles of cascading rubble. The Spartan's roof rang with impacts as small boulders and shards of masonry rained down from the never-ending succession of detonations. Krendl fed Achorax and Vhosk targets with increasing speed and fury. *Escutcheon* led the way through the hellish beauty of annihilation: an entrancing, multicoloured miasma of dust, ash, soot and sand.

It was twenty-two minutes into the assault before Krendl detected any evidence of resistance, which surprised even him. There were a number of reasons why, and it behove the warsmith to catalogue them in the interests of comparison and strategy development. Krendl had to accept the possibility that the princely overlords cared little for their people – at least the minions who inhabited the slums and city districts between the five concentric palace walls.

The local guard, conversely, had been sluggish to respond to the encroaching legionary threat as siege guns continually brought down the walls, fortifications and weapon emplacements set inside. As the tank column thundered on, leaving a dust-swirling path of destruction in their wake, Krendl took the precaution of having *Obliteratus* cover their rear. Krendl did not want regrouping palace soldiers or scrambled vehicles working their way behind the column. As *Eradicant* blasted walls, toppled towers and collapsed archways from the path of their advance, the warsmith had *Obliteratus* turn its attentions upon the catastrophic trail they had left behind. The craters and demolished wasteland of dumbstruck, wounded Euphorosians, shellshocked palace guards and wrecked repulsor-drive vehicles were turned to vaulting infernos of rock and flame, just as those victims began to celebrate their unlikely survival.

Smashing through ornamental gardens and plazas, the column of IV Legion armour took to the broad, elevated avenues and grand, arched thoroughfares of the inner palace. The Euphorosian guard there had established a gauntlet for the oncoming tanks. Krendl could not use *Eradicant* to decimate the road ahead, for such a barrage would destroy the columned avenues they were traversing.

Up until now, the Spartans had weathered the disorganised small arms fire of palace guardsmen stumbling from demolished buildings. They had withstood the gunfire of the half-smashed emplacements that soldiers had managed to jury-rig and establish across the tank column's path.

Through the blood-splattered viewport, Krendl could see the palace soldiers in reflective scale-mail plate, cloaks and the baggy silk of their uniforms swarming the thoroughfare ahead. Some sat astride repulsor-bikes or in tent-topped personnel carriers. Dish emplacements of sonic weaponry were manoeuvred into position, ready to blast the tanks back.

'We stop for nothing,' he told Gholic and the other Iron Warrior drivers across the vox. 'We are iron. We are fire. We ride the storm. Authorise your vehicles to engage the enemy as we pass. Fire all weapons!'

The barrels of twin-linked heavy bolters barked to furious life. *Escutcheon*'s armour sang under the enemy's return fire, the command tank bucking and bouncing as it forced its way on. The Spartan's thick tracks chewed up the avenue, but blast after sonic blast from the dish emplacements hammered the vehicle and slowed its advance. The tank's lascannon gunners fired, blazing the mobile emplacements to scrap. The palace guards' scale armour was principally designed to deflect low-level energy weapons and offered little protection against the storm that was now directed towards them.

Without stopping, the armoured column punched through the gauntlet, smashing aside derelict weaponry and antique vehicles. Droves of palace soldiers went down before the fury of heavy bolter fire, their cloaked and lightly armoured bodies torn apart.

The monstrous artillery fire of *Obliteratus* and *Eradicant* continued around them. The warsmith directed Achorax and Vhosk to drop cataclysmic barrages on guardhouses, landing pads and arterial avenues sighted from his position; feeding the Techmarines an almost constant stream of coordinates, Krendl increased the siege guns' rate of fire but left the elevated avenue intact.

Suddenly, he heard a blast over the vox-channel, and the roars of dying Iron Warriors.

'*Ferrico*?' the warsmith said. '*Ferrico*, call in.'

'*Ferrico has been knocked out by enemy gunships*,' the commander of *Truculent* reported.

The unfortunate Spartan had been hit by a sonic

cannon that had smashed in its side and knocked it into a skidding roll off the side of the elevated avenue. Plummeting down through the arches and towers, *Ferrico* hit the dome of a citadel before its engine exploded. Elegant gunships swooped in on the rest of the tanks, keeping pace with the racing column.

'Engage enemy aircraft with rockets,' Krendl ordered. He nodded to Siege-Captain Krugeran, who sent an Iron Warrior from his squad up through the hatch to man the multi-launcher. As the Spartans surged on through colossal archways, Iron Warriors blasted the gunships, so elegant in flight, from the sky like wounded birds.

Krendl felt a shudder work its way through the battered superstructure of *Escutcheon*.

'What was that? All tanks call in,' the warsmith ordered.

'We just lost *Unbreakable Litany*,' the Iron Warrior manning the launcher reported as he climbed back down into the troop compartment and secured the hatch. 'Ordnance knocked down a tower across the avenue. It took out *Litany* and smashed through the thoroughfare, trapping *Ictus* behind it.'

'Warsmith?' said Gholiç. 'Should we slow for them?'

'We stop for nothing,' Krendl snarled.

'Then at least call off the ordnance,' Siege-Captain Krugeran implored him.

'No. Ironfire will intensify.'

'That's insane–'

'It's necessary!' Krendl roared back. 'This is a live simulation. The real siege will change the galaxy as we know it. There is no going back – not for the primarch, not for Horus and not for us.' He pointed at the viewport. 'The enemy cowers in the inner palace, and we almost have them. Increase our speed. Step up the bombardment. We shall ride this storm right into the Third Legion's nest of decadent deviance. Do you understand?'

Krugeran gave him the blankness of his helm lenses. He turned and retook his position with the siege squad. Krendl eyed him warily.

'Brother Gholic, have the squad aboard *Ictus* disembark and follow us on foot into the inner palace.'

'Yes, warsmith.'

As the armoured column left the elevated avenue, Krendl gave *Eradicant* coordinates for a colossal gated archway that delineated the interior of the Great Selenic.

'What is that I hear?' he asked across the vox. 'It sounds like defensive fire.'

'*Limited enemy forces have left the palace and engaged us, warsmith,*' Mordan Vhosk reported.

'Legionaries?'

'*No, warsmith. Palace soldiers and some light vehicles. The flak batteries and mega-bolters are taking care of them now.*'

As the archway was replaced with the fury and flame of a renewed bombardment, *Escutcheon* plunged into the inferno, followed by the remaining Spartans. The compartment ceiling thundered with the crash of masonry, and fiery destruction scorched their reinforced plating. *Escutcheon* bounced on its tracks through the wreckage, before punching out the other side.

The architecture of the inner Selenic was grand and beautiful. Krendl had his siege guns destroy it all. Palatial pyramids and statues raged up into the skies in colossal fountains of rock and flame.

Lascannon quads cut through the columns of smaller structures, bringing down the roofs of temples, sanctuaries and arenas on palace guardsmen that took cover in the buildings. Heavy bolters chuntered through the

Euphorosians, their rag-doll bodies blasted this way and
that by the flesh-shredding assault.

Shattering their way across statue-lined plazas and
along balcony platforms, the armoured column worked
its way towards the colossal domed structure that
crowned the Great Selenic. Taking his tanks up flights
of carved steps and through the interior of ornamental vaulted halls, Krendl had the Spartans smash their
way through.

'*Obliteratus*,' Krendl voxed finally. 'Grid IF 2-54 69-00.'

'*Grid IF 2-54 69-00, confirmed*,' Vhosk answered.

'Confirm. Target – the palace dome. Ordnance adjust,'
Krendl said. '*Escutcheon* out.'

The sky flashed white.

The blaze of the artillery detonation faded to reveal
a fireball of blast-shattered masonry rocketing skyward.
The domed roof was gone. All that remained was the
smoke-streaming foundations of the ornate building. Billowing clouds of dust and pulverised stone choked the air.

Escutcheon's tracks reached over the lip of the devastated palace before bouncing into the cratered, derelict
remains. The great support columns of the dome were
now stubby, soot-stained remnants sticking out of the
shattered structure. The crowning glory of Euphoros had
been huge and built to last for all eternity. It had not,
however, been built to withstand a direct hit from one
of the Iron Warriors' mighty siege guns.

The assault tanks crunched through the palace foundations, while fiery rubble rained down about them.
Slowing *Escutcheon* to a gritty crawl, Gholic negotiated
the columns that sat like the stumps of felled titanwoods.

'All stop,' Idriss Krendl announced to the compartment
and the open vox-channel.

The warsmith thumped the battered compartment controls and the reinforced door fell to form a disembarkation ramp – the warriors within were treated to the utter devastation that the siege guns had created.

Krendl smiled. It was an ugly sight.

'Brothers, we have won. Ironfire *works*. You proved that. We rode the storm and were one with obliteration, instead of being distant observers. Now we must finish the task and destroy the enemy command structure still present within these ruins.'

'How could anyone survive… *this*?' Siege-Captain Krugeran muttered.

'The Phoenician's sons are weak of will and deviant of flesh, but they are not stupid. They sent their playthings to meet us in battle and die by the fire of our iron. The Emperor's Children wait for us here. I know it. Just like Dorn's dogs will wait for us on Terra, they will be skilled and they will be deadly. For the purposes of our simulation and the integrity of the data we bequeath our primarch, and him to his Warmaster – I would not have it any other way. But we shall prevail, brothers. There are legionaries here who still proclaim themselves sons of the Emperor, in name if not in deed. Find them and kill them.'

'You heard the warsmith,' Siege-Captain Krugeran said, stomping down the ramp. 'The entire palace is coming down on us. We must be swift and resolute. All Iron Warriors disembark. Pattern Obduros – disperse and search by demi-squad. Shields and boltguns.'

Iron Warriors filed out from the battle-scarred vehicles, their studded and riveted plate held in close behind their shields. Resting the snub muzzles of their boltguns in the firing slots, the legionaries advanced.

Standing on the ramp of *Escutcheon*, Idriss Krendl clutched his data-slate. He narrowed his remaining eye, peering through his wire face-cage at the blasted palace foundations. Unlike the Iron Warriors filing down the smashed grand staircases and the smoking scree slopes leading into the structures below, Krendl was a broken warrior. His bones were held together by the iron rods shot through his body and the bolts and screw heads that covered his plate. It wouldn't take much to demolish him once again.

Slipping a fat bolt pistol from his belt holster and with his ragged mail cloak clinking in the breeze, Krendl followed the legionaries, carefully negotiating a demolished staircase that descended into the lower levels of the foundation. Even a fall might be fatal for him here.

He picked out four Iron Warriors and a sergeant that he had met before – an officer named Torrez. Suit lamps cut through the murk of shadow, soot and dust. The Iron Warriors moved expertly from corner to corner, covering one another and protecting themselves from potential attack with their presented boarding shields. They moved with belligerent purpose, eager to be done with the search and get into battle – a state of being for which they had been specifically designed and trained.

Down in the bowels of the palace principal, the artful design and craftsmanship was gone. Here the corners were pleasantly angular and the walls unadorned. As the light from his own suit lamps stuttered between thick metal bars, Krendl realised that they were in a dungeon. He could hear the rattle of war-plate as Iron Warriors tensed behind their weapons.

There was movement here in the darkness.

Hundreds of wretched, drug-addled Euphorosians, who had been obscenely mistreated by the sons of Fulgrim.

Every pleasure, amusement and satisfaction had been taken out upon the prisoners. From the appearance of their clothing they had been selected on rancid whim from the rich and poor, the young and old – and relatively recently. It seemed that prisoners did not last long in pleasing the Emperor's Children. With a planet of deviant pleasures to enjoy and a small civilisation upon which to visit the horror of their desires, it was all too apparent to see why Lord Commander Lelanthius and his legionaries had lingered on the paradise world instead of following their primarch to the meeting with Lord Perturabo.

'Siege-captain, what do you have?' Krendl voxed.

'A dungeon for prisoners, warsmith,' Krugeran confirmed, having moved with squads deeper into the bowels of the palace. 'They look to be in a sorry state.'

Krendl slowed. He peered through the bars of the communal cells. The filthy enclosures were full of the used and abused, all huddled like livestock. Their faces were afflicted with a haunted look of dread, but still they moved forward as a wretched collective to clap their misty eyes on the Iron Warriors.

Something wasn't right. Krendl could feel it in the dull agony of his shattered bones.

'Eradicant,' he said, 'Obliteratus. Same grid reference. Sheltering targets. Ordnance adjust. Stand by.'

Seconds passed. The prisoners drifted forward until their foreheads touched the bars and their clouded eyes squirmed about in their skulls. Krendl's gaze travelled down the bars. In front of him, some mess of a woman had slammed her body into the cell door, rattling it back and forth.

It was open.

'The Emperor's Children are hiding behind the prisoners,' Krendl voxed across the open channel, his tone flat and emotionless. 'They're in the cells. Open fire.'

Every Iron Warrior had heard the order. With transhuman reflexes, they moved to obey.

However, the Iron Warriors were not the only ones in the dungeon with transhuman reflexes.

The ragged prisoners were torn apart by gunfire from behind them. With boltgun muzzles pressed against their spines and the backs of their skulls, the Emperor's Children blasted straight through the Euphorosians.

The dungeon became a scene of even greater horror as the Iron Warriors returned fire. Rounds sparked off bars and shields as the Emperor's Children and the Iron Warriors fought to annihilate one another.

It was brief and bloody, with legionaries of the III and IV falling to the cacophony of point-blank fire exchanged through the bars of the dungeon. Iron Warriors were thrown back against the wall, bolts plucking at their helms and heads. As the remaining huddles of screaming prisoners fell like a curtain, bolts that had thudded through their flesh found purple-plated deviants hiding in the shadows.

In some cells, the Iron Warriors managed to maintain their shieldwall, hammering the trapped sons of Fulgrim back into the darkness. Elsewhere, the surprise attack had decimated the siege squads with peerless accuracy and broke the line. Within moments, the Emperor's Children were out of the cells and working their way up the passageways, forcing Krendl's legionaries back. When bolters ran dry, sabres flashed and sparked off ceramite. In return, the Iron Warriors hammered their

enemies with the unforgiving surfaces of their boarding shields.

As fresh shots blazed up the passageway behind Krendl,
the warsmith clutched his data-slate to his chest and
stepped back behind a corner. Bolts sparked off the brute
simplicity of the stonework, and he chanced a few more
shots in return before his pistol also clunked empty.

'*Warsmith,*' Victrus Krugeran said across the vox, '*we
should withdraw to the Spartans.*'

'Withdraw?' Krendl replied. He could hear the captain's exertions as he fought enemy legionaries almost
faceplate to faceplate, but he was unimpressed. 'Do you
think Perturabo will withdraw, standing in the rubble
of the Imperial Palace? Do you think Horus will withdraw, moments from a hard-fought victory? We stand,
we fight and we win!'

In the gloom and strobing light of gunfire, a singular
warrior swept out to strike the head from an Iron Warrior trying to reload his weapon. He wore the cape and
ornamental battleplate of a III Legion officer – a lord
commander, no less. He was helmless and looked at
Krendl through the long, straight, white hair that framed
his burning gaze. Even blood-splattered and murderous,
Lelanthius wore his sharp, youthful looks like a planetary
prince. But like the Euphorosians, his eyes were misted
by some foul local narcotic.

Lelanthius' face contorted around a noble snarl at the
death of so many of his legionaries, then softened to the
dreamy daze of a fantasy-addicted lunatic. He ejected
the empty clip from his own pistol before dropping the
weapon as well. In his other gauntlet he held a long
blade that glinted in the gloom and dripped with Iron
Warriors' blood.

'Are you out of your mind, turncoat?' the lord commander said, spitting his words with aristocratic venom. 'We have greater matters to contend with in this war.'

'Yet here I find you, deviant,' Krendl spat, 'looking to your prisoners. You will no longer find Iron Warriors garrisoning the galaxy for you. Perturabo has let his sons off the leash.'

'Our primarchs are allies,' Lelanthius seethed before his anger softened once more to hallucinogenic hilarity. 'Our Legions are brothers in service to Warmaster Horus. Who do you think you are, to spill the precious blood of Fulgrim that flows through the veins of every warrior of the Emperor's Children?'

'It seems something else entirely is flowing through your veins right now, lord commander…'

Lelanthius brought up the razor-sharp edge of his sabre. 'You should look to what is flowing through your own, Iron Warrior,' he warned Krendl, 'for you shall soon see it all over my dungeon floor.'

'Stop.'

The word was spoken with searing belief and confidence. Krendl had commanded, and incredibly the lord commander obeyed. The two officers paused as their warriors murdered one another in the darkness around them.

'*Eradicant? Obliteratus?*'

'*Standing by, warsmith.*'

'You might have a blade as well as the will and ability to kill me, swordsman,' Krendl told Lelanthius. 'But one word from me and my siege guns will fire once more on this position. I'm ready to return to the iron and the fire. How about you, lord commander?'

Lelanthius' face twisted with doubt. 'I don't believe you,' he spat.

A bolt pistol swung out from the cover of an adjoining passage, and pressed to the lord commander's temple. Lelanthius froze, his eyes darting to the side.

'Trust me,' Siege-Captain Krugeran said, 'he would have done it.'

The bolt pistol barked, blasting the deviant legionary's brains all over the wall. Krugeran limped around the corner. He had taken a bolt-round to the stomach and his helm had been cleaved open by a blade. Idriss Krendl nodded his appreciation, and the two officers waited amidst the smoke and stench of death as the last clashes of brutal fratricide played out in the dungeon gloom. In the end, only Iron Warriors limped from the darkness to present themselves to their siege-captain and warsmith.

THOUSANDS OF PALACE guards were flooding the avenues, stairways and thoroughfares, intent on surrounding the invading Iron Warriors. Victrus Krugeran joined Krendl once more as they made for the Spartans.

'You can send for the Thunderhawks to evacuate your warriors,' Krendl said. 'Orbital lifters too, for the siege guns.'

'The live simulation is over?' Krugeran asked.

'It's over. Ironfire was a success. Our father, perhaps even the Warmaster too, might learn something from it. Perhaps, siege-captain, you and I might do this again on distant Terra.'

'Primarch-willing,' Krugeran murmured, but he didn't sound as though he meant it.

'Meanwhile, I have other duties for you,' the warsmith said, looking down at Krugeran's wounds. 'During your restoration.'

'Yes, warsmith?'

Krendl handed the siege-captain the data-slate. 'Take this to Lord Perturabo. Appraise the primarch personally of Ironfire's success. Tell him this stratagem is a gift to atone for my past failures.'

'Would you rather not go yourself?'

'No,' Idriss Krendl said, eyeing the siege-captain's injuries. 'As you well know, our father abhors a cripple.'

RED-MARKED

Nick Kyme

Guilliman lies.

*He has deluded himself into denying an inconvenient truth.
He says that Ultramar no longer burns. He says that we won
the war, and turned back the Shadow Crusade. He says that
we must forge a second empire.*

Guilliman is wrong. None of this is true.

*On Macragge, he believes that order reigns. That is also
wrong, the denial of another inconvenient truth. Because out
on the fringes, farthest from the light, only two things are true.*

Anarchy reigns.

And the war for Ultramar isn't over.

AN EXPLOSION LIGHTS up the gloom, throwing the burned
armour of Thiel's men into relief. The blue of each is
streaked by grey. Acid has scorched through to the bare
ceramite beneath. Clouds of incendiary smoke fill the air
around the Protus listening post, turning the rain into a
sulphuric haze. The stench is more than acerbic. It *burns*.

Muzzle flare sears through a soot-black pall released by the explosion. Magazines cook off, and the air thunders as two nearby bunkers go up. Gunfire lashes the slab-sided armoury tower. It looms above Thiel through the murky air. Bolter shells splash against its walls.

They are trapped here, in this dead man's gauntlet.

They must advance. To survive, they must advance.

The dense nest of grey silos, bunkers and walled magazines reminds Aeonid Thiel of Calth. Packed so close together they form a labyrinthine *zone mortalis*. Choke-points and bottlenecks… it's merciless.

But wasn't that what this was all about? Leaving Calth, doing something with purpose? Thiel raises his power sword, and it blazes like a beacon.

'Forward!' he cries. 'On my lead! Wide dispersal. Keep fighting, damn–'

A sniper's bullet cracks against his shoulder guard, but he barely flinches. Then the sword's down again, and he's leading the vanguard.

The legionaries in his charge begin to move, edging from behind steel-plated munitions crates, bolters roaring in the darkness.

A targeting icon flashes up on his retinal feed, right over the tower. Crowned with razorwire and reinforced with ablative exterior armour, it shrugs off the fusillade coming from Thiel's men. 'Inviglio, I need those heavies – now!'

'I see it,' Inviglio replies.

Thiel switches vox-feeds. 'Thaddeus?'

Inviglio shakes his head. Gunfire is flashing across the munitions yard, so close that the transit heat is palpable. The Ultramarines keep moving, hugging walls, hunkering down whenever they can.

A distant scream resounds above the battle noise. Two ident-markers on the tactical feed go from green to red. Haldus and Konos. With the others, that makes six. Thiel catches the briefest glance of a scope's reflection above, before it's gone again.

'Get a response! There's recon in that nest. Tell Thaddeus to take them out, or it's over.'

Solid shot and mass-reactive shells carom off a nearby bunker wall, as Inviglio tries again. 'Thaddeus, are you with us?'

More dead air scratches across the feed, before a crackle of noise announces a broken reply.

'*Apologies… pinned… This is Petronius. Thaddeus is dead… moving up… support…*'

Thiel's jaw clenches as he feels the noose tighten. 'How long?'

'*…three minutes…*'

'Can we hold for that long?' Inviglio asks. 'Do we fall back, find a different ingress?'

Thiel shakes his head. 'If we fall back, that sniper team will cut us apart. Our only chance is forwards.'

Ahead, the smoke parts to reveal several power-armoured forms advancing in unison. Bolters are braced against their shoulders in a firing lock.

Shots ring out, forcing Thiel down. 'Return fire!'

The air is seared by an intense weapons exchange. Even the dust burns.

'Break them! Out of the kill-box! Out, out!' he urges his warriors. 'Grenades, then hard assault on my lead!'

Three-round bursts spit from behind their rapidly disintegrating barricade. Finius waits for a gap in the chaos before throwing a grenade.

It detonates deep into the enemy's ranks. Erontius is

clipped as he rises, but then his throat is torn open in a welter of blood by a stray bolter shell, his gorget split and hanging wide like a snapped hinge. He falls, still holding the primed grenade.

Thiel roars over the din. *'Down–'*

Thiel's warning is obliterated by the blast, as are the two legionaries closest to Erontius. Then comes the silence.

White light. White pain. Retinal lenses overloaded.

Thoughts become instincts and impressions, and for the next few seconds, Thiel's world is a magnesium-bright flare of searing agony.

Then the pain suppressants kick in, and get him moving again. His audio is down, but his retinal display still functions and shows him the bodies. There is blood on their armour. The stench of cordite and hot, wet copper fills his nostrils.

Sound returns after that, but it's distant and submerged. It rings hollow inside his skull.

Inviglio is shouting. He was far enough away from the blast to escape the worst of it. The words are so distant at first. *'Get up, brother-sergeant! They're coming!'*

The warriors emerging from the smoke and darkness are running. Thiel counts twenty. Wounded and barely conscious, his vision blurs, but he sees them well enough. Cobalt-blue and gold, a freshly painted Ultima on their shoulder guards.

Ultramarines. He wants to laugh at the insanity of it, but the next explosion hits and Thiel is off his feet. Flying. Burning. And just before he's about to die, he remembers what Captain Likane said to him on Oran.

There is no war in Ultramar.

✠ ✠ ✠

'REQUEST DENIED,' LIKANE says flatly, before looking back down at the stack of data-slates on his desk currently in review. It's dark in the office, but the shadows can't hide the captain's tensed jawline.

After a few moments, he speaks again.

'Is there something else you wish to say, brother-sergeant? You are not long returned from Calth. Are you having difficulty functioning in light, and with order?'

Thiel looks directly ahead. His arms are folded behind his back, and his head is bare out of respect. 'I would like to know something, sir.'

Unlike many of the officers at Oran, Likane is a war veteran. His battle scars are a testament to his experience, as is the bionic that forms part of his jaw. His bile is all natural.

'Yes?'

'Our purpose, sir.'

Likane doesn't look up. He's not paying attention to his cargo manifests, station reports and duty logs either. 'On Oran? We are a garrison. Our purpose is to guard and be ready. Weren't you told that when you arrived?'

'Ready for what, sir?'

'For whatever our primarch deems necessary. That is what it means to be Thirteenth Legion, to be an Ultramarine. Duty. Honour. *Respect*. You are here until a ship can bear you to Macragge – you and that ragged suit of war-plate you brought with you. Until then, you're mine.'

'I understand, sir,' Thiel replies. 'But any threat, however remote, should be investigated.'

Likane sets down the stylus and regards Thiel sternly from under thick, dark brows. His eyes are the colour of iron, and just as unyielding.

'There is no war in Ultramar,' he growls. 'Beyond our fight to liberate Calth, that is. You've been in the underworld too long. It sticks to you and leaves a mark. I should know.'

Thiel meets the captain's gaze at last. 'I am ill-suited to guard duty, sir.'

'Are you about to lecture me on how I deploy the warriors in this facility, Thiel?'

'No, sir.'

'You'll do as bidden until I say otherwise, or that bloody ship rids me of you,' Likane sighs. 'Your service record grants you *some* leeway, Thiel, as does your recommendation from Captain Vultius. But do not think me tolerant of insubordination. Oran runs to my order. We are a garrison, here at our primarch's command. I won't sanction a mission that countermands that directive because you believe yourself to be above it. You are not. This is Imperium Secundus, sergeant. Get used to it.'

Thiel nods curtly, salutes and turns to leave. Likane looks back down at his reports, when Thiel's voice makes him pause.

'What's Nightfane?'

It's faint, but Thiel hears the slight catch in Likane's breath. The captain's face is pinched with anger when he looks up. 'What do you know of that word?'

'Just vox-chatter.' Thiel gestures to the reports. 'How many in that stack relate to listening posts or watch stations within our purview that we have lost contact with in the last few months, captain? Was it one of them who sent us Nightfane?'

'Are you seriously expecting me to indulge this, sergeant? I know you and the other veterans are struggling to reintegrate with the recruits, but I won't–'

'I would gladly resubmit myself for censure, if you would grant me this one concession. Sir.'

Likane grits his teeth, but stays calm. 'I suspect censure holds little concern for you any more, sergeant.'

Thiel raises an eyebrow. 'So… The listening posts?'

'You want purpose? Duty, Thiel?' Likane scowls, as the already thinning veil of composure collapses. 'You have no concept of either. I look at you, Thiel, and do you know what I see? That we have erred as a Legion. The demands of the Great Crusade were heavy, but men were needed. Lots of them. Our standards, however rigorously we tried to apply them, slipped. I suppose it was inevitable that *lesser* aspirants passed indoctrination.'

'Are you suggesting I should not be here, sir?'

'I am.'

'Then we are in agreement on one fact.'

Likane shakes his head. He's smiling, but out of disgust. 'More than that, Thiel. Much more. You bring shame to us, to this Legion. You are not an Ultramarine – you're a mistake.'

Thiel nods, but shows no emotion. 'And the listening posts, sir?'

The captain clenches his fists. But rather than angry, his voice is resigned.

'You are fortunate that I don't enact a fitting punishment myself. I would *enjoy* it. But then I'd be fit for the mark too. Take whoever is free and able. But I warn you now, you have sanction to perform a single recon mission. Volunteers only. Do not pull anyone from active duty.'

'That's a shallow pool, sir,' Thiel murmurs.

'Yes, it is. You should feel at ease in it. Now, get out.'

✠ ✠ ✠

SMOKE STINGS HIS eyes. His throat is burned raw, and he's lost his helmet. It takes a few seconds for Thiel to realise he isn't dead. His bolt pistol is on fire. It scorches the ceramite of his gauntlet as he seizes the grip.

The tower is down, reduced to a crumbling ruin. Bodies are trapped in the wreckage – the corpses of their enemies, though some of them are still moving. Dazed, they stagger through the fog of agglomerated dust, grit and soot. Lying on his back, Thiel guns them down.

Inviglio is by his side. So are Venator and Bracheus. Thiel hears Venator shouting coordinates down the vox, and realises what has happened.

A second missile barrage hits the ruins of the tower. The explosions shake the earth, blooming brightly before black smoke smothers the light. A few more disparate bolter bursts echo, their muzzle flashes like stars of fire, before it's over.

Inviglio offers Thiel a hand as Bracheus stays on sentry. 'Can you walk, sergeant?'

'Recall… everyone…'

Croaking and hoarse, Thiel does not recognise his own voice. Venator turns to scan the ruins.

'Petronius says we're clear. He's on his way.'

Thiel laughs out loud, and its hurts badly. But he's alive.

Inviglio hauls his sergeant back to his feet. 'At least those bastards are dead.'

Thiel grimaces as he recovers his blade, and looks back to Inviglio. 'We need to make sure. You have a knife?'

'Of course, sergeant.' He cocks his head. 'Do you intend to stab them?'

Thiel limps towards the wreckage of the tower. 'No. I want to see what's under their damn helmets.'

✠ ✠ ✠

AS HE ENTERS the barrack house where he instructed his recruits to gather, Thiel realises that Likane wants him to fail. There are over two thousand legionaries garrisoned at Oran. The captain has afforded him twenty-two.

For Ultramarines, they look less than exceptional. Thiel recognises Inviglio and Bracheus, the Calth veterans. The others are strangers, and marked for censure. Pettiness, in Thiel's opinion, has become the Legion's singular weakness – every infraction, any deviation, however minor, is met with the red. It's not a tool for rehabilitation or even punishment. It's a noose choking the life from the XIII Legion.

Inviglio meets him at the door. 'I think Likane has raided the brig...' he murmurs.

'I see warriors,' Thiel replies quietly. 'He has honoured his word. In kind, at least.'

'In eight hours, this is all we could get?'

Bracheus approaches them, nodding his acknowledgement. 'You sound concerned, brother. There is no shame in adversity.'

Inviglio frowns. 'I feel none.'

Thiel ignores them. His gaze roams the barrack house instead. 'Not exactly what I had in mind. But they will serve.'

He raises his voice.

'You know who I am, and you know what Brother-Captain Likane thinks of you. I have need of men of purpose and skill.'

'For what, brother-sergeant?' asks a legionary with a peppering of dark stubble across his scalp. He stands with his arms folded. He has shell burns, and Thiel suspects that an Apothecary sheared the warrior's hair while digging out shrapnel. He nods, but does not salute. 'Drenius.'

Thiel notes that Drenius also holds a sergeant's rank, and his entire squad carries the red mark.

'A remote listening station called Tritus has gone dark,' he replies. 'I want to know why. I can't man the walls at Oran in a polished suit of armour, waiting to be called to arms. I don't believe any of you can either, or you wouldn't be standing before me now, your helms striped in red.'

A hulking legionary at the back of the room raises his voice.

'Standing at the walls, sitting in a cell, it makes little difference.' He is daubed with the red mark, worn either proudly or dismissively. 'What is this all about?'

'Purpose.' Thiel walks the length of the room to stand in front of him, not quite eye to eye. A pugilist's face looks down at the sergeant, but with intelligent eyes. The red is crisscrossed over his features like an X. 'What's your name, Ultramarine?'

'Petronius.'

Inviglio can no longer hold his temper. 'The sergeant outranks you, legionary!'

'I see the mark,' Petronius growls. 'Do you see mine?'

'Disobedient cur! I–'

Thiel's raised hand stalls any further remonstration. 'You want to leave Oran? I can give you that. Someone told me today that I was not worthy to be an Ultramarine. I think you have been told something similar before, brother. For, make no mistake in this, we *are* brothers.'

He looks around the room again.

'All of us. This is our chance to cast off our shame – whether we deny it, whether we confess to care about it. I believe we are under attack, only we have yet to realise

it. I hope I am wrong, but I don't think so. It begins
with Tritus.'

'And if we find something there?' Sergeant Drenius
asks.

Thiel turns to him, and sees in his eyes a need to atone.

'We kill it, brother. But not before we make sure it tells
where its friends are hiding.'

THE CUNEIFORM ON the dead legionary's face is Colchisian. Bracheus scowls in disgust.

'Carved with his own blade.'

Inviglio looks on. 'That's how they did it on Calth…'

Thiel's face is a mask of cold anger. He taps the dead
Word Bearer's armour with his boot.

'They planned for this. For us.'

'No Ultramarine would fire on one of his own,' says
Bracheus. 'More false colours.'

The wounds are still fresh for all of them. The betrayal,
the sheer loss.

'Fighting from shadows, behind masks,' spits Inviglio,
casting aside the Word Bearer's helmet. 'We hesitated,
and nine of us are dead because of it.'

Bracheus turns to him. 'And if there's doubt? If there
are other Ultramarines at large out here? Do we fire first
and ask questions later?'

'No,' murmurs Thiel. 'We adapt.'

'A call sign, then? Something we can–'

Thiel shakes his head.

'Too ambiguous. And if we're already engaged, it's not
practical. It has to be instantaneous. Immediate visual
recognition.'

His eyes fall upon the helmet he was given at the Oran
garrison – it lies split open on the ground, the red of

censure painted across the ceramite. He smiles, only half grimacing in pain.

'It has to be symbolic. We have to be ready.'

A LONE GUNSHIP sits in the deployment bay surrounded by menials and servitors. Thiel's watching the preparations from a gantry, lost in his thoughts, when he notices Inviglio approaching.

'The *Spirit of Veridia*.'

'Sir?'

Thiel gestures to the Thunderhawk below. 'So named for Calth's lonely star. How it burned…'

'A few hours and we'll be airborne,' says Inviglio. He clearly finds the memory uncomfortable.

Thiel nods. 'Aye, and then we shall see.'

'See, brother-sergeant?'

'See what matters more – a red mark or a blue one.'

A moment of silence passes between them, filled by the drone of industry below. Missile payloads and ammo hoppers are being readied.

'It was Likane, wasn't it,' says Inviglio.

'Who claimed I was no Ultramarine? Of course.'

'He's wrong.'

'I know that.' Thiel gestures down to the legionaries on the muster deck going through their weapon drills. 'But some of *them* don't.'

Bracheus leads them, as harsh a taskmaster as Thiel knows – with the exception, perhaps, of Marius Gage. Petronius wields his chainblade with raw aggression, favouring strength and a two-handed grip over skill.

Drenius stands out for another reason. His sword mastery is exemplary, his form and power without a fault that Thiel can see. Bracheus cajoles and bellows at the other legionaries, but he only nods to Drenius in appreciation of his art.

'Who could ever claim that *he's* not a warrior? Not an Ultramarine?'

Inviglio looks on. 'Sergeant Drenius fights to forget.'

'We're all fighting for something, brother.'

'And what if... What if it's nothing, and there is no great threat within our borders? What then of our purpose?'

Thiel leans close to Inviglio, keeping his voice low.

'Have you heard of Nightfane?'

Inviglio shakes his head. 'What does it refer to?'

'I have no idea, brother, but it came from one of those stations. I don't think they went dark of their own accord. I think they're being silenced.'

Down in the deployment bay, the servitors withdraw and the ready signal is given. Thiel nods to Bracheus, to indicate that their practice is over.

Now for the real thing. Now for Tritus.

'Let's hope Likane is right, and those stations going dark is nothing more than it appears,' Inviglio says with a sigh.

'We're about to find out, brother.'

THE GUNSHIP BANKS hard. Plumes of smoke are leaking from its portside thruster and there are tears in the fuselage from where the flying shrapnel struck it. Thiel can feel the air venting through where the Thunderhawk's structural integrity has been compromised.

'So much for leaving the war behind!' Inviglio laughs.

'We are still in it, brother!' Thiel calls back. They have barely left Oran and already they are on fire. Auto-defences on Tritus, rigged for anti-aircraft patterns – not an auspicious start. 'There is no *leaving* it, brother. There is only war now, or so I've heard it said.'

The air in the gunship shrieks through the breached hull, buffeting the legionaries. Thiel's boots are mag-locked and he stands, feet apart, braced upon the deck.

Petronius chimes in from across the hold. 'I, for one, rejoice.'

He sits with his chainsword clenched in a firm grip, ever belligerent.

Venator, a marksman, sits beside him. Like Inviglio, he's from Konor, but wears his highborn origins like a badge of pride. 'We know you too well, my pugnacious brother. Patience is not a virtue for you, is it?'

'No. But wrath is.'

Petronius makes to rise, but Thiel's stare stops him. Perhaps Likane's words about the needs of recruitment outweighing a desire for the highest standards carry some mote of truth. In most cases, it is why these men have been censured.

Disobedience, defiance, insubordination. Shame.

'Quieten down. Once we're on the ground, I want your attention on the mission – not each other. That turret might not be the only hostile thing on Tritus.'

'*All brace,*' the pilot's voice crackles through the vox, cutting the conversation. '*Coming in hard, in five, four, three...*'

The engine scream reaches a crescendo, before the heavy lurch of metal takes over. Landing stanchions have already peeled from their housings on the ship's belly. Thiel hears them strike dirt, a tremor rumbling through the fuselage, shaking men and metal.

The warning light flashing by the exit turns from red to green. A pneumatic pressure release sounds, and natural light is admitted into the troop hold as the ramp lowers.

'Weapons ready,' Thiel orders. 'Move out on my command.'

He has twenty-two men – three squads, including support armed with heavy weapons. Missile launchers. Another carries flamers, and like stands shoulder to shoulder with like.

It is the way of the Legiones Astartes.

A network of battle-scarred structures is revealed through the widening aperture of the rear access hatch. Whatever is out there, Thiel hopes that twenty-two men will be enough.

THE CORRIDOR IS strewn with the wreckage of improvised barricades. Low light from the legionaries' suit lamps reveals bullet holes and shell craters in the walls. A lumen strip, half ripped from its casings, flickers overhead.

Sergeant Drenius cuts a coil of razor wire.

'This must be where they made their last stand.'

Thiel nods. The ravaged Tritus facility is eerily quiet and to speak too much seems disrespectful to the dead. Something cracks underfoot, and he looks down at thick brass casings scattered across the floor.

His and Drenius' squads are advancing down two transit corridors that lead to the core of the listening post. The entire station has seen heavy fighting, but here it is at its worst. Dense shelling, grenades and thermo-incendiaries have taken out most of the internal dividing wall between the transit ways. Thiel and Drenius' men can see and talk to each other through the ragged gaps.

The other sergeant in Thiel's group, Thaddeus, is back at the gunship. His missile launchers are reinforcement only.

They won't need them. The battle here is over, the

crew of Tritus lost. Mangled bodies litter the place, half drowned by the spent casings. They are the facility staff, including human security officers.

'Chainblade wounds,' Drenius notes.

'They were facing legionaries.' Thiel sees a rune crudely carved into a dead man's face, and scowls. 'Word Bearers.'

Inviglio, standing second in the line, shakes his head sadly. 'Then you were right, sergeant – Lorgar's Shadow Crusade isn't over.'

'That's not what I said, brother. This isn't the Shadow Crusade at all.'

The access gate for the main hub is ahead, half torn from its industrial mountings. Drenius points to the gate on his side. 'We might find some answers in there.'

'There's one thing we'll find for certain,' says Thiel.

'What's that, sergeant?'

'The dead.'

Thiel is right. As the Ultramarines break through into the main hub, they enter a killing room. More of the dead crew of Tritus are here, at the site of their desperate stand.

Instead of just makeshift barricades, the defenders used the heavy metal of their listening stations to hunker behind. The entire hub, a large octagonal chamber, is filled with these bulky communication devices. Desks and chart tables have been turned over. Stacks of hard data cartridges are piled up like sandbags.

None of it was enough to stop whatever hit them. Most of the equipment is destroyed.

There is shattered plastek across the floor. Cables and shorn wiring hang from the ceiling in intestinal loops, but cataracts of sparks suggest the generator or its backup still functions. Hololith arrays, large data-corders and banks of vox-transponders lie broken apart, much like Tritus' engineers, comms-officers and armsmen.

There are no other bodies. Their killers either took their dead with them or sustained no casualties during the assault.

Inviglio curses quietly. 'Have you ever seen such butchery?'

'Been party to much worse,' Drenius replies, staring at the corpses. 'Twelfth Legion. I'd stake what's left of my reputation on it.'

Inviglio turns to him, inviting further explanation. The sergeant removes his helmet.

'We were under orders. Joint engagement with the Twelfth, late in the Crusade. They hit hard, overran the enemy defences, and cut them down as we followed. A praetor by the name of Harrakon Skurn was in charge.'

Drenius smiles, but there's no humour in it.

'*Harrakon Skurn*. With names like that, how could we not have known what they were? What they *truly* were, I mean?'

'What happened?' Inviglio asks.

Drenius' war-torn face darkens with memory.

'They kept going, on into the civilian camps. Widespread heavy shelling earlier in the campaign, you see, and the natives had moved their people into fortified compounds for protection. World Eaters couldn't tell the difference, not with how they were. Perhaps they didn't want to. Skurn let them, anyway – said they had to burn it out of their blood, or something.'

Inviglio nods. 'You broke command. Intervened. That's why you and your squad were censured.'

Drenius shakes his head. His voice barely has the strength of a whisper.

'No, brother. Actually, we didn't. We obeyed our orders and did nothing. *That* was how we earned the mark.'

Inviglio has no words, and Drenius no stomach for further questions or conciliation. He walks away, but Thiel is looking at Inviglio.

'Sergeant Drenius has a heavier burden than most,' he says.

'You knew?'

'I did. I have data-slates from Captain Likane on every legionary in this unit.'

'Is that what this is all about, then? Rehabilitation?' Inviglio asks.

'No, brother. It's about doing something that actually matters. I can see Drenius' shame in his eyes every time he reaches for the bolter that he should have used in defence of those civilians. His red mark is a brand he carries with sorrow. He needs purpose again. So does Petronius, and Venator, Finius. Even you and Bracheus. Even me. Can you honestly tell me you thought you were making a difference on Calth? Can any of us?'

Inviglio stiffens. 'Calth was a jewel of the–'

'Calth is an irradiated hellhole of underground caverns and bitter darkness. It's only fit for ghosts.'

'I never thought you a glory hunter, Aeonid,' Inviglio murmurs. He shakes his head, disappointed.

'I'm not, Vitus, but I do want to make some kind of difference beyond propaganda. I have no stomach for politics. I am a soldier.'

Venator interrupts before Inviglio can reply. 'Apologies, brother-sergeant, but you are both going to want to see this.'

He takes them to a blood-spattered console.

'This one still functions.'

He indicates the cracked data-screen – it's flawed by static, but an image flickers there still. Thiel steps up to the screen.

'Data-screed. Some kind of manifest?'

'There are audio logs, reports and chatter compiled from the other listening stations linked to Tritus.'

Thiel glances at him. 'You think they missed it?'

'Our errant renegades? Yes, I do.'

Two further listening stations are depicted on the screen as Thiel brings up a trinary system map – Oran is marked clearly to the galactic south-east, shielded by the remote stations at Quorus, Protus and Tritus. The three together comprise a half-sickle arc that serves a small region of the coreward aspect of Imperium Secundus.

They are distant outriders, early warning posts. Sentries. Some still refer to them as 'the Old Watchmen of Ultramar', as they had stood untouched for many decades before the coming of the Legion.

'Their next targets,' says Inviglio, grimly.

Thiel's eyes don't leave the screen. 'Vox Thaddeus. We're moving. Now.'

THEY SMELL THE pyres before they see the heaped bodies.

At least, this time, the traitors burned the dead after they mutilated them. Inviglio sees only further insult, to these poor souls and his injured pride. His fist is wrapped so tight around his bolter that it almost cracks the stock.

'Too late again.'

Bracheus stands at Inviglio's shoulder. 'Easy, brother.'

The wind changes direction and washes the wretched flesh-smoke over the Ultramarines. Inviglio shakes his head.

'We have to end this slaughter. End *them*.'

'We will,' Thiel reassures him. The sergeant is standing on a low ridge, surveying the destruction from the wreckage of a broken pylon. Quorus is no more. Only a burning, empty shell remains. Its outer wall has been reduced to rubble, avenues lie cratered by shelling and smoke thickens the air, obscuring the worst of the carnage.

But the bodies are there. Hundreds of them. Skeletal, charred remains, bone being slowly reduced to ash.

No ceremony, no ritual, no last stand of glory. Just death. This is… was a small installation with its own artificially created atmosphere. The generators still turn, but none now live who need to breathe the air.

Venator crouches in the blood-soaked earth as he eyes the blackening horizon.

'They had armour – heavy vehicles, I think. Like using a chainsword to tear parchment.'

Thiel climbs down to rejoin the others. 'They are gathering materiel. Weapons, explosives… even tanks.'

'And the rest,' says Bracheus. 'An arsenal, brother-sergeant.'

Thiel nods, and turns to Venator. 'Well, brother?'

Venator tastes the ash from one of the pyres. It takes a few seconds and there's an instant when he connects, a moment of memory not his own, that registers as a nerve tremor below his left eye. 'Not long ago. I taste fresh agony.'

Thiel turns away from the horror, removing his helmet as he heads for the Thunderhawk idling on a scrap of landing apron behind them.

'Back to the gunship.'

'And if they are arming up?' says Inviglio, halting Thiel mid-stride. 'Are we prepared for that?'

Bracheus steps in. 'We should alert Captain Likane. Have him send reinforcements.'

'I already sent the request,' says Thiel, 'but there's no way of knowing how long it will take to reach him, or if our brothers are incoming. They might even reach Protus ahead of us, Throne willing.'

Drenius shrugs. 'And if they don't?'

Thiel sags, his armoured back still to the rest of his men. 'What do you say, Petronius? If we meet the chainsword that tore through this station, what will we do?'

Petronius' jaw clenches. There's a fervour in him that was lacking before, suggesting that his anger is turning into something useful.

'Blunt its teeth.'

SERGEANT THADDEUS EYES the warren of bunkers and munition silos warily. Protus is unlike the other listening stations they saw on Tritus and Quorus. It's more of a weapons depot.

Petronius hefts the heavy launcher onto his shoulder guard, and lodges into the firing ridge. 'This place is a labyrinth,' he mutters.

Thaddeus ignores the belligerent legionary. 'Up there. Higher ground.'

Amongst the hangars, the gantries, the piled crates and ammunition sheds is a wide ramp that leads to an even wider circular platform. More crates are stacked up here, together with fuel drums and supplies tied down on steel pallets.

The overcrowded landing pad will make the perfect vantage point for the heavies.

Leading the squad out, Thaddeus hails Thiel. As ever, his mood is curt and his tone borders on disrespect.

'Moving to high ground. Will vox again when we have overwatch on the street.'

He cuts the link without waiting for a reply. They take the ramp two abreast with launchers slung low or braced to shoulders.

As he picks his way through the crates and drums, Thaddeus notices movement below. He's about to sound the alarm when he realises the armoured figures are Ultramarines.

Not Thiel's or Drenius' though.

He's only distracted for a second, but the confines on top of the landing pad are relatively tight – by the time Thaddeus sees the *second* group of legionaries having already taken the high ground ahead of him, he is almost on top of them.

Thaddeus relaxes when he sees blue armour again, and raises his gauntleted hand as his squad reach for their side-arms. 'Stand down. Likane has sent reinforcements.'

It's only when he gets up close that he realises his mistake, and the newcomers' bolt rounds tear him to pieces.

As ordered, they take Protus' command centre swathed in red. It is both war paint and baptism – the mark of their new brotherhood and the blood of their enemies.

Thiel crouches low as he peers through the incendiary smoke left behind by the breacher charge they used on the door. 'What's the count?'

He still rasps a little from the explosion back at the armoury, but that's behind them now and the next target beckons: Protus, the third out-system watch station. The third also to go dark. At least now, the Ultramarines know why.

Inviglio stands two paces back, watching the corridor behind with Venator.

'Twenty-eight,' he calls out. 'All dead.'

Most of the bodies strewn behind them wear the cobalt-blue of the Ultramarines, though all but *two* are not of the XIII Legion. Not just Word Bearers this time – some of the dead have the gang-tattoos of Nostramo, or carry Barbaran kukras.

This is *not* the Shadow Crusade made anew – it is something else. They are guerrilla fighters and insurgents, a canker in the midst of the new empire.

And now that he has uncovered it, Thiel means to cut it out.

'Hostiles!' shouts Petronius.

Bolter fire resounds from both ends of the command centre. A final few renegades are dug in behind a barricade, putting up a little more resistance before they die.

If they weren't such loathsome traitors, Thiel might even respect that. Instead, he calls for Bracheus. 'Burn it, legionary!'

Re-fitted and re-equipped, the squad is leaner and more flexible. Bracheus wields the flamer to deadly effect, stepping in from the side of the breach and bathing the entire room in superheated promethium.

Only one of the renegades falls, collapsing to his knees as he burns alive inside his power armour. But the fire's not meant to kill. It's only meant to distract.

As Bracheus steps back into cover, Thiel bellows again.

'Move, move! Rapid fire. Take them down!'

Thiel joins in as Inviglio, Petronius, Finius and Venator open fire. Bolter shells scream hot as they pummel the room and tear the meagre barricade apart. A defender tries to rise, but is hit simultaneously in the neck, chest and head.

Venator reloads fluidly. He takes a second renegade with a precision shot through the eye.

Snap fire comes back in reply, striking wide and scoring only glancing hits. Two more enemies remain and they've hunkered down, lying in wait for Petronius as he barrels recklessly forwards. One of them leaps up, sword in hand, but Finius throws his knife and pierces the warrior's throat.

The second legionary reaches Petronius, though, and hacks his burring chainaxe into the Ultramarine's bolter. It cuts through the stock in seconds, and is about to rip open Petronius' torso when Thiel shoulder-barges the warrior to the floor.

The legionary tears off his helm to reveal the abject scarification of the XII Legion, World Eaters. 'Come on then, Guilliman's little curs!' he roars.

Thiel raises his hand. No one fires.

Inviglio edges forwards, his bolter ready. 'What are you doing? You are injured.'

'No,' says Thiel. 'I'm *angry*.' He eyes up his opponent as he returns his sidearm to its holster, and draws his sheathed longsword.

Petronius' blunt concern is written upon his features. 'He'll kill you, fool.'

Thiel rolls his shoulder to loosen his sword arm, his eyes on the World Eater now.

'We have to show them who rules Ultramar. Sometimes that means doing it bloody.'

Inviglio is unconvinced. 'Who will know, other than us?'

But Thiel's reply is too low to be heard by anyone but himself.

'I will.'

He salutes, earning a savage nod in reply.

The World Eater is fast, and he moves aggressively. Thiel is immediately on the back foot, forced into a hasty defence. A heavy blow swings in, and sparks spit from Thiel's sword and his opponent's chainaxe. The burring blades smother the sound of Thiel's hard breathing.

He pummels the blood-soaked butcher, as relentless as a metronome. Each axe blow is crafted differently to the last, in search of a weakness to exploit. Thiel gives him none, but he's not winning – he's hanging on.

He realises he is being played with. So does Petronius, who goes to intervene.

'Stay back!' Thiel orders. 'Do it!'

Reluctantly, Petronius obeys, and so do the others.

Angry, perhaps. Disobedient even, but loyal.

The World Eater is slurring his words, succumbing to some blood-mad rage. 'Little cur... I'll... slake my blade... with you...' His eyes glaze, the pupils shrinking to tiny black dots of hate. Thiel knows he must end this quickly.

'You are the cur... *war dog.*'

He backs off, and lets the maddened warrior come at him, dodging as much as he's trying to parry effectively. It frustrates the World Eater, goading him. Gripped in two hands, Thiel's electromagnetic longsword holds its own better than any chainblade could. It is his only by dint of a father's indulgence, but no less potent for it.

The butcher's onslaught is ferocious, but each blow is telegraphed now and less reasoned. It's pure rage, a desire to break his enemy through sheer aggression and persistence. Thiel smiles, despite the battering.

'Now, I have y–'

Then he slips, down on one knee as blow after blow

hammers down. His brothers move to intercede, but he roars at them again.

'*Stand fast!*'

Bloodied, hurting, Thiel is struck hard and his arm swings out. So does his sword. The blow leaves him open.

The World Eater lifts his chainaxe like a blood-priest poised before the sacrifice, his hungry grin mimicked by the weapon's ruddy teeth. Faster than he looks in that moment, Thiel thrusts his sword into the other warrior's chest. It tears right through the armoured plastron, piercing both hearts.

Blood boils up the World Eater's throat as he violently convulses, and comes out in a gruesome spray. He roars, teeth so bloody they're crimson, but the axe still falls from his nerveless grip. Four Ultramarines gun him down in unison before the weapon hits the floor.

Thiel rises, taking Petronius' help to get back to his feet. 'Well *that* was reckless,' says the legionary. 'But impressive.'

'I thought you'd approve,' Thiel replies, wiping the blood from his blade.

Inviglio stops him as he approaches the body. 'Were you proving something to him or yourself, sergeant?' He doesn't bother to mask his consternation.

Nor does Thiel.

'Neither. Both. He died, I lived – that's all that matters now.' He looks at Inviglio squarely. 'May I?'

Inviglio gives him room to crouch next to the body. There's a rank tattoo on the dead warrior's face, and some kind of cranial implant in the back of his skull.

'He was an officer. But I have no idea what–'

Then he stops cold. The World Eater isn't dead. He clings on, kept alive by his anger. Not a threat, but enduring nonetheless.

He's murmuring something, and Thiel cranes his neck. Inviglio edges forwards. 'Sergeant…'

Thiel leans closer, grimacing at the dying legionary's stench. He utters one word, over and over. It puts a chill in Thiel's soul.

'Night…fane…'

Only silence follows. The World Eater's bitten tongue lolls in his ugly mouth, but he's smiling in death. Venator has a haunted look in his eyes. 'I have never seen them smile before,' he murmurs.

'Then you've never seen them killing in earnest,' says Thiel, moving up to the command centre's hub.

The data-screed is comprehensive. There is obscurity in its sheer overwhelming detail.

'These aren't raiders. This is organised.'

Finius, Venator and Petronius secure the room. Inviglio joins Thiel at the primary command console. 'Nightfane again… But what is it?'

Thiel shakes his head.

'I don't know. A place, a leader perhaps? They're getting orders from somewhere.'

'I think I know where,' calls Bracheus. He is standing by one of the other bodies. He waits for Thiel and Inviglio to join him. 'Look at the armour. There's a manufactorum stamp. A forge-temple.'

Thiel looks at the symbol. 'That's from Phraetius.'

He's seen the name on the data-screed. He recalls that it used to be the main munitorum depot for Crusade operations in this region, now marked as decommissioned and deserted. It appeared that neither was true.

'They're forging a supply chain, and that's their base of operation.'

'What operation?' asks Bracheus.

'Nightfane.'

FOURTEEN LEGIONARIES SIT silently in the hold of a gunship. Only the glow of retinal lenses alleviates the abject dark. The low hum of their power armour is barely audible above the muffled shriek of dead-drop turbulence.

Phraetius hurtles to meet them, or rather them to it. It is only a minor forge-temple, but it is both fortified and garrisoned. Stab lights lance the gloom as *Spirit of Veridia* plummets earthward, the pilot coaxing it like a glider with the turbines low and the engines cold.

A white glare lights Thiel's face through a vision slit just before he dons a replacement helm. His jaw is set, his voice iron hard.

'We end it here, or die trying.'

No one argues. No one utters a word.

They strike deep. The gunship pierces banks of gritty smog, dropping like an arrow until a siren starts to wail. Running near cold, the gunship was rendered invisible to sensors, but the smog was the last veil of camouflage before the naked eye could spot them. With their discovery, rapid action is needed.

Sudden engine thrust hits the hold like a hammer, and would have thrown the Ultramarines except that they are mag-locked to the deck.

Now they are dropping in hard, right down the enemy's throat. Flak fire is already chipping at the gunship's outer armour, but the anti-air guns are slow to kick in as the defenders rush to man their stations.

As of this moment, surprise is Thiel's greatest asset.

'On your feet, legionaries!'

There are two five-man squads and Drenius' four, with

specialists and heavies in each. The shuddering hold makes Thiel's voice tremulous, but his will is unshakable.

'Now we fight. For primarch and Emperor. For the lost sons of Calth, and those yet to be born on Macragge. This is your hour, brothers. Banish shame. Banish doubt. Banish anger. Show these traitors what it is to be an Ultramarine!'

The side hatch slides back to admit the stench of hot las and incendiary. The sky is night black, but the stab lights converging on the gunship make it feel like day.

Ten feet from the ground, Thiel jumps from the hold with Petronius and nine others in tow.

A blitzkrieg of fire greets them, pranging off shoulder guards and plastrons. The ricochets are so heavy it practically rains sparks. The squads led by Thiel and Petronius hit a gantry after the drop, Petronius' men heading down into a flagged square to deal with the troops coming out of the barrack houses.

Thiel presses on, his first target the interceptor autocannon that's reloading after trying to destroy their gunship. Engine noise roars behind him as he rushes the gun nest, the Thunderhawk taking to the skies with Drenius' squad on board.

A ragged group of flak-armoured soldiers move to block their ground advance, at the urging of an officer standing with the panicking gun crew. Bracheus unleashes his flamer.

The men are still burning when Thiel crashes through them, knocking them off the gantry to a merciful death below.

The officer fumbles desperately for his chainsword. Thiel cuts him shoulder to hip, cleaving two equal slabs of meat. The gunners have their cannon loaded and swing it to bear – one aiming, another pumping the turning crank before a third hauls on the triggers.

The triggerman's head explodes before he can fire. Venator puts two more bolt shells through the other crew. Inviglio spikes the nest and the squad moves on to the sound of frag grenades in their wake, tearing apart what's left of the gun emplacement.

In the square below, an armoured vehicle rolls through a gated entranceway. Another ragged soldier sits in the cupola, muzzle flare tearing from the mouth of his heavy stubber.

One of the barrack houses is in flames, its sides blown out by a missile hit and corpses strewn around it. Petronius is shouting to his squad. One legionary is down, but another hauls him onto his feet and they keep moving.

Thiel jabs a finger at the armoured vehicle converging on Petronius and his men. 'Finius! Heavy support! Now!'

Finius sinks to one knee to brace himself on the trembling gantry, and fires his launcher. The missile streaks brightly across the square and hits the armoured vehicle in the flank. The whole thing goes up in a writhing ball of flame before crashing down a moment later. Petronius gives a casual salute, before urging his squad on.

Dead men in rough soldiers' garb litter the square. Tan uniform is turned black. They hang from the gantries too – more than sixty. The Ultramarines cut down these mortal rebels in under a minute.

Thiel's thoughts are fluid in his mind, running from one tactical decision to another, but a moment of reflection still creeps in.

Their foes weren't ready. Not for this.

Nothing could have prepared them for this.

Above the gate, crouched behind an armoured parapet, a

second battalion has gathered. They wear the same grubby uniforms, but these men are split into heavier weapons teams. Amongst the wretched throng, Thiel sees legionaries too. Not in false colours this time – they wear deep red, blood-spattered white and shadowy, midnight blue.

Petronius has drawn them out, and now Thiel commands their attention. The gantry abuts the gatehouse, although its terminus is strung with razor wire and the outward facing teeth of a tank trap improvised as an infantry deterrent.

The Ultramarines meet the cannonade head on. Power armour absorbs the punishment in a flurry of rattling shell impacts and sparking metal.

'Advance!' Thiel roars into the hurricane. 'Advance!'

He moves almost on instinct, guided by the thunder of the guns. His bolt pistol barks in response, the electromagnetic longsword low by his side. They're running hard and fast along what's left of the gantry, but it feels slow, like pushing against a gale.

Bracheus takes a solid hit. The legionary's shoulder drops and he staggers, but keeps on running.

Thiel is first to the wrecked barricade, barging through the twisted metal of the tank trap. He cuts down a traitor legionary in lightning-wreathed armour, splitting the Night Lord almost in two. The human gunners die just as quickly.

As Thiel shakes blood from his blade, a second Night Lord emerges from a gatehouse tower. He's alone, and his pale Nostraman skin looks gelid as he points a serrated sabre at Thiel.

'Show me your honour,' he hisses. 'Match swords with me, legionary!'

His armour scratched and scored, Thiel wearily eyes

the other warrior. Then he raises his pistol and guns the
Night Lord down.

'There's no room for honour here. Only vengeance,
only justice.'

Below, Petronius has secured the courtyard and fixed
charges to the main gate. A dull plosive tremor shakes
dust from the parapet's battle-worn crenellations.

Thiel activates the vox, as the armoured shapes below
hurry through the broken gate. 'Drenius, we're though.'

After a few seconds, the other sergeant replies.

'Head north-east, through a bank of silos.' He fights to
be heard over the air rushing across the feed. It sounds
like he's airborne and the side hatch is open. 'Follow the
roadway to a manufactorum. Two flak cannons, so we're keeping our distance.'

'Affirmative. We'll meet you at the outskirts, brother.
Touchdown and regroup with us there.'

An icon flashes up on Thiel's tactical display.

'I've laid a marker,' says Drenius. 'It's well fortified, Thiel.
They'll be dug in, now they know we're coming.'

Thiel smiles. 'It won't matter. They can't hide from
death.'

'There's something else…' Even through the vox, there's a
change in Drenius' demeanour. A sharpness. 'Their officer.
I have seen him, brother. I know him.'

Thiel guesses what Drenius is about to say.

'Harrakon Skurn.'

'He's mine, Thiel.'

Thiel nods slowly. He knows vengeance. He remembers Kurtha Sedd.

'I'll pave the way to his neck in blood. They'll all burn,
brother.'

✠ ✠ ✠

THE FLAK GUNS are torn apart in a flurry of glorious explosions, and *Spirit of Veridia* soars low across an ashen sky, its contrails blazing. The roar turns into a scream as its missile tubes ignite and a lethal payload streaks towards to the manufactory wall.

A chain of detonations stitches a line across a bulwark of plasteel and ferrocrete, leaving a gaping breach. The gunship gets lower, angling impudently towards the gap, heedless of the streamers of fire raining ineffectually against it.

Drenius' voice crackles over the vox. *'Thiel, I'll see you on the other side.'*

Thiel looks up at the Thunderhawk as it spears into the fiery darkness of the manufactory complex. 'Good hunting, brother-sergeant.'

'I feel reborn. Forged anew.'

'You sound like a Nocturnean,' Thiel laughs.

'I am an Ultramarine. Let us tear these bastards down, and with those same hands raise ourselves back up in the eyes of our Legion.'

Thiel is already running. Assuming Drenius' sabotage mission achieves its goal, he needs to take full advantage of the inevitable confusion that will follow.

Two flanks emerge from the Ultramarines' battle plan. Petronius, his willingness to lead and tempered aggression making him the perfect successor to Thaddeus, takes the right and the vanguard. Thiel has the left.

They rip through the outer defences with ruthless ease. The manufactory soldiers are poorly equipped and ill-disciplined. Many flee at the sight of the vengeful legionaries charging towards them.

A throaty rumble resonates overhead, and Thiel smells the stench of engine wash and heat before he sees *Spirit*

of Veridia roar back through the breach. Its part in the
assault is over.

Gantries and silos burn, and the air is choked on the
death of the vehicles ranked up in the assembly yard
where the Ultramarines are making their advance. Strategic missile strikes have destroyed most of the armour,
which was in the midst of refit and mechanical overhaul.

The centre of the yard is dominated by a tall column
that serves as an overseer's nest. About two-thirds of the
way up is a wide viewing ring that runs the entire circum-
ference of the column. Thiel gestures to it with his sword,
to the bulky silhouettes moving behind the dimmed
armourglass. 'Up there.'

A staggered ramp and stairway leads up to a pair of
blast doors in the nest.

'That's our objective. Whatever Nightfane is, the
answers are inside.'

Thiel has Inviglio and Bracheus behind him, moving past the wreckage of blazing tanks. Bodies litter the
ground, slumped against the armoured hides of Rhinos
or scattered in groups facing away from the battle. None
wear legionary war-plate. Few mortals ever have the stomach to face those that do.

Petronius' voice comes across the vox. *'Advancing right.'*

Thiel takes cover as the crack of bolter fire resounds
around him.

'Received. Circle around the column. I need some clearance to effect a breach.'

That just leaves Drenius. Over the tactical feed running
across Thiel's right lens, he sees that the other sergeant
has stalled somewhere up ahead.

'Venator, do you have eyes on Drenius?'

'Negative.' The marksman has moved into an advanced

position and taken high ground. *'He's deep, behind the nest.'*

'He's out for blood…' Inviglio mutters to himself.

'So are we,' replies Thiel, moving them on with a curt battle-sign.

Defenders are moving through the oil-black clouds spilling over the vehicle yard. A gout of burning promethium hits them before a single shot is fired in retaliation.

'Cleansed,' Bracheus grins.

Thiel acknowledges him, still pushing forwards. 'Keep going! Nothing stops us. We win or we die!'

He eyes Venator, who has just marked eight more targets on the tactical feed.

Inviglio sinks down next to Thiel as the Ultramarines take cover again. 'Renegades close. At least two squads.'

'We knew they'd be here in force.' Thiel sees them through the gaps in their sporadic fire. Word Bearers and Death Guard. 'Petronius, engage. We'll move on the primary target.'

There's a feral humour in Petronius' voice. *'With pleasure, sir.'*

Bracheus laughs. 'At least we haven't *completely* civilised him.'

Thiel nods to the blast doors. 'I want answers.'

Just beyond the column, Petronius has engaged the renegades. The fire fight is close, but has drawn the enemy off. The way is clear.

'Be ready to breach!'

ARMOURGLASS BLOWS OUTWARDS in a concussive wave. Thiel leads the squad through the breach and wastes no time in gutting the sentry too slow to raise his sword.

Inviglio and Venator gun down the others – two more stunned Word Bearers, reaching for their bolters.

Bracheus holds at the ruined blast doors, while Finius maintains position with his missile launcher at the head of the stairway.

In the middle of the circular room, a servitor is attempting an aggressive data-scrub of the facility's logic engine, infecting it with scrapcode. Thiel cleaves its cyborganic skull in two, silencing its machine chatter.

Instead it stammers out a phrase, over and over, through its damaged vox-grille.

'N-N-Nightfane. Nightfane-fane. N-Nightf-fane. Ni–'

Venator finally silences it with a bolt round.

Removing his helm, Thiel moves to the logic engine, retrieving what he can about Nightfane. He finds schematics, partially corrupted plans, lists of ships and troop dispositions.

There are many names he doesn't recognise. Malig Laestygon. The *Furious Abyss*. Janus Hellespont…

'This is a prelude to invasion. The silenced outposts provide a crucial blind zone for our enemies to exploit. Phraetius was to be their staging ground.'

'An invasion of where?' asks Inviglio.

'Where else? Macragge.'

'Guilliman's blood…'

'Aye, it might well have been.'

Venator calls out. 'Brother-sergeant!'

Thiel glances to where he is looking out through the shattered viewing ring. The marksman gestures, and Thiel follows his gaze.

Sergeant Drenius emerges from the smoke.

He duels Harrakon Skurn inside an inferno. The World Eater is as ferocious as the warrior Thiel fought and just as unhinged, but Drenius matches him with the refined skill of a swordmaster.

Thiel admires him – not for his blade-work, but his composure. The one who robbed his honour and cast him into disgrace stands before him, and yet Drenius looks calm as a statue.

Venator braces his bolter on the rim of the shattered ring, but Thiel puts a hand on the stock.

'I can execute that madman from here,' the legionary insists.

'I know. But I made an oath to Drenius. Skurn is his to kill.'

'What if he dies trying?'

'Then it will be with honour.'

So they watch as chain-teeth spit sparks and grind against one another. Drenius gives a muted cry as the World Eater breaks his guard and sinks his blade into the Ultramarine's shoulder.

The riposte is emphatic, though. Even half-cleaved, Drenius rams the point of his chainsword into the renegade's snarling mouth grille. Blood erupts in a spray, spattering down the blade, the teeth quickly clogging with gore.

But the World Eater's chain-teeth are still howling, the weapon's trigger locked in the renegade's death grip. They chew through Drenius' armour, ripping flesh and bone.

Thiel cries out, cursing himself. 'Shoot! Damn it, Venator – shoot!'

The bolt takes the World Eater in the chest, tearing apart his torso, but it's too late. Drenius slumps to his knees, wrenching the horrific chainblade from his chest while still clinging to his own weapon and using it as a crutch. Bleeding, beyond reach, surrounded by fire, he hails Thiel on the vox.

'It's over… brother…'

His breath and his words come in gasps, but he sounds at peace.

'We can reach you, Drenius!' Thiel replies.

The other sergeant shakes his head. 'I'm… done. Thank you, Thiel. For my… honour… For…'

The link falls silent. Thiel closes his eyes, then opens the squad-wide feed.

'We have what we came for. Phraetius is finished. We leave. Now.'

He spares a last glance at Drenius, on his knees but defiant even in death, before the smoke rolls in once more.

TEN CASKETS LIE in two equal rows in the middle of the chamber, waiting for an Apothecary. Thiel's breath ghosts in the cold air.

'It wasn't easy getting you back, brothers.'

He feels Bracheus' gauntleted hand on his shoulder. 'Their legacy will live on.'

'Ave legiones,' Thiel intones with a sigh. 'They sacrificed their lives for this. Now I must ask for others to do the same.' He allows a moment of silence before he turns to Inviglio. 'We are ready?'

'They are waiting, sergeant.'

A muted hubbub emanates through the barrack house doors. The last time Thiel was here, twenty-two legionaries swore their loyalty to him and his mission. They had halted an incursion, but the rot within Ultramar was far from excised. It would require more, much more.

Bracheus and Inviglio push open the heavy doors, allowing Thiel to step through.

Over two thousand legionaries stand in readiness. Every warrior of Oran garrison has mustered. Thiel sees Petronius and shares a nod with the warrior. He sees the others who followed him to Phraetius, amongst them Venator and Finius.

Captain Likane is here too, his war-helm in the crook of his arm and a sword sheathed at his side.

'I misjudged you, Thiel,' he says. 'I spoke ill, and recognise my error.'

'Sir, I–'

'You are a leader, Aeonid Thiel. Two thousand Ultramarines stand ready to heed your command. I am one of them. Lead *us*. We won't stand idle while Macragge and Ultramar are threatened. So, we shall all be Red-Marked.' Likane gestures to the assembled warriors. 'That's what you're calling yourselves, isn't it?'

Thiel smiles wryly, and nods.

'It is. You can join us. You can all be Red-Marked… *if* you're worthy.'

MASTER
OF THE FIRST

Gav Thorpe

THE COMMANDS OF the recruiting sergeants drifted through the open window, harsh alongside the bucolic hiss of the wind and the buzz of insects that drifted through the hot summer air. The clump of boots was almost perfectly in time. Almost, but not quite, and this became a cause for more shouting from the sergeants.

If he closed his eyes, Astelan could almost believe that he was back on the plains where he had been born. He *had* to close his eyes to ignore the towering fortifications of Aldurukh that surrounded him, and the comm-panels and data displays of the guard post command chamber. If he did that, concentrating on the flitting insects and the heat coming in through the narrow glass window, he could picture the broad waters of the Dynepri meandering between pale-leaved trees, and the silvery shimmer of the camp hab-covers reflected along her banks...

A chime came from the door panel, and the memories disappeared like the morning mist had on that fateful day, so many years ago.

Astelan opened the door locks. Though the Legion had brought many of the technological miracles of the Imperium to Caliban, much of Aldurukh remained unchanged, still using basic pre-Imperial systems and mechanics. The lack of voice-activation in particular still irked the Terran-born warrior.

The door slid open with a rumble of well-oiled gears, revealing Captain Melian, one of Astelan's company commanders. The captain bowed his head in greeting.

'Chapter Master, you wanted to see me?'

'Former Chapter Master, captain. My rank is still held in abeyance. My summons was in reply to your request that we might have a conversation in private.' Astelan waved a hand at the unthinking dials and screens and automated systems of the guard chamber. 'There is nobody here to observe us.'

Melian glanced at the open doorway. Astelan activated the control and the door groaned back into place. He gestured to Melian to speak.

'I... I am not sure how to express myself on the matter I wish to discuss. I have reservations.'

'Doubts?'

'Yes, doubts, Chapter Master. Regarding the Calibanites.'

'There are no Terrans and Calibanites any more, Melian. We are all Dark Angels.'

Melian did not have a chance to reply before an alert beeped onto one of the comm-panels, and Astelan turned to acknowledge the incoming message. He read it in silence.

'Hmm. Interesting.'

'What's that, Chapter Master?'

'A departure. The Lord Cypher and Brother-Librarian Zahariel, unscheduled shuttle run. Launch permission is sealed by Luther himself.'

'This is exactly what I mean,' Melian sighed. 'And why does Luther maintain this superfluous position of "Lord Cypher"? It's antiquated.'

Astelan scanned the details. The shuttle's flight plan was registered to take them west, but their trajectory was plotted for the northern transits. He said nothing to Melian, but it was a disturbing thought that Zahariel and Cypher were undertaking a secretive mission so near to the abandoned Northwilds arcology.

The sound of the shuttle's engine drifted away but it stirred Astelan's memory again. Melian shifted awkwardly.

'I am intruding, my lord. Forgive me.'

'I was just thinking, actually, of the day the Emperor's gunships fell upon my people. I remember the chatter of chain guns and the screams of the dying. The anti-air cannons on the backs of our megaphaunts thundered in reply, driving off the aerial attack, but soon the ground troops stormed in. Thunder Warriors, Melian – did you ever see their like?'

'I did not.'

'Crude compared to the warriors of the Legiones Astartes that would later recruit young Merir Astelan, but far stronger than any techno-barbarians that the poor Sibran nomad clans could muster. It was a massacre.'

'Did you not mourn your blood-kin?'

Astelan smiled. 'Only until I was recruited into the Emperor's Legion.'

'The First Legion.'

'The *only* Legion. I was one of the first five thousand. You will never know how it felt to claim that honour.'

Melian nodded respectfully. There were many Terrans within the ranks of the Dark Angels, but most had been recruited after other Legions had been founded. They were not the sharp arrowhead, but rather the shaft that followed it.

Astelan returned his attention to his subordinate.

'So, you were saying something about Calibanites?'

Melian's list of deficiencies and accusations was specific, and betrayed at least a year of cataloguing such misdemeanours.

'And you know, my lord, that not all the Calibanites are even Dark Angels. Well, not Space Marines.'

'You speak of Lord Luther and the others who were too old to become true legionaries?'

'I do. They should never have been part of the Legion.'

'Anything else?' Astelan asked, barely suppressing a sigh.

'No. I thank you for your time, Chapter Master – I am sorry to have wasted it. I knew you would not be interested. I did not wish to disturb you, and voiced my concerns to Brother-Captain Galedan instead. I have to admit, he told me to stop worrying about Luther and to concentrate on keeping my own company sharp for battle. Then, later, he suggested that I speak to you after all.'

Astelan regarded Melian carefully, disguising his interest with feigned boredom. There had to be a reason why Galedan had sent him to their Chapter Master. Perhaps he hoped Astelan would chastise the captain and dissuade him from further meddling.

Or was there more to it than that?

'Galedan was right that you come to me,' he assured Melian. 'You have spoken of incidents, infractions. But, more generally, what concerns you?'

'The recruits, my lord. They are being trained in the warfare of the Legiones Astartes, but they are being taught the old culture of Caliban. They are being raised more like knights of the Order.'

'The Order? The group that once took the young Lion as its Grand Master? It is defunct. Only a few titles and ceremonies remain, to honour the primarch's past.'

Melian's agitation grew and he strode to the window and gazed out, brow furrowing as he watched the Calibanite recruits below.

'It's more than that. There is no mention of the Emperor in the new oaths of dedication. The recruits swear to defend Caliban against all foes instead.'

'The Lion returned Luther to Caliban as its guardian. We no longer even have any warships – we are a defence force in all but name. The Lion will receive proper testimonies of allegiance, when he returns.'

'You approve of these changes?'

'I am ambivalent, Melian. Let us be honest, we've become irrelevant. The Lion sent us here to rot while Luther creates the Legion of tomorrow. A Legion from Caliban.'

Melian turned and shook his head, not in denial but annoyance.

'But you know the galaxy has changed. The last supply ships brought word of–'

'None of this matters! Those supply ships left years ago. We have been forgotten.' Astelan sighed. 'What do you want from me? Should I insist that Luther reinstate the old oaths? Should I conjure the Lion from the aether so that he can put things right?'

Looking away again, Melian hesitated. Astelan was about to berate him for wasting his time but some instinct told him to wait. There was more to this than a captain frustrated at being trapped on this Throne-forsaken world.

'You spoke to Galedan. Have you shared these thoughts with any others? Others that might feel the same as we do?'

'We? You agree with me then, my lord?'

'With your concerns? Of course. You know I have no particular love for the Calibanites and that my loyalty has ever been to the Emperor, first and foremost. The fact that we languish on this planet is proof of that. I often wonder if there was more to Luther's return than we know. But that is of no concern for now. Are there others that share our view?'

'Quite a few, I am glad to say. Mostly from the old Legion – from Terra, like us. But a few of the veteran Calibanites too. We've not yet decided on a course of action.'

'Action?' Astelan replied, glancing around. 'Careful, Melian – this is a dangerous path to walk. Luther is Grand Master now, second only to the Lion. He has unquestioned authority, legally if not morally.'

'Luther isn't the problem,' said Melian, voice dropping to a conspiratorial whisper, though there was no one to overhear them. 'We already know how we can isolate him, and remove him from power. It's the others, the recruits and those loyal to Luther, that cause the problem. They are too many, and we are too few to force the issue.'

Astelan thought for a moment. 'Then we need a mandate to act. The only way we can get that is from off-world. A message from Terra, or perhaps even the primarch himself, would go a long way towards justifying what needs to be done. If Luther has no authority to remain, his followers will back whatever action you take to remove him.'

'You really think we might be able to do something?'

'I confess I did not know there was wider support for our opinions. It would help your cause a lot if a former Chapter Master, one appointed by the Emperor and held in high regard in the old Legion, was to be the figurehead.'

Melian nodded. 'Your experience, your reputation, would be a tremendous boost to our efforts, Chapter Master.'

'It is settled then. I need you to assemble a gathering. Not everyone, just the officers who can speak confidently for the forces under their command. I'll leave the details to you. You know these loyal warriors best, and I am sure you'll continue with the same circumspect approach. Best not to invoke my name at this stage, until we know who we can trust.'

'As you wish. I am truly grateful for your understanding and participation, my lord. I know we face a difficult time, but with your leadership we shall return the Legion to the right path.'

'I am sure of it, captain.'

When Melian had left, Astelan used the comm-panel to establish an unlogged, secure vox-link.

'Galedan, report to the guard post immediately.'

AS THE HATCHWAY of the magazine creaked open, the soft conversation within fell to silence. The room was emptied of stores save for just a few boxes scattered on the metal shelving units. Astelan stepped over the threshold, to be greeted by more than a dozen pairs of inquiring eyes in the yellow gleam of the artificial lights. He recognised most of the faces – half of them he had fought alongside for almost two centuries. A few, Calibanites to a man, were unknown to him, but he had to trust in

Melian's judgement. They were all of company command rank and higher. Two of them, Neriedes and Temur, were Chapter Masters – like his, their commands had been suspended for undisclosed reasons.

Melian moved to the front of the crowd and held up his hands.

'Brothers, Master Astelan is the reason you have been brought here. He is sympathetic to our cause, and desired to be heard.'

There were no objections. Astelan took this as his cue to speak.

'We are all here because we share a certain viewpoint – an opinion regarding the nature of the Dark Angels Legion and what it means to be a true servant of the Emperor. These past years have been hard, but we have borne our reduced status with stoic dignity, as would be expected of any warrior of the First Legion.'

There were murmurs of agreement. He went on.

'But a time is approaching when such stoicism will not be enough. A tipping point will come. Those who believe in what the Emperor has created must face a choice, or else be swept up by events beyond our control.'

Temur, a long-serving Terran legionary with a bionic left arm and a heavily scarred face, stepped forwards, his voice electronically rendered through a vox-grille. There was a hint of confrontation in his expression, a testing of Astelan's assured demeanour.

'And you are the one to lead us past this tipping point, Merir?'

'I will force nothing upon you, that is not my purpose. I come only with a suggested course of action. If you adopt it, I expect you to follow my lead until it is done.'

'Very well, what do you propose?'

Astelan put a finger to the vox-bead in his ear. 'Please, come in.'

Brighter light broke into the dimness as the hatchway opened again, silhouetting a short, slender woman in the uniform of the Imperial Army auxilia that had been stationed on Caliban since the arrival of the Imperium.

She pulled off her cap to reveal greying auburn hair cropped close to the scalp, and nodded in deference to the Space Marines that greeted her with suspicious looks. Her dress jacket bore the badges of high rank, and the ribbons of several meritorious awards and combat medals.

'My lords.'

Astelan closed the hatch behind the woman and took up a relaxed stance next to her, dwarfing the officer with his bulk.

'Marchesa-Colonel Bethalin Tylain, my brothers. If you do not know her, she is vice-commander of the garrison forces. Redundant on a world now populated by more than thirty thousand battle-ready legionaries, you will agree – but she shares our concerns about Luther's loyalties.'

Temur looked unimpressed. 'The garrison is not enough to swing the balance of military power in our favour. What use is she to us?'

Astelan did not speak, but looked at Lady Tylain, nodding for her to answer the question.

'The Caliban defence force regiments were created to provide internal and planetary security,' she explained, 'allowing the warriors of the Legion to prosecute their own wars safe in the knowledge that the home world was secure. These duties have, as Master Astelan put it, become redundant with the presence of so many legionaries on

Caliban. Since the unrest at the Northwilds, we and the Jaegers have been rendered mostly ceremonial, restricted to the guarding of non-Legion facilities.'

There was discontented muttering, and Astelan held up a hand.

'Silence, brothers. Lady Tylain is a senior officer of the Imperial Army and is deserving of your attention and respect. This behaviour is symptomatic of the division and poor discipline brought about by our extended posting here. You would do well to lead better by example.'

Some of the officers looked suitably chagrined, Temur amongst them. A few glared in irritation at Astelan, but no further objections were raised and Lady Tylain continued.

'While the Dark Angels maintain their own chantry within the walls of Aldurukh, there is another astropath tower located not far from the Rock for the use of Imperial personnel, mercantile interests and the like. Since the unforeseen removal of the Northwilds administrators, the tower at Redevakh has gone largely unused, and is most likely forgotten. The guarding of this facility falls to a corps of the defence forces under my command.'

Astelan could see the glimmering of understanding in the eyes of the others, and took up the final part of the explanation.

'Captain Melian informs me that there are already plans afoot to isolate and confine Luther. While that is in progress, another task force consisting of our loyal companies will secure the tower at Redevakh, and will send messages both to Terra and to our primarch. We seek confirmation that original Legion protocols are to be restored and, in the absence of the Lion, the former command structure is to be reinstated until his return.'

Melian raised a hand and Astelan nodded, granting him permission to speak. 'Warp communication has been sparse, almost impossible for several years, my lord. I am sure it is the only reason we have received no word from the primarch's fleet.'

'Which is why we must take the tower with a sizeable force. With Luther removed from command, there are few of his senior officers that would be willing to initiate conflict between different elements of the Legion. The day-to-day defence of Caliban and the ongoing recruitment process will continue unaffected, but we will have restored access to external communication. Communication that is currently the sole purview of Luther and his coterie from the Order. Who knows what communiqués they have withheld from us, until now?'

A thin smile on his lips, Temur nodded in appreciation.

'Apologies, Merir – I think I did you a disservice. Forgive my earlier doubts. Your plan seems eminently suitable, avoiding direct conflict with the bulk of Luther's forces whilst securing our own position. I do have just one further remark.'

'Please, speak freely.'

'You mentioned that we would reinstate the standard Legion protocols and structure until the Lion's return. Correct me if I am wrong, but with Luther removed would that not make you the highest and longest-serving officer of the Legion? You would, I believe, become a Legion Master...'

Silence fell. Astelan shrugged.

'It had occurred to me, to be truthful,' he replied. 'I was marked for leadership before we discovered Caliban and the old Legion hierarchy was altered to the Wings. To allay any fears about my ambition, in the event that we are successful and a restructuring of the Legion takes place, I must insist that a council of Chapter Masters confirm *any* promotion.'

Tokumon looked at the others and though there were some doubtful faces, most of the officers nodded their assent. 'I cannot see any further objections at this point. We will continue to sound out those under our command to identify any who cannot be counted upon in the days ahead. We will find suitably distracting duties for them when the time comes to make our move.'

As the gathering broke up, the Space Marines leaving in ones and twos, Lady Tylain turned to Astelan.

'It seems we have a consensus, my lord. I confess I did not expect things to go so smoothly.'

'Be careful what you say – there are plenty of opportunities for complications still to come. Remember what I told you. Luther must not have any suspicions of what we are doing, or why. Surprise is essential.'

'Why thank you, Chapter Master,' she said with a sneer. 'And perhaps you would like to instruct me on how to field-strip a lasgun too?'

Astelan offered no apology and the marchesa-colonel did not wait for one. Melian came up to him just as she left.

'She has a wicked tongue at times, Chapter Master. You should not accept such insolence.'

'I need her assistance,' Astelan replied. 'Better that she feels in control. For now, at least.'

Melian leaned closer and spoke more quietly.

'Forgive me, Chapter Master, but I could not help but notice Galedan's absence.'

'As Master Temur said, there are some that perhaps would not agree with our decisions today. I spoke with

Galedan, and thought it prudent that he... received different orders.'

'A shame. I liked Galedan.'

'I am sure he will come to our way of thinking soon enough. For now, do not speak to him again of your concerns. Let him think that I have silenced them.'

'As you wish. And what would you have me do next?'

Astelan placed a hand on Melian's shoulder. 'Nothing, other than keep your eyes and ears open.'

'And you, Chapter Master, what are you going to do?'

'Mustering a sizeable number of armed legionaries so close to Redevakh is going to arouse interest. I have a training exercise to organise. Live ammunition, of course.'

IT WAS PERHAPS a sign of Luther's growing arrogance that although he commanded tens of thousands of the Legion's finest, only five of their number were tasked with guarding his private quarters in the citadel of Aldurukh.

Confronted by three Chapter Masters and the same number of company captains with pistols and blades drawn, it was little surprise that they chose not to fight – except one. Astelan watched with detached resignation as the warrior at the security console outside the doors drew his sword.

He hung back, allowing Temur to take the lead.

'Stand aside, by order of your superiors!'

The warrior vaulted the console, slashing his sword towards Temur's neck. 'For Caliban, and the Order!'

The Chapter Master, who had fought in more than a hundred campaigns, blocked the strike easily and, with similar lack of effort, turned his blade back and held it against the legionary's throat.

'Do you yield?'

Temur's demand was made while the others were being disarmed by Neriedes and the rest. The legionary's only reply was a wordless snarl and a fist, which glanced from Temur's breastplate as he stepped back.

A second later, the Chapter Master's energy-wreathed sword protruded from the warrior's chest, illuminating his face from below with a blue aura, his features a mask of pained surprise. Temur pulled the blade free with a look of genuine regret, letting the body clatter to the floor. Neriedes and Astelan accepted the necessity of the Space Marine's death without reaction, but the lesser captains paled, realising only now that their coup could never have been bloodless.

That was the tipping point, Astelan noted. There could be no turning back for them.

He pushed forwards to the security console while the remaining captives were secured with electro-manacles.

'No alarm raised, no lockdown.'

His fingers moved across the keypad and behind him the security bolts on the doors snapped open.

Temur's blood was up and he led the way, thrusting open the double doors without delay. They searched the reception hall and the bedchamber and found them empty, although reports had confirmed that Luther would be in his quarters at that hour. Only one room remained – the Grand Master's sanctum, located on the floor above.

Astelan was the last up the stairwell, power sword and bolt pistol at the ready. When Temur reached the doorway at the top he did not pause, but crashed shoulder-first into the timbers, splitting the jamb and sending the door splintering from its hinges.

Luther was stood at a high window, looking south

across the lower halls and towers of Aldurukh. He had been a large man, broad at the shoulders, thick at the neck, even before the augmentations wrought upon him by the Legion's Apothecaries. There was a dry, cracked quality to his skin, and artificially reinforced veins bulged in his neck as he tensed.

The Grand Master of the Order held a large book bound in deep red leather, a small dagger used as a bookmark on the open pages. He snapped the book shut and turned calmly, his expression guarded as he looked at the intruders with a raised eyebrow.

'What manner of entrance is this? If you had but asked, I would gladly have granted you an audience.'

Temur was in no mood for Luther's humour, and held his bolt pistol to the Grand Master's head. 'By the authority of the Emperor of Mankind, I charge you with perverting command of the First Legion, for insubordination to the orders of your primarch, and sundry other charges to be detailed at a later time. You are to disarm yourself and relinquish all command of Caliban and its forces.'

Luther's gaze settled on Astelan, standing by the door.

'You too, Merir? I thought you were wiser than this. Do you know what manner of calamity you are about to unleash? You cannot possibly believe that this farce will succeed.'

'I thought you might harbour doubts about my sincerity,' Astelan replied. 'Permit me to allay them.' He placed a small hololithic receiver on the desk and activated his vox. 'Begin transmission.'

It was Lady Tylain that answered. '*Connection established, Chapter Master. Ready to move on your command.*'

The hololith sprang into life, showing a needle-like

tower that rose from lightly forested hills. Luther looked more closely at the grainy image. 'Redevakh? The astro-path facility...'

'It is.'

Astelan manipulated the display to focus on the main valley leading to the tower. Several thousand legionar-ies were advancing through the hills, flanked by battle tanks and walkers from the defence force. Even in the projected light of the hololith, it was clear that most of the Space Marines were clad in the black livery of the original Terran Chapters, but some sported plates of dark green showing that they had been raised on Caliban.

Luther straightened, his expression unreadable.

'I see.'

'Not yet. Continue to observe.' Astelan activated the link again. 'Marchesa-colonel, please execute your orders. This instruction cannot be countermanded.'

'*Affirmative, Chapter Master. All units are in position, commencing action immediately. Let us hope that history remembers us fondly, or not at all.*'

The lead elements of the rebel Space Marine force were almost in position when a succession of bright flashes broke the gloom beneath the treeline. A moment later detonations bloomed among the ranks of advancing warriors, followed almost instantly by the reverberat-ing impacts of shells over the vox-link. The escorting armoured vehicles ploughed to a stop, and turned their turrets on the Dark Angels.

Jets screamed in from the clouds and more tanks rumbled into view while detachments of defence force soldiers emerged from the trees at a run. With them was a full Chapter of Space Marines, the company banner of Captain Galedan flying above the command section.

More concussive blasts shook the advancing rebels as bombs and tank cannons laid down a carpet of destructive fire.

Temur was aghast. 'Damn them, what are they doing?'

He and the other rebel officers in the sanctum chamber were transfixed by the holo-display, but Luther's stare snapped up to Astelan. In that instant, there was recognition in his eyes.

Armour shattered and flesh sizzled as Astelan's first cut took off Temur's pistol hand. Luther was already moving towards Neriedes, the dagger from the book held before him. Astelan's sword parted Temur's throat even as he turned in shock towards his attacker, and a third strike lanced through the chest of Captain Azraphal. Luther pushed the point of the dagger into Neriedes' left eye, driving it up to the hilt in the socket as he rode the collapsing Space Marine to the ground.

The bark of bolt pistols seemed deafening in the confines of the chamber and Astelan flinched, feeling an impact on his left pauldron. He spun and returned fire, dropping Captain Gosswyn at close range.

Captain Orhn backed away from him, readying his sword to strike instead at Luther, before the Grand Master could rise. Astelan did not hesitate, hacking off the captain's head with two ragged blows.

He glanced back at the hololith, seeing the rebel ranks capitulating to Galedan and Lady Tylain. Surrounded by Imperial armour divisions and their Legion brothers, with devastating airpower above, Astelan did not blame them.

'I hoped more of them would surrender...' he murmured breathlessly.

Luther watched them throwing down their weapons,

the column disintegrating in shame before Astelan's forces. The vox-link brought confirmation from Lady Tylain.

'*Captain Galedan is formally accepting the surrender, Chapter Master. The rebels have little desire to fight other Space Marines. My forces will continue to provide overwatch and support.*'

'My thanks, marchesa-colonel,' Astelan replied. 'You have done us a great service today. Have the rebels brought to Aldurukh for the judgement of Lord Luther.'

Luther grunted in derision. 'Twice-cursed, to be traitors *and* cowards. However, I praise your foresight in not ordering them all executed.'

'It seemed wasteful. They might be taught to see the error of their ways. I hear that the Order can be... very persuasive.'

'Indeed. Though I am not sure where we will keep so many prisoners.'

'There are dungeons beneath the Rock. I suggest you carve out more cells.'

Luther turned his head to regard Astelan coldly. 'Why not alert me to this uprising before now? All bloodshed could have been avoided, had you informed me when you first learned of the rebellion.'

'I drew out those truly committed to your downfall. Open action against you justifies this response, without question.'

'And at what point did you choose to betray them?'

'I prefer to think that I "remained loyal", my lord,' Astelan replied, bowing his head.

'You did not answer the question.'

'From the outset, of course.'

'I find that curious. You are Terran, and your distaste

for Caliban and its people is known. Was it out of loyalty? Perhaps you saw that the rebellion was doomed
from the beginning and wished to curry favour with the
winning side. Was power your desire, to return to the
glories of command and… relevance?'

'Nothing so devious, my lord. My reasons for support-
ing you are simple – I do not know everything that has
transpired between you and the Lion, but I can tell that
you no longer work to his aims.'

Astelan gathered his thoughts.

'When the Emperor exterminated my people, I did not
lament. I saw that the execution of power could be righteous, even if it brought misery. To oppose it was pointless,
a meaningless act of vanity that would end in death. When
I was drawn into the Legion, I became a facet of that
power – an element of its application. Now I see that a
different power is rising, and it is similarly futile to decry
it.' He rested his sword's tip upon the floor. 'I prefer action
to clever words, Grand Master. The Lion is a taint. All
that has befallen the First Legion since we discovered your
benighted world is due to his misguided influence. To
oppose him, to set myself against the woes he has caused
us, I would pledge allegiance to a more worthy lord. Tell
me I was wrong, that you are fully committed and loyal
to the primarch, and I will join those prisoners right now.'

Luther's thoughtful silence proclaimed more than any
words ever could.

THE REBEL LEGIONARIES were interred in barracks and
guard rooms, watched over by Luther's troops, while the
most senior dissenters were escorted to the cells beneath
Aldurukh. Astelan waited at the main gate with Galedan,
watching the procession of dejected warriors filing past.

'Luther approved your promotion to Chapter Master, then.'

'He did,' Galedan replied. 'The first favours spilling from the hand of our new overlord?'

'No. Confirmation that he shares my faith in you.'

Astelan saw Melian, but the captain turned his head away in disgust, not willing even to look at his former master. Astelan looked back to Galedan.

'I'm glad he survived.'

'Melian? Yes, he's a good captain – it's a shame he got himself caught up in this mess. He'll be useful later.'

'Later? What do you mean?'

'You can't fool me, brother. I know that Luther is our ally for the moment, but don't expect me to believe for a second that you really think he is your *superior*.'

'I am shocked at the suggestion,' Astelan replied. 'There can only be *one* Master of the First. I will not suffer the Lion any longer, so that leaves us with Luther.'

Galedan looked unconvinced, and Astelan could not meet his gaze without a smile.

'For now, at least.'

STRATAGEM

Nick Kyme

Footsteps echo down a solemn hallway, foreshadowing his arrival. Phosphor lamps flicker, burning low, snapping at the darkness.

This is the second time he has walked this public gallery to the Residency, or so he has been told. The first time he did so accompanied by a squad of nine others clad in cobalt-blue. Now, he walks alone and his armour plate is not so marred by war. *That* suit is missing, and has been since he returned to Macragge. He had intended it as a gift, but it is lost now to whatever petty bureaucracies hold sway over Ultramar, taken by servitors the moment he arrived.

A procession of eyes is upon him. They stare from marble countenances, half hidden by alcoves, and he cannot help but feel the judgement in their gaze. He is not given to whimsy – it isn't practical – but he wonders if they recognise him from the other that claimed his name.

A portal looms ahead, rendered in steel and brass. Gold

engraving describes the foremost Battle King of Macragge on the large wooden doors. It is Konor, father to Roboute Guilliman. The artisan has captured a stately but fierce aspect in the work. Perhaps this is what awaits Thiel on the other side.

He finds it curious that this place holds with tradition and retains the old cultural style of Macragge. Everywhere else now claims a broader aesthetic, as if stone and steel can speak to the alliance of many Legions and make them one under the unified ideal of Imperium Secundus.

He wonders if this is why he is here, to discuss his role, to suffer further censure for what he has been doing since coming back from Calth.

Two of the Invictus guard the doors, bringing him back to the present.

'Relinquish your weapons, brother-sergeant,' barks one.

Their purpose is singular, clad in all-encompassing XIII Legion Terminator plate, visors down, bladed polearms barring entry. They are protectors, but there is an underlying tension to their movements and the tone of their words that hints at a past failure.

They take his battle-helm, that he has clasped in the crook of his arm. He hands it over without hesitation.

The blade upon his back, the longsword, they let him keep. This is also curious. Another unanswered question to add to the many already posed. So many theoreticals – it should not make him this edgy.

At an unseen signal, the guards step aside and the doors yawn open. Thiel steps quickly across the threshold before they shut behind him again.

Shadows persist in the Residency. They have been allowed to remain in an effort to mask the damage. Less so are the scars of the attack, the fractional splinters still embedded in the wood of picture frames, or the dust from the shattered bust of Konor only recently restored. More is the pride of a primarch blinded by misplaced sentiment and hubris.

Roboute Guilliman cuts a powerful, impressive figure. The primarch is standing next to his desk. Fresh stone from the Hera's Crown Mountains making up its impressive mass has been recently freighted to the Residency. Some areas are lighter, more lustrous than others. New replacing old. There are many scrolls and papers upon it – a diligent, exhaustive work.

'Sergeant Thiel.'

The primarch gives only a curt greeting, though the brightness of his eyes suggests more warmth as they assess and calculate.

Ceremonial armour has replaced his battleplate, a deliberate statement of confidence over protection. The plastron carries the ubiquitous Ultima of the Legion, a pair of shoulder guards clamp a crimson cloak in place. He has neither bolt pistol nor blade.

I am not afraid, it says. *This is, and shall always be, my domain.*

'My lord,' says Thiel, and bows.

Guilliman smiles but his strong jaw is set. Parts of his fair hair look uneven in colour, lighter in places where the healed wounds have left it inexplicably mismatched.

Wounds heal, scars do not.

Another armoured figure watches from the shadows, but Thiel pretends not to notice. A new life-ward, possibly? He doesn't detect the scent of wet canine, so it can't be Faffnr. Maybe Drakus Gorod has finally convinced Guilliman that he needs a shadow.

'May I see the sword?'

Thiel obeys and draws it from his back. Its blade catches the low light and flashes brightly. He briefly activates the electromagnetic edge. It is not a flinch that Thiel sees in the primarch but there is a reaction, a subtle tremor in the cheekbone.

'Do you wish it returned?' Thiel asks.

Guilliman gives a single shake of his head. 'Sheathe it, Aeonid. It is your blade now.'

Thiel wants to thank him but it would seem churlish to do so when he stole the weapon in the first place. Instead, he nods and graciously accepts the gift. The sound of the blade deactivating punctuates a brief but awkward silence between father and son.

'May I speak freely, my lord?'

'Of course. Do you wish to sit?' Guilliman offers Thiel a chair as he sits down behind the desk, ostensibly at ease.

'I would prefer to stand.'

Guilliman shrugs as though it matters not.

'Was it in here that it happened?' asks Thiel.

'I think you already know the answer to that.'

'Then why come back? Why not take greater precaution? Why relive it?'

'Because a lord must be at his ease in his own domain. This is my private residence. I won't let it become a prison cell with Gorod and Euten as my wardens.' Guilliman steeples his fingers. His gaze is stern, penetrating. 'When a legionary claiming your name last walked into this chamber, he came to kill me. He did not come alone – nine of his comrades were with him. I invited them in. I survived. That's powerful. It sends a message. I want it to resonate.'

The primarch's outward confidence and disdain will dissuade, not encourage, another attempt. It is a very practical reaction, reminding Thiel how fiercely intelligent his father is, how he is always calculating, assessing, planning. To think on it is staggering.

Guilliman points to the large windows that overlook Macragge Civitas.

'Do you see beyond that glass, Aeonid?'

It is night and much of the city's magnificence is shrouded in darkness but one structure dominates this vista, made visible by stark ground illumination.

'The Fortress of Hera.'

'Aye,' Guilliman murmurs. 'The seat of an emperor who does not take up his throne on the counsel of his men.'

'Lord Sanguinius.'

'Finding my brother is no easy task. I know the Lion has had some difficulty of late.'

He smiles at that. His intent and his mind are difficult to discern, but Thiel thinks he detects some fraternal rivalry and amusement at the Lion's misfortune.

'I realise I have enemies at large amongst what is left of the Five Hundred Worlds,' the primarch continues, 'but I refuse to show them anything other than my defiance and power.'

Another tremor. Anger this time, not trepidation. The statesman in Guilliman counsels consolidation and the raising of an empire, but the warrior still demands vengeance.

Thiel knows that such a debt could never be paid. It does not stop him from trying, though.

'Is that why we still contest Calth, to send a message?'

Putting his palms flat on the desk, Guilliman narrows his eyes.

'You and I adopt a different position on this matter, a fact well known to us both.' He pauses to emphasise his impatience. 'What is it you really want to ask me, Aeonid?'

Deception is not Thiel's forte, so he opts for the truth. 'Why am I here?'

'Because I need your help with something.'

'I am at your service, lord.'

Guilliman smiles again. It is warmer this time, but hides something deeper. To the primarch's credit, he doesn't wait long to reveal what it is. 'Tell me, Sergeant Thiel, what are the "Red-Marked"?'

Thiel allows himself an indulgent grin. 'Is that what they are calling us?'

'Us? So you admit the existence of this group?'

'I do. I formed them, my lord. Volunteers only, men who can be spared–'

'Is it not *my* decision who can be spared, Aeonid?'

Thiel bows his head, but quickly raises it again. He does not wish to wallow long in contrition.

'I saw what was necessary and acted.'

Guilliman tries but cannot fully mask the admiration he feels at his sergeant's temerity. It is what makes Thiel such a singular warrior.

'And what, in your eyes, is necessary?'

Thiel answers boldly. 'The defence of our realm and borders. You said yourself, lord – you have enemies. I agree. They are hiding in the ruins of our former worlds. Some have vessels and gather in warbands. Left unchallenged, they will unite once more. The Red-Marked are dedicated to rooting out these renegades.'

Guilliman leans forwards. 'Tell me about the Red-Marked, Aeonid. How do they operate?'

It is unusual to be questioned by someone who would

normally provide the answers, to be pressed for knowledge by such a peerless leader and tactician.

Nevertheless, Thiel answers.

'Smaller divisions. Two or three squads, sometimes fewer.'

'It is faster that way? Deployment, reactivity?'

'Yes, it provides flexibility. One legionary can do the job of many in some situations.'

'Thus removing redundancy,' Guilliman asserts.

Thiel nods again.

'And their composition?' asks the primarch.

'Adaptable. Tactical with provision for almost countless potentialities,' says Thiel. 'I assigned a specialist to every squad.'

'So you broke with convention and ignored the tenets of the Principia Bellicosa.'

This statement rings like an accusation to Thiel's ears. He expects to suffer sanction.

'I did, my lord. If I have erred then I–'

'No, Thiel,' Guilliman cuts him off, 'you have not. I want to give this endeavour my support. Take the men you need for the Red-Marked, cleanse our lawless borders and know that you shall receive the authority you require.'

Authority.

Thiel glances at the other figure in the room, the one he has been ignoring until now, the one who has neither moved nor spoken since he entered the Residency.

'Is this the reason why we are not alone?' Thiel gestures to the silent warrior. A stronger, more experienced – no, *less reckless* – hand at the tiller, no doubt. 'Please introduce us, lord, and tell me which worthier legionary is to be my superior.'

Guilliman laughs. 'You misinterpret my intent, Aeonid.'

A directed lumen ignites, throwing light onto the legionary that Thiel assumed was his replacement. He recognises the empty armour, because it belongs to him – a suit of battleplate inscribed with Thiel's own tactical argot.

Guilliman stands. 'Your gift?'

'One I thought lost.'

'Do you know what this is?' Guilliman makes a sweeping gesture across the many scrolls and papers on his desk. 'Tactics, doctrine… *Stratagem*, Aeonid.'

He approaches the armour.

'These markings…' Guilliman traces them with his eyes, absorbing and cogitating. He looks up and says something that Thiel never thought he would hear from his primarch's lips. 'I recognise the tactics they describe, but I can see a methodology emerging from them I had not considered before. Does the juxtaposition of one stratagem to another have meaning also? I believe there are correlations to my own work.'

Thiel is bewildered by his primarch's ability to decipher meaning and even interpret fresh purpose from such an idiosyncratic set of instructions. He had not considered for himself how the relative position of each piece of tactical doctrine could affect another. He answers as fully as he can.

'I used it as the foundation for the Red-Marked. Every practical, everything I learned on Calth.'

'A smaller, more flexible structure. Expertise spread amongst squads, not divisions and companies.'

Thiel nods, realising that he will need to provide little to no spur to Guilliman's formidable logic.

'We were few, and fighting a guerrilla war. It is the same for the Red-Marked. Practically, it made sense.'

'Efficacy?'

'Exceeding an acceptable mean.'

'Optimal, then.'

'Situationally speaking, yes.'

Guilliman is voracious in his appetite for knowledge. His intellect and military mind has uncovered a partial revelation, one he wishes to embrace, adapt, hone and modify to strategic perfection.

Thiel realises that *he* is the catalyst for this quantum leap in his father's unfathomable thought process, and cannot help but feel humbled.

'I have been wrong about several things...' Guilliman returns to his desk and gathers up the scrolls and papers. He tears them apart, intending it as a gesture rather than a practical means of destroying them.

Thiel's horror is obvious.

'What are you doing? That is your doctrine, your work!'

'It is flawed, Aeonid, and it took you to show me the error in it.'

'It is? I mean... I did?'

'To function as we have, in our unwieldy Legions, is no longer tenable. I thought these tenets inviolate. I believed them to be the most efficient way to deploy and yoke our strength in battle. But in my hidebound blindness, I missed the utility that was in front of my very eyes.' Guilliman nods at Thiel. 'You, Aeonid.'

Thiel frowns. 'I do not follow, my lord.'

'We are not akin to the armies of old, a warlord and the horde that follows him. We are not one Legion, not any more.' Guilliman smiles and his eyes alight with belligerent possibility. 'We are hundreds of thousands of individual legionaries, each in support of the others, adapting, reshaping. Moulded not to a single purpose but to many, to *any* and *all*.'

Thiel is taken aback. He has never seen his primarch so animated. Guilliman isn't finished.

'Until I saw the armour, and heard of your Red-Marked, I thought us a hammer. We are, we can be, but we do not *need* to be.' He makes a fist, making as if to deliver a mighty blow. 'A hammer takes effort to heft with skill. It requires strength. It is inefficient, profligate.' He opens his hand again, fingers straight and knifelike. 'A rapier kills with a single thrust. Surgical. Efficient. Deadly.' He punctuates each word as if stabbing them. 'We must become the quick death, the blade stroke to the heart.'

Guilliman approaches Thiel. He places a hand upon his shoulder, looking down at his son, grateful for the revelation he has given him.

'You are the practical to this theoretical, Aeonid.'

They part as Guilliman turns his back, his thoughts laid open for Thiel to hear.

'Lorgar outmatched me once. I had no theoretical that countenanced his treachery and no practical responses ready. That won't happen again. Practical, theoretical... Fresh thinking must prevail over these outmoded concepts. We must become more *tactical*.'

Thiel finds that he agrees, and asks the obvious question. 'How?'

Guilliman turns and faces him once again.

'The Codex, the sum of all practical knowledge and its application. For if this war has taught me anything, it is the danger of hubris. That is *your* wisdom, Thiel.'

Thiel bows and sinks to one knee, overwhelmed. His pride overflows.

'You honour me beyond all possible aspiration.'

'That is well, for you have earned it. Now rise. Our work begins now, in earnest. I have a Codex to finish. Your insight has inspired me, and the future of the Legions will not wait.'

THE LONG
NIGHT

Aaron Dembski-Bowden

'JAGO.' THE GIRL'S voice breaks the silence. 'Are you still alive?'

Sevatar sits with his back to the crackling force barrier, ignoring its incessant caress. Around him, only darkness. Not the darkness of a sunless night, but a blackness so absolute that even his eyes cannot pierce its veil. They keep him in this lightless cage, deactivating the barriers and awakening the illumination globes for fifteen minutes each day cycle. That's when he's permitted to eat. They bring him nutrient-rich gruel that tastes of bland chemicals and sticks to his tongue like wet sawdust. He grins at his captors every time, telling them it's the finest thing he's ever eaten, and that each meal is better than the last.

There's comfort here in the darkness of his prison cell. Like silk against his bare skin, the blackness soothes his aching eyes. Unfortunately it does nothing for the pounding throb straining its way through his skull. Since his

369

capture, only her voice has relieved the pain. Just one voice among many – the voices of the slain, dredged from his subconscious.

Sevatar has dreamed of the dead a hundred times and more. In those first heartbeats after waking, he sees their staring eyes in the darkness of his cell, and hears the echo of their cries inside his skull.

None of it is real. He knows that.

In the long watches of the night, boredom is his only true companion. The dead lie in their graves, silent and rotting, righteously punished. When he hears them in his restless sleep, it is nothing but the misfiring throb of his own imprisoned dreams.

'Jago? Are you still alive?'

But not her. Her voice is the only one that lingers when he wakes. Stronger than any other echo. It has been a long, long time since he spoke with a ghost, and he wonders if she died in this very cell, with her shade now lingering within its walls. Perhaps she was killed nearby, and she comes to him now because her spirit smells his curse. She clings to him, the echoing voice of a strange and curious child, whispering to a murderer in the dark. He doubts she even realises she's dead.

'Jago?'

'I am here,' he says to the cold air. There is blood running from his nose, hot and thick and slow. He wipes it away with the back of his hand. 'I am here, Altani.'

'Is it the pain again?'

It takes effort to speak past the pressure grinding down on his brain meat, but he forces the lie past his lips. 'It has been worse.'

'It feels like you're dying.'

He chuckles at that, but doesn't deny it. 'I am still here for now. What do you want?'

'Just to talk. I'm lonely.'

'I am sorry to hear that, little one.' He hesitates, already uncomfortable yet wishing to keep her near for a while longer. Is this the fourth time she has come to him? The fifth? The pressure in his head defies his attempts to focus on even mundane tasks like tracking the passing of time. 'Yours is the only voice I welcome. Did you know that?'

'I don't understand. You hear other voices? Even when you are awake? I thought they came only in your dreams.'

'Yes, and no.' He shrugs in the darkness, a futile gesture if ever there was one. As a child, he had always heard voices. The sounds of desire and anger inside other people's skulls. The murmuring emotions that boiled behind their eyes. The raucous songs of the city's crows as they fought over food.

Worse than any of them was the whispering of the dead. The burning flashes of someone else's memories when he glanced into the eyes of a body in the gutter. The pleas of unseen voices, begging for him to avenge them. The strangling red torment he would feel in his throat when he passed beneath one of the Night Haunter's victims hanging in public, disembowelled and crucified.

Sometimes they would speak with him, in that nameless place between slumber and consciousness.

Telepathy. Necromancy. Psychometry. A thousand cultures had a thousand words for such psychic gifts, but the words themselves didn't matter. All of the music of sentient thought had been his to hear, until the Legion sealed it away, leaving him in blessed silence.

No longer did he overhear others' thoughts.

No more did he hear the beckoning offers of the slain.

Yet now the dead begin to whisper once again. The seals around his mind are breaking.

'Jago? Do you hear the other voices when you're awake?'

'I have a gift. One I do not want. One I tried very hard to lose, long ago.'

'That isn't what I asked, Jago. I know you have the talent. How else do you think we are speaking like this?'

His skin crawls at her knowing tone. 'What child has the right to sound so knowledgeable about such things?'

'I watch,' she says, as calmly and peaceably as ever. 'I listen. No wonder you're in so much pain. Did you truly seek to banish your talent?'

'I tried. And for a time, I succeeded.'

'It cannot be banished. To try damages the brain, the heart and the soul.'

'I was willing to risk it, Altani.'

'But why?'

'Those with a sixth sense among my brethren are hollow and bitter beings, always wretched with melancholic blood. They do not lead the Night Lords Legion. They *cannot* lead it – their misery leaves them too mournful and unreliable. So I buried this gift rather than allow it to grow. My father and his viziers helped me to seal it away. I hoped it would decay in disuse.'

'I see. And instead, it is killing you.'

'There are worse deaths than this,' he says aloud.

You should know, he thinks, refusing to voice the thought. The dead do not like to be reminded they are dead.

'You sound... different tonight, Jago. Is the pain worse than before?'

'Yes,' he admits freely, 'but your voice eases it. What is it that you wished to speak of?'

'I have questions. Who is the Prince of Crows?'

Sevatar takes a breath, letting her voice wash against his mind the way the darkness brushes over his flesh. Her words quench the crushing fire raking through his thoughts. None of the dead voices in his dreams do that. None of the others bring relief.

'Did you pluck that name from my head, little one?'

'No. You spoke it last time, when the pain was fierce. You moaned it out loud. Who is the Prince of Crows?'

'I am. It is what my brothers call me.'

'What is a crow?'

'You ask the strangest things.' He closes his eyes and thumbs their sore lids with bloody fingertips. 'A crow is... Nnh. On what world were you born?'

'Terra. But I was taken by the First Legion when I was very young.'

'Ah, one of the Earthborn. I'm honoured. If you are from Terra, I assume you know what a bird is.'

'Yes. I've seen them in books. Is a crow a type of bird?'

'Black of feather and dark of eye. It feeds on the bodies of the dead, and sings in a raw, croaking caw.'

'Why are you a prince of birds?'

Another chuckle leaves his parched throat. Sevatar leans his head back against the force field, feeling its angry hum vibrating through the back of his skull.

'It's a title. A joke between my brothers and I. Crows feed on corpses... and I make a lot of corpses.'

The dead girl is silent for a time. He can feel her in the back of his mind sometimes, even when she says nothing. Her presence is like the sweep of invisible searchlights. He knows when he waits beneath the ghost's unseen gaze.

'Are you lying to me, Jago?'

'No, little one. It is true, but it is not the whole truth.'
Sevatar licks his cracked lips, tasting the blood upon
them. 'It is, however, enough truth for now.'

She falls silent again, though her presence doesn't
recede from his mind. He feels her watching from the
room's unbroken blackness.

'Altani?' he asks after several minutes have passed.
'Where is your home world?'

The breath he draws into his lungs is spiced by the
scent of his own sour sweat. What he wouldn't give to
be able to bathe.

'Gone. Dead. Destroyed years ago.'

'What was it called?'

'Nostramo. A lawless and sunless place. It burned not
because it was guilty, but because we failed to keep it
innocent. Our laws failed the moment we sailed away
to the stars, and in desperate embarrassment our father
incinerated the evidence of his failure.'

'Your father killed his whole world?'

'He wasn't alone. Every one of our ships fired on our
home world. I watched him give the order aboard the
Nightfall. We rained death down upon the city of my
birth. Have you ever seen a world die, Altani?'

'No. Never.'

He's almost breathless now, lost in the heat of memory. 'It's beautiful. Truly, honestly, beautiful. I've never
seen anything that stirred me the same way as the
night I watched my home world burn. It is de-creation
incarnate. You unmake the very threads of the universe,
pulling apart a body of rock and fire and life that the
galaxy itself conspired to create. You see the world's
burning blood through the cracks in the breaking tectonic plates.'

Silence answers his heresy. He is a traitor among traitors, his confession given at last.

Finally, the dead girl speaks, her own voice much softer now.

'Jago,' she says, 'I don't understand you.'

'That is because I am the only simple man in a complicated galaxy. Now the Imperium burns and trillions die in the trenches of Horus' ambition and the fires of the Emperor's hypocrisy. Hnnh. To the abyss with them. I spit on them both. The Lords of the Night, they call us. The nobility in the darkness. That is where we were born to be. I am not a soldier, beholden to a master. I am justice. I am judgement. I am punishment.'

'That isn't what you are, it's what you wish you were. What you should have been.'

'I am not on trial here.'

'But who do you judge now? Who do you punish?'

Before he can reply, she adds one last sting - a judgement of her own.

'Jago, whose side are you on?'

Sevatar presses his pounding forehead to the cool stone floor, ignoring the blood that runs from his mouth. 'I am not on anyone's side.'

Once more, there is a long silence.

'You used to try to escape. I think I know why you stopped.'

His grin is knifelike. 'Do you now?'

'You think you deserve to be here. This is justice, for all the things you've done. So you sit alone in the dark, while your brain rots inside your skull. Accepting it as your execution.'

He swallows, unable to speak for a moment. 'As I said, I am a simple man–'

'Someone's coming,' she interrupts him, and with a flicker that sends spikes through his skull, she's gone. Blood starts running from his ear, a trickle as slow and thick as the one from his nose.

A mechanical voice comes from above. *'Illumination.'*

He knows to close his eyes as the lumen globes flash into stark life. Even his gene-forged sight is blinded by bright light. The last time he refused to close them for this daily ritual, he spent the hours afterwards seeing smears of scarlet pain written across his retinas.

The power field dissipates with a waspish crack and the drone of a de-cycling engine. Sevatar lifts his head to sit in patient composure, eyes closed, as the cell door grinds open on squealing tracks.

They must not see his weakness. They must not witness how he suffers.

'Feeding time already?' He greets his captors with a smile as unlovely as a rusted blade. 'Such wondrous hospitality.'

His captors have long since ceased replying to him. In silence they stand by the door, their active battle armour thrumming, mechanical joints and machine-nerves snarling with each movement they make. Even without opening his eyes, he knows that two of them are standing there with their bolters levelled at his head, while the third – standing between them – is about to leave the gruel bucket on the cell floor. He can smell the oils they use to clean their weapons, and the charcoal stink of the incense they use in their knightly reverences.

'Please convey my compliments to the chef,' he says to them. 'The last bucket was the finest yet.'

He hears the twin crunches of bolters braced against shoulder guards and can't resist a smile even as his blood runs cold. 'Well, this is new. Is there a reason you're taking aim at me?'

'We heard you speaking before we entered. Has madness come so swiftly to the great torturer now that he languishes in captivity?'

'So it would seem.'

'Who were you speaking to, Sevatar?'

'The ghosts that share my cell. When you're left alone for such a long time, you tend to conjure your own company.'

'Are you aware that you are bleeding again?'

'Am I? My thanks for your concern, cousin.'

'It wasn't concern.'

'I know. I was imagining you were from a Legion where your primarch gifted you with manners. Can I have my nutrient slime now, noble knight? I'm ever so hungry.'

He manages to open his eyes, just enough to let in a sliver of vile light. Three blurred figures stand before him, just as he'd expected. Three Dark Angels, clad in their Legion's black war-plate. His generous, caring captors.

But he has to close his eyes again. The light is acid against them.

'I've not seen you before,' he says to the first of his wardens. 'I recognise the others, but not you. What brings you to my chambers, cousin?'

'Do you find yourself amusing, traitor?'

'You keep calling me that. Show some respect, Angel. I outrank you, you know.'

The warrior gives a disgusted grunt. 'We are watching you, Sevatar.'

'Seeing as I'm caged like a prized pet, I can't imagine that makes for interesting viewing. Shouldn't you be out there, fighting your little war?'

They don't rise to his bait, as he knew they wouldn't. The Dark Angels leave his container of protein paste on the floor, before retreating back through the door. Sevatar waits for the charged hum of the power field to crackle back into life. Only then does he move, eating as a beast would eat, feeding from the gruel in his cupped palm.

For a time he's alone once more, shovelling the nutrient gruel into his mouth. There's nothing to relish in its cold, chemical un-taste.

'Jago,' comes her voice again. The relief of her gentle tones is immediate and absolute, ice water poured onto a burning wound.

'Dinner is served,' he tells her. 'Are you hungry, little one?' He holds out his dripping hand, offering the protein slime to the darkness. 'If you wish, you can share this glorious repast.'

'No, Jago. Please listen to me. The knights of the First aren't blind. They fear something is wrong with your mind.'

'I am told there are many things wrong with my mind.' He bares his gruel-wet teeth in a vile grin. 'I'm afraid you'll have to be specific.'

'Because of the blood and the pain, they suspect your secret. One of them had the talent. He knows you're hiding something.'

Calm and suddenly cold, he licks the bland, grey taste of the protein paste from his lips.

'One of them was a psyker? How... how could you know that?'

'I could feel him in here, with us. He reached out for you with his mind, just as I am.'

So, the I Legion are using their Librarians to watch over him now. That is an unforeseen threat he will have to deal with. But it isn't the Dark Angels that leave his blood running cold.

'Altani,' he says cautiously, as close as he's come to fear since he was taken and reshaped by the VIII Legion. 'Tell me something, little ghost. How did you die?'

'What?' Shock colours her tones. 'I'm not dead, Jago.'

His blood is cold, like the frost that scales over power-less shipwrecks drifting in the deep void, far from the light of any sun. He breathes through clenched teeth, his hands trembling in helpless, weaponless unease. She's in his head. This girl, this *creature*, has forced herself into his head.

'Who. Are. You.'

'Altani. Altani Shedu, Second Voice of the Choir.'

The choir. Realisation grips him in talons of black ice. She isn't some wraith lingering on the wrong side of the grave. She isn't the spirit of a girl that died aboard the Dark Angels flagship. She is–

'An astropath. You are an *astropath*.'

'I thought you knew. How else would I reach you, if I didn't possess the talent?'

He finds himself laughing for the first time in this tor-turous ordeal, laughing through the diminished pain at the games that fate seems so keen to play.

'You thought I was dead?' she asks. She is faceless in his imagination but he can almost picture her innocent, open-mouthed surprise. 'One of the dead voices that you dream?'

'It doesn't matter, Altani. None of it matters. Will you not be punished for this contact?'

'Yes, if they discover it. But I am the Second Voice, and the strongest of the choir. I would be the First Voice, were I older.'

For a child to be raised to the rank of Second Voice, her psychic strength must be almost beyond measure. That makes her precious to her masters, without a doubt, but Sevatar wonders just how safe she really is, speaking so intimately with the imprisoned enemy.

'Why, girl, do you risk your life speaking with me?'

'I saw your dreams. All of us have felt them intruding into our work – your dreams are destroying the rhythm of our choir's astropathic song. The others turned away, guarding against the pain of your mind. I alone did not.'

'Why?'

'Because of what I saw in the redness of your nightmares. I knew I could ease your pain. I cannot teach you to master the talent, but I can keep it from killing you.'

His reply is a blade cast out into the dark, made vicious by his anger. 'Is this a game you play with the First Legion's prisoners?' He feels the words flash from his tongue like throwing knives, hurting her – wherever she is – but anger steals what little guilt he is capable of feeling. 'Is this some pathetic attempt to breed gratitude towards an ally of my captors? Some scheme to break me with kindness rather than privation?'

'No. Not for that. Not for any of those reasons.'

'Then *why*? Why would you do this?'

She doesn't break in the face of his fury. 'Listen to yourself, Jago. Unable to feel gratitude without suspicion. Unable to even understand why someone would help another soul in pain. Your home world has poisoned you.'

'That is no answer at all.'

'Not to you, no. You're a broken soul, Jago – always thinking of yourself, always judging yourself. You've lost the right to judge anyone else.'

Her words hit him with the force of a blow to the head.

He stares blindly into the darkness as if he might see her there, but she recedes from his mind. This time, for the first time, he chases her, reaching out with the untrained, instinctive sense he swore to never use.

But she is gone, and his invisible grip does nothing but dredge the empty silence.

DAYS PASS IN isolation. The pain is harsh enough to leave him drooling, murmuring words of madness as spit runs from his mouth in slow strings. Dazed and nauseous from the pressure in his skull, Sevatar lies in the centre of his cell, the fingers of his left hand quivering in the onset of another muscle spasm.

The pain transcends feeling – it's fierce enough to hear, hot and wet against the inside of his skull, dragging and squealing like fingernails on porcelain.

All he can see is red. All he can taste is blood.

Sometimes, in his agony-stained dreams, he hears the girl screaming. She never answers when he calls for her.

The doors open and close, open and close. He can't tell how many times. He doesn't smirk at his captors, nor does he reach for the buckets of gruel that they leave.

'Jago. Are you still alive?'

He doesn't rise. He has the strength, but any movement stirs the sick heat in his head. The reply slithers from his lips.

'Still alive,' he says, 'though I've seen better days.'

The pain begins to fade. He doesn't know if she does it consciously or if it's merely the effect of her voice in his mind. Right now, he doesn't care.

'Thank you,' he says. It is the first time he has said those words and *meant* them in many years. 'I wasn't sure you would return.'

'He caught me, Jago.'

Sevatar hears it then, some new tension in her voice that was never present before. Some new discomfort. It focuses him, drawing his wandering thoughts together in a blade of concentration. Despite the queasiness, he sits up in a slow, smooth motion.

'Who caught you?'

'My overseer. The Master of the Choir, and First Voice. He sensed our contact. I thought I was careful enough…'

'Hush, now,' he says softly. The sluggishness leaves his words. His tone grows as cold as his concentration. 'They punished you, didn't they?'

'Yes. And not for the first time. But it's over now.'

'Tell me. Tell me everything.'

'There's no time. They're coming for you. They're taking you and your surviving brothers to a prison transport.'

'No.'

Sevatar is on his feet without realising that he intended to rise. Strong hands, a killer's hands, curl into claws. He misses his spear, but he's killed plenty of men and women without it.

'No. *I* am not leaving this ship until you tell me what they did to you, Altani.'

'There's no time! They're coming!'

His voice filters into something savage and predatory, as hungry as the eyeless white sharks of Nostramo's blackest depths. As he speaks the words and reaches for her mind – a gesture that feels no different from breathing in a scent or recalling a memory – he uses the connection to plunge his thoughts into her distant consciousness.

+*Tell me,*+ he commands her.

He feels her flesh, elsewhere, as a husk of battered meat and broken bone.

In that moment he knows what they did to her.

He feels the utterly human panic of being beaten while help-less and blind, unable to raise a hand against the incoming blows. He feels the lashes of a whip crackling with electrical discharge across his unarmoured body. He feels something give in his spine, a crunching snap of dislocation, and the numbness that follows...

He knows everything. They scourged her for seven days and seven nights. She can no longer walk, but even paralysed she is still of use – an astropath needs no legs to sing her warp-borne song. Sevatar feels his lips peel back at the punishment; it is an ugly sentence fit for the madmen of the Martian Mechanicum, who are known to do such things to their disobedient thralls.

He releases her mind and faces the door. He hears them now. Their boots echo on the iron deck, sending minute shivers through the floor.

'Let them come.'

'You can't fight them all.'

'I have no intention of fighting them. You said it yourself, girl. I earned this punishment.' There's no self-pity in his words. No melancholy, no torment. Only vindication.

'*Illumination*,' declares a familiar mechanical voice. Sevatar closes his eyes against the coming razor-kiss of the light. The power field expires with a de-powering crack. A moment later, the bulkhead opens on its grinding tracks once more.

He keeps his eyes closed. Bootsteps enter his cell. He smells the metallic tang of the flexible machinery in power-armoured joints. He tastes the scent of battle-worn ceramite upon his tongue.

'Cousins,' he greets them.

'Come with us, Captain Sevatar.'

'Of course. May I ask where we are going?'

'The prison transport ship *Remnant of Brotherhood.*'

'What a dramatic and wholly appropriate name.'

'Can you see, or do you need to be dragged?'

Sevatar smiles, opening his eyes to slits, bracing against the pain piling against his retinas. Ten of them. No, twelve. All armed with blades and bolters.

'My eyes will adjust in a few moments. Have patience, cousin.'

They allow him the courtesy of letting his vision adjust. The pain diminishes but doesn't vanish. It's enough for him to walk unaided without the indignity of being carried.

'Move, prisoner.'

THE INVINCIBLE REASON is a Gloriana-class battleship, a city in space, and they spend almost an hour traversing its hallways. Through tunnels and corridors, they walk on in silence but for the thud of armoured boots. Sevatar never sees any of his brothers being similarly escorted. It seems that the Dark Angels are taking precautions.

Slaves, serfs, thralls and servants all ignore him, never sparing him a glance, never even looking up from their hooded robes. He has to admit, the I Legion has its minions trained very well indeed, though it's a wonder they can go about their duties with their gazes forever cast at the floor in a peasants' sign of respect.

After a time, he feels the child-astropath drawing near once more. Watching him, as she always has. Watching him... and more.

'Jago,' says the Dark Angel closest to him.

All twelve warriors stop in the same moment, standing motionless in the red-lit reaches of a tributary corridor. He stops in their midst, looking at each of them in turn.

'You'll die if they take you onto the prison ship,' says one of the other legionaries. 'I can help you...'

'...but I cannot hold them like this for long,' says yet another.

'How are you *doing* this?' Sevatar murmurs in astonishment. 'How strong are you, child?'

'One of them is a Librarian. He fights me every moment, and his strength is immense.'

Sevatar looks to the head of the column. The lead warrior's black armour plating is etched with elegant Calibanite runic script, and he stands unhelmed, his features shadowed beneath a hood of ivory cloth.

As the Night Lords captain draws near, he sees the warrior's face drawn in a rictus of effort. Narrowed eyes quiver with the strain of fighting an unseen battle, and sweat forms diamonds on the Dark Angel's brow.

'Hello, cousin,' Sevatar breathes softly. 'Don't struggle. This will only take a moment.'

The Librarian's eyes roll with exquisite, trembling slowness to gaze upon the other warrior.

'No... You are–'

Sevatar snatches the pistol holstered at the Dark Angel's hip, and puts a bolt between his eyes. The headless corpse remains standing, but he feels Altani's sigh of relief in his mind as he throws the pistol to the deck.

'You didn't have to kill him, Jago,' one of the other Dark Angels says.

'No, but it suited me to do so.'

Yet another warrior turns to him. 'You're almost at the ancillary hangar deck. I can help you steal away on a cargo hauler or a tug moving between the vessels at anchor over Macragge. You can hide on board one of the warships making ready to–'

'Little one, enough. There is only one thing I need to know.' Even as he speaks, he's reaching for the chainsword sheathed on the closest Dark Angel's back.

'What is it?' the warrior asks, turning to face him.

Sevatar's fingers tighten around the handle of the legionary's war-scarred blade. He knows that a long and confined journey through the ship's maintenance ducts lies in his immediate future.

And she will have to help him, as best she can. But it will be worth it.

Justice. Judgement. Punishment.

'Just tell me where you are, Altani. I want to hear your choir sing.'

THE ASTROPATHIC CHOIR is in session. Its twenty members commune in absolute harmony beneath a great, reinforced dome that offers a breathtaking view of the star-scattered heavens.

Usually, all is peaceful here. And inside the twenty locked, ritually etched gnosis pods, all is still at peace. They are hermetically sealed against outside air and the raving wail of siren alarms now washing the deck with shades of warning red. The astropaths sleep on, their minds linked in communion, ready to do as their overlords desire – to reach out into the boiling storm and spend their energies in another futile attempt to send word to distant Terra.

Only one of the slumbering forms stirs, though she doesn't awaken. Her consciousness stays on the edge of the choir's perfect psychic orchestra, and she lets their voices wash over her, as she adds her own harmony back into their shared song.

Outside the wall-mounted pods, an intruder roams the halls of the choir chambers.

Dozens of adepts labour frantically beneath the screaming sirens. They work the chamber's arcane machinery, preparing to ease the pain of their charges when the choir's song can safely be brought to an abrupt end.

And they work to seal the inner sanctum. One of them shrieks into a vox-console, crying out for warriors of the I Legion to come at once, to cut their way through the doors if they must. In the halls where no Space Marine is permitted to tread, their presence is demanded for the first time in living memory.

Sevatar moves amongst the fleeing slaves and thralls in a muscled sprint, sparing them from the fall of his blade. They are insects to him, so irrelevant that they may as well not exist.

He pauses at *her* pod.

He knows that he has only seconds at best, and each heartbeat spent with her is a heartbeat wasted, but still he finds himself compelled to remain.

She sleeps inside: a girl-child of bruised skin, strapped foetal in the cushioned gnosis pod. Bio-data wires, muscle needles, and sustenance cables puncture her temples, spine, and limbs in too many places to count with such a brief glance. The fall of her ragged hair hides her empty eye sockets.

Though she is almost motionless in the atmosphere-controlled life cradle, Sevatar lingers just long enough to see her fingertips twitch. Soft, smooth fingers that will never know the grip of a weapon.

He almost presses his hand to the glass of the pod, but a traitor's bloody palm print would only incriminate her further.

+So that's what you look like,+ she says in his mind. Within the gnosis coffin, the girl sleeps on even as she projects the words into his mind. She doesn't speak of the hundreds of scars lining his pale flesh, or the unnatural blackness of his eyes. +You look tired, Jago.+

His only reply is a bloodstained grin.

Then he's gone. Duty calls.

AS THE CHAINSWORD bites into the choir's primary gnosis pod, it vents oxygen as pressurised gas and coolant as a spillage of clear, fizzing liquid. The occupant, a wizened and grey-haired revenant of a man by the name of Mnemoc, is thirty Terran-standard years old. He looks fifty, and has the health of a man of seventy.

Astrotelepathy is an unkind vocation. The brighter a mind burns, the more voraciously it eats through the body's resources.

This ruined man screams in blind panic as he's pulled from his cushioned cradle. Far greater than the shock of being unhooked from the muscle needles and bio-feeds is the devastating shriek as he falls out of the choir's harmonic song. Fire rakes across the surface of his mind, moving into the veins of his brain like a flood of burning oil.

But even weakened by disorientation and stunned by pain, instinct doesn't desert him entirely. As he is hauled into the air by impossibly strong hands, he reaches for the lash at his hip... only to find that it isn't there.

Unlike most astropaths, the overseer's eye sockets aren't empty. Crude bionics whirr and click as they seek to refocus, offering him the distorted image of a towering man he doesn't know, staring into his face with black eyes that he doesn't recognise, whispering in a voice he's never heard before.

'I have come for you.'

Overseer Mnemoc's first word after awakening is a single syllable. He asks what many men in his position might well ask. 'Why?'

His first word is also his last. Sevatar collars him with his own lash, garrotting the helpless man with the same weapon Mnemoc used to beat the youngest member of his choir until her spine gave out.

Jago Sevatarion is an experienced murderer, well familiar with the force required to kill a man in any way the mortal mind can imagine. He strangles the master of astropaths slowly, lovingly, his gene-enhanced muscles barely straining, using just enough strength to drag out the execution without breaking the psyker's neck.

The overseer's psychic sense is a maddened, feral thing, pathetically flapping against the Night Lord's mind as uselessly as his thin fingers claw at Sevatar's unyielding flesh.

His eyes bulge. The flesh of his face darkens from red to purple and finally to blue. His struggles weaken, become twitches, and finally cease.

Sevatar doesn't let go. Not yet.

For all his flaws, he's a thorough soul when it comes to duty.

Huge ornate doors, sealed against intrusion, finally open to admit a phalanx of knights in black armour. The Dark Angels surround him, ordering him to the deck, raising their bolters to take aim.

'I am justice,' Sevatar calls out to them. With a last wrenching twist, he breaks the corpse's neck and casts it onto the deck by his bare feet. 'I am judgement. I am punishment. And I surrender.'

✠ ✠ ✠

HE SITS ALONE in the blackened stillness, listening to the slow rhythm of his breathing. A sense of serenity cloaks him, and a feeling of cold, cold focus that has eluded him for decades.

When he dreams now it is not of the dead, but of the endless night between worlds. The deepest void, where a thousand threats drift, away from the light of loyal suns. The domains of aliens and monsters forced into exile by the Great Crusade, still crying out to be extinguished once and for all. The true threats to mankind.

'Jago,' the girl's voice comes to him again at last. 'Are you still alive?'

And in the darkness of his cell, Sevatar smiles.

SINS OF THE FATHER

Andy Smillie

In my darker moments, I do not love my sons.

Sanguinius was unmoving as the blades clashed around him. His thoughts weighed upon him like the press of time. They rooted him in place, immobile at the centre of the duelling stone as the two combatants exchanged blows.

In these moments, I dwell on what is to come.

Garbed in a simple robe, the beauty of his form eclipsed the many statues and sculptures bordering the chamber, deep within the Fortress of Hera. A numinous, angelic being, he was an ode to the beauty and strength of the Emperor's creations.

And to all save his father, the furrow in his brow would have gone unnoticed.

My sons will never rise to my virtue. They will remain as tarnished mirrors, shining in poor reflection of a greatness my death will rob from them. They do not have the valour to rise against the curse of their blood. Except…

Except, perhaps, for these two.

The Tempest of Angels was a perilous ritual. Sanguinius stood at its eye, as the blades of the Flesh Tearer and the Saviour whirled about him. He followed the ebb and flow of the duel, appraising the strength and skill of the pair as they snarled and railed against one another.

My father cast me in the image of an angel. A divine protector or a wrathful destroyer, he has never said. It is a quirk of his nature to create that which might surprise his knowing. He has left it for me to decide how history shall record my deeds.

Sanguinius closed his eyes, letting his mind drift back to the Triumph at Ullanor. He had always felt alone. Even then. Even in the presence of so many of his brothers. He saw each of their faces, caught the glimmer of unfolding destiny in their eyes.

My brothers suffer from no such indecision. Magnus is no warrior and Angron no tactician. Their paths were chosen for them, freeing them from the burden of such questions.

Sparks danced across Sanguinius' face as the combatants' blades clashed once more. The twin slivers of Baalite steel were anger-hot with friction.

Destroyer. Protector. I am cursed to see the ends of each of these paths, and I know of the pain to turn from either. In my weakness, I tread the line of both.

He opened his eyes. The combatants fought almost on top of him, their furious cuts and thrusts warming his skin.

But these two, these flawed sons of mine, they walk only a single path.

Driven by murderous intent, a blade angled towards Sanguinius' throat. The primarch remained still, and lived – the Flesh Tearer's kill-stroke denied by the blade of the Saviour.

Azkaellon, chief among my Sanguinary Guard, is my greatest protector. The gold and bronze of his armour serves as an echo of the purity he carries in his hearts. Driven by duty, by pride, he is a masterful swordsman, his strokes balanced, measured and poised.

Azkaellon grunted with effort and shouldered his opponent back away from the primarch.

Amit, Captain of the Fifth Company, a warrior born. He would fight until the stars burned cold. His armour carries the scars others reserve for their souls. Caked in blood, it is stained the deepest crimson. He is a destroyer, fighting with the fury of a berzerker. His brutal blows allow for no defence.

Amit growled, regaining his footing and redoubling his attack.

Their single-mindedness will see them outlive me. It gives them the strength to do what others cannot.

And yet, I have foreseen a future without angels…

Ka'Bandha roars in triumph as my body breaks against the ground. Satisfied in his vengeance, he beats his wings and hurls himself into a distant melee.

I lie still.

'No!' Azkaellon's cry is one of rage and anguish.

He runs to me, ignoring the calls of his warriors as he abandons them.

'L-lord…' he stammers, and falls to his knees.

He pulls me close, cradling my body against his own. My head rests upon his sculpted breastplate. My features are as they are now – virginal and unbroken.

'Father,' Azkaellon shakes me, driven frantic by grief as he searches for the life that no longer beats within me. 'He is dead…' He turns his gaze skyward, searching for some

deity who would denounce his claim. 'Our father Sanguinius is dead!'

Around him, parts of the Palace blaze incandescently in their death throes. Fire consumes the ground and broils over the towering walls. Ichorous flesh burns like oil, stripped from corpses and the still-living by gods bent on annihilation.

'How... how can this be?' *Removing his helm, Azkaellon casts his gaze around, as though seeing the world with his own eyes might change its appearance. It does not.*

Hell surrounds him. An absence of hope so absolute as to render the Blood Angel prostrate, his blade slipping from his grasp. His brothers are dying. Red-skinned daemons eviscerate them with barbed claws, while others hack them apart with obsidian blades. So fast are their enemies that the Blood Angels seem to fight in slow motion, the bark of their boltguns drowned out by the snarling of the beasts that they fight.

It is a mosaic of carnage and madness, a nightmare made real. It is the end of all things.

'Lord! Lord Azkaellon, you must fight.'

Azkaellon glances up at the Blood Angel standing over him. The warrior's armour is scorched black, charred by unnatural fire.

'My lord, we need your blade.'

Anger mixed with desperation twists the Blood Angel's face into a snarl.

'He... he is gone. We are undone,' *Azkaellon's voice is hollow, stripped of emotion by despair.*

'Commander Azkaellon, we need you! We cannot–'

The Blood Angel's head and torso vanish in a flash of crimson lightning, vaporised by some ensorcelled weapon of the enemy.

Azkaellon looks down at the Blood Angel's remains, losing

himself in the expanding pool of blood as it spreads across the floor.

'We are lost...'

Amit stumbles forward. Alone in a vast desert, lost amongst the shifting red dunes that stretch in every direction, he has only his rage to sustain him. He has followed his prey there, bleeding his own warriors into annihilation to do so. The sand beneath his feet is not crushed rock – it is a reminder of that gore-riven battle. He walks on the dust of the dead, hills of blood that have been dried and baked by the eight suns blazing overhead.

'I will find you.'

Amit's voice is a rasping snarl, worn raw by those same four words.

The daemon laughs in response. It is a mocking growl, a rumble of contempt that echoes all around like primal thunder.

Amit thrusts his blade to the sky. 'You cannot hide from my blade, daemon. Not forever. I will find you, and I will kill you.'

The crimson heavens crackle with fire. A lash of the daemon's will tears across it, opening a ragged wound in the firmament. Blood, crimson and dark, falls in a vengeful downpour.

'That will not stop me,' Amit snarls.

He is wrong.

The blood-rain falls in a thickening torrent, driving Amit from his feet and churning the dunes beneath him into a thick sludge.

'Face me, daemon,' Amit spits, grunting with effort as he struggles forward, fighting in vain to keep his bulk from sinking into the mire. 'Coward. Fight me!'

Frustration cuts him like a blade as the ground drinks its

fill, and becomes as an ocean. Helpless, the lord of the Flesh Tearers sinks into the crimson abyss.

'No!'

Amit's cry is practically inaudible, swallowed by bloody waves that growl as they break.

He tries to rise, to swim to the surface, but the blood is too thick, his armour too heavy. He sinks downwards, down into the depths of murder that form the world.

'No…'

The thick, arterial liquid fills his lungs, dragging him downwards until he strikes the sea bed – an undulating landscape of polished skulls. Hundreds of thousands of them crowd the bedrock.

And yet, there is space for one more.

'STOP.'

At Sanguinius' command, Amit and Azkaellon put up their blades.

'Switch places.'

'Lord?' Azkaellon's brow creased in confusion.

'Azkaellon, you will attack. Amit, you will defend me.'

'Lord, I have not the temperam–'

'No, Amit, you do not,' Sanguinius' voice was hard but his eyes held no malice. 'You fight to kill with no concern for survival. And you, Azkaellon,' Sanguinius shifted his gaze to the other Blood Angel. 'You fight only to protect with no consideration to what survival might mean.'

Azkaellon held up a hand in protest. 'I fight for the Legion, for the memory of the Emperor and the Imperium-that-was.'

'No, you do not,' Sanguinius shook his head. 'You fight for your own honour. You fight for me.'

Azkaellon looked pained, as though stung by a blade. 'And what cause could be greater?'

'It is not a sin, and it has served you well. But it is not enough. When this new Imperium falls, and we have all been cast down... When I am gone, who will you fight for then?'

Azkaellon's eyes flashed with anger. 'Lord, that will not–'

'You are so certain of a future that was hidden even from my father?'

'Lord... forgive me,' Azkaellon bowed his head in deference.

'And you, Amit, you fight because the din of battle brings you peace.'

Amit looked away, unable to hold his lord's gaze.

'There will come a time when the cries of those you have led to death will drown out the roar in your veins. There will come a time when you must defend what little we have left.'

Amit said nothing, his jaw clenched tight.

'Now...' Sanguinius returned to his position at the centre of the duelling stone. 'Switch places.'

Without another word, Amit and Azkaellon changed positions, and readied their blades.

'My life is in your hands, my sons. Do not waste it.'

THE EAGLE'S
TALON

John French

///SAMPLE FROM *EAGLE'S TALON* VOX FRAGMENT
(VII).///
///PLEASE REVIEW AND CONFIRM RECORDING
CLARITY BEFORE ACCESSING FULL ARCHIVE.///

TH-144: <<*Chokepoint breached. They are
coming through!*>>

GA-739: *How long until they are past you?*

AR-502: <<*Commander Gammus, this is
Arcad. Their auto-defences are back
online. Advance on target stalled.*>>

TH-144: <<*This is Theophon - chokepoint
one has failed. Pulling back to
chokepoint two. They are going to be into
prime arterial corridor in six seconds.*>>

AR-502: <<*They are behind us!*>>

GA-739: *All units, this is Gammus. I
am cutting prime arterial corridor.
Charges firing in five, four, three, two...
Detonate.*

TH-144: *<<Detonation good. Prime arterial corridor closed. That should slow them down.>>*

GA-739: *Theophon, how long until they bypass the wreckage?*

TH-144: *<<Best guess - one hundred to one hundred and fifty seconds, commander.>>*

GA-739: *Arcad, are you at the bridge atmosphere control?*

AR-502: *<<We have heavy resistance, commander... we... Brother... We are...>>*

GA-739: *Arcad?*

TH-144: *<<This is Theophon, chokepoint two reached and holding.>>*

GA-739: *Arcad, what is your strength and status?*

AR-502: *<<Commander, we...>> /// TRANSMISSION TERMINATED.///*

TH-144: *<<They are on us. By Dorn, there are too many of them! We cannot hold this position!>>*

GA-739: *Arcad, what is your strength and objective status?*

TH-144: *<<Commander, this is Theophon. Chokepoint will be overrun in thirty seconds.>>*

GA-739: *Arcad?*

TH-144: *<<He is gone, Gammus! What are your orders?>>*

GA-739: *Arcad!*

TH-144: *<<We are losing this, brother! There is no other choice. If we do this, then it must be now.>>*

```
///RECORDING CLARITY CONFIRMED.
PROCEEDING.///

///ACCESSING FULL RECORDS DESIGNATED
"EAGLE'S TALON".///
///AUTHORISATION ACCEPTED.///
///RETRIEVING INITIAL FILE COMMAND
NOTATION...///
///FILE ACCESSED.///
///PRAISE BE TO THE MACHINE. PRAISE BE TO
THE SEEKER OF SECRETS.///
```

ONE HUNDRED AND ninety-seven days, ten hours, seventeen minutes and thirty-one seconds from the first strike of the Battle of Tallarn, the macro-transporter *Eagle's Talon* impacted onto the surface of the planet. The effect on immediate ground operations on the southern continent was profound, and has been recorded extensively elsewhere. However, the incident's role in the course of the wider engagement is difficult to judge, the Battle of Tallarn still a recent event in the ongoing civil war.

At the time, the fall of the *Eagle's Talon* was thought to be the result of action by an element – or elements – from the loyalist Imperial Army warships within the Tallarn System, or a catastrophic failure of the ship's own protocols.

Both of these presumptions are false.

The vox file attached to this record consists of signals captured from a VII Legion strike force onboard the *Eagle's Talon* prior to its atmospheric re-entry. Signal capture was accidental, and the result of passive operations in place throughout Perturabo's forces. This record, like the means by which it was obtained, remains unknown to all outside of our Legion.

The strength of the Imperial Fists strike force is estimated to have been three squads, designated as Gammus, Theophon, and Arcad. All three squads were of recon configuration, with light armaments only. Infiltration onto the vessel is believed to have been by gunship and micro hull-breach. Mission command was embedded within the strike force as part of Squad Gammus.

///ACCESSING *EAGLE'S TALON* INCIDENT, VOX FRAGMENT (I).///
///RECORD PROCEEDS. PRAISE THE MACHINE.///
TH-144: <<*Squad Theophon at waypoint one. Zero resistance, no signs of detection.*>>
GA-739: *Confirmed, Theophon.*
TH-144: <<*Proceeding to arterial corridor beta.*>>
GA-739: *Theophon, hold position.*
TH-144: <<*We are exposed here, commander. The plans were not accurate. There are four spurs off this junction, and the marked gantries have been removed. There are cutting- torch marks on the walls and floor. We have no cover, and this ship is waking up to drop a lot of armour onto the surface. If anything comes through, we will be compromised.*>>
GA-739: *Understood, Theophon. The order stands. Hold your position.*
AR-502: <<*This is Arcad. Conveyor shaft breached. Grav-chutes active. We are ready to ascend.*>>

GA-739: *Ascend, Arcad. Hold at the second waypoint.*

AR-502: *<<For Dorn, and the Emperor. Squad Arcad at waypoint two. High levels of crew and servitor activity. Zero resistance, no signs of detection.>>*

GA-739: *Confirmed, Arcad. Theophon, you may proceed.*

TH-144: *<<By your word, commander.>>*

AR-502: *<<This ship is vast.>>*

GA-739: *You should have familiarised yourself with the layout, Arcad. I hope you will not be surprised by other details.*

AR-502: *<<"Awe is the gift of the eye and the ear, not the mind or the cold numeral.">>*

GA-739: *Heh, I suppose I can hardly dispute the words of the primarch. This ship is in the top displacement class for a vessel of its type, but it is not unique.*

AR-502: *<<It is impressive though. Even to the likes of you, commander.>>*

GA-739: *The likes of me, Arcad?*

TH-144: *<<I think Sergeant Arcad is meaning to respectfully use this tactical communication channel to imply that you are... long in the tooth, commander.>>*

GA-739: *I do not take compliments from my subordinates, Arcad. Even if our units have a reputation to maintain.*

TH-144: *<<Squad Theophon entering*

arterial corridor beta now. It is in use,
commander. Floor vibrations. There is a
tracked unit moving nearby, but out of
visual.>>
GA-739: *Closing or moving away?*
TH-144: *<<Moving away. Vibration is*
reducing.>>
GA-739: *Can you reach the hatch to the*
power conduit?
TH-144: *<<Yes. If we move now.>>*
GA-739: *Proceed, Theophon.*
TH-144: *<<Do we need to do this? We can*
discard this objective and advance on the
primary->>
GA-739: *Proceed to the power conduit and*
set the charges, Theophon.
TH-144: *<<Aye, commander. Squad Theophon*
proceeding to secondary objective
gamma.>>
GA-739: *Confirmed, Theophon. Arcad, hold*
your position. One step at a time,
brothers.
AR-502: *<<By your word, commander.>>*

///RECORD ACCESS PROCEEDING.///

THE IMPERIAL FISTS' infiltration onto the *Eagle's Talon*
occurred simultaneously with a major but unnamed
engagement in the centre of Tallarn's southern continent. This engagement was dominated by Titan and
Knight-class war machines and, at the time, it was the
largest since loyalist reinforcements had arrived in-system.
Given the weight and power of the forces involved, it was

possible that if either side achieved a decisive victory then they might be able to derive an overall tactical advantage, and then claim victory on Tallarn as a whole.

The *Eagle's Talon* was the largest of a number of transports positioning to drop forces onto the southern continent. Had it succeeded, it could well have tipped the battle in favour of the traitor forces.

///ACCESSING *EAGLE'S TALON* INCIDENT, VOX FRAGMENT (II).///

///RECORD PROCEEDS. THE MACHINE DREAMS. THE MACHINE KNOWS ALL.///

TH-144: ///VOX ENCRYPTION ACTIVATED.///

<<Squad Theophon at port-side power conduit, designated secondary objective gamma. Zero resistance, no signs of detection.>>

GA-739: You are using a direct link, Theophon. Is there a problem with your vox equipment?

TH-144: <<The vox is clear, brother.>>

GA-739: Then proceed to complete the objective, and return to the approved mission frequencies.

TH-144: <<I wanted to speak without Arcad hearing...>>

GA-739: The time for that has passed, Theophon. You have made your misgivings known. I have heard and understood your concerns, and deemed them of less weight than the needs of this operation. Proceed with the secondary objective. That is my will.

TH-144: <<If the primary mission fails...
will you do it? You will detonate the
charges?>>

GA-739: If this ship completes a full
tactical deployment onto the surface, the
battle below will be lost.

TH-144: <<And if that battle is lost?>>

GA-739: Theophon, this is not the time.

TH-144: <<If it is lost, then what will
happen? Will the war for Tallarn end?
Will the Imperium be lost? Or will
everything simply continue as it was
before?>>

GA-739: Victory is made by every
detail, every battle great and small.
Never forget that, brother. No fight is
insignificant, and we cannot know what
deeds the fate of all might rest upon.
All we can do is fight, when we can, with
everything we have.

TH-144: <<And if we detonate a charge on
this power conduit it will cut the ship's
engines and push it into the planet's
grasp. It will hit the surface. The
immediate blast will flatten everything
across half the southern continent. What
of our allies down there? What of the
battles they fight? Fire from the sky does
not care who it burns.>>

GA-739: Most forces loyal to the Emperor
are already in shelters beneath the
surface.

TH-144: <<One crack, just one, and the

*poisoned air of Tallarn will get in, and
then... And then there will be a shelter
for nothing but corpses.>>*

GA-739: *There are always prices to be
paid in war, brother.*

TH-144: *<<I know, Gammus. I remember.
Phall is far away, but I have not
forgotten what survival costs. But it is
for us to bear that cost, not mortals.
This is our war, a legionary war. Our
kind began it, and we should pay the
price for our own victories.>>*

GA-739: *It is not what I intend, brother.
If the primary objective is met, then
none of this will be necessary.*

TH-144: *<<And if that fails?>>*

GA-739: *Then this ship falls.*

TH-144: *<<And those below?>>*

GA-739: *No one lives on Tallarn,
brother. Only the dead who have yet to
go to their graves. Place the charges as
planned, Theophon, detonation vox-keyed
to my control.*

TH-144: *<<By your word, commander.>>*

///RECORD ACCESS PROCEEDING.///

THE TAKING OF a large spacecraft is not a simple task.
The number of troops involved to successfully control or purge a population of thousands – even tens of
thousands – of human crew are similar to those needed
to conquer a conurbated city. Combined with the
issues of fighting in a confined and profoundly hostile

environment, boarding missions are well named in the Imperial military doctrine as zone mortalis. The ground of death.

The most common method of taking a ship is the targeting of either the primary or secondary bridge. Without effective command elements, even a warship is just a lump of metal drifting in the void. Because of this vulnerability, command points are the most heavily defended locations on a ship. To take or destroy a bridge by boarding action is normally a matter of slow attrition by specially equipped troops, or a lightning fast strike by an elite force with overwhelming strength.

To try and take a ship by infiltration is… unusual. The actions of the Imperial Fists on the *Eagle's Talon* indicate a lack of suitable forces, but also a degree of imagination that we have not previously credited to the sons of Dorn.

As in all things, assumption is the seed of ruin.

///ACCESSING *EAGLE'S TALON* INCIDENT, VOX FRAGMENT (III).///
///RECORD PROCEEDS. THE MACHINE IS ALL. ALL IS THE MACHINE.///
AR-502: <<*Commander Gammus, this is Arcad.*>>
GA-739: *What is your situation, brother?*
AR-502: <<*We have a problem. We are moving through the rear spinal levels, but the plans were not accurate, commander. The layout is totally different. We have had to divert, and the only option was to use the vents in the*

upper crew decks. We are right on top of
the enemy.>>

GA-739: What is the enemy strength?

AR-502: <<Uncertain, but substantial,
and they are at battle readiness. They
may be human, but a lot of them are
naval armsmen, plus there are hundreds
of mustering tank crew. We came close
to compromise three times. We are
holding position in a cavity above the
companionway marked as six-seven-gamma-
two on the original plans. As far as I
can tell.>>

GA-739: There is... a sub-arterial
passage leading to the primary target,
not... ten metres from your current
location. Can you shuttle your squad
across the passage to it?

AR-502: <<Enemy activity is constant.
They move without pattern, and the
longest gap has been six seconds.>>

GA-739: Can you work your way back and
take a different route?

AR-502: <<We can't go back. A crew muster
moved into the last location we came
through, and... And there is another
problem.>>

GA-739: Tell me.

AR-502: <<There is a Mechanicum presence
in this area, at least cohort strength.
Thallaxii and Myrmidon troops, and Legio
Cybernetica maniples. They are on full
alert, sensors primed.>>

GA-739: *Your suggestion, sergeant? Speak plainly.*

AR-502: <<First we need a diversion, commander. Something to get their attention, but not jeopardise the mission. Something that could just be a severe accident.>>

TH-144: <<We could blow the hoist on the main port conveyor. Drop it down fifty decks. Potentially a lot of damage, but they should not realise it was deliberate for at least fifty to seventy minutes.>>

GA-739: *My squad can reach the conveyor shaft from our current location. Go on, Arcad. What is the next step?*

AR-502: <<Even with the diversion, we are going to need to eliminate two of the crew before we can proceed.>>

GA-739: *That is a substantial risk. Why?*

AR-502: <<Because there are armsmen posted within five metres of the vent we would have to drop through.>>

GA-739: *You have planned both kills?*

AR-502: <<Yes. Sniper shot for the first, through the grate. We drop through at the same time. Take the second, pick up both corpses, take them with us.>>

TH-144: <<The guards' absence will be noted, even if the kills are clean.>>

AR-502: <<Correct. I estimate that we will have no more than seven minutes until their absence is discovered.>>

GA-739: *You will have to reach the*

primary objective inside that time, and
destroy it. You can do that?
AR-502: <<*Yes.*>>
GA-739: *Very well, Arcad. We will proceed*
as you suggest.
AR-502: <<*Thank you, commander. You*
honour me.>>

///RECORD ACCESS PROCEEDING.///

THE PREOCCUPATION WITH honour amongst many of the
Legions is a factor which can only be seen as a weakness in the current climate. In the time of the Great
Crusade, it had merit in bonding warriors together
to a single purpose, and maintaining the ideals for
which the Crusade was supposedly being waged. Now
it can be seen only as a flaw in those that still carry it
and, more importantly, an advantage ripe for greater
exploitation.

What function does honour serve, other than to create hesitation when there should be swift action, and to
create doubt when there should be none?

The following is a pointed illustration of this flaw.

///ACCESSING *EAGLE'S TALON* INCIDENT, VOX
FRAGMENT (IV).///
///RECORD PROCEEDS. THE MACHINE SEES ALL.
EVERY DEED IS ILLUMINATED IN THE EYE OF
THE MACHINE.///
TH-144: ///VOX ENCRYPTION ACTIVATED.///
<<*You are worried, brother. I could hear*
it in your silence after Arcad spoke of
honour.>>

GA-739: *We are in the middle of a mission, and you think this is the best use of a personal vox-channel?*

TH-144: <<*I am your brother in blood and bond, Gammus. Need I list the battlefields that we shared to earn the right to question if my commander harbours unspoken doubts? I do not think I need request that right. It is mine already.*>>

GA-739: *Yes. Perhaps it is.*

TH-144: <<*You need not doubt Arcad, brother. He is young, that is all.*>>

GA-739: *He is not. No one remains young in this war.*

TH-144: <<*He never knew the Great Crusade. He is one of the first of us who have only ever known war with ourselves. In time all Space Marines will be like Arcad. That he still thinks of honour in such times should give you hope.*>>

GA-739: *There is no honour in what we are doing. Only necessity.*

TH-144: <<*I know some amongst the Legion who would say that our kind have no place claiming honour. Shadow-dwellers and assassins, some call us.*>>

GA-739: *We fight our battles in silence, not dishonour. If the primarch believed otherwise then the recon squads would never have been adopted.*

TH-144: <<*You seem to make an argument against your own worries, brother.*>>

GA-739: *We are old, my friend, and we*

*were old when we went into the shadows
to make war...*

TH-144: <<But Arcad is no aspirant,
brother. He was blooded at Phall. I
have seen few better as a squad leader,
even among those with decades more
experience.>>

GA-739: But from that battle he came
to us - to a war against our enemies,
fought without ever looking them in the
eye. This should not be the cradle in
which the young learn to fight. It should
be where the old come to die. Where we
come to die.

TH-144: <<A more melancholy way of seeing
ourselves, I cannot imagine.>>

GA-739: The chances of success are slim,
brother. The chances of survival even
lower. If we die here, who will carry
our names back to the Temple of Oaths?
Will there even be a Legion to remember
us? And if there is, what type of
warriors will they be?

TH-144: <<I cannot help wondering,
brother, if it is not Arcad's honour that
worries you, but your own.>>

///RECORD ACCESS PROCEEDING.///

WE CAN DEDUCE that the VII Legion operation on board
the *Eagle's Talon* had as its focus one of the crucial command and control systems of the ship, most likely the
communications trunk that linked the bridge to the

stations which enacted its orders. If the communications on a ship of such size can be cut, then it leaves the whole vessel frozen in action – the bridge unable to give commands, and the crew and systems without commands to enact. In a living creature we might liken it to severing the nerves connecting brain and body, leaving both alive but paralysed, the mind locked within its skull.

Such a plan requires a high degree of precision and nerve, but these qualities have never been in doubt when it comes to the Imperial Fists. There is, though, the self-evident truth that the more precise and delicate an operation, the more it is prone to error.

And once disrupted, the chances of mission collapse expand at an ever-accelerating rate. As we know well, the boundary between disaster and triumph is a razor-cut line.

///ACCESSING *EAGLE'S TALON* INCIDENT, VOX FRAGMENT (V).///
///RECORD PROCEEDS. THE MACHINE IS ETERNAL. THE ETERNAL IS AN EXPRESSION OF THE MACHINE.///
GA-739: *Squad Gammus in position. All units confirm readiness and location.*
TH-144: <<*Theophon in place. Holding at chokepoint on prime arterial corridor.*>>
AR-502: <<*Squad Arcad. We are ready.*>>
GA-739: *On your word, Arcad.*
AR-502: <<*Confirmed, commander. Detonate conveyor shaft charges on my mark. Standby. Detonate.*>>
TH-144: <<*Alert sounding on port decks.*>>

AR-502: <<*Corridor beneath our position cleared. Squad standby to engage. Execute. Targets down, moving to->>*

GA-739: *Arcad?*

AR-502: <<*Thallaxii and automata engaging us. Returning fire.>>*

TH-144: <<*Full alert active. Blast doors sealing on our level!>>*

AR-502: <<*We are pinned down on a gantry complex at... junction five-one-zero-seven.>>*

TH-144: <<*Commander, permission to close chokepoint?>>*

GA-739: *Permission denied.*

TH-144: <<*The ship's auto-weapons are activating. Commander->>*

GA-739: *Arcad, advance on the primary objective.*

AR-502: <<*Receiving fire from two arcs. Correction, three arcs. Effective squad strength at four.>>*

GA-739: *Move for the objective. You must reach it.*

AR-502: <<*We will not reach it. The auto-turrets will rip us in half.>>*

GA-739: *No, you will reach it. I will give you an opening.*

AR-502: <<*How is that possible? Half the ship is trying to kill us.>>*

GA-739: *Because my squad is about to hit the servitor controls for your sector.*

///RECORD ACCESS PROCEEDING.///

THE ADVANTAGES OF a force operating covertly against a more powerful enemy are few, but chief amongst them are the twin elements of surprise and confusion. If one individual can visit destruction across a large area in a short space of time, then that individual is not merely one in the minds of their foes – they are *many*. With planning and aggression they can seem to be everywhere.

Though the attached records are only auditory, it can be simply deduced that the three squads of the strike force were spread at different locations through the decks of the *Eagle's Talon*. Squad Arcad, having taken casualties and under fire, had been attempting to reach the mission's primary objective. Squad Gammus, the command squad for the mission, is located in the machine spaces of the higher decks. Squad Theophon is standing ready to cut the primary route by which enemy reinforcements can move into Arcad's location.

///ACCESSING *EAGLE'S TALON* INCIDENT, VOX FRAGMENT (VI).///
///RECORD PROCEEDS. KNOWLEDGE AND THE MACHINE ARE ONE. THE MACHINE IS THE CHILD OF KNOWLEDGE.///
AR-502: <<*Fire intensifying, commander!*>>
GA-739: *Detonating!*
TH-144: <<*Auto-defence weapons are reported as down.*>>
GA-739: *Arcad, move now!*
AR-502: <<*Squad Arcad mov- Argh!*>>
GA-739: *Arcad! Arcad, what is your status?*
AR-502: <<*Squad strength now two.*>>
GA-739: *You are wounded.*

AR-502: <<*I don't need my left arm to run. Enemy forces are at our heels.*>>
GA-739: *Estimate time to target.*
AR-502: <<*Two minutes. But we will not make it if they keep coming.*>>
GA-739: *Theophon, close the chokepoint.*
TH-144: <<*By your word. Squad Theophon engaging now. Full fire. Cut them down!*>>
AR-502: <<*Target in sight. Forces are pursuing us. Turning to engage.*>>
GA-739: *Keep moving!*
TH-144: <<*This is Theophon - we have enemy forces closing through our fire.*>>
GA-739: *Strength, and direction?*
TH-144: <<*All of them, and every direction!*>>

///RECORD ACCESS PROCEEDING.///

AT THIS POINT, the probability of the mission succeeding without the loss of all forces was zero-point-zero. This fact would have been known to the Imperial Fists, but it would not have inhibited their ability to function. They, like all of us raised by the gene-seed of our sires, are not bound by the weaknesses of lesser beings.

They would have known that they would not survive. The only question would have been whether or not they *could* still succeed.

///TIME ELAPSED FROM PREVIOUS RECORD: 00.00.24.///
///ACCESSING *EAGLE'S TALON* INCIDENT, VOX FRAGMENT (VII).///

///RECORD PROCEEDS. THE MACHINE IS ALPHA. THE MACHINE IS OMEGA.///

TH-144: <<*Chokepoint breached. They are coming through!*>>

GA-739: *How long until they are past you?*

AR-502: <<*Commander Gammus, this is Arcad. Their auto-defences are back online. Advance on target stalled.*>>

TH-144: <<*This is Theophon - chokepoint one has failed. Pulling back to chokepoint two. They are going to be into prime arterial corridor in six seconds.*>>

AR-502: <<*They are behind us!*>>

GA-739: *All units, this is Gammus. I am cutting prime arterial corridor. Charges firing in five, four, three, two... Detonate.*

TH-144: <<*Detonation good. Prime arterial corridor closed. That should slow them down.*>>

GA-739: *Theophon, how long until they bypass the wreckage?*

TH-144: <<*Best guess - one hundred to one hundred and fifty seconds, commander.*>>

GA-739: *Arcad, are you at the bridge atmosphere control?*

AR-502: <<*We have heavy resistance, commander... we... Brother... We are...*>>

GA-739: *Arcad?*

TH-144: <<*This is Theophon, chokepoint two reached and holding.*>>

GA-739: *Arcad, what is your strength and status?*

AR-502: <<*Commander, we...*>> ///
TRANSMISSION TERMINATED.///

TH-144: <<*They are on us. By Dorn, there are too many of them! We cannot hold this position!*>>

GA-739: *Arcad, what is your strength and objective status?*

TH-144: <<*Commander, this is Theophon. Chokepoint will be overrun in thirty seconds.*>>

GA-739: *Arcad?*

TH-144: <<*He is gone, Gammus! What are your orders?*>>

GA-739: *Arcad!*

TH-144: <<*We are losing this, brother! There is no other choice. If we do this, then it must be now.*>>

GA-739: *Arcad, can you hear me? Arcad, you have to reach the target.*

TH-144: <<*Chokepoint two breached. Falling back into ventilation system. It is now, Gammus. The primary target is lost.*>>

GA-739: *If Arcad can reach the target-*

TH-144: <<*Arcad is gone! If you don't blow the power conduit now, then we will have failed.*>>

GA-739: *I will not do it, Theophon. You were right. We do not slaughter our own allies for victory. I am a son of Rogal Dorn. I will not be the bringer of such annihilation.*

TH-144: <<*Then we die here, in failure.*>>

GA-739: *We all die as we were meant to.*
TH-144: <<*No. We were made for a different age, brother. It was not me that was right. It was you. If we fail even for an instant, even in the smallest of things, then there will be no future.*>>
GA-739: *Better to be no more, than to betray what we once were.*
TH-144: <<*The choice is not yours, Gammus. The charges are not keyed to your command. I thought I would stay your hand if we reached this point. But now the hand that will fell this ship will be mine.*>>
GA-739: *Brother, no!*
TH-144: <<*And this is not victory, or betrayal. It is sacrifice.*>>
TH-144: ///TRANSMISSION TERMINATED.///
GA-739: ///TRANSMISSION TERMINATED.///

///FILE ERROR.///
///VOX CAPTURE RECORD ENDS.///

THE EAGLE'S TALON fell from Tallarn's sky. The blast wave from the initial impact travelled over three hundred kilometres. Winds of over a thousand kilometres an hour spun debris from the ground, and scattered into the burning air. The engagement on the southern continent was ended in an instant. Earthquakes split the ground, and tidal waves surged across the sludge-clogged seas. Nucleonic fallout from the reactor failure rose up and spread across the atmosphere.

On any other planet this one event would have doomed

all life to a slow death, smothered beneath a blanket of ashes. But this was Tallarn, and the dead planet could not die twice.

The consequences of this one incident are difficult to judge. Would events have unfolded differently if these few scraps of valour and foolishness had taken a different shape?

Perhaps.

For our purposes, it is enough to know that it happened. Will this split in character repeat within the Imperial Fists? Can advantage be taken from it? The questions remain open, but one thing can be certain – for this intelligence to be useful to our Legion it must remain *unknown*.

I tender my advice to you, my lord father, that once you have reviewed this record you consign it to oblivion.

///INITIATING RECORD PURGE.///
///ENTER THE WORD OF OBLITERATION TO PROCEED.///

///PURGE PROCESS COMPLETE.///

///SEEKING ALL ARCHIVE RECORDS DESIGNATED "EAGLE'S TALON"...///
///NO RECORDS FOUND.///
///THE MACHINE KNOWS ALL. ALL IS KNOWN IN THE MACHINE.///

IRON CORPSES

David Annandale

THE BLAST WAS a roar beyond all storms. It was bigger than sound. It shattered coherence. It was war in paroxysm, and it tore the battlefield apart.

It brought no triumph, only loss. And it stole a victory that had been in sight. The warsmith had *seen* it. Koparnos had seen the enemy falling.

But then had come another fall. An immense shape from the skies. Fire lighting the clouds. A shadow falling over the battle.

And then the blast.

The roar.

After the roar came only the shriek of the wind. It scoured the murdered land, kicking up dust clouds so thick that day and night were indistinguishable. Five days of wind. Five days of the unending howl of a war's collapse into madness.

On the sixth day, the wind dropped just enough that day returned in the form of a deep, withered twilight.

It was time to abandon the Rhino. Koparnos was the only survivor. The troop hold had been breached. Sealed in the driver's compartment, he had held out this long, but the poisons of Tallarn were working their way inside even here. His body temperature rose as his system fought to keep the weakened viruses out. There was no real shelter in the Rhino's blasted shell, only a more prolonged end. Koparnos could hear the wind whistling through the rents in the armoured hull.

It was taunting him. It was the sound of defeat and death.

And it could outwait him.

For those five days, he had fought with the Rhino's systems, trying to coax life back to its engines. His struggle was futile. The tank was as dead as his brothers. But during those days of night, there had been nothing else to attempt. Now he had a choice of endings.

He chose to go. Doing so would hasten his death, but he would act as though there were a real chance of shelter. His war was not over. Not yet.

Koparnos slid the driver's door back and entered the troop compartment. His brother Iron Warriors were seated on the benches – they created an illusion not of life, but of discipline. Though their bodies had turned to sludge, their power armour remained upright, as if their corpses were still ready to march into battle at his command.

The dust and ash of Tallarn spiralled around their boots and fell upon their shoulders. It had already turned the iron gleam of their armour to a dun shadow. There was strength in the silhouettes, but it was slowly being buried. The wind would blow the dust into the Rhino until it filled the interior completely.

Koparnos climbed through the torn side hatch and out of the tomb.

The wind greeted him with its full howl. The dust clouds swirled around and past him, revealing and concealing the landscape. From one moment to the next, visibility went from zero to a thousand metres, and back to zero again. He saw the battlefield through shifting veils – huge, tortured shapes were a deeper black against the grey.

Those shadows were Titans.

Some had been melted into slag. They were now low, jagged hills. Others still stood, frozen in mid-combat. Allied and enemy alike, they had all died in the great roar. Between the motionless colossi were the tanks. The blast had hurled them across the plain. They lay variously upended, on their sides, and torn open. Koparnos had been lucky, then. Not many had landed intact.

The dust swirled over a portrait of a single moment of war, arrested in time. Koparnos was surrounded by towering gravestones. They were an iron cry of agony, preserved, extended, and given voice by the mindless shriek of the wind.

Koparnos' visor display flashed its warning runes. The radiation levels were extreme. Even protected by his power armour, prolonged exposure would be lethal. The blast had also scoured the land of the worst of the viral toxins that had killed this world, but the contamination was still present. It was still reaching through his rebreather. His fever spiked, but his body was holding fast. The deliquescence had not yet begun. The clash of poisons had bought him some time. Not long. A few minutes, he guessed.

He would spend every second fighting, and he would fight for a few seconds more.

The situation was no different, except in degree, to any number of suicidal campaigns that his Legion had faced. That was what the Emperor, in all his perversity, had decided the Iron Warriors were good for. How many times had Koparnos and his battle-brothers struggled through impossible sieges and over the landscapes of death worlds, leaving a wake of their own blood, only for Dorn or Guilliman or one of the other pampered favourites to swoop in and claim credit after the fact? If Koparnos died now, his end would have no substantial difference from the rest of his life.

At least he was free of the Emperor's hypocrisy.

'Do you call this a victory?' he shouted to absent enemies, and a demigod as distant as he was false. 'You choose to destroy your own forces along with ours? That is weakness. That is why you will lose.'

He started walking. He had a vague impression of a great shadow not far to his right. It was a destination. It was a goal to strive for, futile though it might be. He would have a purpose even as his organs disintegrated.

His boots kicked up puffs of ash that flew off in the wind. As he walked, he switched though the vox-channels. He had been doing so for days, and the results were the same: nothing but static, an electronic echo of the wind. Death in the air, on the ground, in the vast and tortured shapes, and in the aether beyond.

The wind pushed against him, mocking. It shouted at him that he was alone, the last thing moving across the ruined battlefield.

'Look at me!' he cried back. His voice sounded too thick. His breath rasped. There was liquid in his lungs. It grew thicker. They were beginning to disintegrate, turn into fluid, seeking to drown and suffocate him at once.

Speech was difficult, but he would give voice to his defiance. 'Look at me! I live. I fight on. You will not stop us. You made us too well. We will march until... until we *crush* you!'

He coughed, straining for more of the deadly air beyond his suit's reserves. He marched faster. The huge shadow gathered definition and mass. He could distinguish the gigantic limbs from the trunk. Then the way before him cleared for a moment, revealing the Titan.

It was a Warlord-class, named *Ostensor Contritio*. Over thirty metres tall to the carapace, and almost as wide, it was a hulking mass of immobilised destruction. Its arms bore great cannons, pointed forwards. Koparnos glanced in the direction the Titan was facing. Some distance away, there was wreckage. A battalion of tanks. *Ostensor Contritio*'s final kill.

As the dust rolled back in, Koparnos saw a faint red flicker in the viewports of the Warlord's head. Just one weak flash, but that was enough.

A trace of power. Koparnos could use that.

He wasn't marching out of bitter defiance now. He was racing against his death. He had a hope of survival. More importantly, he had a hope of vengeance.

He reached *Ostensor Contritio*'s left leg. Overhead, above the Titan's waist, the lower access hatch was partly open. What was left of a Mechanicum acolyte lay halfway across the threshold – robes in a vaguely human form were drenched in black, organic soup. A pair of limp mechadendrites hung beyond where the head had been, as if trying to reach an imagined salvation. Death had reached into the Titan, and this fool had been panicked into thinking that it did not also await him outside.

A fluid, multiplying pain was spreading out from

Koparnos' core and into his limbs. His movements were becoming sluggish. His joints felt loose, and burned with acid pain. He didn't have much longer. Scaling the seized pistons of the leg, he hauled himself upwards towards the hatch, seeking hand and footholds wherever he could.

Once inside the Warlord, he slid the hatch shut. Adamantium armour many times thicker than the Rhino's hull now shielded him from the poisoned world outside. All that remained was to purge the viral taint from the interior.

His helmet lamp lit the confines of the dark space. There were more biological remains here. He guessed they had been servitors from the limited, specialised tool limbs that sat in the sludge.

Further in was another door. He grasped the wheel at its centre, turned it and hauled it open.

He crossed the threshold into the engineering deck. There were more Mechanicum dead here, tech-priests who had stayed at their posts until the end. Their servo-skulls littered the floor, eyes dark and wide as though in shock. Koparnos staggered to a workstation that faced the core of the Titan. It was beside a large cluster of ducts running to and from the Warlord's reactor shields. The station's screen was dark, and one of the liquefied operator's servo-arms was still resting against the keyboard. Koparnos moved the limb aside and examined the controls.

The pulse from the blast could well have shut down the Titan's systems – perhaps the priest had been in the process of restarting the mechanical heart of the god-machine. Something had begun, or at least survived, for that light in the Titan's head to have been possible.

Koparnos found the circuit controls. One of them was

open. He turned the others on one by one. A groaning, hissing life returned to *Ostensor Contritio*. Lumen orbs strobed, then settled at a dull crimson glow. The deck and walls shook, as the Titan's heart struggled to beat once more.

He would grant it life, and in return it would gift him the same.

The hollow, automated voice of the machine crackled from the emitters.

'Primary systems activating. Reactor failsafes engaged. The blessings of the Omnissiah be upon us. Warning. Warning. Malfunctions in secondary and tertiary nodes. Locations One-One-Seven to One-Three-Five...'

Koparnos examined the tech-priest's servo-arms, found a plasma cutter, and fired it up.

He examined the ducts, eventually tracing one that vented the power plant's heat upwards into the exchange system at the rear of the carapace. He deactivated the failsafes and cut though until a rush of superheated, radioactive steam burst from the pipe. Within seconds it had filled the engineering chamber.

'Warning. Warning. Extreme hazard. Heat spike detected. Coolant system failure imminent.'

Alarms howled. Koparnos dropped the cutter and began to remove his armour.

'Warning. Warning. Radiation levels in excess of working maximums. Evacuation advised for all organic personnel.'

'Poison... against poison...' he gasped as the scalding death hit his exposed skin.

He stood in the middle of the cloud, a fresh clash of pain erupting in his body as his genhanced biology absorbed the radiation. His melanchromic organ went into overdrive, his skin pigments blackening instantly.

He breathed deeply, and the burn reached into his lungs. It scoured the slow rot from him with an even more deadly agony.

Poison against poison.

He stood in the lethal cloud for a full minute before the dose overwhelmed his ability to process toxins. The virus was dead, and he began to die in a new way.

He dropped to his knees and vomited out a black, stinking mass that began to eat its way through the deck. Then he stood again. Little more than the force of his own will kept him conscious. The steam was damaging him much faster than he could heal, but he waited another full minute before he reached for his battle-plate once more. If even a trace of the virus remained, he would be done.

His mucranoid began a last-ditch attempt to preserve him. A waxy shield oozed from his pores, sealing him off from the lethal atmosphere of the chamber. He fumbled with the armour, his fingers growing slick. Carapace. Chestplate. Power pack. One piece at a time, he took sanctuary from the radiation. His vision greying from exhaustion and pain, he closed the manual redirect valves to reroute the exchange system leak.

When he was done, the radioactive fog lingered. He felt as though it had penetrated his skull, and his senses were overwhelmed by a grand mosaic of pain. He was one shock away from falling into a sus-an coma, but he stood still and tried to force the darkness from his mind.

His work was not done. He had shelter, but it would serve no purpose if he could not fight...

'Iron within, iron without,' he muttered. Both had carried him this far. They would see him back into war. The loyalists no doubt thought that they had turned the Iron

Warriors' victory into a mutual defeat. All they had done was throw more of the same hopelessness at the Legion that it had battled and surmounted for centuries.

He would show them their error. He would show them his Legion's iron.

The vow made, his pain took him into the night. He fell, unconscious even before he hit the cold deck.

'Enginseer Meridius?'

Crackling woke him. An electronic scrape in his ear. The internal vox was active. There was a gasp, someone drawing a deep breath before finding the strength to speak again.

'Enginseer Meridius, we have power again. Are you well?' The woman's voice was that of a mortally wounded warrior.

Koparnos dragged himself back to the workstation in silence. He was no adept of the Mechanicum, but he was a warsmith. Though he was not privy to the most arcane mysteries of the Titans, he knew how to shape a battlefield. He knew how to shape war itself. So he would make *Ostensor Contritio* answer to his will. One way or another.

'Meridius?' the voice called again.

Koparnos was surprised by the strength of it. The speaker was dying. The alchemy of desperation and hope was the fuel for the cry.

He would answer, but not yet.

He succeeded in running a rough diagnostic of the Warlord. Power appeared to be reaching most quadrants. The potential for movement and attack was there. That left the most important motive force: the princeps. If this woman was only one of the moderati, there would be little he could do. He would be stuck in an immobilised shelter, no better off in the long term than in the Rhino.

He worked his way to the upper levels of the carapace. He found the pods of the moderati minoris. They were closed, but they had not been sealed from the contamination of the virus. The gunners were dead. They left behind ruined uniforms and the stinking slurry at the bottom of their pods. Koparnos wrote off the secondary weapons.

'Meridius! Why don't you answer?'

Koparnos reached the reinforced hatchway to the Titan's head. Outside it were the remains of another tech-priest, twin servo-arms slumped against the door, and the metal marred with scratches and burns. Another sign of mindless panic. What had the adept hoped to accomplish? The bridge space beyond was a sanctuary only as long as the door did not open.

Koparnos turned to the comm-link on the wall to the right of the door. 'Meridius is dead,' he said.

At first there was only silence. Then the voice spoke again. *'Who is this?'*

'I am Koparnos, and I am your only hope. Identify yourself.'

'Princeps Benrath,' she answered without hesitation, recognising the deep reverberations of his voice. *'You are of the Legiones Astartes.'*

'Are the moderati majoris still alive?' Koparnos asked.

'I'm not sure. They were an hour ago, but they haven't spoken since. They don't answer any more.'

'You are unable to confirm one way or the other?'

'I can't move,' she said. *'When the pulse hit us, there was a surge before the power went down. The neuro-feedback was... devastating. I am paralysed.'*

'What about your connections to the Titan?'

'I'm not sure. Until the power returned, I was linked to a void. I can feel its life now, but not the machine-spirit. Ostensor Contritio is as paralysed as I am.'

The fact that Benrath was severed from the machine-spirit was to be expected. Koparnos had seen the system breakdowns in the diagnostic. The machine-spirit was still alive, but isolated.

'I saw light in the cockpit earlier,' he said.

'The head has enough reserve power to function in isolation for an extended period.'

'You didn't eject.'

'What purpose would that have served?'

'None,' he agreed. Good. Benrath was fully conscious of her situation. Separating the head from the crippled body of the Titan would only have shifted the position of the survivors in the blasted land. There were no retrieval teams coming. Not for anyone. Whatever events remained to play out here, they would do so cut off from the rest of the planet.

'Princeps,' Koparnos said, 'I can end your paralysis. I can give you back your purpose.'

The phrasing did not come naturally. To offer rather than to command went against his training and his being. But he needed her consent, along with that of the moderati majoris, assuming either was still alive. If they were this close to death, a struggle of any kind could be lethal.

'You can restore Ostensor Contritio to us?' She sounded understandably sceptical.

'Not exactly. I can restore you to it.'

He waited for Benrath to deduce what he meant. He gave her some space to approach the idea on her own, to assimilate its reality and its implications. He was standing still but, all the same, he was reshaping the battlefield.

'We have no neural bus, no amniotic tank,' Benrath said. She knew what was coming, then, and was already half-way to acceptance.

'I am aware of that.'

'You are able to proceed without one?'

'Yes.'

'And the process is irreversible?'

'Would you ask that of a Legion Dreadnought, honoured princeps?'

'No. Forgive me. The weakness of my body is not the weakness of spirit.'

'Then I will begin. Know this – the interior is highly radioactive.'

'I understand. Once I open the seal, there is no going back.'

There never is, Koparnos thought. *Everything is irrevocable.*

There was a metallic *clunk* and a hiss of air as the circular hatch parted in the middle. The two halves slide aside. There was little room for the warsmith to enter the compartment.

The two moderati majoris sat in thrones to the rear of the space, flanking the one occupied by the princeps in the forward section of the Titan's skull. The armour-glass eye ports looked out over the broken landscape. The wind had dropped a little more since he had entered the Titan. Obscuring dust clouds still billowed over the field, but he could see further now. The graveyard of gigantic corpses was endless. On and on and on went the ranks of iron monuments, preserved in their rage.

But he also saw flashes of distant gunfire amidst all the death. He was not the only one seeking to bring the corpses back to a semblance of life.

He had won time for himself. He wasn't dying any more, but he had stopped one countdown only for another to begin. A new battle was coming. The embers of the war for Tallarn were struggling to reignite.

He would not be found wanting.

He checked the moderati. They were unconscious, their breathing laboured, but there was enough life there to suit his purposes.

'Are you there?' Benrath asked.

Koparnos could see the top of her shaved skull above the back of her throne, and her hands resting on the ornate arms. She didn't move. Her paralysis was as extensive as she had said.

'I am here,' Koparnos told her.

He began his work. It took time, and he had precious little of that. Even so, he shut that concern from his mind and focused solely on the task. He had a foundation upon which to build: the interface cables connecting Benrath and the moderati to the Titan's manifold were still viable.

He moved back and forth between the Warlord's skull and the workstations of the engineering deck. He never set foot beyond the moderati stations. He never saw Benrath's face. The princeps was a voice behind a throne, growing ever weaker. He required her consciousness a bit longer, though, and prepared the diagnostics to track the flow of neural data. The machine-spirit was there, silent but raging. To give it a voice, he had to find the point where the communications had been severed.

'Speak to it,' Koparnos urged Benrath over the vox when he was ready.

'I can't.'

'I know. Your failure will be instructive.'

'*I hope so.*'

She fell silent. A moment later, traceries of power lit up the workstation's screen. A few seconds later, Benrath gasped and the screen dimmed.

'Princeps?' Koparnos asked.

No answer. She was unconscious. Not dead – her life still registered on the screen in the form of faint pulses from her cerebral cortex. They barely registered, their paths fading into darkness almost immediately, but her effort had shown him the problem. Strong as her mental command had been, it had run into a damaged interface tangle one level down from the skull.

Koparnos found a maintenance hatch not far from the location of the interface. He opened it, expecting to find a crawlspace much too small to accommodate him. Instead, there was a narrow catwalk that twisted into the gap around the Titan's reactor housing. Koparnos moved inside, surrounded by pistons the size of pillars, cables as thick as a Thunderstrike's cannon. The connections stretched into the gloom above and below him.

'I am coming for you,' he called out to the raging machine-spirit. 'The princeps bent you to her will. I will do the same. You seek to vent your wrath? Good. You will do so at my command.'

The damage was not hard to find. Above his head, to the right of the catwalk, was a cluster of torn and fused cables. With the tools he had salvaged from above, he cleared the pathways as best he could. Some lines were torn beyond repair. Some connections had melted together in a mass that could never be differentiated.

He was satisfied when he made his way back to the primary workstation and examined the new energy tracks that appeared. He had not expected to restore all the pathways between Benrath and the machine-spirit to their original state. Nor did he wish to. He had merely created the possibility of communication. Now he would shape the nature of that dialogue.

He would shape the battlefield.

It took him another day to make his preparations. It was now the seventh since the blast. On this day, there would be no more rest for the dead.

IN THE SKULL of *Ostensor Contritio*, the princeps and the moderati majoris were still unconscious. They did not stir as Koparnos amplified their life-support and performed rough intubations. The mechanism that had kept them alive this long would now preserve the spark of life in their bodies for as long as the Titan survived. It would also hold them prisoner.

He was most careful as he worked on Benrath. He would have rejected the word *gentle* to describe the operation. It was *precise*. It was calculated. Unnecessary and premature shocks could easily defeat his purposes. His approach was as tactical and merciless as any siege he had ever led.

In truth, what he was attempting *was* a siege.

Little by little, he embedded her into the machinery. He could not install more ports into her skull and spine, but he jacked more cables into the existing ones. The resulting drain on her mind could shatter the body, so he increased the energy load even as he reduced its need.

He augmented.

He cut away.

He made the princeps one with the god-machine.

And when he was ready to open the links between

Benrath's mind and the machine-spirit of *Ostensor Contritio*, she awoke. He was standing between her and the window ports, and she saw him for the first time.

She saw the colours of his armour, and her eyes widened. 'Traitor!' she hissed.

Koparnos leaned in, savouring this fragment of justice reclaimed from the inferno of defeat. Corrupting a loyalist Titan was a fine act of reshaping, and a successful siege. But he wanted the princeps to know.

His victory would have its witness. An eternal one.

'You trusted blindly,' he snarled. 'So did we, once. But we learned our lesson in time. Have you? I think not.'

She was too weak to struggle. Even so, she tried. The skin around the sunken orbits of her eyes tightened as her will raged against a body withered and bound. Koparnos waited. With his task on the verge of completion, now he *did* have the luxury of time. He wanted to see Benrath realise the full extent of her powerlessness. He did not regard his triumph over a single loyalist as petty. His wrath was as justified as hers was futile.

'You will be defeated,' Benrath whispered.

'Not by you,' Koparnos grunted. 'No, not by you.' He completed the last of the connections. 'And so I keep my promise,' he added, then restored the neural link between the princeps and the machine-spirit.

Benrath screamed as her consciousness flowed away down into the manifold. It left her body behind. The flesh became nothing more than an organic bag, a conduit of fuel to keep the mind alive. She was cocooned in cables, vanishing into the mechanism of her throne, and only her face was visible.

Its final expression, before it fell into the slackness of living death, was one of utter horror.

Koparnos knew why. He could not experience the fusion that Benrath was undergoing. He could not conceive of it. But he understood exactly what he had set in motion. Before the blast had shut the Titan down, the machine-spirit's fury had been forced into compliance by the great will and discipline of the princeps. But she had been weakened, and he had stripped away the manifold defence mechanisms, leaving Benrath vulnerable to a machine-spirit so maddened by its injuries that its sole purpose was nothing more than unceasing, indiscriminate destruction. Given free rein, however, it would send *Ostensor Contritio* on a rampage as uncontrolled and unpredictable as the winds of a hurricane.

Benrath was now immortal whether she liked it or not. She was locked in a perpetual struggle against the anarchic rage of the machine. Koparnos had linked her mind to those of the moderati majoris, comatose but still neurologically viable. She retained just enough strength to channel the power of the Titan. She could direct the Warlord's movements, but she could not choose their purpose or their target.

Koparnos had reserved that power for himself.

He stood at the rear of the bridge space, looking beyond the thrones, through the armourglass eyes. The control mechanism he held was crude, little more than a collection of electronic prods, each with a different function. It would be sufficient.

He depressed a trigger, delivering a synaptic shock to Benrath. He impelled her to walk.

And so *Ostensor Contritio* walked.

The Warlord lurched with the bone-shaking growl of an iron city on the move. For the first time in seven days, the Titan's earth-cratering steps resounded throughout

the machine. *Ostensor Contritio* began its march through
the land of corpses. In the twilight distance, appearing
through the curtains of dust, other half-glimpsed giants
were moving. Koparnos saw the flash of giant guns.
Death had not had its fill on this battlefield.

And nor had he.

The vox was still consumed by static, but Koparnos had
confidence that he would know brother from enemy. He
depressed triggers to the left and right, and the Titan's
great arms rose, weapons cycling up.

He had no illusions. He was entombed within the Warlord as thoroughly as Benrath was. He would never leave
this cursed place. But his war was not over. He was in
command of a terrible wrath indeed.

This was a triumph, of a kind. It was the one that he
had sought.

And so he wondered about the new dread that
descended over him as a battle lost and finished now
lumbered once more into a grey, nightmare un-life. He
felt the shadow of the future fall over him – the shadow
of a war as futile as it was eternal.

THE FINAL COMPLIANCE OF SIXTY-THREE FOURTEEN

Guy Haley

'The Emperor has lied to you.'

The Warmaster's voice sounded from every public address system, vox-horn and comms device on the planet. His face spoke from the giant screens on the sides of starscrapers in place of exhortations and announcements. Rich with reason, mellifluous and persuasive, Horus addressed the world of Goughen, once known to him as Sixty-Three Fourteen.

'I request your fealty. We bring no rebellion against righteous authority, but make a stand against a tyrant who cares only for himself. Join with us. You have been deceived. Throw down your arms and follow me as a peacemaker upon the path of truth. Pledge yourselves to our cause and be free of the great deception. The Imperial Truth is a rank falsehood. The Emperor has lied to you.'

Planetary Governor Mayder Oquin glanced from his cabinets of trophies to his adjutant, Attan Spall. 'Is there no way of turning that damned racket off?'

'No, sir, I'm afraid not,' said Spall regretfully.

Still he called him sir, even thirty-six years after the compliance. There were some habits you could not leave behind.

'A pity,' muttered Oquin. He stood tall despite his age, with his wrinkled hands clasped behind his back. His uniform – he still wore his Imperial Army dress uniform when acting in an official capacity – exhibited all the hallmarks of a military man's habitual neatness, as did his moustache, still black, and his otherwise unruly shock of white hair, which he battled into submission daily. The gallery was intensely lit, full of mirrors, with light-coloured walls and gleaming floors of marble, so that the objects within the cabinets might be fully appreciated. Such illumination would make even the smartest man look shabby, but not Oquin. Instead, it highlighted his immaculate appearance. Age had garlanded him with wisdom, not frailty.

His voice, gruffer than it had once been, was nevertheless still strong and commanding.

'What to take, what to take?' he murmured.

'Sir?' asked Spall. Every word Oquin spoke sounded like an order, and demanded a response whether he desired it or not.

'Hmmm? Oh, I intend to take something with me. Perhaps as a gift for our visitors. Something to remind them of our shared history.'

'Is that really necessary, sir? Only, we should give them an answer soon.'

'Oh, it is, Spall! Very necessary.'

The governor let his eyes wander over his collection. Items taken from a dozen worlds. Relics from long-dead civilisations sat beside artefacts from societies incorporated into the Imperium. The blackened mementos of those who had resisted.

'...*the Imperial Truth is a rank falsehood...*' the Warmaster's voice repeated.

Oquin examined them all, carefully displayed in their crystal glass cabinets. They were his pride and joy. An austere man such as he had little use for trinkets or adornments – the decoration of the palace was the work of his subjects, not to his taste at all. The collection was Oquin's only indulgence, memories of a life given gladly in service to a higher ideal.

'Lest I forget,' he always said. Spall had heard it many times, and he knew exactly what Oquin meant.

The governor pointed to a stone mask – a long, oval grotesque of exaggerated lips and fangs and wide, staring eyes carved from glossy carnelian.

'That one, I think, is my favourite.'

'Sir?' asked Spall.

'The Bathranin war mask,' Oquin explained, although Spall knew perfectly well what it was. 'Before your time, Spall. Tribesmen of Sixty-Three Three.'

Spall was getting nervous. He pressed a finger to the vox-bead in his ear and listened. 'Sir, the delegation is growing impatient, as is the prime minister. The council insist on knowing what you are going to tell the Warmaster before you leave. I shall not tell you to hurry, sir, because it's not my place–'

'Not for any aesthetic reason, you understand,' Oquin interrupted, ignoring Spall's concerns. 'For I'm sure you can see as well as I that it is a damnably ugly thing.' He shook his head and smiled. 'You should have seen them, thousands all arrayed against us, voices booming behind the stone. Can you imagine it? Terrifying, in its way. That was my second compliance after my own world joined the great dream of the Imperium.' He snorted, as if at some private joke. 'I was a common foot soldier. No idea what to expect. Even having met the Legions and seen their primarchs, even given the wondrous weapons of Terra, it took a while to get over the shock of it. Primitives painted in red mud, riding those beasts of theirs. Hopeless, really. For all that display, they had no chance. The Bathranin were brave and proud and they would not give up, and so we slaughtered them. Bloody work. Sad, in its way – they were savages after all, and knew no better.' Oquin cast his eyes ceilingwards, as if he could see through the plaster mouldings to the lights of the war fleet in the sky. 'The unity of mankind. Neither innocence nor bravery is protection against such a vaunted cause.'

Spall cleared his throat. 'Sir, I do not mean to chivvy you, but we have to give an answer. They've been outside for a quarter of an hour.'

'They can bloody well wait five more minutes, then!' shouted Oquin. 'This is my world, given to me to rule by Horus himself!' His hand snapped up into the air and back, as if he batted a fly away from his ear. 'If he wants our pledge of loyalty so badly, he could have come down here and not sent his lackeys. I am not an old man who has forgotten what has been asked of him. I am a commander of a planet of the Imperium! Is that clear, Spall?'

'Crystal clear, sir.'

'Very good,' said Oquin, calming himself. 'And turn your vox-bead off. I have.'

A wing of heavy gunships flew low over the governor's palace, momentarily drowning out Horus' echoing address. The vibration caused the collection of trophies to tremble tinkling across the glass shelves. Oquin tutted and smoothed his jacket. The threat to go with the promise. Always the way.

Last time Oquin had checked, there were fourteen warships in orbit. That was threat enough. Beyond the ancient veterans that had settled there, Sixty-Three Fourteen had precious little of a standing army – no fleet, few orbitals. Horus had grown unsubtle. Heavy-handed.

He looked next to a dress of silvermail from Sixty-Three Six, a garment made of tiny rings of precious metals linked together most cunningly. Not armour, but a fashion in the capital at the time of the compliance. He had liked his wife in it. She was gone now. Disease. Peril did not cease with war's end. Building a world brought its own troubles.

It was a blessing that she did not have to see this day.

'Beautiful,' he said at the memory.

Spall followed his master's eyes. 'Yes, sir,' he agreed.

Oquin nodded. Spall had been with him since Sixty-Three Six, first as a sergeant, then his lieutenant, then a captain, and so on, following him up through the ranks, always one step behind. Oquin could not say he liked Spall. The two could never be friends, but Spall was dependable. That was why Oquin had been such a good leader – he could see past personal likes and dislikes to the real quality of the man beneath. He still liked to think that he was respected for it. He was not mistaken.

Next to the silvermail were tech-armlets from Sixty-Three Ten; deactivated and inert, of course. Oquin had made sure of it personally. By the armlets were worn pieces of metal dug from the forest loams of the barely inhabited worlds beyond Sixty-Three Thirteen. The metal was covered in hieroglyphs that remained undecipherable. The mystery of their provenance was intriguing, but their real interest was that once a year, on the very same day according to the solar cycle of their world of origin, the markings would flow and change.

'Fascinating,' said Oquin, taking a sideways step. 'Absolutely fascinating.'

Displayed now in front of him on a long, purpose-built rack were a host of artefacts of common design: glass, metalwork and technological devices that, if simple, were still beautifully fashioned.

'Sixty-Three Seven,' he said, tapping the glass. He smiled. 'I was less discriminating in my choices then. The personal storage I received seemed so capacious after my lieutenant's quarters. Do you remember? It was there that they made me a captain.' He had been proud that day, and still was. 'Such nights! Such joy. After the initial battles, the common people welcomed us with open arms. They were the sensible ones.'

'Yes, sir,' said Spall. 'I remember.' He was becoming less anxious, being drawn in to the former lord commander's nostalgia. 'The flowers and the pools.'

'And the women, eh?' Oquin added with a smile.

'I thought it impolite to comment, sir.'

Oquin laughed. He bent low to inspect a set of clay fertility figures bartered on Sixty-Three Four. 'We're old,' he said.

'Yes, sir.'

'Do not think that I grumble,' said Oquin standing ramrod-straight again. 'More than a century of life is far better than I expected. And such a century it has been. I always wondered, when I was a boy, what it was like up there in the void. Did you?'

'Yes, sir,' Spall replied. 'Every night, sir.'

Oquin nodded at his aide. *Of course*, his expression said. *Of course you did.*

'Up there, wherever he is, I'll bet Horus has not aged a day. Such insects we must seem to him, our lives as fleeting as summer days. It can't be healthy. Men were not meant to last forever – not even men like him.'

'Sir?' asked Spall cautiously.

'This is what occurs when the mighty are immortal, Spall. Inevitable, I suppose. Ambition is poison to loyalty, in the end.'

'Sir.'

Oquin tapped his upper lip with an extended forefinger. 'No,' he said decisively. 'Sometimes the singing rocks of Sixty-Three Nine are my favourite, but today the Bathranin have it.'

'Are you taking that then, sir?'

Oquin stopped before the central items of his collection. In a case as tall as a man were the governor's arms and armour, lovingly maintained. A bronze-coloured cuirass with attached faulds and spaulders, and a helm crowned with the laurels of a conqueror were displayed on an armature, as if worn by an invisible warrior. On an ornate wooden stand in front were a laspistol, a volkite culverin given to him by the Mechanicum component of the 63rd Expedition after the battle for Sixty-Three Eleven, and a power sword. The holsters and scabbard were upon a belt girdling the placard of the cuirass. Oquin passed his hand over the hidden locking mechanism.

'Not today, Spall. I will greet them as I left them, as a hero of the Imperium. Help me into this would you?'

'Sir... I...'

'Don't just stand there dithering, man. Help me. The armour is heavy and I am not getting any younger.'

Spall hesitantly joined his commander. Together they

brought down the armour and placed it over the governor's head and Spall tightened its fastenings.

Oquin smiled fiercely. 'It is *damned* heavy! A lot heavier than I recall. I am weaker, I expect. But...' He admired himself in one of the room's many mirrors. 'It still fits.' Spall handed him his helm, and Oquin slid it carefully on. He turned right and left. 'Aha! If I squint, I'm still the crusader I was forty years ago. Dashing, eh Spall?'

'Yes, sir.'

'Hand me my gloves and my weapons. Just the pistol and the sword, if you would.'

Spall did as requested. Oquin looked the blade up and down, wonder upon his lined face, as though it were the first time he had held it. Spall stood back, his stomach knotted with anxiety. As he had feared, Oquin did not sheath his sword or holster his pistol. Instead he stroked the activation stud on the gun, and green lights tracked up its charge indicator. The sword's disruption field hissed into life, the air crackling faintly around it, generating a smell of ozone.

'Sir, what are you going to tell them?'

Oquin stared levelly at him.

'*The Emperor has lied to you,*' Horus' smooth, recorded voice was still saying. The voice of peace. '*I request your fealty...*'

'Loyalty, Spall. I fought for the Warmaster. He elevated me, he trusted me, and I loved him. But my loyalty is to the Emperor. The Imperial Truth is the only truth.'

Slowly, Spall unholstered his laspistol. The scrape of metal on the leather as he pulled it out seemed monstrously loud, louder even than Horus' cycling message. He raised the gun with a shaking hand to point at his master. Tears ran freely down his face. Oquin did nothing to stop him.

'Please, sir. They'll kill us all,' he said. His voice cracked.

'Yes. I expect they will.' Oquin smiled sadly. 'A harsh reaction when refusal is given, but far from abnormal in a compliance action. That's what this is. A compliance for the Warmaster's new Imperium.' Oquin deliberately turned his back on Spall. 'But as I learned when I took part in the slaughter of the Bathranin, Spall, some things are worth more than life. Perhaps worth more than the life of an entire world.

'Now, I am going to walk out of that door and give them my answer. Feel free to shoot me in the back. I am confident you won't. Not if you remember even dimly what we were fighting for.'

Oquin strode down the gallery, his bearing proud. Spall made a strangled noise in his throat. He kept his gun trained on the governor the whole way. The weapon wavered, his aim blurred by tears.

He couldn't do it.

Mayder Oquin disappeared through the doors.

Spall was still staring dumbly at his weapon when the din of boltgun fire echoed up the palace halls.

Sixty-Three Fourteen had replied.

THE HERALD
OF SANGUINIUS

Andy Smillie

IT TAKES TWO deaths to keep a secret.

This truth is as old as time itself, and far more cruel. It is a truth that will see me break the bonds of a Legion. And it is for this truth that I stand here, my blade poised at my brother's throat.

His name is Hakael, and this is the last time that I shall speak of it.

He is an honoured veteran of the Sanguinary Guard, a stalwart champion of Baal, yet this fate will steal away everything he has fought for. All of his deeds, his triumphs and glories will be forgotten. He will receive no burial, and his name will not be recorded in the Litany of Heroes. He will die here. He will die *completely* and, like the long-distant past, he will go unremembered and unmourned.

To his credit, he welcomes this fate. He stands before me, his chin lifted, throat exposed, hands loose at his sides. But his eyes are firm with conviction, his pupils the flat black of acceptance.

He senses my hesitation.

'Duty demands this, Azkaellon,' he urges me. 'Do not dishonour me with pity or regret.'

I nod. 'The Blood keep you.'

My blade removes his head in a single stroke. He is dead before he hits the floor.

I bite down the grief that swells in my throat, and turn to face the chamber's only other occupant – Aratron, another of my Sanguinary Guard. His jaw is locked tight, his eyes fixed on the short length of kindling in his hand.

'It seems ill-fitting that fate and nothing more decided who lived and who died here,' he murmurs, hesitantly. 'Had we determined this with a blade, it would be me lying there...'

I sheathe my sword. 'Your deeds brought you to this room, as did his,' I remind him. 'But in the end, Aratron, our skill and zeal only carry us so far. We are all of us subject to the whims of fate.'

Aratron's face creases, though he says nothing. It is rare for a warrior to admit that his life is not in his own hands, but we have both seen too many stray rounds steal away a life unintended. I give him no time to reflect on that possibility.

'And make no mistake – from here, you are as dead as he. Your name will never again be spoken or heard, and your life as it was is over. Though my blade will not part your flesh, your fate has already been sealed by the rise and fall of an artificer's hammer.'

I step to the brazier burning in the corner and reach into the fire for the helm within. Flame kisses my gauntlet as I lift it free – it smoulders faintly, as though angry at my touch. Its faceplate is an intricate mask, a perfect replica of the one worn by our father, Sanguinius. I regard it for a moment, awed by the craftsmanship. The primarch had fashioned it himself.

'Are you ready?' I ask, turning back to Aratron.

Aratron nods, and kneels before me. I grip the back of his head with my free hand and hold it firm.

'The Blood grant you the strength to endure,' I add solemnly, before pressing the mask onto his face.

THE AIR IS over-charged, feeling set to explode. A fight is imminent. Blood may be spilt, and this uneasy alliance of brothers will crumble. The walls of this fortress could be cast down. Imperium Secundus would fall and, with it, all that remains of the Emperor's realm.

I move to intercept Sardon Karaashison as he tries to force his way past Neria and Vual. There is anger in his glowing eye lenses.

'Get out of my way, *Angel*,' he spits. 'I will not ask you again.'

I step close to him, keeping my voice low. 'You would allow yourself to become the catalyst for our undoing, kinsman?'

'What? Speak your mind, Azkaellon.'

I gesture to the cordon of Sanguinary Guard spanning the breadth of the chamber. 'Look around you, sir.'

The thin line of golden armour ripples and shifts as my warriors struggle to hold back the press of other legionaries clamouring for an audience with the Emperor Sanguinius.

'We stand on a knife-edge. Uncertainty, frustration and mistrust are foes we are ill-equipped to defeat. What Lord Guilliman has built here is a fragile kingdom. A single brick knocked from its foundations by your anger is all it would take to topple it.'

The Iron Hand begins to see what I see – a new war in the making.

I place a hand upon his shoulder. 'Would you really give Horus the satisfaction of *that*?'

He steps back, shame lowering his eyes. His outrage is all but forgotten. 'We have stood here a day without audience. Lord Sanguinius cannot ignore the Tenth Legion.'

'He will not,' I assure him. 'You will be heard. But not now.'

'When?'

'I will see to–'

A commanding voice rings through the din of the chamber, and my words are cut short. 'Tell my brother Sanguinius that *I* would speak with him.'

I recognise the speaker at once. The soft menace in his tone is one that I am well acquainted with. I steel myself, and turn to face *the Lion*. The primarch of the Dark Angels is fully armoured – one hand cradles his helm, the other rests upon the pommel of his sword. Around him, ten of his veteran warriors are clad in hulking Terminator armour.

I speak with as much authority as seems appropriate when addressing the lord of another Legion. 'Other matters demand the Emperor Sanguinius' attention. When he is available I–'

'*Now*, commander.'

The Lion towers head and shoulders over me. Like all primarchs, he is a warrior god by any definition. And still, I have to fight the urge to draw my blade. His rash display of force endangers us all.

In the end, it is duty and not fear that keeps my temper in check. 'With the greatest respect, lord, you know the rules. One cohort may enter the throne room at a

time except under direct instruction from Lord Sanguinius. I have received no such instruction.'

The primarch's seething rage is an almost primal thing.
'You will not defy me.'

For the first time in weeks, there is silence. I know
without looking that all eyes are now upon us. I must
choose my next move carefully – if I back down then all
semblance of order here will be lost.

If I defy the Lion, I risk fragmenting this alliance
further.

'I cannot disobey my father. Wait here, lord, and I will
petition him to receive you.'

'Do not dally...' he sneers.

I turn from the Lion and make for the vaulted doors
behind me, opening a vox-channel to the Sanguinary
Guard as the first murmuring of the crowd builds once
more. 'Hold them here. No one passes the line. *No one.*'

I EXIT THE receiving hall into an antechamber. It is only
a few dozen strides across and tall, clear-glass windows
run the length of the walls on either side of me. The centre of the space is dominated by a marble statue of the
Emperor – the original Emperor. It is not the finest rendition of the Master of Mankind that I have seen, but
then it is more than a mere ornament.

Fused within the marble, fine beads of explosive await
detonation. I look again at the windows, imagining
the panes of glass shattering as the statue explodes at
some unseen trigger. I picture the lethal shards shooting
through the air to sever limbs and end the lives of *any*
intruders. I feel a shiver run down my spine.

'The Blood keep us from such desperate measures...' I
whisper to the shadows.

This room, like all in the Fortress of Hera, is at its core like Guilliman. Cold. Calculating. Functional. Wreathed in just enough finery to lower the guard of its guests. I allow myself to be fooled for a moment, to enjoy brief solace before walking through the heavier doors ahead of me and into the throne room beyond.

I address my father as I enter, bowing as I cross the threshold.

'Lord Sanguinius.'

This is the second of Hera's great throne rooms. It is a long slit of a chamber, the ceiling held aloft by serried rows of granite columns, and cut down the centre by a length of crimson carpet. The principal throne room remains Guilliman's, for he is Master of Ultramar. Even as the new Emperor, my father would not disrespect him by claiming it.

No, there is more to it than simple respect. This *position* sits uneasily with Sanguinius. Remaining here is his protest, a silent objection against a role he had little choice but to accept.

My father sits at the far end of the chamber, ensconced upon his throne. His wings are pulled tightly back behind him, tucked into a recess in the chair. 'I have told you before Azkaellon – there is no need for you to bow here.'

I straighten. 'I shall try to temper my disobedience, lord.'

Sanguinius rises and descends the marbled steps to meet me. His battleplate is gleaming gold, his wings spread out behind him like a cloak of virgin snow. I cast my eyes low, humbled by his majesty. Were hope a tangible thing, he would surely be the manifestation of it.

'What trouble do you bring me this time?' he asks. His

face is unreadable, yet I know enough of him to sense the weariness in his tone.

'The Legions gathered here grow restless,' I report. 'Sardon Karaashison of the Iron Hands demands an audience. As does Sergeant Raln of the Seventh Legion, and the sons of the Khan, as well as many more of Lord Guilliman's own Ultramarines and officials. Yet I cannot in good conscience let any of them into your presence. Any one of them could be working to carry out some foul threat that we cannot yet perceive.'

He sighs. 'But I cannot rule from behind a wall of mistrust.'

'Then let us simply be cautious. Let the Sanguinary Guard shoulder the risk in your stead. Let us act as your heralds.'

Sanguinius considers this for a long moment.

'Very well.'

I nod, and make to turn.

'Wait,' he calls out. 'There is something else, Azkaellon. Speak your mind.'

I wish to Baal that I had worn my helm – that my face had not betrayed me. 'The Lion...'

I pause, choosing my words with care.

'Curze's escape... It *claws* at him.' I swallow hard and force the rest of the words from my mouth. 'His fingers stray close to his blade...'

Sanguinius' face darkens. 'My brother's loyalty is not in doubt. He is Master of the First Legion. He is beyond reproach.'

'I do not doubt his intent, lord. But what of his judgement?'

'Leave this alone, Azkaellon.'

Sanguinius leaps into the air, a single, powerful beat

of his wings carrying him high up into the darkness of the chamber's balcony. In his absence, I bring my fist to my breastplate and salute the throne.

It is only then that I notice the long blade, which had rested there when I entered, is missing.

'This honour should be yours, Azkaellon. It is only fitting that you–'

'No, Aratron,' I say firmly, shaking my head. 'I cannot be herald *and* safeguard our father. You ten are the greatest of the Sanguinary Guard. Exemplars of Baal's heritage, first among the Legion of Sanguinius. This honour falls to one of you.'

I let my eyes move across the ten Blood Angels standing in the chamber with me. I have fought beside each of them. We have shed blood and faced horrors unimaginable. They are my brothers and my friends, and I would send them into harm's way without a second thought.

Yet what I ask of them now weighs upon my soul like an armoured boot on my throat.

Hakael nods with a grim resignation. 'Then let us decide this.'

He is first to step forwards, an act typical of him. His eyes meet mine, but we say nothing as he pulls a length of bound parchment from the bunch held in my hand. Unrolling it, he holds it up for his brothers to see. It is stained with a single blood-drop.

One by one the others follow, until Aratron draws the other marked lot. He nods in silence and takes his place next to Hakael.

I take the lengths of parchment from them and move to the lectern. Upon it sits a small metal inkwell, a slender quill and a golden chalice. The quill is magnificent, a single feather of purest white, plucked from the wings of Sanguinius himself.

'By our father's body is the truth written,' I intone. 'By his blood will it be remembered.'

The well is warm, the blood within heated to prevent it from drying. I remove my gauntlet, take up the quill and dip it into the well. With long strokes, I write Aratron and Hakael's names onto the pieces of parchment.

'And by our blood will it be honoured.'

I place the pieces of parchment into the chalice, and draw a knife across my palm. Clenching my fist, I squeeze a thick drop of blood into the cup.

The eight Sanguinary Guard who will leave the chamber do the same, adding their blood to mine. I wait until they are done before dropping a small, lit taper into the chalice. It ignites with a blue flicker, burning the paper to ash. I use my fingers to scoop the ash-blood mix into my mouth, tightening my lips at the acrid taste. It is not wholly unpalatable.

The thought strengthens me.

It is well that I can bear the taste of sorrow.

I swallow hard, using my tongue to drag the mixture back towards my throat.

'It is done,' I say. 'May our Lord Sanguinius grant us the strength to endure.'

'Glory to Baal,' the rest of them call out in unison.

The eight Sanguinary Guard salute and exit the chamber, leaving me alone with Aratron and Hakael.

I stand there a moment, unmoving, anchored by questions. How is it that I have come here to strike down two of my own? Are my actions born of necessity or paranoia? Will the blood that I am about to spill be justified? I look inside myself for answers, and find only the hollow stab of doubt.

Perhaps, I muse, when I am dead and gone, my blood and bones naught but dust in the wind, history will ask these questions again. Should that be the case, then I hope that there comes an answer.

I hold out my hand, proffering two lengths of kindling to Aratron and Hakael.

'May the Blood guide you.'

THE LION ROUNDS on me, his eyes narrow. 'What is this deception?' he demands, thrusting a finger at the golden-armoured figure sat upon the throne. '*That* is not Sanguinius.'

Beside him, his Deathwing honour guard tighten their grip on their weapons. I hold up my open palms in appeasement, speaking calmly and clearly.

'You are correct. We have not sought to conceal ourselves with lies. His likeness to our father is born only out of respect.'

The Lion thumps his gauntleted palm in frustration. 'Where... is... my... *brother*?' he demands.

'With respect, if the Emperor Sanguinius wanted you to know, he would have told you.'

'*You* will tell me.'

His eyes are like blazing brands. I hold his gaze. 'I will not.'

He steps close to me as his temper frays. 'There is steel in your heart, Angel,' His is an intimate anger, his threat personal. 'But my blade will pierce it as surely as it has a thousand others.'

Nestled amongst the anger lines creasing his face, a slit of raw flesh draws my attention. The wound is slight, a hairline laceration. It is–

No. I feel my eyes widen as I realise that it is not simply a wound.

It is an *insult*, an indignity made with the very tip of a blade. No mere legionary could have marked the Lion in such a way.

I pause politely, taking a measured breath. 'I do not fear death, lord – by your hand, or any other. Duty demands I do far worse than hurl myself at oblivion.'

He regards me coldly for what feels like the longest moment of my life. Then he nods, with what seems to be a grudging respect.

'Were it only that my brother understood *duty* so clearly...'

He brushes past me, stepping to the foot of the throne.

'And how should I greet this... *herald*?'

I hide a smile.

'If it pleases you, my lord, you may address him as the Sanguinor.'

ABOUT THE AUTHORS

Graham McNeill has written many Horus
Heresy novels, including *Vengeful Spirit*
and his *New York Times* bestsellers *A
Thousand Sons* and the novella *The Reflection
Crack'd*, which featured in *The Primarchs*
anthology. Graham's Ultramarines series,
featuring Captain Uriel Ventris, is now
six novels long, and has close links to his
Iron Warriors stories, the novel *Storm of
Iron* being a perennial favourite with Black
Library fans. He has also written a Mars
trilogy, featuring the Adeptus Mechanicus.
For Warhammer, he has written the Time
of Legends trilogy *The Legend of Sigmar*,
the second volume of which won the 2010
David Gemmell Legend Award.

Aaron Dembski-Bowden is the author of the Horus Heresy novels *The Master of Mankind*, *Betrayer* and *The First Heretic*, as well as the novella *Aurelian* and the audio drama *Butcher's Nails*, for the same series. He has also written the popular Night Lords series, the Space Marine Battles book *Armageddon*, the Black Legion novel *The Talon of Horus*, the Grey Knights novel *The Emperor's Gift* and numerous short stories. He lives and works in Northern Ireland.

Chris Wraight is the author of the Horus Heresy novels *Scars* and *The Path of Heaven*, the Primarchs novel *Leman Russ: The Great Wolf*, the novella *Brotherhood of the Storm* and the audio drama *The Sigillite*. For Warhammer 40,000 he has written the Space Wolves novels *Blood of Asaheim* and *Stormcaller*, and the short story collection *Wolves of Fenris*, as well as the Space Marine Battles novels *Wrath of Iron* and *War of the Fang*. Additionally, he has many Warhammer novels to his name, including the Time of Legends novel *Master of Dragons*, which forms part of the War of Vengeance series. Chris lives and works near Bristol, in south-west England.

Gav Thorpe is the author of the Horus Heresy novels *Deliverance Lost*, *Angels of Caliban* and *Corax*, as well as the novella *The Lion*, which formed part of the *New York Times* bestselling collection *The Primarchs*. He is particularly well-known for his Dark Angels stories, including the Legacy of Caliban series. His Warhammer 40,000 repertoire further includes the Path of the Eldar series, the The Beast Arises novels *The Emperor Expects* and *The Beast Must Die*, Horus Heresy audio dramas *Raven's Flight*, *Honour to the Dead* and *Raptor*, and a multiplicity of short stories. For Warhammer, Gav has penned the End Times novel *The Curse of Khaine*, the Time of Legends trilogy, *The Sundering*, and much more besides. He lives and works in Nottingham.

Matthew Farrer is the author of the novella *The Inheritor King*, which appears in *Sabbat Crusade*. He also wrote the Warhammer 40,000 novels *Crossfire*, *Legacy* and *Blind*, along with numerous short stories, including 'The Headstone and Hammerstone Kings' for *Sabbat Worlds* and the Horus Heresy tales 'After Desh'ea' and 'Vorax'. He lives and works in Australia.

Rob Sanders is the author of *The Serpent Beneath*, a novella that appeared in the *New York Times* bestselling Horus Heresy anthology *The Primarchs*. His other Black Library credits include the The Beast Arises novels *Predator, Prey* and *Shadow of Ullanor*, the Warhammer 40,000 titles *Adeptus Mechanicus: Skitarius* and *Tech-Priest*, *Legion of the Damned*, *Atlas Infernal* and *Redemption Corps* and the audio drama *The Path Forsaken*. He has also written the Warhammer Archaon duology, *Everchosen* and *Lord of Chaos* along with many Quick Reads for the Horus Heresy and Warhammer 40,000. He lives in the city of Lincoln, UK.

Nick Kyme is the author of the Horus Heresy novels *Deathfire*, *Vulkan Lives*, and *Sons of the Forge*, the novellas *Promethean Sun* and *Scorched Earth*, and the audio dramas *Censure* and *Red-Marked*. His novella *Feat of Iron* was a *New York Times* bestseller in the Horus Heresy collection, *The Primarchs*. Nick is well known for his popular Salamanders novels, including *Rebirth*, the Space Marine Battles novel *Damnos*, and numerous short stories. He has also written fiction set in the world of Warhammer, most notably the Time of Legends novel *The Great Betrayal* and the Age of Sigmar story 'Borne by the Storm', included in the novel *War Storm*. He lives and works in Nottingham, and has a rabbit.

Andy Smillie is best known for his visceral Flesh Tearers novellas, *Sons of Wrath* and *Flesh of Cretacia*, and the novel *Trial by Blood*. He has also written a host of short stories starring this brutal Chapter of Space Marines and a number of audio dramas including *The Kauyon*, *Blood in the Machine*, *Deathwolf* and *From the Blood*.

John French has written several Horus Heresy stories including the novels *Praetorian of Dorn* and *Tallarn: Ironclad*, the novellas *Tallarn: Executioner* and *The Crimson Fist*, and the audio dramas *Templar* and *Warmaster*. He is the author of the Ahriman series, which includes the novels *Ahriman: Exile*, *Ahriman: Sorcerer* and *Ahriman: Unchanged*, plus a number of related short stories collected in *Ahriman: Exodus*, including 'The Dead Oracle' and 'Hand of Dust'. Additionally for the Warhammer 40,000 universe he has written the Space Marine Battles novella *Fateweaver*, plus many short stories. He lives and works in Nottingham, UK.

David Annandale is the author of the Horus Heresy novel *The Damnation of Pythos* and the Primarchs novel *Roboute Guilliman: Lord of Ultramar*. He has also written *Warlord: Fury of the God-Machine*, the Yarrick series, several stories involving the Grey Knights, including *Warden of the Blade*, and *The Last Wall*, *The Hunt for Vulkan* and *Watchers in Death* for The Beast Arises. For Space Marine Battles he has written *The Death of Antagonis* and *Overfiend*. He is a prolific writer of short fiction set in The Horus Heresy, Warhammer 40,000 and Age of Sigmar universes. David lectures at a Canadian university, on subjects ranging from English literature to horror films and video games.

Guy Haley is the author of the Horus Heresy novel *Pharos*, the Primarchs novel *Perturabo: The Hammer of the Olympia* and the Warhammer 40,000 novels *Dante*, *Baneblade*, *Shadowsword*, *Valedor* and *Death of Integrity*. He has also written *Throneworld* and *The Beheading* for The Beast Arises series. His enthusiasm for all things greenskins has also led him to pen the eponymous Warhammer novel *Skarsnik*, as well as the End Times novel *The Rise of the Horned Rat*. He has also written stories set in the Age of Sigmar, included in *War Storm*, *Ghal Maraz*, *Call of Archaon*, and *Legends of the Age of Sigmar*. He lives in Yorkshire with his wife and son.